INDIGO FIRE

I0678858

Book One
Of
The Indigo Brothers Trilogy

VICKIE McKEEHAN

Published by Beachdevils Press

INDIGO FIRE
The Indigo Brothers Trilogy
Published by Beachdevils Press
Copyright © 2016 Vickie McKeehan
All rights reserved.

beachdevils
PRESS
ISBN-10: 0692643532
ISBN-13: 978-0692643532

Published by
Beachdevils Press
Printed in the USA
All Titles Available at Amazon
Cover designed by artist, Jess Johnson

You can visit the author at:
www.vickiemckeehan.com
www.facebook.com/VickieMcKeehan
http://vickiemckeehan.wordpress.com/
www.twitter.com/VickieMcKeehan

also by Vickie McKeehan

The Evil Secrets Trilogy
JUST EVIL Book One
DEEPER EVIL Book Two
ENDING EVIL Book Three

The Pelican Pointe Series
PROMISE COVE
HIDDEN MOON BAY
DANCING TIDES
LIGHTHOUSE REEF
STARLIGHT DUNES
LAST CHANCE HARBOR
SEA GLASS COTTAGE
LAVENDER BEACH
BENEATH WINTER SAND

The Skye Cree Novels
THE BONES OF OTHERS
THE BONES WILL TELL
THE BOX OF BONES
TRUTH IN THE BONES

The Indigo Brothers Trilogy
INDIGO FIRE
INDIGO HEAT
INDIGO JUSTICE

For Pancho,
who enriched my childhood beyond measure.

The most powerful weapon on earth is the human soul on fire.

~ FERDINAND FOCH

The First Warrior looked out on the land and his Home.
He saw the hills
And the stars
And he was happy.
For giving him his home, the First Warrior told the Great Spirit
That he would fight and win many battles in His honor.
But the Great Spirit said, "No, do not fight for me.
Fight for your tribe,
Fight for the family born to you,
Fight for the brothers you find.
"Fight for them," the Great Spirit said, "for *they* are your
Home."

~ HENRY STANDING BEAR
Longmire TV series

Part One

Jackson

Prologue

Wednesday, September 23rd
11:45 p.m.

Olivia Indigo Buchanan had reached her thirty-third year.

Unfortunately, it would be her last.

Her eyes fluttered open.

Darkness.

She couldn't focus. Every time she tried, she saw two of everything. There were shadows and the shadows kept moving—dark to light, light to dark—and back again.

Her head pounded like she'd been drugged. The surface where she lay felt hard, cold, damp. Was she inside a basement with a dirt floor or outside lying on the ground in the woods? The air seemed muggy, almost fetid. Maybe that meant she was outdoors.

She struggled to raise her head, tried her best to move her arms. But it was just too much effort. She began to squirm and realized her hands had been bound behind her back. She did her best to work them free but couldn't budge whatever held her hands together. She tried to scream, to lick her lips and met the foul, pasty taste of duct tape covering her mouth.

She caught movement to her left. Relief moved through her in bits and pieces knowing she wasn't alone. But that was short-lived when she realized it was a stranger she didn't recognize. He stood ten feet away chopping at something...no, no, that wasn't right, he kept hitting something, no someone. She watched, she listened as the thwack, thwack, thwack sound repeated, over and over again.

The other victim on the ground fought for his life, the punishing blows coming fast. Olivia heard what sounded like bones crack and snap. His effort to survive became a pathetic attempt until finally his desperate mutterings and pleas for help got weaker.

Through heavy lids, she thought she heard her name. Livvy. For one precious moment, the nickname fluttered on a sunny breeze from the past. Her mind tried to reach out and grab hold of that lifeline, that memory of the life she'd lived.

But then, she watched in horror as her captor took out a plastic bag and slipped it over the man's head to silence him once and for all. The man put up another weak struggle. But it was brief. Terror moved through her when she heard him take what sounded like his final gasp of air.

She needed to get away from this monster. With tears streaming down her face, she used the last bit of energy she had to roll as far away as she could. She shoved along using her legs to get away from this brutal asshole. She inched on her belly over uneven ground. It occurred to her every muscle in her body ached. Had she already suffered some type of debilitating injury that prevented her legs from working, from going faster?

As she edged along over gravel and loose dirt, Livvy thought of her children. Where was Blake, her eight-year-old son? And where was Ally, her six-year-old daughter? If she got away and they were still here somewhere, if the monster had them hidden away in this horrible place, what would happen to her kids if she left them alone? Were they alive, being kept somewhere in the darkness where she couldn't see them?

The last thing she remembered was being at home, tucked in her own bed. She desperately tried to recall what had happened after that. How long ago had that been? Hours? Days? How long had she been kept here tied up in this torture chamber?

Where was her husband, Walker? Why wasn't he helping her? She looked back at the battered man on the ground. A sick feeling overpowered her. The man looked like Walker. She realized he'd stopped moving, stopped moaning. Her last real glance told her all she needed to know. Walker's face had been beaten, his body brutalized and tortured. All that was left was a mass of bloody clothing wrapped around flesh and bone.

She felt her stomach churn as she began to push herself farther along over the hard, dirty surface to get away. But something impeded her progress. She felt pain in her head, felt the monster on her back.

With a massive force grinding into her spine, Livvy realized he'd used something heavy to hit her across her shoulders. She felt something jab into her kidneys. The blow put an end to her moving. It felt like a crowbar came down on her skull. Metal connected with her head. A thousand needles pierced her brain.

With his foot, he kicked her in the side and turned her over to face him. For one brief moment she locked eyes with the man. He tore off the duct tape that sealed her lips. Profanities sailed out of his mouth. He kept yelling at her to tell him…something.

She tried to raise her head to ask him why he was doing this, but she couldn't speak. Her jaw refused to work. In that moment Livvy knew for certain she was about to die. She thought of her mom and dad and all her brothers. She thought of Walker, and Blake, and Ally. She thought of the perfect life she'd once had. What had she done to deserve this kind of death? Why such torture and brutality? She'd always thought she'd lived a good life, been a good person.

But the blows kept coming. The smell of iron overwhelmed her. Blood trickled into her eyes and ran down her face, so much that it felt like she became bathed in the stuff. She took another hit to the head and then another. Olivia's world became a sea of sharp pain.

As the plastic bag slid over her head, her last thought was of her children. She wanted to cry out, to ask God to spare her babies. She tried to yell at the top of her lungs to not let this monster get his hands on her kids. *Please don't let him do this to Ally and Blake. Please!*

Her last stand was a desperate attempt to fight, to buck, to live. But she was slowly running out of air. Her breathing became more labored until finally blackness descended. Darkness took over. Her body no longer felt anything at all. Not the ache or the agony of pain. A peace settled over her. No more thoughts rushed through her mind. But the terror and pain remained in her vacant, open eyes, eyes that would never see again, at least not in this world.

Where life had once been, now there was nothing left but an empty canvas of black.

Chapter One

For Jackson Indigo it had been a nerve-wracking forty-eight hours. Ever since his mother's phone call the day before telling him that his sister Livvy, and her family had gone missing, his mind had been a scattered mess of fear and panic.

He'd caught the first available flight out of New York for Miami International and then boarded a puddle jumper that would take him to the southern tip of Florida.

Even though he'd long since left behind his childhood home for life in the Big Apple, it didn't mean he'd hesitate coming back to tiny Indigo Key when the situation warranted it.

Sure, he'd spent holidays and birthdays here. It was impossible not to. His last visit to the area had been in the spring to help his parents bury his beloved grandmother. But he never stayed in town for longer than a five-day stint. With his busy schedule it wasn't practical.

Even as a kid growing up, there'd been a restlessness brewing inside him. Much to his mother's dismay, it had been enough to push him out of the nest completely at eighteen.

Always at the top of his class—even when that class was a mere sixty-five students—Jackson had always known what he wanted to do and set his sights on making it happen. Because Lenore and Tanner Indigo had four kids to put through college—a difficult task for a self-employed carpenter and a bookkeeper—Jackson had always known it would be an uphill battle.

As a smart, but rather nerdy guy, he'd headed north and worked his way through four years at Columbia University. Thanks to a slew of scholarships and small grants and a work-study program, he'd survived his undergrad years.

Once he got to grad school, he'd made do bussing tables and washing dishes in the school cafeteria until a research assistant job opened up. There'd been all-nighters of hard studying where he'd gone to class bleary-eyed and exhausted. But he'd made the best of his situation.

On the way to getting his Masters, he'd taken a research position that eventually turned into a teaching assistantship and an increase in pay. During most of those college years he'd held down two jobs on his way to an Environmental Science degree before moving on to MIT for his doctorate. There, he'd studied marine ecosystems. When the Woods Hole Oceanographic Institute offered him a spot on board the research vessel, *Constantine*, he'd hit the bigs as far as the world of science recognizing Jackson Indigo as an oceanographer.

After getting his Ph.D., he'd taken a job in downtown Manhattan with the Ocean Shield Institute, a nonprofit dedicated to protecting coastal watersheds and shorelines, ecosystems and marine life. The work kept him in the field most days, doing what he loved, studying catastrophic storm events and the effects on the coastal ecology and soil erosion.

Staring out the window past the wing of the jet, his eyes landed on the blue-green waters of Florida Bay and the sugar-white sand along its shoreline. It suddenly hit him that this is where his love of the ocean had started, drumming through his veins at a young age. He had a fondness for the Key—barely three and half miles long and not quite that wide.

So when his commuter plane touched down on the tarmac of the little airstrip that served the Florida Keys, memories from childhood came flooding back to him.

He'd spent his early years trouping alongside his father to fish for snapper or sea trout, or spending time snorkeling with his siblings. There had been something amazing about hitting the waves as a teen with his surfboard and spending hours lazing at the beach, ogling the girls.

There'd been an Indigo in these parts for three hundred years or more. Ever since Koda Indigo—a swashbuckling pirate—had taken refuge on the island with his captive, a Spanish countess he'd spirited away from a rival. As local legend went, when Koda had refused to ransom the beauty as planned, his crew turned on him with daggers and flintlocks to prove a point. The mutiny had forced Koda to jump overboard gripping the arm of the lady in question and swimming into the night until they'd made their way onshore to the nearest land mass. Somewhere through Jackson's ancestral heritage Indigo blood had merged with Spanish, and later, with the Seminole tribe, producing a long line of forceful, independent, stubborn mavericks— male and female alike. It occurred to him his sister, Olivia Shay Indigo Buchanan, fit that picture to a tee.

With a plunk, the Gulfstream came to an abrupt stop. It put an end to the mulling over family history and brought him back to the reason he was here.

For two days, Livvy and her husband, Walker, had been unaccounted for, which meant her two kids, Blake and Ally, had missed a couple days of school. It was out of character for his sister not to call their mother. And since no one had seen or heard from the family since Wednesday afternoon, his parents were growing more frantic by the hour. Overwhelmed by the situation, Lenore and Tanner Indigo had reached out for help from their three sons.

As soon as the pilot gave the all clear, Jackson stood up, his six-two frame taking up most of the headroom in the aisle. He grabbed his carryon from the overhead as the pilot, Bryce Kimmel, appeared from the cockpit.

"I'm sorry about Livvy and her family. It's been all over the local news. Everyone's been trying to do what they can for your mom and dad."

That one sentiment caused reality to sink in. Jackson's mouth went dry. A surge of fear lodged in his gut. Jackson stared at Bryce, a man with a linebacker build, but who had in fact played fullback in high school. "From what I understand no one's seen or heard from any of them since Wednesday evening. Livvy was supposed to bring the kids over to Mom's house on Friday night for a sleepover. It never happened."

Bryce slapped Jackson on the back with a sympathetic nod. "At least you're back home now. This is a time for family. Your mama and daddy need you here, all of you, no doubt about that." To lighten the mood, he added, "I never did understand why you or your brothers didn't go out for football. You'd have made a helluva receiver."

Jackson slipped on his Ray-Bans. "Tell that to Coach Burton. As I recall, at the time, Coach thought I was too slow, way too slow. Turtle slow is how he phrased it. Mitch's game was always baseball. And Garret, Garret just loved the water. You couldn't get that kid out of it. He even slept with his surfboard. We're pretty sure Garret must be one part amphibian, one part alien."

"That might explain local boy making good. Livvy is awful proud of him. She always submits the photos he sends from his competitions to the *Indigo Dispatch*. Over the years we've got a good look at the world through Garret's travels. Look, I know you're worried sick, but Livvy and Walker will turn up, you'll see. Why, I bet by the time you get home, your mama's already heard from them and they just got away for a few days."

Despite Jackson's head bob, he'd exchanged text messages with Mitch and knew for a fact his parents hadn't heard a thing. But he put on a brave face anyway and said, "Let's hope Livvy has a good explanation as to why they've been gone all this time."

Bryce followed his passenger down the steps, pointed across the pavement. "If I'm not mistaken that looks like Mitch waiting for you by your dad's old beat-up Ford pickup. How long's Tanner had that thing anyway?"

Jackson grinned for the first time in two days. "It's almost as old as Garret."

"Go on," Bryce directed. "Go greet your brother. I'll get your luggage, bring it over, load it up."

"Thanks, Bryce."

Jackson shifted his gaze, spotted his brother standing next to a twenty-year-old gray Ford 250 with streaks of peeling paint on the hood. He made his way over to the man who was a mere eleven months younger than he was. "I thought you were somewhere in the Bahamas."

Mitch tossed out an arm, gave his brother a man hug. "I was. We were diving near Little Bahama Bank for a treasure-laden ship we think went down in 1658. After Mom called, I caught the first flight into Miami, then took a jumper home, same as you."

"When did you get in?"

"Last night. Left my crew in the middle of the best hunt I've been on in two years. When Livvy does turn up, she better have a good explanation for taking off like this, scaring the hell out of Mom."

Jackson nodded. "Let's hope she's back home right this minute explaining herself to Mom and Dad." But the notion fell flat. Jackson's eyes bored into Mitch's. It was then he noticed how gaunt his brother looked and the dark circles that showed the strain of the past two days. There was something about that one fact that caused him to divert the topic from Livvy. "No one has keener instincts at finding a ship's location than you do. It doesn't take much for your pirate instincts to surface. I can tell you'd rather be out on the water instead of dealing with this."

Lack of sleep had taken its toll and Mitch's face showed every line. "Look, I have to keep my mind on something other than Livvy and those kids or else I'll go nuts."

"Understood. So what fortune was listed on the ship's manifest?"

Mitch's golden-brown eyes, so much like his own, gleamed with the pride of a treasure hunter. "Records show it held gold doubloons stuffed into fourteen chests, precious gems along with snuff boxes, each one made from gold, each weighing five ounces or more."

"Nice haul."

"Gotta locate it first. No good to us unless we find it."

When Bryce brought over the luggage, Jackson helped him load it into the bed of the truck, making room for his stuff among his dad's toolbox and ladder.

Bryce offered his hand. "Y'all need anything, your mama has my number. Anything Michelle and I can do, you be sure to let us know."

"Thanks," Jackson said again, as he weighed Bryce's grip. "We appreciate the offer. Would the wife still be Michelle Gretzel?" Jackson asked, his tone teasing remembering a busty brunette cheerleader whose measurements had kept him up nights.

Bryce grinned. "She's been Michelle Kimmel now for eight years. We have two daughters. One's in Blake's class at school, the other in Ally's."

Jackson ran a hand through a mop of hair the color of rich espresso and let out a sigh, the playful tone gone. "It makes me sick at my stomach just thinking about what might've happened to those kids. Surely someone knows something."

"Or saw something," Mitch tossed in. "That's the kicker. Why hasn't anyone come forward with information, a sighting, a tip of some kind?"

"They'll turn up," Bryce assured the brothers. "Maybe it's as simple as Walker and Olivia heading out of town for a few days to grab some downtime and forgetting to call."

Jackson's disdain for that idea showed on his face. "Not this time of year with school just getting started. Ask yourself, would you and Michelle do that with your kids?"

Bryce scratched his head. "No, probably not. We usually wait for three-day weekends to go exploring."

"Exactly. And if you wanted downtime, you'd need to arrange for someone to sit with the kids. It doesn't make sense that they'd take Ally and Blake and go off without telling anyone."

Mitch shifted his feet, impatient. "Sorry to break up this little reunion, but we need to get moving. Mom and Dad are waiting for us."

After another round of man hugs from Bryce, the brothers crawled into the Ford to head for home, Mitch behind the wheel. "Funny, I don't remember the football player being so warm and fuzzy the day he beat me up in eighth grade and demanded that I give him my lunch money."

Jackson snorted. "Maybe Bryce is getting soft in his old age. Or maybe he secretly still has a thing for Livvy. They went to junior prom, as I recall."

It was Mitch's turn to laugh as he turned the pickup south onto the Causeway that would take them into town. Glancing out the window at the Key that was a slice of paradise to all of them growing up, Mitch added, "Please don't put the image of Bryce and Livvy making out in my head. I'm the one who caught them tonsil diving on the front porch steps. That almost stunted me for life."

Jackson was too tired to reminisce. He let his head fall back on the headrest, eager for a chance at a quick nap. "How are they holding up, Mom and Dad?"

Worry flicked in Mitch's eyes. "About like you'd expect. Mom's trying not to bawl all the time and Dad's trying to hold it together for her. Neither one has been to work since this thing started. For days now, they've been sitting around that house imagining the worst. While he's making sure Mom doesn't break down every time the phone rings. There's something you ought to know. You're walking into a hornets' nest. Dad insists Walker's responsible for Livvy and the kids going missing."

"Not such a surprise there. Dad never did warm up to Walker."

"That's an understatement."

"So what exactly does he think Walker's up to?"

"I'll let him pitch his own case."

"Okay, so what's the battle plan? What exactly do we do first?"

"We find Livvy and the kids."

Jackson scrubbed his hands over his face in a gesture that spoke volumes about how drained he felt and he'd only been on the ground less than thirty minutes. "Some part of me hoped that by the time I got here, Livvy would drive up to the house with a big smile for all of us and say how they took off on a fishing trip."

"That didn't happen. Walker's boat is still sitting in Sugar Bay."

"That's what Mom said. This morning as I waited to board my flight at JFK, I looked up at a TV monitor only to see Olivia's name and picture come across the bottom of the screen. 'Olivia and Walker Buchanan and their two children missing from their home on Indigo Key,' that's what the tagline read. And that's when I realized this was for real and I needed to get my ass back home."

"This whole thing is surreal to me, too. I mean, where are the kids? Like you said back at the airport, Livvy wouldn't just take off without letting someone know her plans. She'd tell mom for certain."

"Yeah. And that kind of thinking made me realize that if my adventurer brother—who loves treasure hunting more than anything else in the world—tells me we have a family crisis back home, I know better than to argue with him."

Mitch sent his brother a scornful glare. "Since when did a brain like you start holding a poorly educated sailor like me in such high regard?"

Sensing the familiar sore subject building between them, Jackson took off his sunglasses so he could look his younger brother in the face. "Come on, that's not fair. Was it wrong of me to want you to go to college instead of working on a salvage ship right out of high school? As your older brother it was my duty to encourage you to do something more with your life, something better."

Mitch's face closed off at the same excuse he'd heard for years. "I had my fill of school even when I was in school. I couldn't wait to get out. I tried to make you understand that. College was something you wanted, not me."

"Fair enough. You're obviously good at what you do. Finding that Spanish galleon off the coast of Jamaica three years ago made you a wealthy man."

Mitch made a derisive noise in his throat. "I had to split the booty with a team of ten. Besides, it wasn't that much of a challenge. We found the ship in sixty feet of water where it had run aground. Didn't even take that much to clean up."

Jackson sent him a lopsided grin at the obvious attempt to downplay the importance of the find. "You've never been one to beat your chest any more than Garret. You're both fairly level-headed, a little quick to anger but still..."

"Maybe so, but when the athlete in the family agrees to leave Australia in the middle of a competition where he's going after another world surfing title, I know something's way off. I may not have a bunch of degrees like you or the athletic ability Garret possesses, but I'm pretty sure Livvy's disappearance tops a treasure hunt any day of the week."

Mitch exited toward the downtown section of town, driving past the marina where a twelve-foot bronze statue of a pirate, sword drawn, one foot resting on his pirate chest, stood tall above a flowing fountain at its base.

Carved from quartz and red Italian marble, the swashbuckling landmark had greeted tourists at the corner of Pearl Street and Seafarer Way since 1896. For more than a hundred years the sculpture had marked the entrance to the port.

With the installation of lights in 1956, the distinctive fountain lit up at night and could be seen for several miles offshore. It made for a popular backdrop where tourists could pose for snapshots.

From the point of the statue, if you wanted to venture into the business district, locals knew to hang a right onto Pearl. Take a left on Seafarer Way and it would lead you straight into the residential section of town.

Mitch kept heading right, reducing his speed past the Winn-Dixie, the bank, Mattito's Bar, a nightspot called Theo's that proudly advertised a live band seven nights a week, and several little boutiques lining the way to the strand. From there a row of restaurants gave way to a grill house that specialized in steaks, a pizza place, a barbecue joint, a hamburger stand, and a taco eatery.

Jackson saw people he recognized milling along the sidewalks sweating in the heat, either making their way from the beach, or coming back from an afternoon of fishing.

The inlet known as Sugar Bay glistened in the sun as it swelled with catchy-named sloops and sleekly-built catamarans that bobbed in the gentle waters. The sight of it all brought fond memories rushing back in a montage of snapshots from the past. The foundation of his childhood had been built on these shores, on these streets.

The smells of local cuisine caused Jackson's stomach to rumble. "Right about now I could use the biggest, juiciest cheeseburger from Charlie's that I could shovel in my mouth."

"I wouldn't mention that to Mom. When I left home she was cooking up a batch of cornbread and a pot of gumbo."

"That'll work, too. Look around. Everything seems so normal. Everyone's going about their business as usual as if nothing's wrong."

"Except Livvy and the kids aren't here."

"Exactly. When's Garret due in?"

"Tonight. And you're picking him up."

"My little brother's become bossy. Why me?"

"Hey, we're more like twins really. And you're doing the hauling because there are a couple of people I want to talk to."

Jackson's temper flared. "Not without me you don't. And I'm sure Garret will echo that same reaction. So whatever it is you're cooking up, you might as well push it back until we can go as a unit."

Mitch let out a low growl. "I was afraid of that. I should've kept my big mouth shut. You know, when I called Dad ship-to-shore to get more detail about what happened, I'm sitting out in the middle of this dive spot and decided that if you and Garret could chuck what you were doing to come home and help look, I couldn't stay away either. So while I'm not crazy about leaving my crew to get into, God knows what kind of trouble, you should know that I'm in this for however long it takes."

"Glad to hear it. What do we know for certain so far?"

Mitch ticked off the list and it was short. "That Livvy left the Vitamin Hut to pick the kids up from school on Wednesday afternoon just as she always does. She made a stop at the Winn-Dixie to pick up something for dinner. The kids were with her."

"They have surveillance of that?"

"Yep, including all three of them loading the sacks of groceries into that minivan she drives and taking off out of the parking lot. After that, Livvy heads home. We know that because she talked to Mom around five o'clock, said she had to go so she could fix dinner for the kids. And that's the last time anyone talked to her."

"What about Walker? When did he leave the health food store?"

"Walker closed up the Vitamin Hut at six o'clock. There's video of that, too, from the bank across the street. But there's nothing that tells us what time he reached home."

"Or if he ever did."

"Right. What I want to do is arrange a face to face meeting with Jessup Sinclair, get his take on all this up close."

"Is that old man still police chief?"

"He is. And Jackson, get this. Sinclair told Dad he doesn't think they disappeared on their own. That's his take, which could mean something's seriously wrong here. Like you said earlier, considering the worst-case scenario makes me sick at my stomach. We both know Livvy would call if she could. It's been seventy-two hours since she got off the phone with Mom. Something isn't right."

Jackson rubbed his tired eyes. "I talked to Mom this morning before hopping on the charter. I'm pretty sure she said there was no sign of blood found in the house, no evidence of foul play. So that's good, right?"

"Doesn't mean it isn't there. If Livvy and Walker up and left, what happened to make them do that? Crime scene techs are still turning that place upside down as we speak. Who knows what they'll find?"

"But will they share anything? That's the major question. Not likely," Jackson surmised. "That's why we need to prepare to go it alone, maybe hire us a private investigator if that's what it takes."

"I can tell you this," Mitch went on. "Blake and Ally were marked absent on Thursday and Friday. By Thursday afternoon the school called Mom when they couldn't reach Livvy or Walker to find out why the kids weren't in school. That's when Mom got worried and went over to the house. The minivan wasn't in the driveway. So she decided to use her spare key to go in and look around."

"And?" Jackson prompted.

"Nothing. Mom saw nothing out of the ordinary. The rooms downstairs were left tidy, nothing out of place, nothing missing, clothes still in the drawers, suitcases still in the closets."

"That's odd. It doesn't sound like they left on their own to me." Jackson chewed his jaw. "But where's the minivan?"

Mitch shook his head. "That's the thing. There's been no sign of it anywhere around town."

After reaching the end of the row of businesses in downtown, Mitch gunned the truck toward the corner of Blue Fin and Windward giving Jackson his first glimpse of the media craze. Scads of journalists, neighbors, and onlookers had invaded Livvy and Walker's neighborhood. Like an annoying swarm of mosquitos, the reporters fluttered around the two-story house that Livvy had painted a soft green.

Jackson sucked in a breath, remembering how ecstatic his sister had been the day she and Walker closed on the property five years earlier. She'd emailed everyone pictures of the interior, room by room.

"This is anything but normal," Jackson muttered. "Just look at those vultures standing out here while the state police try to keep everyone back."

The crowd was so thick the closest Mitch could park the pickup was six houses away on the other side of the narrow street.

"Why are all these people hanging around here anyway?" Jackson grumbled. "What do they hope to gain or to see?"

"Hey, don't knock it. Many of these on-air personalities made the trip all the way from Miami and Tampa to cover Livvy's story up close and personal." Mitch pointed a finger at a good-looking platinum blonde. "And she's down here from Jacksonville. Getting the word out is part of the process. You'll have to figure out a way to deal with it. Someone has to be the family spokesperson. These guys have already been bugging Mom and Dad to make a statement. Somebody's got to do it."

Jackson wiped his brow beginning to sweat at the thought of standing in front of a wall of reporters and microphones. He ran a hand through his hair. "This is nuts."

"More like unbelievable," Mitch corrected.

"That too. It's hard to imagine that six blocks from here is where we grew up. Mom always worried about her sons going out into the big bad world. Which meant Olivia should've been the safest since she never left Indigo Key for longer than a week."

"Good point. Her getaway for a week was the cruise she and Walker took on their honeymoon."

"Yeah. It's difficult to believe Olivia married Walker two years out of high school."

In the heat of an Indian summer, Mitch noticed Jackson sweating and reached over, cranked the air conditioning up to max. "No matter what I said earlier, I can't take much of this. I think you should be the family spokesman because, let's face it, Dad is not the most diplomatic person you want in front of the world. You know how he feels about the Buchanans. That's bound to come out in the first few minutes they shove a microphone in his face. Any statement he tries to make will likely be biased and rough. Are you ready to get out of here?"

Jackson nodded. "Yep. Get me home. There's nothing to do here anyway except watch the media melt in the heat of September."

"Not until all these cops clear out and the horde leaves."

Mitch hit the gas and turned the corner. In the shadow of the saltshaker-style lighthouse at the end of the block, Jackson spotted several more newshounds who'd staked out the house where he'd grown up. A few stragglers lined Quay Avenue. One van had lettering from as far away as Atlanta, Georgia.

"Sheesh, these guys are everywhere. They're waving us down," Jackson noted.

The small crowd had Mitch slowing to keep from hitting one of the more aggressive types. "That's because they're looking for a quote from the family they can air tonight."

"I'm not up to making a statement so don't even suggest it. Hell, I just got here, I'm not even sure my brain has engaged yet or what exactly is going on."

"I'm with you there." Mitch maneuvered his dad's pickup past the string of reporters and pulled into the side driveway behind his mother's faded red Subaru station wagon parked under the carport.

Jackson got out on his side, grabbed his bag from the bed of the truck and stood there watching one of the journalists make a mad dash toward him.

"I'm Weston Hunt from Orlando," the on-air personality began.

Even though Jackson recognized the reporter from decades of commentary, he didn't let the man get his question out. "I have nothing to say yet. I haven't even had time to see firsthand what we're up against."

"I don't have anything to say either," Mitch tossed out. "Just give us some time to get a handle on what's happened and we'll appear on camera during your live broadcast tomorrow. We'll make it a press conference. Deal?"

That seemed to appease the newscaster. "A presser? Sure. Okay. Deal. What time do you think that might be?"

Determined to keep his cool, Jackson chose to make his case by glowering at Weston. "We don't know yet, okay? Look, we haven't even had a chance to sit down with our parents yet. When we're able to assess all our options, we'll let you in on our plan. How's that?"

Weston nodded, handed off a business card. "Fine. So you think the police are doing everything they can to find your sister and her family?"

Jackson's temper ramped up. "Now see, I have no idea. We don't know much more than you guys do. So making a statement under those conditions would seem rather foolish on my part, don't you think?"

It was either his tone or the lethal glare that sent the longtime correspondent scurrying back across the street to his van.

"Way to go, big brother," Mitch sang out. "You up to giving a press conference? Those guys can be brutal when they want to be."

Jackson glanced back across the street at the media. "I'm not gonna hide from 'em or run dashing into the house every time they drive by if that's what you mean. When it comes time, the whole family will stand together as a unit just as Livvy would expect us to do."

Having said what was on his mind, he took the time to study the little two-story frame house that belonged to his parents. Somehow they'd managed to raise four kids in a shotgun-type cottage the size of a hamster cage. The original foursquare had started out a mere one thousand square feet. But over time the carpenter had made sure it grew to a roomy fourteen total. The living room always seemed to be stuffed with furniture while the three small bedrooms were always packed to the brim with kids.

Jackson recalled the fights between siblings over every square inch of available space. He also remembered the day his father got fed up with all the squabbles and agreed to add a sunroom-type enclosed porch onto the back, next to the kitchen. It sounded like heaven to Jackson.

As the oldest boy, he dug in and fought for his right to claim that spot for his own. The day he'd won, he celebrated his newfound freedom by cranking up the CD player he'd bought with his own money and declared the room off limits to all who dared to enter. He was twelve at the time, Olivia fourteen. The fact that he'd won the rights to the barebones interior meant he had his own digs, even if he had to put up with basic drywall and whatever leftover paint they had on hand. Which was probably the reason Livvy had passed on entering the fray. As the only girl, she'd already nailed down special treatment anyway—a room of her own without having to share with anyone.

Jackson hadn't cared about the sunroom's décor or lack thereof. He made do with a hand-me-down twin bed from a cousin and an old dresser his aunt donated to the cause. To cover the barren walls, he saved his allowance and bought Pearl Jam posters and world maps to use for wall art.

Since settling into his nirvana-like digs, the two oldest Indigo kids could proudly boast they had their own rooms, while the grade-schoolers, Mitch and Garret, still languished in shared living quarters.

Score one for being born ahead of his other brothers.

Now, Jackson gazed at the bungalow's paint job. The house had weathered eight hurricanes, losing the entire roof only once in 1992, when Hurricane Andrew ripped through town carrying winds in excess of a hundred and seventy miles an hour. In 2005, Dennis caused the carport to give way. It collapsed on top of his mother's old Chevy. All that didn't take into account how many tropical storms had blown through the region and left them having to rebuild some part of the house. Like the time his dad had commandeered his three able-bodied sons to add on a balcony to the top floor. The addition had been his mother's birthday present. Owning an older home meant the house always seemed to need a repair job of one sort or another.

Last Christmas, as a gift to his parents, he'd hired someone to give the native heart pine a fresh coat of creamy white. The shutters still bore the pastel blue his mother favored giving the family home its Caribbean zing along with a dose of Jamaican gingerbread lace and a touch of Victorian arts and crafts. He liked to think that only Lenore Indigo could make it all come together and work like it did.

He hadn't taken two steps when his mom burst out the front door and bounded down the porch steps. The sight of her running to give him a hug reminded him how she'd reacted on his first visit back home after a year in New York. She'd given him what amounted to a hero's welcome, complete with banner. The only thing missing at the time was a marching band. The whole thing had been a gesture that embarrassed him at the time. But that was Lenore Indigo. She had a habit of putting everything she had into making a small thing an event, especially when it came to one of her kids. At five-three and fair-haired, Jackson had always thought of her as an indomitable pixie.

"You made it," Lenore sighed, taking her son's face in both hands and kissing both cheeks. "I'm so glad you could come home. I can't wait to have all three of my sons here to help look for Livvy."

"Don't cry," Jackson pleaded. On instinct, he wrapped her up in his arms. When he scanned the yard he zeroed in on his dad who watched from the railing. It wasn't difficult to remember his parents had been sweethearts since high school. His heart broke to realize how vulnerable they were now. It triggered a promise. "We're home now. We'll find them."

Lenore dabbed at her eyes. "Just when I get my boys here, my girl's gone along with my grandbabies. You know as well as I do that there's no way Livvy would ever take off with the kids like this. Walker wouldn't leave his health food store closed for three whole days unless something drastic had taken place."

Tanner Indigo stepped off the porch, his usual trademark stoic attitude wiped from his face, replaced by worry and lack of sleep. "Mark my words, Walker had something to do with this."

Jackson exchanged a look with Mitch, their coffee-colored eyes simmering with a newfound concern. But it was Jackson who moved the four of them along inside. "Let's table this discussion until we get out of the watchful eyes of the media. I don't think giving the reporters a show right now is a very wise move on our part."

One by one they trailed into the house. Jackson followed and waited until his father had shut the front door. "Why do you say Walker was involved in this? Was he abusive toward Livvy?"

Tanner gazed at his son. "Because his business was in serious trouble. The Vitamin Hut was bleeding debt."

Jackson chewed the inside of his jaw. "But Royce Buchanan is one of the richest men on the Key. Why wouldn't he bail Walker out like he has all the other times?"

Mitch spoke up. "Maybe Walker's old man finally got fed up and reached his loan limit."

"Then we need to find out for sure. Tell me where to stow my gear. Same place as last spring?"

"I'm not sharing a room with Jackson or Garret," Mitch declared in protest.

Tanner pointed a finger at his sons. "You'll both bunk where I put you. Jackson Lee, you'll take your old room out back. No argument. Mitchell Taylor, you'll sleep where you did last night. Garret gets Olivia's old room. Are we happy little campers now?" Tanner barked.

"Yes, sir," Jackson and Mitch replied in unison.

Jackson left it at that and made his way toward the back of the house, past the kitchen. He decided this living arrangement would take some getting used to. How long would it take for a thirty-one-year-old man to get used to taking orders from his father again? Holidays were one thing, but an indefinite stay might mean a move into a hotel.

He dumped the two suitcases he'd brought on the same futon he'd slept on for five days last April and took out his cell phone. He was about to send a text message to his coworker and sometimes bedmate, Rachel Tarleton, when he looked up and saw Mitch standing in the doorway.

"I know what you're thinking," Mitch announced.

Jackson paused in mid-text and decided to table the idea of connecting with Rachel. For now, it seemed like too much effort for very little gain. Mainly because she'd never been big on dealing with family issues, mostly hers, certainly not his. For over two years Rachel had made one excuse after another not to accompany him back to Florida, not even to meet his parents. During Thanksgiving and Christmas, she'd go her way and he would go his. That said all anyone needed to know about the on-again-off-again relationship.

Jackson gazed at his brother. "I doubt you know what I'm thinking."

Mitch plopped down almost on top of the luggage. "Sure I do. Right about now you're trying to figure out how the hell you're going to deal with sharing space again with Mom and Dad over the long haul. But we have bigger problems than letting Dad get under our skin."

"I know that," Jackson muttered, irritation laced in his tone. "Believe me, if I could have figured out how not to disappoint Mom, I would've had you drop me at the hotel on the way here. But it's best if we stay close, keep Mom happy and make this place our war room."

"Agreed. What do you think about what Dad said? Could Walker's financial difficulties be the reason they took off?"

Jackson dropped down on the mattress. "Honestly, I'm not buying that. How bad could the finances have been when they had Royce Buchanan to go to if things got tight at the Vitamin Hut? With Royce's wealth do you really think he'd ever let his son flounder in debt?"

"Maybe he squandered whatever Royce gave him."

"Now that I believe. But I'm not ready to make Walker the bad guy yet. Let's get Dad to finish dissing on what he knows and decide how much is fact or fiction. Then we go find Sinclair and have a little chat with him. By that time Garret's plane should be touching down at the airfield."

Over his mother's sweet iced tea and bowls of shrimp gumbo, Jackson crumbled his cornbread over the soup and listened to his father go on about Walker.

"That son of a bitch always did look out for himself first, the kids second, and Livvy was way down on his list at third. That attitude never did sit well with me. You wait and see. This will turn out to be some scam Walker's involved in that somehow bit him in the ass and burst back on Livvy."

Dubious, Jackson scratched his chin, puzzled. "What specifically?"

"I'll give you an example. Several weeks back, Livvy told me about some guy named Connelly showing up at the store trying to get money out of Walker. When she pressed him for details, Walker clammed up, refused to share with her what was going on."

"Dad, there could be a hundred reasons why…"

Tanner cut him off. "I trust my gut more than I trust a hundred other reasons. Walker takes too much after his daddy. I've known Royce back in his salad days when he'd do anything to fatten his bank account, anything at all. Walker's not that much different."

Jackson leaned back in his chair, drained his glass of tea. "What do you think, Mom? Are you in agreement with Dad's take? Was Walker that secretive? Did he refuse to share those kinds of details with Livvy? She never mentioned that to me."

Lenore put down her spoon. "It's no secret your father's never liked Walker much, downright resented him for a lot of reasons. And there's no denying the recent money problems the two were having. I thought it was because they poured all their savings into the Vitamin Hut. Starting a business puts a strain on finances and a marriage. I know at one-time Walker went out of his way to make Livvy happy. He'd have done anything in the world for her. But lately, that had changed. Is the marriage perfect? Is Walker the perfect husband? No. Livvy admitted there'd been some problems there. They'd argued a lot since starting the health food store. But anyone knows that's normal when you have a start-up. Things are likely slow to take off until you get your feet firmly planted.

Those first few months were lean times. But Livvy told me that the last couple months, the store had been doing much better."

Jackson frowned. "But what about their marriage? It sounds like you both knew there were bad times. Was it doing better than before?"

"No, not really." Lenore picked up her tea with a shaky hand, took a sip and pointed a finger toward Tanner. "Just because you don't like Walker very much doesn't mean he's taken off and done something bad."

Jackson watched as his mother's hand began to tremble more, so much that the glass almost slipped out of her fingers. He reached over and took it from her, set it down on the table as Lenore dabbed at her eyes, now filled with tears.

She began to sob. "Our grandbabies were supposed to spend the night with us last night. Blake and Ally always made coming over on Friday nights special for us. They made us promise we'd make brownies and watch movies. I'd already checked out *WALL-E* at the library, which they hadn't seen before."

The trio of men in the room wasn't sure how to handle the waterworks. Mitch nodded his head for Jackson to do something and Jackson did the same to his father. Finally it was Tanner who got up to pat his wife on the back, not knowing what else to do.

Lenore brushed off the attention and waved him off. "Oh, I'm okay. I just want them found safe and sound."

After several more minutes, Lenore was able to get herself under control and cleared her throat. "So what do we do next? Your father already got Jimmy Don Bates to make us up some posters. People we've known for forty years have started plastering them all over town. So what now? Are we supposed to just sit around and wait and do nothing?"

Jackson reached over, took his mom's hand, squeezed her fingers. "Mitch and I don't intend to sit around and wait. After lunch we'll go see Sinclair, try to corner him to give us an update on what's going on with the investigation. Next, we'll try to track down this Connelly guy and see what happens from there."

"In the meantime you guys keep driving around town looking for Livvy's car," Mitch suggested, wiping his mouth with his napkin. He stood up to put his dishes in the sink as he'd been taught to do from childhood. "By that time, Garret's plane will be here."

Jackson nodded and repeated what Mitch had done with his bowl and utensils. He took one last slug of tea, draining the glass before he turned to face everyone. "After seventy-two hours, we deserve some kind of official update from law enforcement. That means after Mitch and I talk to Sinclair, we'll call or text you with what our next course of action will be."

"Fair enough," Tanner said. "But one of us has to go talk to Royce. And it won't be me."

"Your father's afraid he'll lose his cool and punch him in the face," Lenore explained. "Those two have almost come to blows many times through the years."

Mitch slapped his brother on the back. "Then we'll send in Jackson. He's Royce's favorite."

"Gee, thanks," Jackson drawled. "I thought I was the one taking point with Sinclair."

"Hey, Sinclair still carries a grudge toward me after I egged his car for hassling me and my friends one day after school," Mitch admitted. "Come to think of it, maybe I should wait in the car. He'd probably be more likely to cooperate without me there."

Jackson's eyes sparkled with newfound amusement. "Not a chance. This little meeting was your idea. Besides, we're grown men now. Screw the past."

Chapter Two

Indigo Key had a police force of five—four uniformed officers that reported to a bear of a man named Jessup Sinclair.

The wrinkles on Sinclair's face showed almost seventy decades worth of living. He'd been police chief in these parts since Hurricane Andrew whipped through Florida in 1992 and blew away entire neighborhoods. A plainspoken guy who wasn't always politically correct in how he did things, he'd gotten his start handing out tickets at the Florida Highway Patrol. After retiring from there, he'd settled into Indigo Key in hopes of watching sunsets and spending his time with a rod and reel in his hands.

But that had all changed one day in January 1992 when a prisoner escaped from Big Pine Road Prison fifteen miles from where Jessup had gone fishing for mangrove snapper. He'd no sooner thrown his line in the waters of Sugar Bay when he noticed a man lurking nearby wearing the unmistakable blue prison garb with the white stripe running down the pants leg.

Jessup had simply taken out his cell phone and called the cops. While waiting for them to show up, he'd removed his Beretta pistol from his backpack, the one he always carried with him, and watched as the prisoner made his way over to where he stood on the shoreline. By the time the local police force arrived, Jessup had the prisoner restrained using nylon fishing tape to bind the man's hands and feet.

The incident had gained Jessup instant notoriety and respect from the community. That spring, an election year, the town had voted him in as their police chief.

Those he served described him best as a fair-minded guy, determined to keep the town free of riffraff. Since there wasn't much crime to speak of in little Indigo Key, most people gave him a thumbs-up for a job well done.

When Jackson and Mitch strode into his office, Jessup showed a willingness to gab, mainly because he'd been forced to turn the Buchanan case over to the state police almost from the get-go. Jessup wasn't happy about that turn of events. As he talked, his bitterness was evident in every word.

"Either Walker's daddy got me taken off the investigation, or the state police didn't think I was up to the task to handle this kind of high profile missing persons case."

Jackson exchanged looks with Mitch before leveling a stare at Jessup. "Why would Royce Buchanan want you off the case? That makes no sense. You're the guy in charge who knows everyone around here for miles."

Jessup skewed up his forehead. "Because it sounds like something that sneaky so-and-so would do just to spite me. Royce hasn't given two hoots for me since I ran his boy in for a DUI back when Walker was seventeen."

"Small town politics," Jackson mused. "Always in play even if the event happened a dozen years ago."

Jessup ignored the remark and went on, "Whatever the reason, the state sent some young smartass down here from Tallahassee by the name of Dack Hawkins. What kind of name is Dack anyway? Makes me think of a damn silly duck."

Jackson put a hand on the man's shoulder. "Jessup, we know you're pissed. We don't blame you, but focus. What can you tell us about Livvy's case?"

"You mean other than there's no evidence of foul play in the house?"

"How can that be? Where's Livvy's minivan? Indigo Key is a dot on the map. It has less than four thousand people living here unless it's during tourist season, which ended Labor Day weekend. Before we got here, Mom and Dad spent Thursday and Friday driving up and down the streets combing the area for any sign of the car. How hard could it be to locate Livvy's van?"

"I put a BOLO out for it Thursday afternoon as soon as Lenore called me. At the time, Tanner had rounded up a bunch of his friends to scour the streets. So far, we've got no sign of it. I know you guys are looking for quick answers, but you need to quit getting your britches in a twist and prepare for the long haul. This could take time."

"Please don't tell us that," Mitch grumbled.

Jackson wasn't as diplomatic. "Time's against us. What if Livvy and the kids are in a desperate situation? What if they needed us yesterday? We've already let them down. We're having to play catch up."

Jessup nodded in understanding. "I didn't say patience would come easy. Look, you might want to talk to a woman by the name of Tessa Connelly. She came here to the Key, first of the week from Nags Head, North Carolina, to look for her brother, Ryan Connelly. According to her, three weeks ago, this guy leaves home driving his own Honda Civic and heads down here to see Walker. But when he didn't show back up in North

Carolina on schedule, the sister got worried. After two weeks of no news, Miz Connelly headed down here to check things out for herself. She's made a pest of herself around town ever since."

Jackson's forehead wrinkled into a scowl before he shot a glance over at Mitch. "So you're saying this Connelly's gone missing, too? Could this guy have done something to Livvy and Walker and the kids and then disappeared?"

Jessup shook his head. "Not likely, since Connelly went missing first. I haven't even been able to locate the Civic he was driving. I put out a media release the day his sister phoned me to let me know he'd gone missing. By that time it'd been three days since he'd checked out of the hotel."

"And what did your investigation turn up?" Jackson wanted to know.

"Not a thing. Since then I've checked with the state police in Georgia and South Carolina, which would be along his driving route back home. Nothing turned up. Checked hospitals for matching admissions. Still nothing."

"What did this guy want with Walker, do you know?"

"Fishing. That's the story I got from his sister. Miz Connelly said her brother came to the Key at Walker's invitation to fish for a trophy and hasn't been seen since he checked out of the Mainsail Lodge. This town goes years without so much as a major crime wave and in a short span of time we have a missing family along with a missing fisherman. That's two huge coincidences. I flat out don't believe in coincidences. I'm thinking these two events might be connected. I just haven't found what links them together."

"You mean other than Walker?" Jackson pointed out. "Hmm, since the Key lacks any major hotel chains I'm assuming the Connelly woman went back to the Mainsail Lodge where her brother stayed. Or did she check into the Sugar Bay Motel where she could walk down the strand to be closer to the shops?"

Jessup thumbed through his notes. "She struck me as someone who wanted access to where her brother had been. Ah, here we go. Yep, I have her checking into the Mainsail."

"Does it say there what room she's in?"

"Three-eighteen."

"You don't mind if we talk to her?"

Over his trifocals, Jessup sent Jackson a harsh look. "Honestly, I feel sorry for her because I don't have a single thing on her brother since he checked out of the lodge. There's no trail to follow. It seems Connelly came here and the Keys swallowed him up. The man just up and vanished. As far as anyone knows he could've made it across the state line before something happened to him in Georgia, maybe even South Carolina. I tried to explain all those possibilities to her." He shook his head. "But she didn't want to hear 'em. Wastin' time here if you ask me."

"So you think this guy had an accident on his way back home?"

"I did before Livvy and Walker went missing. Before last Thursday I'd convinced myself that Connelly was someone else's problem." Jessup scratched his nearly bald head and the sliver of gray hair remaining. "Now, I'm not so sure her brother ever left Indigo Key. So why would I mind if you guys touch base with his sister? I've got nothin' to tell her."

Jackson held up his hands in peace. "Just asking. We don't want to step on anyone's toes."

"Since when?" Jessup fired back. "You don't fool me. Everybody around these parts still remembers that wild bunch of heathens known as the Indigos. That includes Livvy. Always thought that was due to the Injun blood you guys have running through your veins."

At the derogatory name, Jackson swapped peeved looks with Mitch. This was the sometimes prejudice side of Jessup he remembered from his youth. It brought out a defensive posture. "I'm sure you already know that in these parts the Seminole tribe beat you here by a few hundred years."

Unfazed at the comment, the police chief went on with his recollections. "That wild blood started up long before your middle school years. None of you ever let up till you left here, course Livvy stayed. Besides, y'all take after Tanner that way. What you guys don't realize is that your daddy had a wild streak in his heyday that would make the hair stand up on your heads. Shame he pulled Lenore into his shenanigans."

Mitch laughed at that depiction. "Oh really? Do enlighten us. That would make for interesting fodder during meal time."

Jackson chuckled. "Are you referring to the rumors that Mom and Dad once crawled up on the water tower before Homecoming and painted it orange to make it look like a giant jack-o'-lantern just in time for Halloween?"

Jessup tried to hide a grin. "That they did. Lenore and Tanner were just as wild and reckless when they were young as you boys. Don't let them tell you any different. Already your daddy's showed he's not afraid to get in the state investigator's face with an opinion about this whole thing. Yesterday he got into it with Dack Hawkins outside Livvy's house. You might want to do more to keep him in line."

Jackson's mouth quirked up and he lobbed back, "As if either one of us could make that happen. Surely you don't fault Dad for being upset? His only daughter's gone missing along with his only grandchildren. What do you expect him to do, keep his cool? We're talking about Tanner Indigo here."

Jessup let the attitude slide. "I expect he'll do what he wants like always. However, there's a way to go about it without pissing off the detective in charge of the case. Tanner's convinced himself that Walker was into all kinds of nefarious stuff and shared that with Dack Hawkins. I gotta tell you, I don't see it. Walker had his problems but I know for a fact that man worked hard every day to get that vitamin place to where it would make a profit, maybe not a fortune but enough to pay the bills. Walker even told me he'd found a contractor to design a website he could use to take mail orders nationwide. Walker had big plans."

"Maybe too big," Jackson stated. "Maybe Walker got in over his head."

Jessup shook his head. "You think what you want. I might not be a fan of Royce Buchanan. But my instincts tell me if that had been the case, Walker's daddy would've bailed his baby boy out of trouble faster than a knife fight in a phone booth."

"Then I guess we'll head to the hotel and talk to this Connelly woman. Promise me, you'll let us know if you hear anything through the law enforcement grapevine, anything at all. I know despite being taken off the case, you'll maintain your contacts with the higher-ups in Tallahassee. I know you have them."

"You betcha. Count on it."

They ended it there and walked back outside to the parking lot. Jackson angled to face his brother. "I didn't want to mention to Jessup that Dad brought up the name Connelly like he was Walker's business partner. I'm hoping we didn't misstep there."

"I don't think we did. We should probably test the water first. It won't hurt to hold a few things back until we figure things out more. We need to wade carefully through the water, find the people we can trust the most. Right now, Jessup's clearly on Walker's side, he made that clear enough."

"I was surprised we found Jessup so cordial," Jackson noted as he got behind the wheel. "I remember a guy who could be a bit of an ass."

Mitch climbed in on the passenger side. "I guess, if you call cordial using his customary slurs when it comes to referring to our Native American heritage."

"Yeah, that sucked, but it's fairly typical of Jessup. I thought he'd probably stonewall us. He was actually friendly. He didn't have to tell us about the Connelly woman."

"Then let's make a stop at the lodge and find out for ourselves if she holds any answers."

"That, or Jessup's sending us off on a wild goose chase."

The Mainsail Lodge showed off its Spanish influence with archways across the front of the three-story building. The pastel blue painted stucco trimmed in banana yellow gave off a cheery invite to what the rooms offered inside. A tiled courtyard surrounded by fragrant calla lilies and pretty amaryllis led guests past a stone fountain and into the tastefully decorated lobby.

The place had changed hands over the years, but still stood as the focal point at the corner of Largo Avenue and Bayside Boulevard. Each room on the front side had a view of the water. Beach access was as easy as a mere trek down a few steps to reach the wedge of pearl-white sand that glistened in the sun.

The September afternoon had warmed to a humid swelter by the time Jackson turned the pickup into the parking lot. The sun banked in the west, giving a golden shimmer to the waves as the fishing boats in the marina bobbed and swayed to a rhythm as old as the tides.

"Should we both go up there and confront her?" Mitch asked, glancing toward the third floor.

Jackson debated their options. "At this point, two against one might not be a smart move. We want to learn as much as we can about her brother's association with Walker, even if we have to lean on her some. Two might seem like we're pouncing on her."

"Okay, then which one of us does the leaning?"

"I'll go. I'm more diplomatic."

"That's your ego talking," Mitch chided as he watched his brother get out of the pickup and walk toward the hotel's portico. But he stayed where he was, grateful it wasn't him making the long trek to confront the woman.

As Jackson mounted the stairs to room three-eighteen, he went over what he wanted to say, reminding himself he needed to show the utmost in tact. That comment proved to be downright prophetic when he rapped on the door.

From inside, Tessa Connelly was in no mood for a visitor. But since she'd come to this wide spot in the road on her own to find Ryan, she was determined to put up with the local yokel attitude, which seemed to run glacial cold toward strangers. For the past week, she'd clearly felt the sting of being the outsider.

Tessa stared through the peephole, only to see a man she didn't recognize. He had tawny skin, a mass of dark sable hair, one shade off from inky black. The amber burnish to his chocolate eyes reminded her of exotic locales. She pegged him right away as having Native American roots or a fair amount of Creole running through his veins. All he needed was a cutlass in his hand and he could easily pass for a seventeenth-century pirate. She recalled walking past a statue near the marina. The resemblance to that monument and her visitor was uncanny. There was a familiarity around the nose and mouth, the same way his eyes were set as if he were on a dogged mission.

Cautious to a fault, but even more so since arriving in Indigo Key, Tessa shouted through the wood, "State your business and tell me who you are and what you want."

Jackson went into his rehearsed spiel, introducing himself in a louder tone to penetrate through the door. Explaining the reason for his visit, he went on, "My sister's family has been missing since Wednesday. Chief Sinclair told me you're looking for your brother. I need to ask you a few questions about what he was doing down here and why he was demanding money from Walker Buchanan."

That statement had Tessa throwing open the door with attitude and bluster. "Demanding money? Are you sure that's the approach to this you want to take right off the bat? Accusing my brother of…"

Jackson didn't hear the last part. He stood back and gaped at the knockout redhead who answered the door. She had long copper-colored hair that swung in a tapered cut down to her shoulders. Her face was like the silky dew of morning, flawless except for a splash of freckles across the bridge of her nose. Her deep sapphire eyes narrowed into sharp crystals. At the moment her lips leaned toward pouty, or maybe just a flat-out ill-tempered mouth.

Tessa stared at the visitor, who hadn't spoken another word. "Well? What's wrong with you? Is everyone in this town just plain rude or what?"

That insult had him shaking off the dazzle, coming back to earth with a sputter. "You're Tessa Connelly?"

"I thought we'd already established that." A measure of sympathy moved through her knowing she'd seen his sister's story plastered all over the local news channels. But she still took exception to the man's accusatory tone when it came to Ryan. "For your information, my brother was looking to get paid. Walker Buchanan hired Ryan to design his website, begged him to create something that really popped. Ryan got half upfront, but that left a balance of five grand. Walker owed my brother the other half of the money. Ryan came down here to collect it."

Jackson whistled through his teeth. "Ten grand's a steep price to pay for a simple site when I can do one for a fraction of that cost."

Tessa's fists curled and landed on her hips. She glared back at him in a fighting stance. "Sure, you could go that way if you preferred tacky. Your brother-in-law wanted upscale and market-friendly, including the ability to shop and order online. He wanted features like a shopping cart and forums where customers could ask questions about the herb and vitamin supplements. Those features jacked the price up. Ryan put together all the bells and whistles while I wrote the copy. That price also came with one year of web hosting and maintenance. If you ask me, Walker got an exceptional deal for all that stuff he requested."

Jackson had to admit upscale sounded like something Walker would demand. "But Sinclair said your brother came down here to fish."

Tessa rolled her eyes and snarled back, "That sounds like something your inept sheriff would focus on instead of the fact Walker owed him money."

"Police chief," Jackson corrected.

"Whatever. The thing you need to know is that Ryan fulfilled his part of the contract, one hundred percent. But after sending your brother-in-law several demands for payment, and getting ignored, Ryan felt like he'd been scammed. Buchanan went silent for almost a month, not a word out of him. But Ryan didn't give up. He kept sending him invoices to Walker's email account. After another week went by and the money still hadn't shown up in the bank as promised, Ryan, went to bugging the hell out of him, this time with phone calls. Then one day, Ryan decided to ratchet up the heat with the only thing he had left. If Walker didn't come up with the money within seventy-two hours, Ryan would take down the website. The day after Ryan sent that email, out of the blue, this Walker guy sends Ryan back a response, all friendly like. He says for Ryan to come down to Florida and they'd settle up the account. It seems Walker wanted to take him fishing during his visit to make up for the misunderstanding about the payment and to show there were no hard feelings."

Tessa started to tear up. "The last time I heard from Ryan was the day he left Nags Head. He drove down here in his own vehicle and now I can't even locate the car. Neither can your chief of police. No one seems to want to cooperate with me or tell me anything. No one seems to care. All I know is Ryan's business arrangement with Walker was amenable up until Walker refused to pay. Now, Ryan's gone missing."

"So you're saying Ryan drove all this way for five grand? That doesn't make any sense. Why didn't Ryan demand Walker send the money via wire transfer?"

"Maybe because Walker never had any intentions of paying Ryan what he owed him. Did you consider that angle? If you want to know what I think, I think your brother-in-law lured Ryan down here with every intention of doing him harm and then followed through with it."

"Over five grand? Walker's father pretty much owns half this town. Walker…"

Tessa stepped closer to Jackson and poked a sharp fingernail into his chest. "Now, you listen to me, asshole. You don't get to come to my room and accuse my brother of wrongdoing, especially since he's missing. Ryan was merely doing his job, a job Walker contracted him to do. Ryan created a beautiful, detailed, artistic work of art for this guy and Buchanan stiffed him. The fishing story was nothing more than a come-on to get Ryan down here…"

Her breath hitched. She had to pause before going on. "All Ryan did was trust the wrong guy. He came down here to collect his money and maybe get in some fishing, something he loved doing and now…"

"But for five grand? People don't go missing over five grand."

"Stop saying it like that! Some people need that kind of cash to—I don't know—do regular things like eat and pay rent. Or haven't you heard?"

When she finally took a breath, Jackson tried to correct his mistake. "You're right. Let's back up a minute. In case you didn't understand the situation, my family is in the same boat you're in, looking for answers anywhere we can find them. That's what brought me to your door, not…I didn't come in here to accuse your brother of any wrongdoing."

Tessa pushed her hair off her face and cut him off. "Sure you did. It's as if you thought Ryan had done something dishonest and pressured Walker Buchanan for money on a whim. If anyone should be outraged here, it's me. I'm the one who should be chucking spears the size of cannons back at you for that accusatory tone. I'm willing to cut you a degree of slack because you have a missing family of four. But that doesn't mean you get to walk in here and accuse my brother of being part of something illegal. And in case you weren't paying attention, Ryan went missing weeks *before* the members of your family ever did."

Jackson's eyes flashed amber hot. "That's been pointed out to me already. For the record, I'm not accusing your brother of anything. I'm trying to figure out what went on and why we've been unable to locate two little kids. And how exactly they could possibly play into taking off like this? Or have you forgotten there are kids involved?"

He let out a long, frustrated breath as he searched her wary blue eyes. "Look, I apologize if I led you to believe I thought your brother was into something bad. Walker wasn't exactly a choirboy. He comes from a long line of slick wealthy operators."

He scrubbed his hands over his face. "I tell you what, let's start over. How about we merge our forces? Come to my parents' house tonight for dinner. We'll sit down and hash this all out and try to get to the bottom of it."

Tessa bit her lip. "Really? This isn't some sort of trick, is it, to lure me out of the hotel and do away with me in the dark of night? Because if you don't mind me saying, so far, this town of yours sucks because it's mostly been unfriendly as hell to me. And I'm not completely sure who I should trust."

"No tricks. I'm sorry about the cold reception," Jackson said in apology. "But we'll try to rectify the friendliness thing. Right now, I need to go pick my brother up at the airport. If you have a pen, I'll write down directions to get to the house. It isn't far. You won't have any trouble finding it."

She sucked in a nervous breath to ease the pent-up stress. "Better still, give me the address and I'll key it into my phone, let my mobile GPS app do the rest."

Jackson took the phone out of her hand and typed in the info along with his number. "There. You get lost, you call."

"I won't. Get lost, that is. I started out as a mapmaker, also known as a field surveyor for the county. At least I used to do that before I found out there's more money in blogging online full time."

"You're kidding. There's money in blogging?"

She lifted a shoulder of indifference. "Yeah, who knew? If you do it the right way."

He cracked a grin. "It's a shame you gave up the mapmaker thing. I use maps all the time."

She finally rewarded him with a half-smile. "Glad to hear it. But doesn't popular myth state that most men forego directions or maps altogether?"

"Only if they want to wander around aimlessly in the wilderness." Curious, he had to ask. "What kind of a blog?"

"DIY projects. One of the local hardware stores back in Nags Head employs me to run their blog, promote business and answer online questions about a variety of projects. Then there's the fact I have an additional in with the owners because my dad's a plumber. He's been a good customer for decades, although he was thinking about retiring soon. That is, if my stepmother will allow it."

Jackson sent her a strange look. "So she's one of those taskmasters who wears the pants in the family?"

"Pardon my being honest, but Suzanne's a bitch, plain and simple, the typical poster girl for wicked stepmothers. My poor dad joined one of those online dating sites and found Suzanne for a twenty-five-dollar membership fee. Not much of a bargain since she reeled him in looking for a lonely sap with a fat bank account, which she now controls. My dad's the sweetest guy. All he was looking for was a little company after my mother died. Instead he got an overbearing shrew who makes him check in every thirty minutes or so."

"Wow, she sounds horrible."

"You have no idea. She has a penchant for sitting on her ass and screaming orders at him like a queen bee. She treats him like her personal fetch boy." Tessa struggled with that description. "I feel so sorry for my poor dad. He'll probably end up working himself into an early grave and have a heart attack standing over someone's plugged toilet and when he dies Suzanne will get every dime of his life insurance. After he's served his purpose she'll likely go online, and do the same thing all over again to some other poor schlep."

Jackson wasn't sure how to respond. So he went with a benign comment. "Families have complicated interactions all around."

"Mine wasn't, not really, not until Suzanne happened on the scene. That was a short two years ago. Ryan and I spent the last six months trying to get Dad to wake up and consider leaving Suzanne. Then before we could complete the deal, Ryan goes missing."

"That's why you should come over tonight and see if we can solve this thing. Remember, you aren't alone in this anymore."

A lump clogged in Tessa's throat at the notion. "So you think Ryan going missing is connected to your sister's case?"

"It's a distinct possibility." It suddenly hit him. "You came down all this way by yourself to look for your brother, alone, in a strange place."

"I'm a big girl."

"I see that. But it's still an amazing feat."

"Why? What was I supposed to do? Leave it to your chief of police to solve and get back to me long distance?"

Jackson smiled. Some people would've done just that. "I'm not sure waiting for Sinclair to act would get you anywhere. That's why your being here is so special."

Chapter Three

On Bayside Boulevard the Life Stone Church sat at the end of the block along a row of historic 1930 Queen Annes built with classic gables and widow walks. Residents in this part of town were known to keep their lawns tidy, their flowerbeds professionally maintained as landscapers toiled with overflowing fragrant hibiscus, wild petunias, and feathery periwinkles.

Lenore strolled along the sidewalk lined with lofty buccaneer and silver palms. In no hurry to get to her destination, she stopped to study the cavalcade of yellow trout lilies that Cozelle Dunfrey had coaxed to grow in containers and set out on her front stoop. She'd tried to grow them a time or two without success. Even Livvy had attempted to get the hard-to-grow plant to thrive with no luck. And Livvy could grow anything.

When she reached the chapel, she took a minute to gaze at the original stone structure, used now for private meditation and prayer. With its stained glass windows and Victorian turrets, it could've been plunked from any Irish countryside or nestled on a college campus. But it was here so long ago, that Lenore had sought out a place to make a spiritual connection, to find a refuge where she could bring her brood and get away from life's pressures.

Balancing other people's books and carrying out a long to-do list raising four kids, she craved that link with others for a couple of hours every Sunday where she could make sure her head stayed on straight. Over the years Life Stone had become a staple in her life as fierce as the vitamin D she took every day to keep her bones healthy. She relied on the people here for inspiration and support.

The walls of the courtyard were awash in warm sunshine as she flipped up the latch on the gate. But instead of heading inside, right now she felt more comfortable standing in the coolness of the shadows. For Lenore, the idea of knowing Livvy and Blake and Ally were no longer just down the street, made the world lose its brilliance.

She didn't really have the strength to open those double doors and go into the empty auditorium to sit confined within another four walls. She could've done that at home. Instead, she opted for a seat on the concrete bench under the burgeoning Jamaican dogwood.

She raised her head upward, blocked the glare from her eyes with her hand. The thirty-foot tree, laden with purple fall blossoms, created such a beautiful sanctuary it made her realize she could pray anywhere without leaving the precious sunshine.

In this beautiful garden, she'd surely get a little peace and quiet for longer than five minutes. Tanner was her rock, always had been. Her boys were coming together to help her through this ordeal. But lord, what a racket they could make when they got together. Livvy would be the first one to attest to that fact.

These past two days had been a nightmare. If she could just sit here long enough to watch the sky fill up with stars, Lenore knew she could get through one more night of anguish. Maybe she'd wake up any minute and it would all have been a terrifying dream. Livvy and the kids would be tucked inside their house down the street again. Maybe they'd be dropping by later for supper. She'd fry up a couple of chickens and make a pile of mashed potatoes. Blake loved her fluffy potatoes. Maybe she'd throw together a key lime pie for dessert. It was Ally's favorite.

She snapped out of her daydreaming, rested her head in her hands. The dull throb of a headache began to pound at her temples. In spite of the pain, she lifted her head to the heavens.

Please, God, please. Let Livvy and the kids be okay. Bring them back home where they belong.

Tears streamed down her cheeks as a thought occurred to her. She realized she'd left her cell phone back home. What if Livvy called while she sat here feeling sorry for herself?

Lenore stood up and scurried across the bricks of the piazza to the street, all the while feeling the need to get back home. She'd make chicken the way Livvy and Ally liked it. She'd fix Blake's mashed potatoes with all his favorite ingredients.

Lenore had one thought in mind. Her daughter and grandchildren would soon be headed back home. She had to think like that. Anything else, made her crazy with grief.

Jackson had a fifteen-minute wait on the tarmac for Garret's commuter to arrive. At six-fifteen he watched the turboprop make its descent, touch down on the runway, and then taxi to a stop at an angle.

Without a jetway, Jackson stood to the side as the hatch of the Beechcraft Super King opened and the steps dropped. His youngest brother appeared at the top, the first one out of the closed up space.

Garret didn't like long flights any more than he liked being cooped up in a claustrophobic cabin. With a flight time of twenty-five-plus hours, the trip from Melbourne to Miami meant Garret had been on a plane for longer than a day. It explained the day-old stubble that could easily be mistaken for the beginnings of a goatee.

Jackson watched his brother heft a bag to one shoulder, sling a guitar case over the other.

Garret's face showed major jet lag, the giveaway was the dark bags under his eyes. His mahogany hair sported a few honey-colored streaks running from cap to tip, evidence of all the time he spent outdoors. Today the pro surfer wore it stretched back in a tight ponytail for easier upkeep while traveling.

It occurred to Jackson that his parents had tagged this one at birth. The name Garret personified the label "brave one with a spear." That was his baby brother, or maybe more apt, "fearless with a surfboard."

As soon as Garret reached the blacktop, Jackson relieved him of the bag and wrapped an arm around a shoulder. "God, am I ever glad to see you. Even if you do look wiped and out of it."

"Somewhere over the South Pacific I took an Ambien to help me sleep. But I got antsy once I woke up. Twelve hours in and I was ready to climb out on the wing. You try sitting on a plane for what seems like two days and then tell me how you'd do."

"No argument from me. Last time I did that I came back from studying the coral reef in Menai Bay, Zanzibar."

"Then you know. Look, I have to grab my surfboard out of the belly and then we're good to go."

"I'll do it." Jackson surveyed the cargo hold. "You brought a lot of stuff with you."

"Hey, when I fly I never leave behind my board or my guitar, no exceptions. Them's the rules I live by."

"But you still play drums, right? I noticed your old set is still taking up most of the hall closet."

Garret sent him an easy grin. "You bet. I'm a drummer at heart. But even I've never been able to build up the discipline to cart them around in the cargo hold of a triple-seven. It's a pain in the butt with this much stuff. How are Mom and Dad holding up?"

"About like you'd expect when one of their own is MIA. Plus, they've been waiting to get a look at their baby boy."

"Yeah, right. I'm pretty sure Dad thinks all I do is bum around the world and surf."

"That's exactly what you do."

Garret grinned again. "You know who taught me to surf? Livvy. She was ten. I was four. I remember one particular summer day. Before that, all I'd done was splash around in the water near shore. Livvy put me up on her board and I sailed through the waves beside her. So blame her. The first time, holding on tight to her. The next time…"

"You had to try it all by yourself. I hate to burst your bubble, but that wasn't the first time you went surfing. That might be your first memory of it, but Livvy used to drag you to the beach all the time. You couldn't have been more than two when she took her first picture of you sitting on top of her surfboard with that old Pentax Spotmatic camera. Mom still has it front and center, hung up on that photo gallery back home."

Garret's lips curved up again. "I remember that thing. For a couple of years there Livvy never left the house without it dangling around her neck, took that thing everywhere she went."

"You ought to remember it. It used to belong to Dad's Aunt Tansy."

"The one who worked as a photojournalist for *Time* magazine?"

"Yep. Tansy used that thing to take pictures of combat nurses assigned to the MASH units during the Vietnam War. They should be in a museum somewhere. Sad thing is, I remember Mom making Livvy and me clean out the attic one summer day. We were being punished for fighting over chores. While we were knee deep in junk, Livvy discovered Tansy's camera buried in a box of pictures. I swear Livvy danced all the way down the stairs to ask if she could claim it as hers, finders keepers and all."

Whether it was the jet lag or the situation, reminiscing about their sister caused Garret's eyes to tear up. "She'll be okay, won't she? Tell me, Livvy will be okay."

Jackson wasn't sure it was that easy of a thing to promise. But he tried to be as upbeat as he could. "Livvy was always one to take care of herself. She didn't take crap off any of us."

"She took plenty of crap off Walker," Garret pointed out.

There was no point denying it. But even as Jackson thought of encouraging words to assure his brother of a hopeful outcome, there was a part of him that couldn't deny the wad of doubt that lodged in his throat.

Later, the setting sun painted the bottom half of the sky a swath of orange and red. Clouds and haze topped off the canvas by helping to create a majestic velvet purple edge. Across the horizon a crown of new stars popped overhead like a ribbon of blue canvas laden with shimmering diamonds. Tessa had never seen the Atlantic such a brilliant bluish green. It reminded her of The Outer Banks back home.

She pulled up in front of a white frame foursquare with blue shutters, parked at the curb under a row of sugar maples and cut the engine. Second thoughts began to seep in. Sitting behind the wheel in her sporty little metallic blue Toyota Coupe, a jangle of nerves made her wonder if this was the right course of action.

She stared up at the well-tended yard. Orange camellias and bright pink azaleas flourished in the flowerbeds next to a crop of colorful coleus. Despite the foliage and curb appeal, the doubts lingered and caused her stomach to churn.

In the five days she'd been on the Key searching for her brother, her options had been limited. It seemed none of the townspeople wanted to talk to her about Ryan. In fact, they'd stonewalled her efforts. So far she'd been unable to get anyone to open up to her satisfaction. How could the people in such a small town not have seen her brother? The only verification that he'd spent five days here had been his hotel bill. Thank goodness the staff at the Mainsail Lodge had confirmed that. Otherwise, there were times she doubted whether he'd been here at all. She'd even considered the possibility that she might've misunderstood Ryan's intent.

Back in Nags Head her stepmother, Suzanne, had already deemed the trip a total waste of time, which didn't help matters. Even though she couldn't entirely disagree with that, sitting back in North Carolina and worrying seemed to make less sense than the journey here. Who was she kidding? There had been times during the past week that Tessa thought about giving up the quest and heading home.

But she'd stuck it out and prayed her luck might turn. Maybe hooking up with the Indigos would do something to jumpstart locating Ryan. If there was a chance that this Indigo brood could accomplish more than what she'd been able to do, and the name alone said they could, it might be the last hope she had of finding out what happened.

Just as she unclipped her seatbelt, a tap on the glass made her jolt. Her hand went to her heart as she looked up to see Jackson standing next to the window.

"Whoa there. It's okay. I didn't mean to make you jump."

"I'm on edge."

"I see that." Jackson flipped the handle and swung the car door open. "I think you'll find the Indigos are an interesting bunch. We're loud. We've been known to vigorously argue our point and defend our viewpoint. Somehow we're always able to make sure we're heard. With six of us it was always like growing up at a political convention, lots of jockeying for position and bartering for votes. But for all our faults, we rarely take a bite out of anyone. So relax and know that my mom and dad are looking forward to having you here."

To prove it, the minute they reached the porch, the front door flew open and Lenore latched on to their guest. "Come on in. Jackson tells us what a tough time you've had getting people to talk to you. Believe me, you won't have that problem with any of us. We'll blather on about anything."

"I appreciate y'all having me over during such a difficult time like this." Tessa's Carolina drawl came through loud and clear. She let Lenore guide her into a small, but orderly living room decorated with comfy but dated furniture. Smells of fried chicken wafted on the air and Tessa guessed right away what was on the menu for dinner.

"You're having your own difficult time," Lenore told her before introducing the others. When she caught Tessa staring at a wall lined with family photographs that took up the length of the parlor, she added, "This is our own photo archive. It documents our past. Livvy's doing. She took most of these at one time or another through the years."

Tessa looked back at the crowd and found a bank of eyes aimed at her. She noted the group of men all bore very similar features, dark hair, striking dark eyes, a definite contrast to their fair-haired mother. Tessa decided she wasn't all that comfortable knowing she was the focus of their interest.

As if sensing that, Jackson took her by the hand and led her into the kitchen. "You look thirsty. Will iced tea do the trick? If not, there's always a cold beer."

"Tea's fine."

Lenore went over to the stove to check on the chicken while Jackson got down a glass from the cupboard, chunked in ice. "Mom makes it fairly strong but the ice should melt and weaken it some."

"I'm sure it's fine," Tessa said again, sniffing the air. "It smells like home in here."

Lenore studied the redhead. "I bet you miss your family, especially your brother. Jackson explained to us how Walker owed him money."

"Told you so," Tanner threw in before their guest could take her first long drink. "I'm telling you Walker is up to no good. This is all his fault."

Lenore waved a hand toward her husband. "Tanner, what do you say we let our guest catch her breath first before we go off on a tangent and air our misgivings about our son-in-law." She turned back to Tessa. "I hope you like chicken."

"I do. I'd like to help."

Lenore patted Tessa on the shoulder. "Don't you worry none about it. I have three strapping boys for that. I spent the better part of this afternoon frying up enough to feed this bunch. I'll get one of my handsome sons to help me get supper on the table. Now you go on and sit yourself down outside where it's cooler. Jackson, you see to it this pretty lady settles in."

"Yes, ma'am," Jackson said, snatching Tessa's hand and pulling her through the back door and out into a large yard.

A thriving vegetable garden took up a slice of landscape along the side. A long stone barbecue grill had been carefully crafted by hand and looked like an outdoor kitchen. It stood next to a circular fire pit with a collection of mismatched chairs arranged in a circle. There was a hammock in the corner, strung from one mighty magnolia to another. Under a pergola sat the biggest round picnic table she'd ever seen. It was already decorated with a pretty blue tablecloth and plates of different colors and set with linen napkins in various shades of green and purple.

"Your mother shouldn't have gone to so much trouble," Tessa noted, taking in the homey atmosphere.

"There's no need to regret your decision to come tonight," Jackson stated. "What's the worst that could happen? You'll eat a home-cooked meal instead of fast food, have some key lime pie to top it off, and get to know my family. My mom has been cooking since Mitch got here last night. He says she hasn't sat down for longer than fifteen minutes at a time before she's bouncing back up again to do something, trying to stay busy instead of worrying."

"All the more reason she shouldn't have put herself out like this."

Garret sidled up to their pretty guest. "Jackson's right. Mom wanted you to get a decent meal. In case you were wondering, we're not all as bad as Jackson. He mostly just scares off women and very small children. He gets that after Dad."

"I heard that, Garret Davis Indigo," Tanner roared from the doorway. With a twinkle in his eyes he set down the huge platter of chicken in the middle of the table and turned to give the stink eye to his youngest boy. "At least Jackson and Mitch had more sense than to ever smoke a whole pack of unfiltered Camels. You got so sick you puked for a week."

Right behind his father, Mitch placed another plate of fried chicken at the other end of the table. "Dad's got you there. As I remember it, your skin even turned green for a week. What were you, twelve at the time?"

Garret winced at the memory. "Yep. And I thought I was so cool when I won those things at the county fair. Last time I ever put a cigarette to my lips, I'll tell you that."

"If only that applied to weed," Jackson murmured in Garret's ear as he slapped his brother on the back.

Garret gave him a brotherly shove. "Get real. I gave that stuff up years ago. To compete on the tour, there's random drug testing now."

"When did that happen?"

"2011."

Lenore appeared holding yet another platter, this one with ears of corn piled high. "Quit your squawking in front of our guest and get ready to eat. Tell us, Tessa, if you favor any part of the chicken over another, say white versus dark meat. Ally and Livvy always fought over the pullybone."

"That's what we call the wishbone," Jackson piped up. "I remember Livvy and Ally refused to touch any other part of the chicken."

"Not me," Tessa offered. "I'll eat dark, white, I'll even eat my fair share of chicken wings drenched in hot sauce. I'm not a picky eater."

"My kind of girl," Tanner said with a wink as he directed Tessa over to the table. "Have a seat and dig in before these big brutes push you out of the way to get to the food. With so many kids scrambling at suppertime you learn to look out for yourself around here."

Jackson noticed his mother's lips trembling and the tears forming at the corners of her eyes. "What's the matter?"

"I miss Livvy and the kids. I thought for sure they'd be back for now."

Jackson sat down next to his mother and wrapped her up in his arms. "Come on now. Don't do that. You need to eat some of this great food you spent all day cooking."

Tessa watched the oldest son interact with his mom. There was something about a grown man comforting his mother that made her heart do an extra flip and flutter. Never mind that he was easy on the eyes. That southern drawl of his brought out a sexual appeal she'd felt only a few other times in her life. That thought was broken when she found a platter of fried meat shoved in her face. She busied filling up her plate until she realized Mitch had said something to her.

"Where were you just now?"

Embarrassed at being caught salivating over his older brother, she stumbled over the words. "I guess I was thinking of better days." When she realized what she'd said might be taken as an insult, she added, "Uh, no offense. I just meant other times back home."

Charmed with the redhead's southern roots, Mitch grinned. "None taken. I'm curious though. Once your brother arrived in town, did you have any communication with him at all?"

Tessa shook her head. "It's something I regret now. But that Labor Day weekend was busy. I went over to New Hope to see a cousin of mine to help her with plans for her wedding next spring. Stayed there all weekend."

She moved the food around on her plate, suddenly losing her appetite. "Your police chief verified that Ryan checked in at the Mainsail on September 1st at six-thirty in the evening and checked out September 6th a little after eleven a.m. That means he had several days to fish and pick up the check from Walker before he should've been back on the road for home. Allowing for stops, it's a sixteen-hour drive up I-95 back to Nags Head. But Ryan never called home to say he was heading back. And he never made it."

Tessa cleared her throat. "There's something else you should know. I hacked into Ryan's email account a couple days after settling into the hotel." She mistook the looks she got from everyone around the table as judgmental. "Before you think I went too far…"

"It isn't that," Jackson added quickly. "As far as I'm concerned, I'm impressed with your expertise. Not just anyone could do that. Do those particular skills come with your bent toward blogging or something you acquired along the way?"

The corners of Tessa's mouth curved up. "Actually it comes in handy in situations like now when you're desperate. I was desperate to find out who Ryan had been in contact with right before he disappeared. Ryan's email trail was one way to do that. One thing popped up right away. Until then, there was nothing to indicate Walker would have trouble paying. That was back in August. As a small business owner you look for red flags. There were no red flags in the exchanges Ryan initially had with Walker, just the normal course of doing business. But by the time your brother-in-law asked Ryan to come to Florida, Walker was blaming his financial woes on his extravagant wife's lifestyle. That would be your sister."

"That's bullshit," Jackson said, tossing his napkin on the table. "Show me the email."

"Us," Tanner corrected. "Show us Walker's email."

Tessa took out her cell phone, thumbed through the messages until she found the right one. She held it out to Jackson. "See, he tells Ryan that he's having cash flow problems because his wife is spending money faster than he's able to make it."

Jackson frowned as he read the accusation with his own eyes. He passed it around for everyone else to read. In that moment of understanding, his razor-thin support for Walker evaporated. "That bastard has no right to make up such lies."

Tanner sat back with a smug look on his face. "I don't want to say I told you so but…Livvy wasn't the one throwing money around like a sailor on shore leave."

"You did try to tell us," Jackson admitted.

Empathy for the family moved through Tessa. "Just a suggestion, but the chief of police could certainly get Walker's cell phone records and make them available to you. That way we could backtrack, go through the timelines and maybe find out what happened three weeks ago when my brother first got to town."

Jackson stared at her. "That's an excellent start. Have you tried that with Ryan's phone?"

"Yes, but the carrier refuses to give me the data without a warrant."

"Then we'll ask Chief Sinclair to do it. There's someone else though who might hold the key. It's time I had a face to face talk with Royce Buchanan."

"Then I'm going with you," Tessa insisted.

"No, you're not," Jackson returned. "And here's why. Royce will be reluctant to talk to me anyway. As you've gathered by now, he's not exactly this family's favorite person. The feeling is mutual. I doubt he'll feel the urge to disclose anything of a personal nature regarding his son in front of you, a total stranger. You've already discovered firsthand how closed-mouthed this town is."

"Fine. But I'm still going even if I have to wait in the car."

"Forty-five minutes is a long time to sit in a hot car," Jackson noted.

Tessa looked out beyond the dark patio. "Not if we go over there right now. I promise I'll open a car window, stick my head out if necessary, and won't wander off without my leash."

Mitch snickered at the levity.

Even though she was getting too tired to play nice, Tessa wasn't opposed to bargaining. "Look, if I don't go with you what else do I have to do but sit in my hotel room worrying? I've done that already. Don't make me spend the evening like that. If this Buchanan guy might hold one small piece of the puzzle, don't make me spend another night wondering about Ryan. I normally wouldn't beg but…"

Garret's heart went out to her. "She has a point. The sooner we hit the ground running proving Walker's charge false, the better off we'll be at finding out where the hell they went. I didn't come half way around the world to sit around and wait for answers to come to us. We have to go out and get them. Royce might know more than we do."

Mitch nodded. "I'm with Garret. We have to be ready to pound the pavement. No one knows this area better than we do or the people living here."

Jackson caught the grim looks around the table. "Okay, okay. I guess I'll talk to Royce tonight." He turned to Tessa. "As long as you understand that it could take an hour or more before I get Royce to open up. He's always been a standoffish sort even on his good days."

"That's okay. I'll take my Kindle with me and delve into the book I downloaded this morning." She got to her feet, but stopped short. "By the way, when do you plan to saturate the area with more posters and officially kick off a search?"

Jackson made a distressed sound in his throat. "A friend of ours started putting up flyers already. I have a feeling that isn't what you're talking about."

Tessa shook her head. "Nope. That's fine for Indigo Key. I'm thinking more along the lines of sending the info across the entire state of Florida. If you agree, I'd like to add my brother's photo to whatever packets you come up with."

Jackson looked at his family, ran a hand through his hair. "I guess we need to talk about all this when I get back. But as far as I'm concerned, the sooner we contact the right agencies the better."

Tanner tightened his jaw. "We have missing kids. That means the center for missing children should be top on that list."

"That's a good idea." Jackson turned to Tessa. "Something tells me you've already done the research on the pertinent law enforcement agencies in the area where to send out Ryan's poster."

"Last Monday I began making a list of all those in the general vicinity. But there's more yet to do since some of the businesses here in town wouldn't let me leave Ryan's flyers to go in their windows."

An appalled look crossed Jackson's face. "Make a list of which businesses gave you a hard time because that kind of attitude is damn well gonna change." He sent a look of unity toward Mitch.

His brother bobbed his head. "I'll make a note of that when I touch base with Jimmy Don about coordinating the search tomorrow."

"What search?" Tessa asked.

"I'll tell you about it on the way to the Buchanan estate," Jackson said, tugging her toward the driveway. "Let's get this business with Royce done and behind us."

Chapter Four

Things couldn't have turned out any better if he'd planned it for a year.

The Indigos were running around their little island clueless. They had no idea what to do. He hadn't bargained on the little redhead, though. The bitch liked to stick her nose into other people's business.

In short order, he'd turned this sleepy knockabout place on its ear, that's for sure.

Payback was a bitch, Karma like a fine vintage merlot when it was finally uncorked.

He'd sat on the shelf long enough, watched all the players enough to know he'd shaken things up and finally entered the game on his own terms. It might've been a lot messier than he'd originally thought. But it was done with and behind him.

How long had it been since he'd enjoyed his work this much? He hadn't gotten his hands this dirty in a long while, not since the '90s at least. Back then he'd been nothing more than an errand boy.

Guns and bombs were for pussies. There was nothing quite like getting a little blood on your hands to make you feel alive, to make you feel an integral part of the game.

Breathing in the ocean air, he felt an exhilaration knowing he'd get to do it again. But probably not with the same kind of panache he'd used with the Buchanan family. That had taken a chunk of his creativity. To watch the shock on the man's face knowing he was about to take his last breath, to watch the woman's eyes flutter closed and the life drain out of her body.

The boss had been pleased. And in this business that was the only thing that mattered.

Chapter Five

There'd been bad blood between the Indigos and Buchanans going back a hundred years or more. That's one reason Jackson wasn't sure how welcomed he'd be at Royce's mansion located at the edge of town. But it was an encounter that couldn't be put off.

The battles between families had begun shortly after the War Between the States when Rufus Buchanan, a reputed opportunist and scalawag, showed up in town and got a lukewarm reception. Right away, the locals pegged him as a carpetbagger. And when Rufus tried to claim a piece of property belonging to one of Jackson's distant relatives, they were convinced the newcomer planned to loot and exploit each one of them.

The contentious confrontation that ensued set off a century-old pattern where the two families bickered over everything from property boundaries to outbidding each other for acreage—precious land where valuable sugar cane could be grown as the crop of choice. They wrangled over the right to smuggle rum by boat up through Sugar Bay. They disagreed at every opportunity over town politics.

More recently, Tanner had gone toe to toe with Royce over the island's future development. Royce fought Tanner for control of the town council because he desperately wanted to get the go-ahead to build a proposed golf course, and ultimately a lavish resort. Naturally, Tanner was vehemently opposed to the idea.

The disputes kept ramping up because neither man liked the other very much. They had little in common. A hundred years hadn't done a thing to soothe ill will.

That's why no one could believe it when Olivia Indigo started dating Walker Buchanan in her senior year of high school. Tanner had objected to the relationship from the start, which probably was the reason Olivia dug in her heels to keep the bond going.

By the time things began to trend toward serious, Tanner had lost the upper hand. Turns out, it was the one thing he and Royce could finally agree on in the forty-five years they'd known each other. Neither father wanted the other for an in-law.

But the marriage forced them to find neutral ground, especially after the grandkids came along. The two men did their best to mellow somewhat during family functions like barbecues and picnics. It wasn't enough to forge a true congenial relationship. They put up with each other, mostly by steering clear of the other.

That tendency to butt heads was the basis for Jackson's uncertainty as he veered his father's beat-up truck along the route to what looked like a dated, antebellum plantation. On either side of the driveway a succession of fragrant magnolias lined the pathway up to the front door, their branches swaying in the scant evening breeze.

"Wow," Tessa said, a bit in awe. "Did we just go back in a time machine to the Civil War? This house looks straight out of a scene from *Gone With the Wind*. I'm expecting Scarlett O'Hara to pop out the front door any minute now."

Jackson gave her a lopsided grin. "No Southern belles here despite the setting. Royce's wife, Carla, succumbed five years ago to brain cancer. It was an awful time, a long-drawn-out sickness that threw Royce into serious depression and Walker into…" His voice trailed off before he decided how best to describe Walker's mindset. "Some kind of funk."

Tessa tilted her head. "Are you aware that's the first time you've said anything halfway decent about Walker?"

"That's probably true. He's not a bad guy, just…not my type of person to be around. He's always been a little too self-absorbed to hang out and have a beer."

"Ah. So what kind of funk?"

Jackson scratched the stubble on his chin. "After his mother died, Walker became more detached from the kids. At the time, he worked for Buchanan Industries, a position he'd had since dropping out of Florida Tech. Livvy said he stopped going to work at all for a while. And when he did go back full-time, there were nights Walker didn't come home. It was almost as if he avoided being there. There's no doubt he experienced some type of an early mid-life crisis, a binge of wild spending mixed with erratic behavior. I'm not sure it ever got any better."

"But you didn't mention any of this to your parents tonight."

"They already know. Livvy couldn't keep that a secret. It was so evident at the time. Besides, Livvy and Mom have always been pretty close and she did live a few streets away. I was made aware of the situation because Livvy reached out to me through emails. I think because she needed a man's take on the situation. Keep in mind this is when the kids were very small and Walker had just lost his mother. Livvy and I talked at length about it. In the end, we brushed it off as going through a weird grief process. Then to top it off Walker lost his older sister in a car accident. Winifred. But everyone called her Winnie. She died before Thanksgiving last year."

In the warm night, Tessa rubbed her arms as chill bumps began to form. A look of horror crossed her face. "My God, I'm beginning to get a sense that Ryan did business with the wrong client."

Jackson reacted by sending her a strange look. "Why do you say that?"

"You're kidding? Think about it. This Buchanan family loses a daughter last year and now a son goes missing under mysterious circumstances, both incidents happening within less than a year of each other. How could you not see the eerie chain as anything but suspicious?"

"But Winnie's death was an accident. She ran her car off the road, sent it flying into a ditch on the way home from celebrating with friends at a bar in Key West. She'd been drinking heavily all evening."

"Doesn't matter. That's an incredible coincidence."

"A coincidence? That's the same word Sinclair used to describe Ryan's disappearance bunched with Livvy's." Jackson chewed his lip. "If you're right, then there's something else at play here, something that drew Livvy and the kids into harm's way."

"And dragged Ryan into it after he got here. Which brings up the question, are you sure you want to go in there and get in this guy's face right now?"

"Not really. But I need to find out what he knows about Walker's money troubles and feel him out about how bad the situation was."

Before Jackson could open the driver's door to get out, Tessa reached into her purse and pulled out a photo of her brother. She handed it off to Jackson. "Do me a favor, ask him if he saw Ryan?"

Jackson took the picture and studied the image. A measure of understanding moved through him. He instinctively reached out and touched her silky mane, wrapped a few strands around his fingers. "Your brother doesn't have the same hair coloring as you do."

"Ryan lucked out. He got the russet version. I got the awful copper."

Jackson ran a finger down her cheek. "Try to understand that I'd take you in there with me if I could, but it would just complicate things."

"Go. Get your questions answered. If Buchanan is as difficult a person to deal with as you say, then I'm happy to wait right here."

As Jackson approached the front door and rang the bell, he realized things had changed quite a bit since his sister had married into this family. For one, while Livvy had been concentrating on taking care of two little kids, Walker had come unraveled after Carla Buchanan's death. By the time Livvy thought he'd recovered, and the situation had righted itself, Winnie had died in the car accident. Had her death left Walker in another funk that he couldn't shake? Had it evolved into a deeper and more complicated psychosis that brought him to a darker side, a side that had him doing harm to his wife and kids?

A housekeeper ushered Jackson into the library where he found Royce Buchanan sitting in front of a roaring fire. The man had always been eccentric but given the fact that the outside temperature still hung in at a warm seventy-five, Jackson figured Royce had found a new outlet for odd. The thermostat had to have been lowered to a chilly sixty-five degrees just to keep the room and anyone in it from melting in the otherwise heat of the September evening.

Jackson stared at the wealthiest man in the county, who sported a thatch of silver hair, a year-round golf tan, and a usual arrogant demeanor. But tonight, Royce looked broken.

Even though it wasn't that late, Royce had on a pair of blue silk pajamas and fuzzy slippers. The overstuffed chair seemed to gobble up his body, a body that had grown frail since Jackson had seen him in town last spring. Was the man in ill health?

"Thanks for seeing me," Jackson began. "I wasn't sure you would."

Royce's eyes were glassy and showed he'd downed more than one glass of the Scotch he held in his hand. "Has there been any word? Did you hear anything? Are you here with news? Have they found my boy yet?"

"I'm afraid not. We're as much in the dark as you are."

Jackson watched as Royce ran a shaky hand over his forehead. "Where could they have gone? Why would they take off like this?"

Either Royce had become an excellent actor or the man was truly mystified by his only son's disappearance. Jackson shifted his feet. What he had to ask wouldn't be easy. The longer he drew out this labored conversation, the harder it would get. So he decided to take the blunt route.

"There are some rumors floating around town that Walker had major money problems. Would that have been enough for him to take his own life? Would he have been in such a desperate state of mind that he would do away with himself and his wife and children? You need to be straight with me now and tell me if we might be looking at a murder-suicide."

Royce's mouth fell open at the suggestion. "The idea is ludicrous. Did that bullshit come from Sinclair? He's full of crap. Walker would never do such a thing. I'm appalled that you would even suggest it. And my son knew he could come to me any time if he had financial woes."

"Look, I'm sorry. But from where I'm standing we have to cover all the bases, otherwise we're out of the loop and playing a desperate game of catch up. So is there any reason Walker might've fled the country?"

"Don't be absurd. You're talking crazy. It has to be a kidnapping. That's the only thing that makes any sense. I've been sitting here waiting all this time by the phone expecting a ransom demand. I put my staff on full alert at the office to make me aware of anything they see or hear out of the ordinary there."

"Okay. So you'd tell us, wouldn't you, if that were to happen? If someone contacts you wanting money, you would share that information with us, right?"

"Of course, your family would surely want to contribute their fair share to the ransom, if there is one."

Jackson's eyes narrowed, he bristled at the old man's callousness. "The Indigos may not have the wealth you Buchanans are used to, but I guarantee if there's a ransom demand we'll come up with our part of it. You know, Royce, those grandkids belong to you as much as they do to us. You haven't said a word about Blake and Ally."

"I'm aware of that," Royce snapped. "Do you plan to tell me who it is that's been saying those awful things about my son's money problems?"

Not wanting to tip his hand, Jackson shrugged. "They're just rumors. You know how people talk in small towns. Besides, in the grand scheme of things rumors are relatively insignificant at this point."

"Jealous, petty people must be dealt with no matter how insignificant they seem. Some people in this town have always been envious of my son and all that he's accomplished."

Jackson wasn't certain he could list Walker's accomplishments in detail, other than a smartass disposition and a belief that he'd been born to an entitled birthright. But he kept his mouth shut and went along with the old man's point of view for now. "That's just it, can you think of a reason Walker would take his family and disappear like this? You know how much Livvy loved Walker. Taking off out of the blue like this doesn't wash. She wouldn't do that to us. Could they be running from something or someone? That might be a turning point for her."

Royce cast his eyes downward refusing to meet Jackson's eyes. The old man shook his head. "Not that I'm aware of."

Jackson took that moment to reach into his shirt pocket and pull out Ryan's photograph, held it out for Royce to study. "Have you seen this man with Walker, say about three weeks ago?"

Royce took the picture and held it under the lamp sitting next to him on the table. "I'm pretty sure that's the man Walker went fishing with over Labor Day weekend."

"Did you meet him?"

"No. Walker owed him five grand for work on the store's website so I wrote the man a check in that amount and Walker was supposed to deliver it to him. Why? What's this man got to do with any of this? Did he do something to my son?"

"Ryan Connelly's gone missing, too. He never made it back to North Carolina. His sister's down here now looking for him, has been since Monday. She hasn't even been able to locate his car."

"That is odd."

"Yeah. There's a lot of that going around. Tell me something. Did the check ever clear the bank?"

"I think so."

"Could you check and get back to me?"

"Sure. Is it that important?"

"Yes. We need to make sure Ryan cashed Walker's check. If he did, it would tell us that he might've been robbed before he could leave town."

"Yes, I see. Okay, I'll have someone look into it first thing Monday morning and get back to you."

"Appreciate it. If there's anything else you can think of, let me know." Jackson turned to leave and then stopped. "And Royce, remember, you don't have to be in this big old house by yourself. You can always pick up the phone and let one of us know that you want company."

In the firelight, Royce's eyes flickered with the depths of sadness. "I'll keep that in mind. God wouldn't do this to me again, would he? Surely he couldn't take my son from me after losing Winnie and Carla so close together."

With no answers to give the old man, Jackson let himself out the front door and left Royce still muttering to himself.

"So, how'd it go in there?" Tessa asked as soon as Jackson got back to the car.

"Weird. Which isn't all that unusual. I get the feeling Royce is stonewalling me in some way. Not a surprise, but still…the thing is, I can't figure out why, when we both want the same thing. Why would he not fully disclose the truth?"

"What is it with your family and the Buchanans?"

"How much time do you have?"

"Apparently, the rest of the night."

"Okay, here goes. For starters, local rich boy, Walker, marries way beneath him, or so he believes. He hooks up with my sister back in high school. From the start, he treats her like she's less, no matter what she does or how hard she tries to please him. And for some reason, she just keeps putting up with the treatment. That's something my dad picked up on and resents to this day. Going back to high school, Livvy was the popular one. Everyone liked her. Walker, on the other hand, had problems making friends. At some point, he makes a play for Livvy, the cheerleader. She ends up falling for his so-called charm and here we are."

"But the town's named after your family. Surely that means something."

Jackson turned over the engine in his dad's truck and started down the long driveway. "That's because we were here first by several centuries. It was Koda Indigo who jumped off a pirate ship one night in the middle of a mutiny—a little misunderstanding over a woman—and swam ashore with his so-called captive, not too far from this very spot."

"Well that certainly demands a whole lot more detail," Tessa prompted.

"According to legend, he and his crew had snatched a woman from a rival, kidnapped a countess by the name of Marissa DeVaga Querida. The plan was to ransom her to the highest bidder once they got to Jamaica."

"I don't think I like your ancestor very much," Tessa noted.

Jackson chuckled. "Different era, different agenda. Somewhere during the plan, Koda decided he'd fallen for Marissa so he decided to keep her in lieu of going through with the plan. Apparently that decision didn't go over too well with his band of brothers. His shipmates turned on him. An uprising ensued. During the skirmish someone took a sword to the gut. That's when Koda grabbed the lady's hand and they both jumped ship into the water, started swimming like mad for shore. Eventually, he and the countess washed up here on the island, hid out and took refuge. Before anyone knew what was happening, Koda and Marissa ended up having eight kids."

Tessa rolled her eyes. "You totally made that up."

"Nope, I just repeated the legend. Hey, you had dinner with my family tonight." He pointed to the mansion over his shoulder. "We're more the shotgun-style house type where the help lives. Buchanans are the plantation-owning moguls. Other than the countess we have no ties to royalty. Add to that, our lineage has been watered down quite a bit since then. So the fact that the town's named for Koda Indigo doesn't really mean all that much when you're dealing with money-hungry land grabbers like the Buchanans."

Jackson turned the truck toward Quay Avenue and to where Tessa's car was still parked. "By the way, Royce admitted he wrote the check that Walker was supposed to deliver to Ryan. One way or another I intend to find out if the check was ever cashed and who cashed it. I'm not waiting for Royce to get around to looking into the matter."

"How do you plan to do that?"

"I know someone who works at the bank in an executive capacity."

"That sounds very close to being illegal."

His lips curved into a wide grin. "It is, sort of, like hacking into someone's private email account. But I figure you won't tell on me since priority one is gaining information anywhere we can get it."

"Please tell me you'll do that first thing Monday morning."

"I won't even wait that long. I'll make the call tonight and see if my old friend, Nathan, can take a peek at Royce's account tomorrow morning."

"A Sunday? I'm impressed. So what's the next step?"

He took his eyes off the road long enough to send her a curious look. "Aren't you ready to crash? It's been a long day for me. I'm sure you're as exhausted as I am."

She scrubbed both hands over her face. "I am tired. This emotional rollercoaster is taking its toll. I'm not even sure how long I'll be able to stay here and keep this up."

Jackson felt a streak of panic in his gut at the thought of her leaving. He wasn't sure why. "How much time were you able to take off?"

"Technically, none, because I blog for a living, remember? So far I've been able to keep up my posts long distance from my hotel room, piece of cake technically. But to tell you the truth I'm completely out of anything creative to write about." She didn't see the point of mentioning that she was almost out of money as well.

"I mean, normally I'd be able to come up with interesting ways to repurpose that castoff chest of drawers found in a back alleyway, or give an outdoor space a cheap mini makeover. But with Ryan missing, all that seems so trivial, so unimportant."

Her voice broke. "How am I supposed to think of DIY projects when my brother is gone and I don't know where he is?"

He pulled into his parents' driveway, cut the engine, and turned to face her. "You can't. I'm afraid until we locate your brother and my sister, our normal lives are pretty much on hold."

Tessa's eyes locked with his. "I never even asked what you do for a living."

"I mostly study coastal erosion and sedimentation, the kind of damage that occurs after a catastrophic weather event, like say, a hurricane, a category three and up, or a tsunami."

"Funny, you don't look like a scientist."

"Gee thanks."

"I mean, you look like a Wall Street type."

"There's a part of me insulted at that description. Scientifically put, I'm a physical oceanographer. Growing up on an island, I always found myself thinking about geophysical fluid dynamics. You know, how weather, high winds and such, create the huge waves that impact the coastal tidelands. I found my calling with buoyancy-driven currents."

"Let me see if I have this right. In other words, how much sand and beach grass wash away after a storm?"

"Geeky, I know."

"Haven't you heard? These days geeks rule the world."

He turned to see the light in her eyes, those kissable lips. He tried to tamp down his attraction. "Yeah, well, while most guys my age were figuring out how to be the next Dan Marino, I wanted to go into creative research and learn everything I could about ecosystems, earth and flora disappearing, stuff like that, and how long it took for the vegetation to come back after devastation."

Even in the waning light inside the car's interior, she could see the eagerness on his face, the enthusiasm he had for his work so much that it resonated outward. It had been a longtime since anyone's passion had been so visible, so apparent to her. Longing moved through her. She recognized that pull in her lower belly, that sense of desire and knew what it meant. On instinct she reached across the bench seat and took his face in her hands. She said nothing before pressing her lips to his.

His mouth worked a kind of magic, jolting her body to life. It felt like silvery stars shattered inside her, each one finding its mark. Their arms slid around each other until there was no space left between them. His hands roamed to touch her hair. His fingers strummed along her spine and splayed down to her hips.

Between the frenzied slip of tongues, she inhaled his scent, rode the fragrance of his aftershave. The kiss was like standing on a mountaintop, creeping toward the edge, and waiting to take the drop into freefall. She floated high, gliding on the prospect of what they could do next.

Jackson thought she tasted like a smooth cognac laced with golden honey, swirled with soft caramels. He angled his head to slow the pace, and understood the moment she yielded to the pleasure of the kiss. Her body melded into his as a reckless want took over. He sought to rush headlong into the white-hot fire.

An earsplitting foghorn sounded offshore. The noise broke them apart. But the air still sizzled, still rippled between them like the glow from a laser beam.

Jackson rested his forehead on hers. "I've wanted to do that since you first opened the door at the hotel."

"Same here, only when I saw you standing outside my door I saw a pirate who looked too dangerous to mess with or let in. Your little speech about your sister is the only reason I opened the door."

"This is probably not the best time to start this kind of thing up, is it?"

"Definitely not. Too much going on."

"Just one problem with that kind of thinking. I'd like to do more than kiss you."

"Ah, good. It's a good idea."

To prove it, they went after each other a second time and then a third, snuggling together until they heard a door slam. A few seconds later an impatient Tanner called out,

"Jackson, that you? What's taking you so long to get out of the truck?"

Tessa let out a belly laugh. "I feel like I've been transported back to fifteen again."

"I haven't made out in a car since I was a freshman in college," Jackson admitted. "Back then I had three roommates. And now I'm sharing a house with four people, the same ones I was with when I was twelve. We might have a problem carving out any time to be together."

A little thrill inched up her spine knowing it hadn't been a one-time event. "I've heard where there's a will, there's a way."

Impatient, Tanner bellowed out again in the direction of the truck, "You in there? Anything wrong?"

Jackson rolled the window down. "Dad, we're fine. I was just saying goodnight to Tessa. I'll come inside in a minute."

"Oh, okay, sure. I forgot Tessa went with you."

Jackson shook his head and watched his father head back into the house. "Yeah, right. Geez, he probably did that on purpose. Your car's still parked at the curb. This'll get old real quick. Want me to follow you back to the hotel?"

"No need, I'll be fine. Be sure to let me know what your friend at the bank says."

"Mitch and I sorta promised a TV reporter we'd hold a press conference tomorrow…early. Mitch is working on setting everything up. How about having breakfast with me in the morning before I face the media?"

"Sure, sounds like a plan. So they're making you the spokesman?"

"Oldest son. I sense I'll be drafted."

As he walked her to her car he realized he hadn't been this happy about scoring a breakfast date since he and Roma Lynn Caraway went out for waffles after senior prom. After a dozen years, he still recalled how he and Roma had spent their time together leading up to the food.

It wasn't until he watched Tessa drive off that Rachel popped into his head. Almost twenty-four hours had gone by and she still hadn't thought to text him to ask about his family crisis. Typical. Their on-and-off-again relationship had been on life support for too long. It was way past time to pull the plug.

As he opened the back door and stepped into the little mudroom, he decided he'd send an email before he went to bed tonight breaking things off for good. No more connecting with each other just to hook up for sex.

From here on out, he'd take it slow with Tessa. It probably wasn't the ideal time for that kind of distraction anyway. The two of them were on a mission, a collaboration to find answers, not to play kissy-face with each other in a parked car sitting in his parents' driveway. Besides, when Livvy and the kids got back home, he'd head to his job in New York. When Tessa located her brother, she'd go back to Nags Head. They were two ships passing each other for a brief amount of time. Hitting the sheets would only complicate things. But under any other circumstance, Tessa would've been a welcome bright spot to an otherwise ordinary visit.

Jackson was brought up short when he found his father and brothers sitting around the kitchen table, a spot where the family had faced down many calamities in the past. They were drinking beers all around.

"Where's Mom?"

Tanner sighed wearily. "She went to bed about an hour ago. Let's hope she can get some sleep."

At the prospect of ragging on his brother, Garret snickered with laughter. "Dad says he's awful sorry he busted in on your make-out session with the hot redhead."

Mitch snorted with laughter. "Yeah. We're in here strategizing, working hard, while you're out gallivanting with a woman and can't keep your hands to yourself."

Jackson glared at his dad. "Thanks a lot."

Mitch straightened him out. "Hey, don't blame Dad. We figured it out when you stayed in the truck so long that the windows started steaming up. Next time, get a room."

Jackson finally cracked a grin. "I don't have to take this. I'm going to bed."

Tanner stopped him. "Not before telling us what happened with Royce. How was the old coot anyway?"

Resigned to a discussion, Jackson snatched another amber ale from the fridge and took it over to the table. To needle Mitch and Garret, he made each brother move their chairs over so he'd have enough room to stretch out his legs. After twisting the top off the beer bottle, he plopped down, guzzled a long drink before breaking into the recap. "Actually Royce looked like he'd taken a punch to the gut and was still trying to digest devastating news, the kind that takes the wind out of your sails right before you crash into the rocks."

With that, Jackson replayed the high points of the conversation. "Despite everything Royce said to me, I got the feeling he wasn't being entirely truthful."

"Now there's a surprise," Tanner said as he stood up. "Want a piece of Key lime pie to go with that beer?"

"Isn't that sacrilegious, drinking a beer with Mom's pie? She takes particular pride in the way she makes a meringue."

"True. It's Livvy's favorite," Garret noted with fondness. "I remember one time she scooped in and grabbed the whole pie Mom had made for her bridge club, snuck off with it and gorged herself on the stuff, ate the entire thing in one sitting. Got so sick she puked her guts out right over the treehouse wall. It was so cool."

A smile crossed Mitch's face at the memory. "You were just mad because Livvy beat you to the punch, swiping it before you could. I remember that old treehouse. That sucker stood until tropical storm Fay blew through here in 2008 and toppled over the big old maple, turned it into a pile of splinters. Sad day for all of us."

Tanner chuckled. "When I built that thing for you guys I wasn't sure the tree could withstand the weight of the lumber, let alone the four of you climbing up and down on its branches every day. Livvy called it her playhouse and you guys referred to it as a fort. Your mother settled the squabbles by naming it Indigo Towers."

Jackson bobbed his head. "It's a shame Fay destroyed it before Blake and Ally got to enjoy everything the fort had to offer. Best treehouse within twenty blocks."

Mitch took exception to that. "Are you kidding? Best in town, biggest, too. I spent hours up there reading, playing with my Matchbox cars, then later when I was fourteen trying to get up the nerve to ask Raine Manning out."

"You must've figured out a way," Tanner said in jest. "Your mom and I couldn't keep the two of you apart the summer you turned fifteen."

Mitch smiled. "Those were the days. Now Raine barely speaks to me."

"Gotta be the Mitch version of Indigo charm," Garret chided.

"Is that why you avoid going into her family's restaurant like it contained some foreign strain of the plague?" Jackson asked.

"Fuck you. What do you know about it?"

"Watch your mouth," Tanner warned. "I didn't allow that kind of talk when you were fifteen."

"I'm not fifteen anymore," Mitch fired back.

"Doesn't matter. My house means my rules."

Stony silence followed. It stretched on until each of them remembered the reason they were gathered around the table in the first place. The unease built up and then dissolved into quiet acceptance.

Four members of their family were not there. And so far no one had done anything to resolve the why of it.

It was Jackson who finally broke the quiet. "I promised Tessa I'd look into Royce and Walker's bank records. To do that, I need to make a call to Nathan tonight. After that we need to come up with a serious game plan. Now's as good a time as any."

Garret laughed a little. "I can't see Nathan Hollister going against bank policy like that. He's the straightest arrow you ever had for a friend."

"That's just it, Nathan and I go way back. I was best man at his wedding."

Mitch cleared his throat. "Okay, I'll say what no one else wants to. We need to get better organized…and fast. There are four of us, including Tessa, and each one needs to do his or her part without bitching. I managed to get the press conference set up for tomorrow morning at eight. Don't expect a lot because I pulled it together with a bunch of favors and phone calls. Let's face it, the reporters might not even show up on such short notice. And it's happening on a Sunday. But it's a starting point. The next step is rounding up more of the locals for a ground search. I've made some calls on that, too. If we get the community involved, we should have a decent turnout. But eventually we'll need to ask around, maybe bring in professionals who do this sort of thing for a living. I have calls into people who do that with a great turnaround."

"You're talking about looking for bodies?" Jackson said before slamming his fist down on the table, fatigue and frustration taking hold. "Where? Where exactly do you intend to direct these people to look? Where do you have them start? Livvy and the kids could be anywhere."

Mitch abruptly stood up, causing the kitchen chair to fall over behind him. "You think I don't know that? You think I don't know that at this point we might be looking for remains?"

"Don't talk like that!" Tanner shouted. "It's too early to think that way."

Mitch sent his father a sad look as he set the chair upright. "Livvy has always been responsible, the one to pick up the phone and call home. Think about it. She's a levelheaded mom herself, a quick thinker. We all know she wouldn't go away on her own without giving you guys a heads-up about her plans." He stared at his dad. "You've already considered the stark possibility. Don't deny it. Mom might not have, but it's crossed your mind a time or two since this thing began."

Mitch paced to the kitchen sink, stared out the window into the darkness of the backyard. "Look, I don't want to fight with you guys, but the truth is, I'm the one person in this room who has the expertise and knows how best to find things no one else can."

He turned to face his family. "I do it all the time sailing the damned ocean. I know what I'm doing. I've already contacted my salvage crew to head back into port. They'll be here Wednesday with enough sonar to scan what's out in Sugar Bay and beyond."

Jackson leaned back in his chair, put his hands on his aching head. "I'm sorry. I'm so tired I'm not thinking straight. Plus I'm scared, scared out of my mind. The search is a good idea, expanding it to the water is an extension of covering our bases to rule out where they could've ended up."

Mitch sat back down. "The plan is to form three groups of volunteers. I'll send one out to canvass the strand and hand out flyers all along the shops. While doing that they'll ask around to see if anyone saw Livvy or Walker on Thursday. While one group pounds the pavement around town the other two will fan out and cover the beach, the right of way that leads to the marshlands, and the woods near the bog."

Tanner exchanged looks with his sons and scrubbed a hand over his face. "My God, I can't believe we're looking for bodies. This is really happening. Please don't let your mother hear this kind of talk yet."

But it was too late. All eyes turned to see Lenore standing in the kitchen doorway. One hand covered her mouth while the other clutched her chest. "You've heard something. My babies are dead, aren't they? Oh my God! Tell me this isn't happening. Tell me this is a nightmare."

Tanner got up, went to his wife. "No, no, we haven't heard a thing, honey. Go back to bed. Mitch is just organizing a search for tomorrow."

Lenore wobbled on her feet and started to sink to the floor.

"Call Vernon Whitten," Tanner demanded. "His number's there by the wall phone. Get him over here now!"

"Shouldn't we call 911?" Jackson asked, panic setting in.

"No, Vernon's two streets over. Do it! Just make the call."

Dr. Vernon Whitten had just settled in front of the flat screen to watch his alma mater, Florida State, finish off the Georgia Bulldogs in the final few minutes of the fourth quarter when the call came in. He'd been the Indigos' family physician for over thirty years. Because he knew what they were going through, he rushed out the door and headed to Quay Avenue.

Vernon beat the paramedics there by ten minutes.

After determining that Lenore had suffered an anxiety attack and that it had nothing to do with her heart, the doctor sedated her and directed Jackson to carry her to bed.

Vernon looked over at an exhausted Tanner and patted him on the shoulder. "She'll be fine. A good night's sleep will go a long way to helping her state of mind."

Tanner eased down into the nearest chair. "Thanks for getting here so fast."

"Not a problem. When this is over and Livvy and the kids are back home, we'll take those kids fishing for a couple days, get away from this bad memory, get us a bucket of chum and see how many redfish we can score."

Tanner wasn't that easily appeased. "Will it ever be that simple again, Vernon? Will the two of us ever get to go fishing without worrying about where Blake and Ally are, where their mother is? Before you got here, we were making plans to search for bodies. Nothing will ever go back to the way it was, not when you're forced to search for bodies of little babies."

Vernon went over to his friend. "They'll turn up. You have to believe that."

"Everyone keeps saying that, but how do I make sure Lenore holds up until that happens?"

Vernon had no answers so he patted Tanner on the back and said, "You need anything you know Jill and I will do whatever it takes to help. You just name it."

"That's just it, I'm not sure what to do, where to start. None of us are."

"You'll figure it out," Vernon said, looking around the room at the glum faces of the Indigo boys. "And these guys, your sons are pretty damn smart. Lean on them to get you and Lenore through this."

After Vernon left, Tanner joined his wife in bed. But the brothers stayed up, huddled back around the kitchen table.

Jackson rubbed his eyes. His head still pounded from the scare with his mother. "This might be the longest day of my life. We're all exhausted, frustrated, and on edge. And so far we've done a piss poor job of this whole thing. We haven't even been here one whole day yet and we almost gave Mom a heart attack just mentioning the reality of a search."

Mitch shifted forward, lowered his voice. "But we have to organize one. There's no way around it. I'm not cancelling everything I've worked out. This has to be the next step. The presser is a perfect opportunity to get attention from the media, which is what we need. We don't have the luxury of waiting any longer, which means we'll need a spokesperson. My vote's for you, big brother."

"Make it two," Garret chimed in, grateful he hadn't been pegged for the job. "As the oldest, Jackson gets to talk to the press."

"But…it should be Mitch. He's the one who reached out over the phone."

Mitch shook his head. "I'm too volatile. You know it's true. You're the levelheaded one, the scientist with the logical approach to a problem. I'm the reactor."

"More like the enforcer," Jackson corrected, combing his hands through his hair. "Great, just great. So I guess if nothing else, we scour the town for the minivan and try to come up with a witness, someone who saw them leave on Thursday. Are we in agreement there?" Jackson sent a look toward Mitch, then Garret.

After getting nods out of them, he went on, "Good, because there's something else. I think we should ask the volunteers to look for Tessa's brother's Honda Civic while they're at it. In my announcement I'll add Ryan's name to the mix. We should include missing posters of him along with those of Livvy, Walker, and the kids. Tessa already has some printed up. Don't fight me on this. It's the right thing to do since Tessa's down here on her own. We have each other to lean on and yell at. She's got no one. Imagine going through this kind of thing without family. I'd be lost."

Mitch nodded. "That's a given. How serious is this thing you have for her?"

Jackson's back went up. "I just met the woman today. Don't be an ass. But even if I wanted to take her back to her hotel and spend the night, it's none of your business. So butt out."

Garret drained his beer in time to play peacemaker. "Doesn't matter. We don't have time for those kinds of complications. And it wouldn't be right to hang Tessa out to dry by leaving out Ryan. The guy's poster should be included in the press packet."

"Okay then, we get some sleep and get up in the morning prepared to hit the ground running."

Chapter Six

Jackson had known Nathan Hollister for most of his life. The two had met on the playground of the day care center down the block at the age of four. Through the years they'd argued over Matchbox cars, fought over video games, clobbered each other roughhousing, suffered through a pesky outbreak of lice together, and that was all before beginning kindergarten.

In first grade they'd broken out with chicken pox days apart and recovered in time to join the same Cub Scout den. They'd slept in the same tents during camping trips where the summer humidity felt like a sauna and poison ivy was part of the packaged deal.

They got into fights with the same group of bullies who either became fast friends or common sworn enemies.

They shared their dreams about what they wanted to be when they grew up. They consoled each other when they struck out in Little League with bases loaded, and later in life, when neither one could get a date on a Saturday night.

It was evident early on the two leaned toward sharing the same nerdy interests, which probably was the reason their bond hadn't ended at high school graduation. They were friends on Facebook, shared regular email updates, and remained close despite the fact Jackson lived fifteen hundred miles to the north.

Even though it was a Sunday morning, he met up with his childhood buddy in the back parking lot of the First National Bank building in the heart of downtown. The area was almost deserted—too early for anyone to be out and about heading for church—the beach maybe, but not church services. Those wouldn't start for another three hours.

At six thirty-five Jackson followed Nathan through the back door and into an office.

"Thanks for doing this," Jackson said as Nathan waited for his desktop computer to boot up.

"Anything for Livvy. Anyone finds out what I'm doing, though, I could lose my job. So remember, you owe me. If I end up in the unemployment line, you're paying for my health insurance."

"Duly noted. Does your wife, Wendy, know you used to steal stacks of *Penthouses* from Junior Morrissey and sell them under the bleachers after football practice for a dollar apiece? I was gonna use that dark secret to my advantage if you hadn't agreed to do this."

Nathan narrowed his eyes at the attempt at humor. "Blackmail works both ways, buddy. I know enough about your past to take the dirty details straight to your mother. I can just see your mom's eyes bug out when I tell her about the times you forged her signature on school notes after multiple offenses. Then top it off with how many times you used to fill your pockets at the Pack N Save with pilfered candy. I doubt that would go over too well with your old man."

Jackson grinned and held up a hand to stop. "No need to dredge up the sordid history on either side."

"You say that now but your seedy past was a lot worse than mine. Let's just do this thing and get out of here. I actually snuck out of the house before Wendy woke up because I didn't want her asking where I was going. If she asked I thought about telling her I decided to take up jogging."

"Not a good idea. That's a lie you'd have to draw out for at least a couple weeks." Beginning to realize what Nathan was jeopardizing, Jackson shifted his feet. "I don't think it's a good idea to tell too many people about this."

"Well. Duh." As Nathan logged onto the system, his nervousness caused him to feel the need to make more small talk. "How's the research project going in the aftermath of Hurricane Sandy?"

"Still taking samples of the estuarine environments impacted by the heavy rainfall. It's amazing how much soil and sediment were washed away and how many pollutants ended up in the coastal and marine interior. Even looking back and studying the devastation of what Hurricane Agnes did to the Chesapeake Bay in 1972 we weren't prepared for Sandy's damage to native grasses, or the change in habitat of the crab and fish. Sandy wrecked marine life that will take years before the coast is able to completely recover."

"Listen to you, the scientist speaks."

Jackson shrugged. "It's what I do. Look at you. Who would've thought you'd get off on debits and credits. And to think I tried to talk you out of majoring in finance in college."

It was Nathan's turn to smile. "I timed it perfect when I graduated from FSU and found out old man Savage was retiring. The bank needed a junior exec and I fit the bill. Since then, I've worked my way up."

"Yeah, lucky you." Jackson looked around at the dull, gray interior walls. To him, the bank's cubicles represented a confined jail cell. "I'm glad I get out in the field. I can't imagine spending eight hours at a time, five days a week in here."

"Hey, don't knock it. I get to help customers secure their futures. I help them with their car loans and home mortgages and CDs."

"Sounds exciting. Not." Standing behind Nathan, Jackson spotted the screen come up with Royce's account information. He went line by line reading the details until he found what he was looking for. "So Ryan Connelly did come into the bank at 11:25 to cash his five-thousand-dollar check. This is the same morning he left the hotel around eleven o'clock."

"If the trustees find out I've done this, they'll have me fired for sure," Nathan groused.

"Since when did you become such a worrywart? Besides, this is a significant clue. Did you bring this up to Jessup Sinclair when Connelly turned up missing?"

"I spoke to Sinclair maybe once. But he didn't ask me anything about a Ryan Connelly. Besides, have you any idea how many people walk through that door after a major holiday to cash a check? It's pretty routine and not possible to keep track of one missing guy's whereabouts. For all Sinclair knew the guy could've marched out of here and hit the Hialeah Park Race Track or dropped the entire amount at the nearest casino."

Jackson thought of Tessa's efforts to find any information about her brother and refused to accept a lazy assumption. "That's one way to look at it. But Nathan, the man had five grand on him in cash and you didn't think to, at the very least, follow up with Jessup about it? What if this was a member of your family who went missing? What if your relative couldn't be found? Did you ever consider the possibility that Ryan might've been robbed somewhere along the way before he could leave town?"

"Sure, make me feel guilty why don't you? But Sinclair never directly came in to my office and made an official inquiry about it or ask to see specific details."

That just pissed Jackson off more. "So while we're standing here arguing the point, can you look and tell me if Livvy or Walker withdrew any large amounts of cash from any of their accounts?"

Nathan eyed his buddy with a snarl on his lips. "You're pushing it, Jackson. Isn't it enough that I already cooperated with the state investigator by giving him Livvy and Walker's bank records? Some guy named Hawkins looked over the transactions and determined no money's been withdrawn from any of their accounts since they went missing, nothing."

"What's the balance in each of Livvy's and Walker's joint accounts?"

Reluctantly, Nathan hit several more keys and brought up another screen. "Main checking has about twenty-five grand. Savings still has another twenty grand. They have several money market accounts with an equal amount, which rounds out to be about forty thousand more."

It didn't sound to Jackson like Walker would've had a problem paying Ryan what he owed him. "Could I take a look at the individual transactions on their main account?"

Protectively, Nathan shielded the computer with his hands. "I can't do that. I told you there was no activity since they went missing. The last was from the Winn-Dixie in the amount of seventy-five dollars when Livvy bought groceries. You'll have to take my word for it because I'm not letting you see more than that. I've already broken the law for you. Don't ask me for more."

Since he'd gone this far, Jackson ignored the declaration. "Exactly. So letting me get a peek for myself won't hurt a thing. Come on, Nathan, a glance, that's all I'm asking."

Nathan gave in again and adjusted the computer screen so Jackson could get a better look.

Jackson frowned at what he saw. "Now see, what you told me isn't entirely correct."

"What? Of course it is."

"Nope. The very last transaction was Wednesday night at six-fifty when Walker made a deposit in the amount of seven hundred and fifty-eight dollars. Cash deposit. I'm assuming that was probably the take for the day from the store."

"So? I thought you were interested in purchases not deposits," Nathan explained. "What difference does it make?"

"About three hours. The surveillance at Winn-Dixie lets us know that Livvy checked out at four-ten with her groceries. This seems like a routine stop by Walker to swing by the ATM to make a deposit at the end of the day. In other words, Livvy's shopping trip was completely normal. She intended to cook dinner. No big deal. Walker's stop by the bank before heading home for the day was another ordinary thing. Which means that whatever happened to make them leave, happened while they were all four inside that house."

"That's good, right?" Nathan asked. "That's something you didn't have before this minute."

"It's something. I'm not sure what yet. This information is just another part of the puzzle. But if Walker and Livvy were planning on leaving town why wouldn't they take some cash with them? In fact, why doesn't Walker keep the cash he has in his hand instead of depositing it into the business account? If he intended to take a trip he's right there at the ATM machine. He could have withdrawn more money then. If they were headed out of town, why wouldn't he take out extra cash from his personal checking account? I mean, yesterday when my mother called and said I needed to come back home, the first stop I made on my way to the airport was the ATM machine for a little traveling cash. Why wouldn't Walker or Livvy have done the same?"

Nathan scratched his chin. "That's a good point. Is that significant?"

"Sure. But it's also disturbing. If they didn't leave town without getting cash ahead of time and there's been no activity since Wednesday night, then where the hell are they without access to their money?"

"Maybe they had an additional account somewhere else?"

"Hmm, it's possible, I guess. We do sit in the middle between Key Largo and Key West. I'll have to ask Mom and Dad to see if Livvy ever mentioned opening up another account." Jackson chewed the inside of his jaw. "I need to see if they chartered a jet out of the same airstrip that serves the area. One thing I've learned about this is that I make a piss-poor investigator. That's the first time I've thought of looking into alternative transportation out of the area."

"The more you think on this, the weirder it gets. It is strange that Walker didn't keep the money he had on him. What exactly do you think happened to them?"

"I honestly don't know. Which reminds me, Mitch has rounded up volunteers for a search of the area beginning at eight o'clock." Jackson glanced at his watch. "I've got an hour to pick up Tessa and get some breakfast and make it there on time. Are you and Wendy coming to help?"

"Absolutely. Who's Tessa?"

"Ryan Connelly's sister."

Nathan gave him a hangdog look. "Ah. It never occurred to me this guy's family would show up down here and want to know these kinds of things."

"Why not? Indigo Key was the last place he was seen."

Nathan abruptly powered down his computer and changed the subject. "Do me a favor, Jackson. Next time you see Wendy, try not mention that I had the hots for your sister back in the old days."

"The old days? Hell, Nathan, back then I thought for certain that one day you would eventually talk Livvy into something other than friends."

"Really? Because there was a time I thought that way, too."

"I was rooting for you."

Nathan grinned. "But then Walker came along."

"Yeah. Walker."

As if thinking back to the past, Nathan went on, "One thing about Livvy, she hasn't changed much since high school. She's still beautiful. No one brightens up a room like she does with that hundred-watt smile of hers. Whenever she comes into the bank, she goes out of her way to be as nice and friendly to everyone, must be that cheerleader personality of hers." Nathan sent Jackson a sheepish look. "Uh, you might not want to mention that last part to Wendy, either."

"Now would I turn on a bro like that?" Jackson said as he wrapped Nathan up in a bear hug. "Thanks, man. Thanks for putting your job on the line like this."

"No problem. Just remember, Indigo, I know where you live and I'm not talking about Quay Avenue."

"Right back atcha. Catch you later. Don't forget the search starts at eight." With that Jackson sailed out of the office and jogged to his dad's truck to go pick up Tessa.

On the way to the hotel, Jackson sent a text message to Tessa. *Ready for breakfast? Got news.*

He had to wait several minutes for a reply.

Starving. I'll meet you out front.

Since he could see the Mainsail Lodge from the bank, the trip took less than five minutes. He didn't even have to honk the horn when he pulled up in front. She was standing on the steps waiting for him wearing a little sweater top that matched her eyes with just enough contrast to set off the pair of dark jeans she wore.

She popped into the front seat next to Jackson, a million questions firing on all cylinders. "What did you find out?"

He rehashed the fact that Ryan had visited the bank the morning he was supposed to have left town.

"If only we had his cell phone records," Tessa noted. "How do I go about getting a copy of his cell activity?"

"If he has an online account with his carrier, you could try to hack into it the same way you did his email account. That way you could bypass getting in touch with his carrier."

Tessa grabbed Jackson's arm. "Great idea. I should've thought of that. I'm pretty sure he signed up for online payment when he upgraded his last phone. But that was almost a year ago, Christmas, I think. If I'm lucky, maybe he even used the same password he did for his email. I need to look that up as soon as possible. Like right now."

"Let's find someplace where we can sit down, grab a quick breakfast and I'll tell you the rest. I don't have much time before I'm supposed to make a statement to the media. I do have a question for you, though. Is it okay if I mention Ryan during the presser? Sort of lump both cases together?"

Tessa's eyes glistened with appreciation. "I hated to be pushy, or to ask last night, but it would be wonderful if you would, if you're sure it won't take the focus off looking for Livvy and the kids."

"You aren't pushy since I'm the one who brought it up. My brothers and I talked about it last night and we all came to the same decision. It's the right thing to do. Besides, if Mitch talks Jessup into appearing with us, it might bring law enforcement around to linking the two events together."

"So you've come to that conclusion, too."

"I have." Jackson pulled the pickup to a stop in front of the local pancake house known as Go Flip a Cake. He led her through the door and faltered when he spotted a flyer of Livvy, Walker, and the kids taped to the side of the cash register. Jimmy Don's doing, he decided.

The poster denoted reality. It smacked him in the face before he finally got his feet to move past it. He tugged

Tessa toward the nearest booth and signaled for the waitress, a tall, thin woman in her fifties who also owned the place. "Morning, Helen, we're in a crunch for time."

Helen nodded. "Got that news conference soon. Mitch phoned me about it last night. Been super busy because of it. Reporters and camera crews got here early. Don't worry. I'll get your order out in record time. That's a promise. I'll see to it you won't be late. What'll it be?"

"A blueberry short stack for me," Tessa said without a glance at the menu. Eager to get back to the conversation, she gave him a look that said hurry up and order.

Jackson took the hint. "Sounds like a winner. Make it two, but I want mine with two eggs over easy and a slab of bacon. And coffee. I could use a gallon of it. And orange juice."

Helen gave him a wink. "You got it. I'll get Merle working on it right away."

After Helen had dashed off to the kitchen, Jackson offered up his report. "Since Ryan had cash in hand the morning he planned to leave, if he wanted to get on the road, what's the next logical thing he would do?"

Tessa thought for a moment and sat up straighter. "He'd have to fuel up his car at the gas station. Maybe someone robbed him there."

"That was my gut reaction, too. But…"

"Wait a minute. I found something out last night," Tessa said and began digging deep inside her handbag. "I wrote it down so I wouldn't get it wrong."

While she searched, Helen returned with a carafe of coffee, filled two cups, and set down two tall glasses of juice. "This'll get you started. Your order will be up in a jiff."

Tessa pulled out a piece of paper, held it up. "I got into Ryan's online bank account, stayed up until two o'clock last night doing that instead of sleeping. But it paid off. I found out Ryan hung around town after he checked out of the hotel. I'm not sure why."

"Now we know he cashed that check," Jackson added.

"But I didn't know that last night because that amount never showed up in his bank account back home. Ryan never made it out of this state, Jackson, maybe not even out of this town. I'm sure of it. Granted there's no branch here in Indigo Key where he could have deposited the money, or for that matter, Florida. And now that I know he definitely got his money from Walker, maybe he paid cash at the pump to gas up his car. I discovered his last debit transaction occurred at 3:45 when he used his card at a hamburger place called Charlie's. Which means he hung around town from eleven-thirty in the morning to at least four o'clock. Why? Why would he not get on the road and head for home immediately after getting his five-grand and gassing up? It's bugged me all night."

"Maybe he had to meet up with Walker one more time?" Jackson prompted.

"Then we're on the same page there. Since Walker's basically the key person Ryan interacted with during the time he spent here, it makes sense that if he didn't leave right away there had to be a good reason. Meeting with the client who brought him down here in the first place is the most logical answer."

About that time Helen delivered their order, two plates each stacked with still steaming hotcakes, Jackson's eggs and bacon.

"Anything else I can get ya?" Helen asked as she refilled their coffee mugs.

"Nope. I think we're good," Jackson said, not waiting before cutting up his eggs and digging in. After Helen trekked off to the kitchen leaving them alone again, he tore into a litany of suggestions. "Getting our hands on cell phone records needs to be a priority because I'm beginning to realize we desperately need to look at either Walker's or Livvy's carrier to nail down what progressed over the past three weeks. That accomplishes two things. We get a picture of Walker's interaction with Ryan and the time leading up to Walker and Livvy's disappearance. It's the best way to focus on their activity. The problem is law enforcement has already gained that information. It cuts us out of the picture entirely before we ever get started."

Tessa frowned. "That might be the case with Livvy but not likely with Ryan's info. I doubt Jessup even bothered to go to that kind of trouble for Ryan."

Jackson stopped eating long enough to reach across the table to put his hand over hers. "I'm sorry your brother's disappearance has gone neglected in all this."

"That's why I'm working on it myself. But it's not as easy to access phone records as it sounds. Ryan must've changed the password recently because I haven't been able to access his billing statement online. I'm sure you'll find out how difficult it is when you try for Livvy's without knowing her user ID and password."

Jackson shook his head. "Not me. That's Garret's job. Last night we agreed to split up the list of things to do. And keep detailed logs on everything we get. And now I know that we're also facing an additional problem because the state investigators have already subpoenaed bank records. Nathan let that slip out this morning. That means the cell phone information will likely be off limits as well."

"How do you intend to get around that?"

"Jessup is our in with law enforcement. We're hoping at some point the investigators will share what they know with him and it'll trickle down to us."

She sent Jackson an incredulous stare. "That's your plan?"

"Feel free to enlighten me. I'm open to other options."

"I'm thinking of hiring a private investigator. Obviously in order to cover the expense, I'd have to get my dad on board and my stepmother—"

Jackson cut her off. "A PI's been on the table since we got here. We're all willing to chip in to get the best. Don't worry. We'll include Ryan in that as well. It wouldn't be right to leave him out."

Tessa let out a huge sigh. "Thanks for that."

He got the sense there was more she wanted to talk about. But when he looked at his watch, he knew they were running out of time. "We need to get out of here. If I'm late to this presser my brothers will string me up." He slapped money down on the table, snatched Tessa's hand in his and led her out the door and into the street.

They walked along the sidewalk toward the Vitamin Hut. Even from this distance Tessa spotted a crowd, which included most of the Indigo clan, already standing in front of the strip shopping mall. A rush of envy overwhelmed her. Livvy and her children, even the questionable Walker, had plenty of support, support Ryan lacked.

Tessa shifted toward Jackson and wanted to know, "Are you nervous?"

He was, but what was the point of admitting to it. Instead, he dismissed the notion with bravado that was far from convincing. "My sister and her kids are missing. I don't have the luxury of being nervous."

She let the show of arrogance slide, glad it was him stepping in front of all the cameras and microphones instead of her. She wasn't sure how he'd ended up tagged as the spokesperson but she had every confidence he'd do the job with a composure she didn't feel.

Suddenly, he tugged her between two buildings and dragged her up against him. Their lips were a breath apart. "What would you do right this minute if I kissed you?"

"I'd...I'd..."

Before she could complete that thought, he covered her mouth. She tasted like cinnamon and warm maple syrup.

There on the streets, a stone's throw from the marina, they used eager mouths to tease each other to the brink of something greater. For him, it broke the tension that had been building all morning. He rested his forehead on hers. "I needed to do that. Let's hope it gives me the oomph I need to deal with the reporters."

She patted his chest and chortled with laughter. "Sure. Any time. Whatever I can do to help. Is there anything special about my lips or will anyone's do?"

He grinned. "I think you already know the answer to that." He snagged her hand and raced around the corner and back to the location Mitch had chosen for facing the media.

The spot seemed significant because it was in front of the Vitamin Hut. Maybe the surrounding area on camera would trigger a witness coming forward. After all, this was an orchestrated effort required to jog the public's memory. Maybe someone had seen something that would help in bringing the family back home.

Jackson looked out over the sizeable crowd realizing that Mitch had done a good job organizing all the volunteers. "I'm surprised so many people showed up." It seemed to him half the town had blown off their Sunday activities to be here. It was almost a rally of sorts.

Mitch took his place next to Jackson, his chest puffed with pride at the turnout. "And to think the Dolphins are playing the Jets on the road. Every man here could be watching the game on TV."

Jackson spotted Jessup and jabbed Mitch in the ribs. "How'd you get the old man here?"

"I appealed to his pride. The guy might have been replaced as top investigator on the case, but it doesn't mean he isn't itching to chip in his two cents at the first opportunity."

Tanner slapped his middle son on the back. "Good job. Having a member of law enforcement standing behind us during the press conference signifies we won't be ignored."

Garret had done his part as well by contacting media outlets throughout the state. News vans and reporters lined the streets waiting to send the live feed back to their viewers.

Jackson put an arm around Tessa as they pushed their way through the throng of people, his hand clutching hers in solidarity. Noticeably missing was his mother.

"How's Mom?" Jackson asked Tanner.

"She's resting. Wanted to be here, but Vernon nixed that idea."

"It's just as well," Jackson agreed, blowing out an anxious breath. He looked around at his brothers. "Are you guys ready to deal with the onslaught? Are we ready to create this monster for real?"

Garret nodded. "Might as well get it done."

At eight a.m. on the dot, Jackson stepped to the bank of microphones he'd so dreaded the day before. Surrounded by his family, he cleared his throat and began his pitch.

"Today, after more than seventy-two hours have passed without any word from them, we face the stark reality of looking for our missing sister and her family. We're asking the public's help to find them. If you've seen any of these people…"

Jackson paused long enough to hold up the last family photograph taken back in the summer. It showed four people in the frame—two adults, two kids—looking tanned and fit and happy as the boy and girl hammed it up for the camera.

While the reporters digested that information, Jackson held up a second photo, this one of Ryan taken with Tessa. "And we have another missing person, a man who's been gone three weeks without a trace." He went into Ryan's physical description and the pertinent facts Tessa wanted everyone to know about her brother.

"The bottom line here, folks, five people went missing and they've left behind loved ones who care about them and are worried for their safety. That's why we're beginning a search today and we'll be here tomorrow and the day after that until we find Olivia, Walker, Blake and Ally Buchanan and Ryan Connelly. We'll keep trying every single day and won't rest until we bring them back home. If anyone has any knowledge, if anyone knows anything at all, even if you don't think it's significant, please come forward. Contact the local authorities or the state police. Or contact us directly. My brother Mitch set up a special phone number for tips. There's no doubt we need the public's help. That's why we're counting on our neighbors to come through for us."

"Do you plan to offer a reward?" one of the reporters shouted.

"We're working on that, still coming up with an amount," Jackson answered. "But the quick response is yes."

Another yelled out, "So you think the case of the missing web designer is also related to the Buchanan family disappearing?"

"I'll leave that determination up to law enforcement," Jackson stated diplomatically without giving anything else away. "But even if the two events aren't connected, the bottom line is we need help in finding Ryan Connelly and getting him back to his family."

Immediately after the session with reporters ended, Mitch led the way next door and into the clubroom at the marina, adjacent to the Vitamin Hut. This made for a short walk so the volunteers could get their assignments and begin the difficult task of covering every square inch of town.

Mitch had designated this place their command center for a reason. It could hold more than two hundred people, including four professional search and rescue teams Mitch had persuaded to participate. The teams came from different parts of the Sunshine State and each one specialized in tracking human scent.

To help the dogs—a border collie, a Lab, and two golden retrievers—Mitch had commandeered a couple of items belonging to Ally and Livvy they'd left behind at his mother's house. One item was Ally's Barbie doll, the other, a pair of shorts Livvy had worn the weekend before she went missing. Of course, the starting point for the canines had to be the house on Blue Fin where the family was last seen.

The sea of faces included several sets of parents with children. Many were Ally's and Blake's classmates from school.

As Jackson spoke with each one he discovered how the kids had spent an anxious and fearful couple of days. No doubt they'd picked up on the tension emanating from the adults. The offers of help touched his heart. He ruffled the head of one freckle-faced boy about eight years old and made sure he felt like a part of the process. "Thank you for helping us out. Don't worry. We'll find a job where everyone gets to pitch in and do their part."

Everyone else crammed into the meeting room and gathered around the grid map Mitch had put up. He began assigning target areas to the first group, given the simple task of saturating the town with more flyers.

The second and third groups would become part of the actual ground search. They would spread out, shoulder to shoulder, and walk through the marshland, from shoreline to shoreline and repeat the same tactical maneuver over higher ground. They would scour alongside roadways and target drainage ditches. All this, while another team went door-to-door, walking up and down each residential street combing trash bins or behind hedges and shrubbery.

Mitch had contacted a variety of seasoned pros who generously guided him through this particular process. He was meticulous when he recounted those instructions to the volunteers. "Each of you will be given a set of bright orange plastic ribbons to use for tagging along with an orange whistle. Remember, as you're going through an area, don't touch or pick up any items you come across that look suspicious. If you find something that might be pertinent to the case, tag the area with the ribbon and let someone know you've located something that might need a second look by blowing the whistle. That also goes for any articles of clothing, any personal items like cell phones you locate, or any jewelry that might be of particular interest to law enforcement. If you find any of these types of things, be sure to let your team leader know. They'll be the ones who'll contact authorities so law enforcement will actually bag the items for evidence. Are we all clear on that?"

Tessa listened, impressed with how the organization had come together in such a short amount of time. She knew Mitch and Garret had gotten the owner of the hardware store to open up at six-thirty that morning so they could stock up on every package of tagging ribbon and whistles the retailer had on hand. It was a testament to what three people could accomplish as a unit versus one lone outsider.

She was about to join the others for her assignment when an elderly man in his eighties approached her, tapping his cane on the floor to get her attention.

"I recognized that picture of your brother Jackson held up."

"Really? Where?"

"Saw him eating a burger over at Charlie's."

A wave of optimism rose in her chest. "Do you remember when that was?"

"Two days after Labor Day. I remember because it was my wife Josie's birthday. Took her in there around four-thirty to get us one of those chiliburgers for supper. Had a coupon for buy one, get one free. Can't beat that deal. On social security we don't eat out much. So when Charlie's runs those coupons in the *Indigo Dispatch* every Wednesday we go without fail. So yeah, it had to be the Wednesday after Labor Day."

Tessa chewed her lip, disappointed with that little nugget. She already knew Ryan's bank records showed he'd eaten there. In fact, it indicated he'd ordered his meal as if he intended to hit the road right afterward.

Which again had her wondering why Ryan had decided to stay so long after he'd cashed the check. Why had he gotten such a late start in the day when he could easily have left around noon? Those were questions that kept nagging at her. There was one more detail the man might be able to provide, though. "Was Ryan eating by himself? Was he sitting alone?"

"At first. But then Walker came in and ordered himself a Coke, joined your brother about midway through his meal."

"Interesting." But it didn't explain the hours Ryan had spent from the time he left the bank at 11:30 to meeting up with Walker at 4:30. None of it answered what happened to him after he left the restaurant.

After thanking the man for coming forward with the information, something occurred to Tessa. If Ryan met with Walker late in the day, could Walker have done something to Ryan after that? She decided to run it by Jackson first chance she got.

That proved to be sooner rather than later. She found him handing out ribbons and whistles to those who'd volunteered to cover ground riding their ATVs.

"Where are they going?" Tessa asked Jackson.

"Greenbelts, fields, parks, along pathways, anywhere and everywhere," Jackson said, frustration laced in his tone.

She told him about the old man's sighting at the hamburger place. "I have to assume Walker might've been the last person Ryan talked to that day."

Jackson tightened his jaw and stared down at the redhead. "You're suggesting he was the last person to see Ryan? You're thinking Walker did something to Ryan to make him disappear?"

Tessa puffed out a sigh. "I guess I am. There's no doubt Ryan had a fair amount of cash on him at the time. What if Walker wanted it back? Is that a problem, seeing that I suspect the guy who happens to be a member of your family?"

"It certainly doesn't help matters," Jackson acknowledged, rubbing the back of his neck where tension had formed in between his shoulder blades. The headache from hell was beginning to ratchet up in his already aching temples. "Right now I'm having a hard time thinking straight. Could we table this discussion until tonight after we get the first search behind us?"

"Sure," she said, more than a little disheartened at his unusual reaction. But then, she was still a virtual stranger in this cliquish town. In the face of family, what had she really expected from Walker's brother-in-law? It was one thing for kin to badmouth Livvy's husband for being a louse, quite another to view him as a suspect in her brother's disappearance.

For now, she rolled up her sleeves and reported for duty. The day had already hit eighty degrees by the time she went out with the first group, a tedious but necessary task of tacking up more posters to as many poles as she could find and as many business windows that would give her permission.

Rubbing elbows with the locals had its advantages. She got to make the case for finding her brother, one on one, armed with a photo to boot. Her pitch seemed to work. She noticed the people acted a hundred times friendlier than before, almost as if they'd had a one-eighty change of heart. As she ambled along the streets, even she understood none of it would've been possible without Jackson. The fact that he'd lumped Ryan's disappearance in with the Buchanans' might trigger a resolve.

But when her group ran out of posters, instead of heading back to the command center with the others, Tessa opted to slip away. She backtracked to the hotel parking lot where she'd left her car. It was time to deal with her own problems, which meant she needed to walk her path alone, at least for tonight.

It was nearing dusk by the time the volunteers began returning in waves to the command center where they'd started out that morning. Muddy and sweaty and suffering from mosquito bites, they streamed through the doors, dejected looks on their faces. No one had found a trace of the Buchanan family, not even a single noteworthy item to tag and hand off to the authorities.

Their lack of success had made them stay out longer than the assignment entailed hoping to stumble on a clue or two. Empty-handed, they hadn't dragged themselves back to the marina until they'd lost the light.

With the first attempt behind them, a downhearted Jackson began to rally everyone for the next day. "Those of you who are able to take the day off, meet back here in the morning. I realize most of you have jobs. But any amount of time you could spare would be greatly appreciated. Keep in mind we're committed to repeating this process until we bring them home."

After the last volunteer had been accounted for, Jackson turned to his brothers. "I just realized I might've spoken out of turn earlier when I declared we were in this for the long haul. It's one thing to say it and another to fully commit. Are you guys prepared to do this indefinitely until we find them?"

Mitch was the first to speak up. "You bet. Looking at the grid map, we've barely scratched the surface. There's a lot of island yet to cover."

But Garret was more pragmatic. "What if we're all looking in the wrong place? What if they aren't on land at all?" He looked out past the marina and beyond to the waters of the Atlantic. "If you wanted to dispose of a body or several, where's the perfect place to get rid of your victims?"

His arms swung wide. "We're surrounded by water. You take out a boat large enough to hold four victims, weigh them all down so they stay down, and then dump them one by one over the side. They wouldn't surface for weeks, maybe months, if they washed up at all."

Mitch let out a sigh. "You're the first to voice what's been in the back of my mind since I woke up at three o'clock this morning and couldn't go back to sleep. The ocean is the perfect dumping ground."

About that time Jackson spotted his parents coming through the door. His father looked downright worn out and his mother looked as though she'd aged ten years overnight.

"Do me a favor," Jackson groaned. "Don't mention that kind of shit with Mom nearby. Besides that, there are certain things we need to address right now, like the reward the press asked about earlier."

"I'll put up fifty grand," Mitch asserted.

"Make it one hundred," Garret offered, lifting a shoulder in a modest gesture. "I signed a new endorsement two months ago for a brand new line of surfing gear."

Pride moved through Jackson. "Might as well make it one-fifty."

Tanner and Lenore gaped at their sons. But it was Lenore who asked, "You guys have that kind of cash on hand?"

Jackson shifted his feet. "We all make a good living doing what we love doing. You guys taught us that, to do what we love. The thing is there's no doubt in my mind that if things were reversed, Livvy would do exactly the same thing for any of us if she were the one standing in this spot."

"That's the truth of it," Garret said in agreement.

Jackson stuffed his hands into the pockets of his khaki shorts. "Look, I hate to shift this discussion into another dire possibility, but it's unavoidable. I was approached this afternoon by a retired sheriff's deputy who suggested that, at some point down the road, we might need to utilize a website called NamUs."

Garret shot his older brother a disgusted look. "But you just got onto me and said you didn't want us talking like that."

Jackson rubbed his forehead. "I know. But it occurs to me that putting the info into NamUs means covering all our bases. It doesn't mean we've accepted that scenario as fact."

Tanner looked over at his wife's face. "So that website is exactly what it sounds like?"

"I'm afraid so. It's a centralized database for law enforcement and medical examiners from all over the country to use as a resource in hopes of identifying remains."

But Lenore wasn't ready to accept that as an option. "What does that have to do with Livvy and the kids? You're wasting your time." Her voice cracked. "I keep telling you Livvy, Blake, and Ally are not dead. They're not," she insisted. "They'll come back to us when whatever scared them off is over with, when they think the danger's passed, they'll come back home. You'll see. There's no doubt in my mind that Livvy's simply waiting for a safe time to call home, that's all."

Jackson studied his mom's face, a mound of resentment welling up. No son should be put in a position where these things had to be explained to a grieving mother, let alone his own.

He scanned the room, got the nod from Mitch and Garret to continue. Choosing his words carefully, he tried an assuring tone. "Mom, in the event this doesn't have the happy ending we all want, NamUs is another tool to connect with other agencies around the country to help us locate them."

Mitch picked up the refrain. "None of us wants to consider the worst case scenario. But if remains are found anywhere in Florida that need identification, this website will know about it. You and Dad won't have to log on. One of us will check it daily for any new leads. And we had to notify the center for missing kids. There's no discussion about that."

Lenore put a hand over her mouth. "Well, I refuse to think that way. Give Livvy enough time and everything will work out. She'll call. I know she will."

"I hope you're right," Jackson said, knowing there was one more thing they needed to cover before everyone headed back to the house. "I say it's time to hire a private investigator before this thing gets out of hand and the case dries up completely. By hiring one now, we take the initiative. We capitalize with the only advantage we have at the moment. Today we captured the media's interest, not just Florida but nationwide. Now we have to keep it by bringing in someone who knows what he's doing. The problem is I have no idea who to contact in that area. I'm not sure we'll get the best man for the job by looking it up in the Yellow Pages. So does anyone have suggestions?"

Mitch cleared his throat. "There's a guy in Miami who fits the bill. He's well known for his work in high profile cases. His name's Anthony Marcelli. He's a former detective with Miami PD and has a decent rep for not giving up until he gets answers. He's the one who tackled that case five years ago where an ex-wife talked some jerkwad into murdering her former husband for the million-dollar life insurance she carried on him."

A pained look crossed Jackson's face. "I remember that case. The woman's name was Amelia Emberson. It was a jumbled mess before Marcelli was able to slog through the leads and find out what really happened."

"Yeah. And Marcelli never quit until he gathered enough evidence to take to the cops who ended up bringing Emberson down. A jury convicted her and now she's serving life in Broward for the solicitation of capital murder."

Garret nodded. "I've heard of Marcelli. He's also the one who did all that work to find that newborn baby abducted from the hospital nursery three years back. It was all over the Internet how he pursued the kidnappers until he solved the case."

Tanner blew out a breath. "It sounds like this Marcelli knows his stuff. You okay with that, Lenore?"

"Anything to bring Livvy and the kids home."

"Then let's go with him. Who makes the call?"

Garret took a step forward. "I'll do it. Mitch organized the search while you took over getting account details out of the bank. First thing in the morning I'll reach out to Marcelli."

"Okay then. We're all exhausted. Let's get some sleep, try to wake up refreshed, and prepare to do it all over again tomorrow."

Chapter Seven

Tessa started her day before eight o'clock with one mindset. Talk to as many boat owners as she could to find the one Walker had used to take Ryan fishing. It sounded like a longshot. But she had to try. And if she did get lucky, maybe she could sneak on board to take a look around, or better still, talk the owner into giving her a tour himself.

She lifted her face to the ocean breeze and found loons and herons diving for their breakfast. The water, an iridescent jade, was a wonder. So crystal clear you could see the sandy bottom below. Any other time she would've loved to park her fanny on the beach, or dip her toes in the water and go snorkeling. But she wasn't here to play tourist.

Walking along the pier, gazing out at the sea-foam ocean currents, a dreadful thought ran through her mind.

She'd been raised on Nags Head, been around the ocean her entire life. She knew exactly what the sea could do to a body. She also knew how often people went missing on the water and the body never surfaced at all. Her heart sank at the prospect. She shivered at the notion Ryan could have ended up like that. The thought made her ready for an all-day quest if that's what it took.

She followed the signs to at least a dozen yacht owners advertising charters. She circled the docks but at each place had a difficult time getting anyone to talk to her.

But then, at the umpteenth stop she got lucky—a charter service operated by a one-man band named Paulie Gruden.

She watched as Paulie stood over a folding table gutting a large tuna he'd caught just that morning. He wore a pair of cutoffs and a green T-shirt that read, "Old Fishermen Never Die They Just Smell Like They Do." A generous growth of beard covered the man's weathered face and went with his shaggy mane of graying hair. When he flashed his smile it showed several missing teeth. But fortunately for Tessa, Paulie seemed affable and liked to talk.

"You look like you're lost. What're you lookin' for there, girl?"

"Could you tell me if Walker Buchanan chartered one of your boats around Labor Day to take a tourist out fishing for marlin or barracuda?"

Because Paulie had a wad of tobacco in his mouth, he had to stop and spit before he could answer. "No, ma'am, Walker wouldn't need to charter a boat for fishing since he owns a real nice one hisself, a forty footer with all the fancy bells and whistles people like the Buchanans could ever wish for."

"Really?" She frowned. Why had Jackson not mentioned that to her before? Would it have made a difference? "Which one is it? Could you point it out to me?"

Paulie raised a lean finger and pointed to Walker's blue and white yacht docked in one of the slips about ten boats away. The powerful cruiser had a wraparound helm and a walk-through flybridge. Etched on the side wasn't the name Tessa expected. It wasn't Livvy's name written in silver letters, but that of another. The *Misty Dawn* rocked in the waves.

Tessa listened as Paulie ran through the boat's list of features. "That one's top of the line, fully-loaded. She's got two staterooms and two heads, and a nice GPS system. Wouldn't belong to a Buchanan if it wasn't first-rate classy."

"Do you have any idea the last time Walker took the boat out?"

Paulie cocked his head and spit again as if thinking. "Probably, near as I can remember, about ten days ago. You know he's missing, right? Been missing since last Thursday. The whole family's up and left town. Didn't take the boat though."

"I heard. What do you think happened to them?"

"Got themselves into a mess of trouble, probably," Paulie surmised. "That boy always did push people's buttons the wrong way, ever since he was old enough to talk."

"Have the police been on board that you know of since the family went missing?"

Paulie scratched his head and tried to tone down his mass of hair. "Not to my knowledge. Nobody's been coming around here asking 'cept you."

"Do you think anyone would mind if I looked around it?"

"You mean go on board? You one of them reporters that's lookin' for a story?"

"No. My brother went missing right after Labor Day. I'm trying to find out what happened to him."

"Is that a fact? Didn't hear nothin' 'bout that on the news."

Tessa did her best to contain the knot of resentment over that fact. "My brother's name's Ryan. I'm Tessa."

Paulie spat again and shrugged, leaning in toward her. "Nice to make your acquaintance. I'll tell you what, Tessa. The *Misty Dawn* ain't my boat so I won't tell nobody if you want to go take a look on 'er. In fact, I'll even stand lookout."

Tessa gave him her friendliest smile. "That'd be great if you could spare fifteen minutes."

"Hell, for a purty girl like you, I'll spare thirty."

Tessa proceeded after Paulie down the wooden pier where she slipped aboard the *Misty Dawn* while her new friend stood guard.

Standing on the bow, she tried to picture Ryan fishing off its railing. She did the same with the man she knew as Walker, trying to picture him standing at the helm, setting a course out to the deep waters of the Atlantic.

She headed below deck. But before reaching the galley, an overwhelming smell of bleach hit her. The antiseptic odor permeated what had to be the boat's deep-sea fishing history. How many tarpons had been caught and brought on board and ended up gutted in this very spot? How much bleach did it take to mask the odor of dead fish?

Tessa pondered that as she went about checking the cabins. The place had a masculine feel to it rather than being suited for family. To her, there was no sign of a woman's touch anywhere. It certainly didn't give off an indication that Livvy and her children had ever spent a great deal of time sailing Sugar Bay with daddy.

But Tessa wasn't done snooping. The galley was so tidy and orderly she moved on to peruse through the library of books sitting on shelves. There were several novels written by noted authors along with a stack of magazines. Tessa got curious and started thumbing through Walker's choices, only to find the sailing publications hid a sizable collection of hardcore men's magazines.

She abandoned the centerfolds and moved into the first stateroom, took a few moments to admire the elegant wood trim and the tasteful décor including all the gold accents. On impulse she pulled out her cell phone to capture the image. While it might not be her kind of design thing, she might be able to get a blog post out of the idea.

There were lockers to check out, so she slid open what amounted to closets. She found the usual men's clothing, the extra pairs of tennis shoes and boots. There were all kinds of fishing gear taking up space. It made her wonder what exactly she was looking for. Everything seemed in locked its place, maybe too nice and tidy for a reason.

She crossed over to the second stateroom and found the same personal touches here that were so prevalent in the first room. She slid open drawers, only to feel disappointment when she found them empty. But as she scanned the floor, something flashed in the corner, a flicker of silver. She got down on all fours to get a better look. By the time she reached out to touch the metal, a lump had formed in her throat. Her fingers held Ryan's medical ID bracelet, a stainless steel mesh band he wore around his wrist to alert people that he suffered from epilepsy.

Tessa got to her feet only to see Paulie standing in the doorway. She slipped the bracelet into the back pocket of her jeans.

"Everything okay in here? You ready to go? Sorry to rush you, but I gotta get back to work."

Even though she felt like throwing up, Tessa nodded, doing her best to play it cool. "Thanks for keeping an eye out there for me."

"No problem. Find what you were looking for in here?"

Tessa shook her head, not wanting to give anything away. "No, there's nothing here."

"I guess that's the reason the cops didn't come snooping around first," Paulie said when they were walking back to the dock. "Nothing here to find."

At Paulie's comment resentment boiled up inside Tessa. She now understood how little time Sinclair had actually spent searching for her brother. The fact that it had been little more than a cursory probe at best made her want to hit something or someone.

While she watched Paulie go back to his gutted tuna, she dug out the medical ID bracelet, rubbed her fingers over the engraving. This was clearly a bad sign. With her other hand she took out her cellular, let the phone ring on the other end until her father picked up back in Nags Head. Tessa heard the familiar Carolina drawl. And it was like music to her ears.

Dwight Connelly was full of questions. "Where the heck have you been? I haven't talked to you since Saturday morning. I knew I shouldn't have let you go down there without me, especially when you won't stay in touch."

"I'm fine, Dad."

"You don't sound fine to me. Look, baby girl, I think you need to come back home before something bad happens to you, too. I don't care what Suzanne says, I'll take the money and hire one of those private investigators to step in and look for Ryan. You get yourself back home."

That sentiment was all Tessa needed to hear before she began to tear up. She opened her mouth to speak and everything came tumbling out about the past few days and what she'd found on Walker's yacht. "So you understand why I can't leave now. Something bad happened to Ryan on that boat and no one else cares, no one is doing anything about it except me."

"That's it. I'm not leaving you down there alone. I'll pack up tonight and be on the next plane out of here."

Knowing Suzanne wouldn't let him do that without a fight, Tessa calmed down to give him the impression she was more in control than she really was. But she didn't want her dad to know how overwhelming the situation was. "Dad, I've met some great people down here. What I could use is an influx of cash. Is there any way you could wire me some money without letting Suzanne know about it?"

"No offense, but screw Suzanne. Of course I will. Are you sure you don't want me to come down there?"

"I'm sure. I don't want you putting your marriage at risk along with everything else."

"That's just it, I shouldn't have to risk my relationship to find out what happened to my son. Will two thousand dollars keep you afloat for another week?"

"That's more than enough. Send it to the Western Union office here and I'll pick it up."

"Not the hotel?"

"I checked out, Dad." So he wouldn't worry about her, she decided to fudge the truth. "I'm staying with the people I met. You know, the ones with the missing family. They offered me a room." The lie hung between father and daughter like a heavy fog.

"You think they're trustworthy?"

"Sure." About as trustworthy as their lying brother-in-law, Tessa thought. But she went on in upbeat fashion putting a pretty spin on things with her father. By the time she ended the call, she decided she'd done a good enough job calming her father's fears.

Now all she had to do was keep her head above water until her dad's money arrived.

The Indigos were embroiled in their own family dynamics inside the house on Quay Avenue. After a second day of searching turned up nothing, the brothers had butted heads on where to send the teams out next. They disagreed on search coordinates, even what time they should schedule the next press conference. Short fuses had them blowing up at each other over every little thing.

The tension of the demanding day was taking its toll. So it was no surprise when tempers boiled over for real as soon as the state investigator, Dack Hawkins, set foot in the living room. Resentment had built up slowly over the questions about Livvy's spending habits and her relationship with Walker. Enough so that Jackson got fed up and glared at the two-piece-suit-wearing Hawkins.

He stepped into the guy's face. "Why don't you talk to Walker's friends? Why don't you grill Royce and ask him about all his ties to those disreputable developers he aligns himself with and has for decades? Because until you do that, until you're willing to dig up all the Buchanan skeletons and trot them out where everyone can get a good look, you have no right wasting time interviewing us. Find out what role the Buchanan name played in this and you'll keep moving forward. Bury your head in the sand and you've stagnated the case. We weren't even in town when all this went down. So what do you think my mom and dad did? You think they did something to hurt their own grandchildren? You're so far off the mark, it's scary."

The thirty-something Hawkins looked steamed but didn't flinch. "We're contacting everyone who knew Livvy and Walker. Everyone. These questions are routine. So I'll ask you to give me the respect I deserve and start giving me the answers without that attitude."

Mitch grabbed Jackson's arm to jerk him into the neutral zone. And then, even Mitch turned on the cop. "You understand the frustration we're dealing with here, right? It's beginning to get to us. We haven't had a lot of sleep since this thing started. We're a little touchy when you waste this amount of time asking us ridiculous questions about what Livvy was involved in. She's your typical soccer mom with a new business. End of story."

Hawkins didn't give an inch. "It's never that simple. And your lack of sleep is no excuse for your surly attitude. I'm just trying to get a handle on how routine her life was up to last Wednesday night. Did she have secrets? Was she having an affair? Was she into anything she shouldn't have been? Stuff like that."

"Okay. Then I should be able to pick up the phone and call Royce to see how long you grilled him about those same things regarding Walker, right?" Jackson snapped. "He'll be able to verify that you asked him about Walker's personal life, about all the secrets he had, right?"

The ringing doorbell interrupted the showdown.

Lenore got up to answer the door and found Jessup Sinclair standing on the porch, his face blank. No one said a word as the police chief sauntered into the living area and surveyed the tension reverberating off the four walls.

Hawkins scowled at the police chief. "What are you doing here?"

"My job. I'm giving the family an update regarding a development."

Hawkins automatically took out his cell phone. "What update? No one's notified me of anything."

With a smug look on his face, Sinclair drawled, "Then maybe you should check to see if your fancy phone's quit working."

Impatient, Jackson got tired of waiting for the two men to get on the same page. "What's the development?"

Sinclair shifted his feet. "Livvy's minivan was found at the Tampa Bay airport in one of the satellite parking lots. Looks like it's been there since last Thursday night."

"Oh, thank God," Lenore blurted out. She turned to Tanner. "They're all right. See, I told you they were okay."

Jackson met his father's eyes. "Tampa Bay is more than seven hours from Indigo Key. If they wanted to fly somewhere why wouldn't they do it from Miami International? It's a lot closer. Or better still, from the local airstrip?"

"I wondered the same thing," Sinclair admitted. "Just so you know, Tampa PD had the vehicle towed where a crime scene team can comb through it this afternoon. In addition to that, the investigators plan to go through the surveillance video around the airport and see if they can spot your sister and her family going through security to board a plane."

Jackson chewed his jaw. He scanned the room, noted the elated look on his parents' faces. But while his mom and dad seemed relieved, Mitch and Garret had the opposite reaction. Like him, they appeared guarded at what the development meant.

Were Livvy and the kids off somewhere truly soaking up some rays? In his mind, it wasn't a likely scenario. No one seemed to understand that Livvy had never done anything remotely like this before in her life, not even during her teen years. She'd never been the rebellious type.

No matter how Jackson tried to make sense of it, the news left him wondering what could possibly have occurred to make his sister take off to parts unknown without letting anyone know her whereabouts, especially in the middle of the night.

"Why would she take the kids out of school?" Jackson said aloud. "Why would she allow us all to worry like this, put Mom and Dad through a string of days filled with hellish anguish?" He did his best to walk that fine line between dashing hope and using common sense. "Does that sound like something Livvy would do?"

Garret shook his head. "I don't see her taking off like this. Not willingly anyway. Whoever parked the van there wanted us to believe she grabbed the kids and left on her own."

Mitch was even more skeptical. He walked to where his mother stood. Towering over her, he dipped his head, tilted her chin up so she'd meet his eyes. "Mom, you said it yourself. When you went in the house that day to check on them, Livvy's stuff was still there. She hadn't taken her clothes. Who takes off without packing a bag? Ally's favorite doll was still in her room. Blake's things were still there. You know more than anyone else what was happening in Livvy's life. Her van left at the airport doesn't seem right to me. Does it seem right to you?"

Lenore's eyes filled with tears. Slowly, she moved her head back and forth. "My boys know their sister. I know my daughter. Livvy wouldn't have planned a trip without telling me, or her dad about where she was going. Something's wrong. I feel it in my bones."

Mitch circled her shoulders for support. Jackson, Garret, and Tanner did the same.

Jackson turned to Jessup and then to Hawkins. "I think that tells you everything you need to know about where the Indigos stand. Finding the minivan parked at the airport makes no sense."

"You're saying it was staged to send us off in one direction?" Hawkins demanded. "That's ludicrous. It sounds to me like your daughter left with her kids on her own. Maybe she and Walker had a fight. Maybe she wanted a vacation."

"Then there should be an airline out there that will back up your assumption," Jackson fired back.

"And you know what they say about assuming," Garret tossed out, eyeing the fresh-faced investigator. "Let's see if your notion holds up when the cops finish going over the passenger manifests."

Confident in everything he knew about his sister, Mitch added, "You won't find Livvy's name on there, so be sure to let us know as soon as you figure that out."

Dack Hawkins stormed out of the front door first leaving behind Jessup to deal with the family's anger.

"What will you do when Hawkins and his team head back to Tallahassee tomorrow?"

Jackson stared at Jessup. "I don't even know what to say to that. Is it possible the state investigators are that inept?" He bobbed his head toward his mother. "Mom went into Livvy's house before it was sealed off. There's no evidence they bought a ticket anywhere."

"Where on earth would they go?" Lenore dabbed at her eyes with a Kleenex. "Everything of value was still there in the house. The family computer sat on the desk. The stereo and DVD player was there, along with Livvy's jewelry left in plain sight on the dresser."

A vein popped out on Tanner's neck as he listened to the exchange. "You should know we're thinking of hiring a private investigator to get to the bottom this."

Surprise showed on Jessup's face. "You guys don't have to convince me that something happened to Walker and Livvy. But until we find something concrete that points to foul play, or we get a helluva lot more evidence, I don't even know which direction to look. It doesn't mean anybody in my office is going to sit on his hands and do nothing. But then I don't exactly have jurisdiction in what's happening in my own backyard."

"You were taken off the case fairly quickly. Why is that?" Tanner barked.

"I wish I knew," Jessup grumbled.

The afternoon rolled into evening as the news spread that the Buchanan van had been found at the airport.

Lenore and Tanner played hosts to a steady stream of well-meaning neighbors who dropped off casseroles. The little house on Quay soon filled with people they'd known for years. Many wanted to pass along good wishes while others offered up stories about Livvy when she was little.

But when a few began to ask nosy questions and want more information that seemed inappropriate, Garret couldn't take the crowd any longer. He left the mass of people to go find the nearest bar and grab a beer. Maybe he'd put in another call to the private eye in Miami and bug the guy.

That left the others to help pour coffee or tea, serve platters of homemade cookies, all the while answering the same tired questions again and again, as friends and acquaintances they'd known for years tossed out an assortment of theories as to Livvy's whereabouts.

The Indigos' longtime pastor, Boone Dandridge, took Tanner aside and told him about the time Livvy admitted she wanted to check out the Molokini Crater on Maui and explore the coral reefs there. "That girl definitely had an itch to see the world."

Tanner didn't take the suggestion very well. "*That girl* was a wife and mom who thought the world of her kids. And besides, when did she tell you this?"

"Must've been about five years ago after Ally came along."

Tanner narrowed his eyes and stared at the man he'd known for more than twenty years. "So you're suggesting that Livvy waited until Ally started first grade to take both kids out of school so she could see the world?"

Boone looked puzzled. "Well, I'm sure the kids would enjoy snorkeling with the sea turtles there. Brownie Collier took her grandkids to the crater and brought back an hour and a half's worth of video memories to prove it." He chuckled. "I had to sit through her entire vacation highlights."

Tanner didn't see the comparison at all or the humor. "I won't even bother pointing out how silly that sounds to think my daughter wanted to check out the sights on Maui. If that's true she had all summer long to do it before now."

It wasn't just Boone who went out of his way to plant the seed that Livvy had taken off to parts unknown. Carson Frawley, the baker at Glazed & Dazed Donuts, retold the story that Livvy had been in his store three weeks earlier to say she planned to take a trip to the Big Apple. "She made a point to tell me she wanted to see Central Park in the fall."

Roger Baskin, owner of the garage on Prospect, claimed Livvy had mentioned to him how much seeing the Golden Gate Bridge meant to her.

Mayor Dave Oakerson went on to say he'd been at the Vitamin Hut buying supplements one day when he'd overheard Livvy say she'd often thought long and hard about moving to Santa Fe.

But it was Antoinette Gray, Livvy's longtime hairdresser, and Cristina Newman, Blake's teacher, who dashed any such notion.

Antoinette pushed back her purple-streaked black hair and puffed out, "That's ridiculous. I just trimmed Livvy's bob ten days ago. She was already talking about buying Halloween costumes for the kids and the matching outfits she and Walker intended to wear. A trip out of state didn't even come up. I've been doing the woman's hair since I rolled into town eight years ago. She would've told me if she meant to fly off the radar just to see the world. It's absurd."

Cristina, a slender thirty-four-year-old with kids of her own, nodded. "Blake never once mentioned taking a trip anywhere, except maybe to go out on his Uncle Mitch's boat. You know, to look for treasure. Blake talked about that quite a bit."

Mitch overheard that last part and his heart dropped. He remembered making a promise last Christmas to take the kid on one of his hunts. But he'd gotten busy over the summer and forgot to follow through.

It wasn't until everyone cleared out that Lenore turned to her family. "Did you get the sense that was a united mission to make sure we believe that Livvy up and left on her own?"

"That was certainly my take," Mitch answered.

"Mine too," Jackson stated. "The question is why? They didn't even bother to get their stories straight. They had Livvy leaving to go all over the country. What's it to them what we believe or where we look? It's as if they're making not-so-subtle suggestions we give up searching."

"Pretty lame if you ask me," Tanner added. "Especially that part where Livvy wanted to see practically every state in the union."

"Then why the full court press? Why make us believe something that flat out isn't true? A lot over the top if you ask me," Jackson grumbled. "It didn't seem to matter to them that their pitch was so obvious. I've no doubt they stopped by just to let their tongues wag." But despite his demeanor, panic began to set in, a realization that they were no closer to having any real answers than the day before or the day before that.

Garret walked into the kitchen holding a legal pad scribbled with handwritten notes.

"Nice of you to show back up again," Mitch muttered. "Where did you disappear to?"

"Not that it's any of your business but I went down to Mattito's for a beer."

"We got a crazy-ass caller while you were gone who claimed they saw Livvy and the kids at Disney World. We passed the information along to Sinclair."

Lenore poured herself a glass of iced tea. "Even I know that isn't true. Livvy didn't like the crowds there. When Blake was five he got lost at Magic Kingdom—for about five minutes—scared Livvy into the next county. She swore she'd never take the kids there again."

Garret rolled his eyes and tossed the legal tablet on the kitchen table. "So let the crank calls begin. A side effect of the large reward we posted." He turned the paper around so he could share what he'd jotted down. "I finally got a callback from Marcelli's office. He'll be here tomorrow. Apparently, he's been keeping up with the case through the media so he's pretty much up to speed. Although I did have to assure the guy I spoke with that Livvy wasn't the type to leave town without letting people know where she was going. He seemed to agree, at least over the phone." Garret looked around the room at the faces for a reaction. "I thought for certain y'all would be whole lot more excited than this. What gives? What'd I miss?"

Jackson helped himself to a beer out of the fridge and twisted off the top. "Well, for starters, a series of performances from the stalwart community we've known and loved for years."

"What do you mean?"

Jackson replayed all the different conversations.

"Sounds like someone wants us to go off on a wild goose chase," Garret snapped.

"Several wild goose chases." Jackson guzzled his beer. "The problem with that load of crap is that if it ever gets back to inexperienced cops like Hawkins. The guy might take it as fact and decide it's further proof Livvy took off."

Lenore's eyes widened as she pulled back the plastic wrap on one of the mac and cheese dishes the neighbors had dropped off. "Well, luckily for us, Antoinette and Cristina set them straight. Surely Hawkins would listen to them over…"

"Livvy's pastor?" Tanner pointed out. "Did the women set Boone and the others straight? Some people will believe what they want to believe regardless of the facts. Boone flat out ticked me off. Why the very idea Livvy would be so irresponsible as to take her kids out of school to fly to Maui to see some stupid crater is not worth my time."

"Then why go out of their way to tell us the stories at all?" Jackson queried. "Why stop by at all? Unless they were purposely trying to send us in the wrong direction?"

"Are we getting paranoid here?" Tanner wanted to know. "These are people we've known for years, people we've trusted."

Jackson lifted a shoulder. "We could stand around trying to figure the why of it but we have bigger issues to deal with, like a third day of searching."

"Which reminds me," Mitch wondered. "Why didn't Tessa show up at the search point today to help?"

"She wasn't there? At all?"

"Nope. I have the roster for each and every person who went out today. Tessa didn't check in."

"That's odd. I thought we'd missed each other. It never occurred to me she was a no-show." Jackson took out his cell phone, flipped through his texts and phone calls. "Come to think of it, with everything else going on, I haven't heard from her all day." He keyed in the message, *What's up? Are you okay?*

But after waiting several minutes without a response, Jackson made a decision. "Maybe I'd better take a spin by the hotel and see what's up."

Tanner took the beer out of Jackson's hand. "Make sure she's okay. I don't want to have to worry about someone else's daughter disappearing."

Lenore patted Jackson's arm. "What he means is invite her back over for dinner tonight. Look at all this food. Now who wants some of this tuna casserole?"

At the Mainsail Lodge Jackson was stunned to learn Tessa had checked out of the hotel. Standing in the lobby he tried calling Tessa's cell phone only to have it go straight to voicemail.

Baffled, he stood there and thought back about their last conversation. Something about her pointing out that Walker had been the last person to see Ryan. At the time he'd been too busy and too distracted with the search to take the time to really listen to her.

But now, unease began to creep its way into his gut. He hoped to Christ he didn't have another missing person to worry about.

He ran back outside to where he'd left his dad's truck and spent the next hour combing the streets looking for her blue Toyota.

In hindsight, he should've asked for her family's phone number back in Nags Head. But who knew she'd do a vanishing act. He racked his brain trying to figure out where she could have gone. After scouring every street near the hotel, he pulled over and sent one final text message before heading home. His last effort of the night read, *Private investigator coming tomorrow. You're welcome to sit in on the meeting. Where are you?????*

While Jackson hunted for Tessa, she'd gone for a drive not far outside town. In fact, at the same moment he dashed off the urgent message, she was sitting down the road from Royce Buchanan's mansion snooping on Walker's father.

If Walker had done something to Ryan, it stood to reason that Royce had known about it, or played some role in getting it done and then covering it up. The Buchanans certainly had the resources.

There might be zero logic to it, but she'd never wanted to leap to a conclusion more than she did now. How else had Ryan's medical alert bracelet ended up on the floor of that stateroom on Walker's yacht? Tessa chose to ignore a reasonable explanation, like it might've come unfastened while Ryan had been reeling in one of those oversized swordfish.

Instead, she'd bought a pair of well-worn but high-powered binoculars for fifteen bucks from a thrift store in town with the sole purpose of using them to spy on Royce. For the past hour, she'd watched several luxury cars pull up and park in Royce's circular driveway.

As a stranger in town she didn't recognize any of the men who'd shown up. It was too dark to make out any of the guests anyway. That is, until she spotted Jessup Sinclair's squad car pulling up. She watched as the police chief got out, adjusted his gun belt, and walked to the front door as if he belonged there.

A lump of mistrust settled in her belly.

When a Mercedes zoomed past the Toyota and parked behind the line of other cars, it made her wonder if all this activity signaled a break in the case that she knew nothing about.

There was one way to find out. She used her cell phone to check local news outlets online. But after several minutes, she couldn't find a single mention of a development, at least none that had gone public.

She thought about calling Jackson, especially after reading his texts. But when she picked up her phone again, it had gone completely dead. All the Internet searching had drained the battery.

The sound of another car made her glance up in time to see a BMW whiz by. The driver of the Bimmer took a position in line behind all the rest.

Something big was going on. She'd bet money on it.

Gut instinct had her rethinking the call to Jackson. Could she really trust anyone in this town? By the looks of the high-end vehicles, Royce's summit embraced a segment of Indigo Key's well-connected higher ups. But if Royce had gathered a consortium of his buddies, the police chief was obviously a part of that.

Whatever the reason for their meeting, it was taking place right in front of her. She'd been in town a week and realized this was the first opportunity that might provide a little insight into what Walker might've been involved in and with whom. Like father, like son. Because the occasion presented itself, Tessa needed to take full advantage.

She decided taking photos of all the license plates on the cars would go a long way to finding out exactly who was on the guest list. She had to wait for the phone to charge to at least twenty-five percent before she unplugged the device and got out to get a closer angle. The trick was not getting caught.

Eager to take the pictures, she walked down the dark road toward the house. On the way, it occurred to her how remote this house was. Anything could happen out here and no one would be the wiser.

"Stop letting your imagination run wild," she murmured into the shadows. "Stick to what you're able to prove."

As she went from one car to the next snapping photos, she wondered if Ryan had made it to this same spot during his visit. Had Walker brought Ryan here just as he had brought him onboard the *Misty Dawn*?

A loud discussion coming from inside the house broke her train of thought. The male voices drew her closer. Ducking into a row of hedges, she made her way past juniper, the rough needles causing her bare arms to itch.

The drapes on the front windows were still open so she peered through the glass and got her first look at the five guests who'd dropped in to visit Royce Buchanan. From

Jackson's description, the elderly man was easy to spot. He looked frail and broken as he sat shriveled in a wing chair in front of a roaring fire.

The heated discussion seemed to be coming from the other men as well while Royce sat back and listened. The men argued about what to do next. Of all the unlikely members bent on getting his point across, Jessup Sinclair seemed the most adamant. Entrenched in his stance, the police chief shouted in Royce's direction. "We shouldn't give up now, not after everything, not after coming this far."

Another man added, "We've invested a lot of time and money in this. Do you know what this could do for the town? Why, we could build one of those megachurches with a sprawling campus, maybe even start a college like you see other towns doing."

It didn't seem fair though to single out these two, Tessa thought. Because the other men seemed just as locked in the same opinion.

"He's right. It would be pointless to go back on our word. We're in too deep to give up now."

Those last words had goose bumps forming along Tessa's neck. On the warm breezy night, the chill she felt went straight to her bones. How deep had these men gone exactly? Had murder taken them all down a deeper, darker path?

Those questions brought her full circle. What the hell was going on in this picture-perfect little town? And at some point had Ryan asked that same exact question?

Chapter Eight

Inside the clubroom at the marina, the third day of scheduled searching began with a disappointing turnout. Fewer than twenty people showed up. And the ones who did began to wonder about Livvy and Walker pulling the kids out of school and taking off for Barbados via the Tampa Bay Airport.

By midday many had decided that the couple had opted for an impromptu vacation, and were, even now, listening to calypso music while sipping mojitos and soaking up rays on sugar-white sand.

Jackson had tried his damnedest to explain that if Livvy and Walker had wanted to sit on the beach, they had only to go down the street to do it. "Why would they take off for the Caribbean?"

But logic didn't seem to make a difference.

What the hell was going on in this town?

If it hadn't been for Jackson and Garret, Mitch would've told the doubters what they could do with their ridiculous theories.

Tanner looked around at the sparse crowd. "Where are the rest of the volunteers?"

Jackson knew the truth would sting. "I'd say we've encountered a major ding in the town's support system. Where's Mom?"

"Where do you think? Sitting by the phone. She refuses to leave the house hoping Livvy will call." Tanner scanned the clubroom a second time. "What do you mean we've lost support? Overnight? How is that possible? There are at least four thousand people on this island. Surely they don't all believe Livvy and Walker left on their own."

Jackson exchanged looks with his brothers. "That's the thing, Dad. You should never underestimate the power of Boone Dandridge and his flock. Rumor, innuendo, and email are powerful tools when you want to get the word out."

Tanner couldn't believe his ears. But after Boone's declaration yesterday while standing in his own living room, it was tough to dispute the results. The tide had definitely turned. "Your mother and I have been members of that church since you guys were little. Through the years we've attended baptisms, weddings, held prayer meetings, baked enough potluck casseroles to feed thousands, sat beside most of them in Sunday school class. We've showed up at the hospital to show our support when members of the congregation got sick. Walker and Livvy did the same. And this is what happens when we need help? Why would Dandridge turn on us like this? Why would he choose to ignore the very real problem that members of his own church have gone missing, disappeared out of their house in the middle of the night? What's going on here anyway? Has everyone gone nuts?"

Annoyed with the turn of events, Garret pointed out, "That's why we hired the private investigator, to get to the bottom of all this. Speaking of Marcelli, the guy should be pulling into town in about an hour. I suggest we grab something to eat and plan on a long afternoon."

Mitch agreed and started packing up the extra posters and other equipment. "Were you able to locate Tessa?"

Jackson looked miffed. "No. She checked out of the hotel without a word to me."

"What do you intend to do?"

"About what? What do you want me to do? Didn't you hear what I said? She didn't exactly leave a fond farewell note behind."

"What if something's happened to her, Jackson? She's the one who got such a chilly reception from this town when it came to asking questions about her brother."

"Well, damn. Thanks for making me feel like a coldhearted jerk for not following up last night."

Mitch rolled his shoulders back, lifted one. "Look, maybe it's as simple as her switching hotels. The Mainsail *is* a tad on the pricey side even this time of year. Did you try the Sugar Bay Motel? They're already offering an off-season rate if you book at least a weekly stay."

Jackson rubbed the back of his neck. "That just shows how much my brain is on overload. I didn't even consider she might be looking at saving a few bucks." He took out his cell phone, searched the motel's number online. "It's worth a shot."

But when the desk clerk checked, he was told Tessa Connelly hadn't registered. Jackson decided then and there it might be time to worry.

Garret noticed the concern on his face. "You look like you took a punch to the gut. What do you want us to do?"

"Get something to eat, recharge, get ready for the meeting. I'll take another spin around town, try to locate her car."

"Okay, but keep us posted." Before turning to head out, Garret added, "Don't worry about her. She struck me as a capable woman who could handle herself. I'm sure she's around somewhere."

"She doesn't know anyone else but us."

"True. But there's always the possibility she got fed up with things around here and headed back to North Carolina."

That option didn't sit right with Jackson. He had to admit he liked the spunky redhead.

"Mitch wants to head over to The Blue Taco. But if you ask me, I think he really wants to catch a glimpse of his old high school flame. Want us to grab you a plate to-go?"

"Sure. I'll meet you there. Order me the lobster roll with an extra side of rice and salsa. If I don't make it there, bring them back with you to the house."

Ten minutes later, the rest of the Indigo men opened the door to a turquoise and gold-trimmed stucco building in the heart of the marina district belonging to The Blue Taco. Family-owned, the restaurant had been around for more than three decades. It began when Diane and Douglas Manning moved to the Key in 1962 and started a food stand near the beach where they served fish tacos.

Through the years, they added versatile dishes to their menu. They boasted low to moderate prices. An affordable meal always appealed to tourists. That's why visitors flocked to it during the summer. It wasn't unusual for lines to form out the door and around the corner at lunchtime.

By the late eighties, the eatery became a popular teen hangout for the high school crowd. It was tradition to dish up a tasty fish taco combo or burrito platter, or offer up their famous eight-inch lobster rolls served with fries cooked in peanut oil.

Mitch let his Dad and Garret do the ordering while he slid into one of the peacock blue vinyl booths under a wall of plate-glass windows. From that spot he could look outside onto the patio and see familiar faces in the crowd. His heart did a little extra thump in his chest when he spotted Raine Manning, her honey-blond head ducked under a bright blue umbrella.

He watched as she bussed one of the tables before wiping it down with a rag. The way her butt wiggled in the tight jeans she wore took him back to another time, back more than a dozen years earlier when they'd steamed up their fair share of car windows in the backseat of his ancient Datsun. They'd been sophomores in high school, their sixteen-year-old hormones driving them to spend every minute they could with each other.

But times change.

People move on.

The last time he'd spoken to her had been at Thanksgiving the previous year. He'd asked her over to his parents' house for a turkey dinner with all the trimmings for old times' sake. She'd passed on the invite. No surprise since she hadn't uttered a kind word his way in more than ten years.

Raine swung through the door carrying a tray full of empty beer bottles. Mitch knew the minute her eyes caught sight of him. There was the same disdain he'd grown used to. A snarl, a look, that said she'd rather serve food to a ten-foot alligator rather than deliver it to the likes of him.

She sent a scowl his way before stuffing the trash into a receptacle and depositing the empties into the recycle bin. Tossing out her chin, she decided to meet the heartless bastard head-on. After all, she was no longer that silly, naïve teenage girl who'd had her heart broken by Mitch Indigo.

Plus, there was also the real fact that no one had heard from her friend Livvy. That's why the grown businesswoman could act like she owned the place and was no longer interested. To her, he was just another customer come in to fill his belly at lunch.

She reached for the bottle of sanitized solution and went over to his table to spritz down the top. She said nothing right before the spray got a little too close to said asshole's face and landed on his shirt and neck. "Oops. Sorry."

Mitch flinched to dodge the mist. "What did you do that for? That stuff barely missed my eyes."

"Please. It's just a watered down two-percent bleach mixture. It won't hurt a thing, might sting for a minute or two, but that's all." She took out her rag to wipe up the excess.

He snatched up a napkin to dab at his face and collar. "You did that on purpose."

"I've been doing this for years. I have excellent aim," she boasted with a wink.

But when Mitch looked up and met her eyes, Raine saw the worry written on his face. A moment of empathy moved through her. But it was the déjà vu flaring up that did the most damage. Despite the little pep talk she'd given herself, she slipped back into youthful harmony from the past. She watched his mouth move and shades of another time and place flashed through her head. She'd forgotten the exact shade of his brown eyes and how the tinge of amber around the iris glinted in the sunlight.

Thankfully she pulled out of "been there, done that" in time to salvage her dignity. She pushed those bygone days into their proper place in history, that era when she'd been so very gullible and stupid.

For Livvy's sake Raine put aside her resentment for the greater good. "Is there any word yet about Livvy and the kids?"

"Nope. Nothing. It's like they vanished into thin air."

She pointed to where his father and brother stood at the counter placing their orders. "Didn't you forget something?"

"They already know what I want, same thing I always order, the Grande burrito with the works. Why don't you sit down and cheer me up?"

Raine tilted her head, sent him her sweetest smile. "Same old Indigo. As you can see I'm working. Actually, I run the place now. No time for chitchat with the riffraff."

"I heard your mother turned the day to day operation over to you."

"Yep. Four years now."

"Raine…" Mitch tried to reach out and take her hand.

She slapped it away in time to glance over and see Tanner and Garret watching the scene play out from a few feet away. Raine didn't intend to give them the satisfaction of a second act. "I'm sorry about Livvy and the kids. You should know I don't believe all those rumors she ran off to Bermuda."

"We heard Barbados," Garret quipped and took the seat across from Mitch.

"Not there either," Raine noted with a smile. She stared at the youngest Indigo brother. "Surfing agrees with you. Your hair's lighter than I remember, not as jet-black. And to think I knew you when you were still afraid to get your feet wet and mess up your perfect locks."

Mitch leaned back and crossed his arms over his chest, listening to the normal, familiar banter between two old friends catching up. Why couldn't the woman do the same with him? She could joke with Garret as if they were siblings or cousins. Why not be as cordial to him? He came out of his funk when Raine tossed out her gold nugget.

"Look, it may not mean anything, but the Wednesday Livvy went missing, she came in here for lunch. She seemed agitated, upset. When I asked her what was wrong, she shook her head and said she was tired of Walker's BS. From that point on, she pretty much proceeded to pitch a downright hissy fit over something Walker had done. Liv said she'd already let Walker get away with way too much during their time together and she was done with it." Raine's voice held a tinge of fondness at the memory mixed with a degree of sadness.

"Did you tell anyone else about this?" Mitch wanted to know.

Raine lifted a shoulder. "No one's asked."

"What exactly upset her that day?" Tanner said as he slid in beside Garret.

Raine took a deep breath. "I hate to admit this, but we were swamped that day and I didn't really pay all that much attention to her outburst."

"For God's sake…" Mitch asserted.

"Don't start with me," Raine warned, stabbing her finger at him. "Look, it wasn't all that unusual for Livvy to rant like that. In fact, she did it quite a few times before. She'd get it out of her system and then forgive Walker for whatever it was he'd done. So don't get upset with me. I'm just the messenger. I hope in some way the info helps find her and the kids. Now, I'll go see what's taking so long with your order."

Mitch watched her storm off before turning to his dad and brother. "See, the people who truly care about Livvy know she wasn't completely happy with Walker."

A sick feeling pounded Tanner's belly. As hungry as he'd been before, the bottom dropped out. "All my accusations about Walker and I'm having a tough time with this."

Baffled looks passed between Mitch and Garret, but it was Garret who pointed out, "I don't believe my ears. For four days now all we've heard is how Walker is responsible for all this, the root of the problem. Now you've changed your mind?"

Tanner scrubbed his hands over his face. "I didn't say that. It isn't as black and white as all that."

"Okay, what then?" Mitch asked.

Tanner huffed out a breath. "I didn't like the guy, okay? At all. But accepting the realization that Walker did something to Olivia means she's not coming back. You don't have kids so you couldn't possibly understand the implication of that. It means… It means I didn't do enough to protect my own daughter and my grandkids? Speaking of which, where are they, the kids? Did Walker really have it in him to hurt his own flesh and blood? If so, then why didn't I see that and do something about it beforehand? It means I let Livvy down. I let Blake and Ally down. I should've had a long talk with that son of a bitch four years ago and straightened him out when I saw how distant he behaved around his family. After his mother died I knew something was wrong. But I did nothing."

"Stop it," Mitch commanded, raising his voice. He angled closer to his father. "No one could've predicted this. No one. Things like this aren't supposed to happen."

Garret held up a hand. "Let's settle down for a minute and stop jumping to conclusions. We're letting our emotions lead this thing and we need to follow the facts, follow the actual evidence we know for certain. That's what the PI is for."

Tanner nodded. "Let's do that. From this point forward I'm taking a page out of your mother's playbook. I'm hoping to God that phone will ring and Livvy will be on the other end saying everything's okay."

While his family stuffed their faces, Jackson repeated his route from the night before, expanding his search by several blocks. He wasn't sure if he felt pissed or rattled. But as each street yielded no sign of her, he hit the fringes of panic.

The clock ticked off the hour till Marcelli showed up. He was running out of time. Should he stop at the police station, let Jessup know he couldn't find Tessa?

Just as he started to head that way, something caused him to rethink the idea. Better still, he'd ask the private detective what to do about her. Maybe the Miami expert would have better luck locating her.

Chapter Nine

Tessa walked through the doors of The Blue Taco barely missing the Indigos by a mere five minutes.

After ordering the taco special, à la carte, Tessa found a booth at the very back for a little privacy so she could take out her laptop. She booted up the computer and logged into her email account. Each time she did so, hope settled in her heart that somehow her brother had found a way to write a brief message telling her he was okay.

But as she stared at the inbox and all the other emails that were *not* from Ryan, she realized one more day had gone by with no word. Tears watered her eyes.

Without warning, Jackson scooted in across from her. "Where the hell have you been? You checked out of the hotel and didn't tell anyone. I've been looking everywhere for you. Where've you been the last two days? And why couldn't you return a text message so I wouldn't worry?"

Tessa frowned. "You were actually worried about me? Why?"

"Why? Five people are unaccounted for in this town. Then out of the blue, you decide to go dark. It made me wonder. I thought I might be dealing with number six."

In spite of her mistrust, tears welled up and trickled down her cheeks. Embarrassed at the display of hormones, she grabbed several napkins to dab at her eyes. "I'm so sorry. I had no idea you'd take the time to go looking for me."

"You're kidding, right?" He held up his thumb and index finger as a measurement. "I was that close to going to Jessup and telling him we had another missing person."

"Don't do that! From here on out, I don't recommend going to Jessup for anything."

Jackson noticed the genuine panicked look in her eyes. He watched her blow her nose and tried to figure her out. "I thought we were hitting a stride, you and me. I thought we'd made a connection other than this craziness we're both dealing with. And then you ignore any communication from me. Why?"

She decided to level with him. "Since Sunday I've been dealing with a few trust issues, okay? My fault."

Dumbfounded, Jackson sat back in the booth, clearly shaken. "You don't trust me or my family? Since when? What gives with you? It's a disappointing fact that everyone else in town pretty much thinks it's a done deal that Livvy hit the beach on some Caribbean island somewhere. But you, with your own brother missing, you don't trust *us*?"

"Just calm down a minute. Hear me out. After Sunday, after our brief talk about Walker, I needed to spend some time by myself. I needed to wrap my head around all my suspicions that kept whirling around in my head." Lowering her voice to a whisper, she told him about finding Ryan's ID bracelet on Walker's yacht. "That's what capped all my misgivings."

Then she told him about the meeting at Royce's, ticking off everything she'd seen for Jackson's benefit.

Jackson whistled through his teeth. "I wonder if that might explain why certain people made a stop at our house yesterday to make sure we went in another direction, to make sure the search got fewer volunteers."

He told her about the cascade of rumors and the stories. "They obviously went out of their way to spread that around town. I doubt it's a coincidence. Would you be able to recognize Dandridge and Frawley if I pointed them out to you?"

"Probably. I got a good enough look at them. The one man I did recognize for certain was Jessup Sinclair."

Jackson's eyes grew wide. "Holy shit. What the hell's going on in this town?"

She lowered her voice even more. "Sinclair, the police chief, the one person I went to and reported my brother missing, and who did nothing about it."

His jaw tightened at the idea he'd trusted the top cop. He glanced down at his watch and stood up. "Right now, I have to go meet with the detective. You need to wrap up lunch and make it there so you can tell him what you saw firsthand. We need to make him aware that we should tread carefully around the local cops. Plus, my family will want to hear all this from you firsthand."

"Sure. Okay."

"Meantime, don't go disappearing on me again." He leaned down and brushed a kiss on her forehead. "Try to stay out of trouble. See you in thirty minutes. It's okay to be late."

After Jackson left, Raine dropped off Tessa's order. But instead of leaving it on the table and vanishing back into the kitchen, she plopped down in the same seat Jackson had occupied. "You didn't tell him you slept in that cramped little car of yours last night."

Tessa made an uncomfortable sound in her throat.

But Raine ignored it. "Don't bother denying what I saw with my own eyes. I recognized your sports car with the Carolina license plate parked over at the corner of Marina Way and Sand Shell. You were tucked up for the night on the cul de sac trying to get comfy in that tiny backseat. That couldn't have been a very comfortable way to sleep. Anyway, before you ask, I wasn't spying on you. The spot you picked is right around the corner from where I live."

Tessa shifted in her seat and looked around to see if anyone had overheard. She was uncomfortable enough with the stark reality of her financial situation without it getting out that she was strapped for cash. "Please don't say anything to anyone."

Raine locked her lips. "It's our secret. But do I at least get to ask why? Why all the secrecy?"

"It's embarrassing and it's a small town. I took off to come here and put my job in jeopardy. In fact, if I can't come up with a blog post soon, I may lose it for good. If I keep hanging around here much longer without results, I'll have to chalk this up as a lost cause. So please, I don't want you mentioning my situation to Jackson until I've had a chance to tell him myself. I'll get around to telling him that I had to check out of the lodge because I'm running low on money. My credit cards are maxed out. The balances are beginning to look like the national debt."

"Okay. Sure. But if you've run out of funds, how do you intend to stay here and still keep up the search for your brother?"

As a distraction Tessa nervously shredded her paper napkin, then cleaned up the mess. "I'm working on that. My dad already sent me some money. After paying on my bills back home—rent, utilities, and making the minimum payments on my credit cards—I'm hoarding the rest. I can sleep in my car until…"

"You could, but you don't have to."

"What do you mean?" Tessa began to babble. "You're right. I could take on a temp job. Don't worry, I'll figure something out. The longer this thing plays out, the more

I'm getting a bad feeling about ever finding Ryan. Even if I could talk my tightwad of a stepmother into extending me a loan it would only prolong the search for another month. That's if I eat peanut butter and jelly sandwiches every night."

"Is that a sure thing with your stepmother, or more like wishful thinking?"

Tessa tried for a laugh but it stuck in her throat. "Honestly, it's wishful *dreaming*. Suzanne, that's her name, holds onto my father's purse strings like a world-class Scrooge. I'm not sure why our dad lets her call all the shots. But he does. It's as if Suzanne neutered him the minute she dragged him to the altar ten years ago."

"Ouch." Raine chewed her bottom lip. "There is a solution without butting heads with the cheapskate, overbearing stepmother."

Tessa finally focused. "There is?"

Raine lightly tapped the tabletop to make her point. "You'll come home with me after I get off work and bunk at my place. It's just two streets over. Everything downtown is within walking distance. You'll save on gas."

Tessa's eyes grew wide. Her jaw dropped. She shook her head. "I couldn't..."

Before Tessa could protest more, Raine leveled a finger at her. "Don't be an ass. I have a perfectly good spare room that's going to waste. The bed there has to be a lot more comfortable than the backseat of your car. The room's yours for as long as you need it."

"Why?"

"Because every time I watch the news all the talk is centered around the missing Buchanans, which is great. But somewhere along the way, I think your brother's been overlooked as a potential victim in all this. Whatever *all this* turns out to be."

"I don't know what to say. You're incredibly generous."

"Thank you usually covers it. By the way, I want you to know, Ryan never came in here during the time frame

Jackson suggested on Sunday during his press conference, at least, not that I know of. Maybe your brother didn't get a hankering for tacos while I was on duty. I don't know. I checked our surveillance tapes myself from around Labor Day. Your brother wasn't on it. But I could ask around to other restaurants and see if they've looked at their security tapes. It'd be a longshot because some businesses tape over their surveillance video right away…but you never know."

"It's something," Tessa stated. "Thank you. Each time there's the slightest bit of cooperation from anyone I get ecstatic." She nibbled on her bottom lip, fought back tears. Emotions took over. "I'm blown away by your offer. Thank you," Tessa repeated. "It comes at a time when I wasn't sure how I was going to stay in town. But I won't hold you to it. For all you know I could be a serious drug addict who has the potential for being the roomie from hell. I'm not, by the way."

A corner of Raine's mouth lifted. "That's good to know. Any sister who'd go to this much trouble for this long to find her brother is all right in my book."

Tessa picked up on a vibe that bore the seeds of something deeper. "So you have a brother?"

"I did. His name was Danny. We lost him in Afghanistan four years ago. It broke my mother's heart so much that I took over running this place for her. My grandmother's still around so she helps my mom get through the day."

"I'm so very sorry." It was then Tessa zeroed in on what Raine had mentioned earlier. "So you don't believe that the Buchanan family just decided to go on vacation in the middle of the week without telling anyone?"

"Nope. I knew Livvy. That woman had just gotten both kids in school for most of the day. Little Ally was so excited about first grade. And Livvy looked forward to making the Vitamin Hut a huge success. She thought it might shore up her marriage."

Tessa tilted her head. "Whoa. So there was trouble there? Was it serious? I mean, serious enough for Walker to do something drastic?"

"Livvy never made a habit of opening up to people about what happened at home, especially to her mom and dad."

"So the Indigos don't know? I ask because I spent some time with them the other night. It's a fifty-fifty split down the middle as to whether they completely trusted Walker or not. Lenore seems to believe there's no way he would ever hurt Livvy or the kids. But then there's the fact that Walker told Ryan in an email that Livvy spent his money faster than he could bring it in."

"*His* money?" The words came out of Raine's mouth like acid. "That sounds like Walker. Selfish bastard. See, that's what I'm talking about. That statement's another Walker lie." She shifted closer and whispered, "There were rumors all over town that Walker was having an affair, some woman who worked at a strip club down in Key West named Harlow. Which makes sense when you think about all the trips the guy made down there at least once a week."

"Really? I don't think the Indigos know about this Harlow woman because it didn't come up, not with me there anyway."

"Hey, Mitch was just in here. He didn't say a word to me about an affair. We've known each other..." Raine stopped in mid-sentence before filling in the blanks. "Let's just say, we go way back. And yet...if he doesn't feel comfortable talking to me about this situation, then I don't feel that it's my job to tell him his brother-in-law was screwing around with some stripper."

"Good point. But I don't have the luxury of tiptoeing around the family's dynamics. I'm not part of their past." She thought back to the kiss she'd shared with Jackson. She couldn't let emotions stand in the way of finding out everything she could about Walker. "For almost two months the man refused to pay Ryan the money he owed him. That's why he came to town, to collect."

"Walker did the same thing to Jimmy Don Bates before the Vitamin Hut opened. It took Jimmy Don almost three months to collect on the print advertising he'd done for the store."

"So Walker was used to doing business like that. Ryan had no idea. It's one reason I get the sinking feeling that something bad happened. Every day he's gone, I'm losing the advantage, if I ever had it."

"I'm right there with ya. Livvy was a good friend, a wonderful mom, a decent person. I'm already beginning to think that something bad happened to all of them. It keeps me up at night wondering what happened to those kids. Tell you what. If you want to wait until tomorrow, which is my day off and I'm off the clock, we could do our own snooping around, maybe drive down to Key West, take one of those missing posters with Walker's picture and see if anyone IDs him as someone who hung around the strippers."

"You'd do that?"

"Sure. I'm thinking I should've done more sooner rather than wait this long. I want to make up for it now. I don't want to force you to go with me, though. After all, this trip to Miami would be more about Walker and less about your brother."

"The way I see it, the more I learn about Walker, the greater chance I have of finding out what happened to Ryan." Tessa gnawed at her lip, wondering if she should mention that she'd found Ryan's medical ID bracelet aboard Walker's boat. Even though this was a new friend she decided to unburden that detail and watched as Raine's mouth fell open in surprise.

"Oh, my God. That has to mean something sinister happened there."

"That's what I'm thinking."

Raine rested her chin on her hands. "Then let's hope my idea yields some viable info. We'll get you settled in first at my house and then hit the road tomorrow." She took out a pen and a piece of paper from her pocket and wrote down her address. "I'll be home a little after six o'clock. Any time after that is fine for moving in."

"Sounds like a plan."

Chapter Ten

At the Indigo house, Jackson devoured his to-go order of now cold tacos while Mitch paced the floor. Garret stood at the window watching the driveway for the private detective's car. Lenore sat at one end of the sofa with her yarn basket at her feet, knitting a mint green sweater top for Ally. Tanner had stretched out in his recliner doing his best to catch a nap.

Eager to take this next step, no one talked about how nervous they were at meeting Marcelli. It seemed too final a step to take. But between bites, Jackson had already shared Tessa's find on the yacht and what her spying on the Buchanan house had revealed. "No wonder trust became an issue for her. We grew up here and I'm wondering if we ever truly knew any of these people."

Lenore's fingers stilled. She let her knitting fall to the side. "I would try to defend that meeting as harmless if not for one thing. I'm still reeling from the email Reverend Dandridge sent out church-wide, an email to all the parishioners stating that Livvy and Walker left on their own. My own pastor suggested how no one had to show up for the search. I wouldn't even believe he could ever do such a thing, if Laura Davies hadn't forwarded me the email."

"It's bullshit," Tanner grumbled, rubbing his eyes. "I'm done with Dandridge. There's no excuse for what he did, even if I'm hoping the man's right and Livvy's alive and well somewhere."

Mitch stopped his pacing back and forth around the room. "You can't have it both ways, Dad. You either have to wonder why Dandridge would go to all that trouble, or believe that Livvy is sipping a piña colada in Aruba."

"This is a nightmare," Tanner declared, running his hands through his thinning hair. "It's not easy accepting the fact that your own pastor is part of some kind of grand conspiracy."

"Suit yourself," Mitch tossed back. "But I don't appreciate him sending a group email and poisoning our well of volunteers. It was a definite, orchestrated effort."

Garret cleared his throat. "Car's pulling up in the driveway, he's here. Whoops. Wait a minute. Person getting out of the driver's side is a female, a total babe."

"Thanks for the play by play, now answer the door," Tanner suggested, as he brought his recliner to its upright position.

Garret bolted to answer it before the woman had a chance to ring the bell.

Tall and slim, she had long black hair that fell in gentle waves around her shoulders. Her big dark eyes were almond-shaped and flecked golden to bronze depending on the angle. To Garret's delight, she looked like an exotic siren, a bit dangerous, and ready to lure any conquest into the rocks.

"Hi there, I'm Anniston Marcelli. The private investigator you hired out of Miami."

"You're not Anthony," Jackson stated.

"No, I'm not. And you are?"

Jackson introduced himself. "We were really hoping for Anthony," he admitted with obvious disappointment.

"Then I'm afraid you'll have a long time to wait. Two years ago my dad suffered a heart attack. He's now semi-retired and mostly working as a consultant."

"But the guy I talked to led me to believe we'd be meeting with Anthony, uh, Mr. Marcelli," Garret corrected. "I'm Garret by the way, and this is my brother, Mitch, my dad, Tanner, and my mom, Lenore."

"Nice to meet all of you. I wish it were under better circumstances. I'm sorry you're in the middle of a horrible ordeal."

"Who was it I talked to yesterday?" Garret questioned.

"That must've been my brother Sebastian. You see, Sebastian's handling a tough case of his own right now in Daytona. To keep my dad's business alive we decided to merge our forces. We return calls, go over the situation with our father and then we decide to either move forward with the case or refer it to someone else, depending on the specifics. But if you'd rather wait until Sebastian is available…"

Garret didn't wait to scan the room or get the go-ahead from the others. "No, no, it's fine, you're fine. We're anxious to kick this thing into high gear. That's why the urgency."

Anniston placed her laptop bag on the entryway table. "If it's any consolation your sister's disappearance intrigued my dad enough that it almost tempted him to come out of retirement and make the trip here. But he's in no condition right now to do that, or to take on such a complicated case that might warrant a strenuous eighteen-hour day. Fortunately, I was able to convince him he could still contribute back in Miami, which he will. He's tasked me to keep him up-to-date every step of the way. So it's either work with me, or start from scratch and find another PI. Your choice. I'm prepared to recommend several capable and trustworthy colleagues."

"Are you fully licensed?" Mitch piped up. "Because we need the best."

Unoffended at the comment, Anniston dug in her bag. She was used to this kind of reception where she had to prove she could take on tough cases and follow in her father's footsteps. She handed Mitch her driver's license, her Florida state license to practice, and her gun permit. "Are we all set now, or do you want to see my Costco card?"

Anniston met Mitch's eyes and saw the doubt had diminished. "So, if we're ready to get started, I came prepared with a long list of questions."

"Sit down and make yourself comfortable," Lenore finally offered, making room on the couch. "Would you like something cold to drink? I have iced tea."

"Not right now, thanks." Anniston took a seat on the sofa next to Lenore. She opened her briefcase and took out the detailed list of everything she needed to cover.

"You'll have to forgive us," Lenore began. "We're a little on edge. We have a lot to tell you and when we finish, you'll understand the reason we're so edgy."

"No need to explain since you've all been through such an emotional roller coaster the last few days."

Jackson got up to throw away his trash. "We're also expecting a friend of ours to join us. Tessa Connelly has a great deal to add to this initial meeting."

"Ah, the one with the brother who went missing? Good. My dad and I happened to catch your news conference on Sunday. I'm glad Ryan's sister will be joining us. Because my father is convinced Ryan's disappearance is connected to your sister's, which means, three weeks ago has to be our starting point. I'll ask for your patience on that because Walker seems to be the common denominator in both cases."

Disappointed to hear that, Mitch wanted to know, "How patient? When will you get around to investigating what happened to Livvy?"

Anniston decided this particular Indigo needed a little more convincing. "I understand how you must feel. But try to look at this from an outsider's perspective. In a town of just over four thousand, in a span of three weeks, five people vanish without a trace. The minute my father handed me this case I did my homework, gathering quite a bit of additional background information on all the parties before I ever got in the car this morning. There's no way to discount the importance of Ryan's dropping out of sight unless we can account for it. If we find out what happened to him then it might tell us why Walker and Livvy went missing as well."

The doorbell rang and Garret opened the door to usher Tessa into the mix.

They all crowded into the small living room listening to Anniston go over the how and why of all things pertinent to hiring an investigator. After all the parties had signed the agreement and she listened to the brothers argue over who'd put up the retainer, Anniston got down to business. "So, who wants to go first?"

All eyes turned to Tessa.

Tessa glanced over at Jackson for a little emotional support. The man didn't disappoint.

"Anniston says Ryan may hold the key to this whole thing."

Tessa inhaled a nervous breath. "Really? Well, I guess that's my cue. I'm not sure where to start. Ryan came down here for two reasons. Walker owed him five grand for the website he designed. Plus, Walker offered to take him fishing. Ryan loved to fish. And he'd never been to Florida before, let alone to the Keys, so it seemed like the perfect way to spend his Labor Day weekend. He was so excited about making the trip that he forgot to arm the security system at his condo."

Anniston jumped in. "Did he often forget that little detail?"

"Not at all. Ryan was a techno geek who latched onto anything new in software or computer hardware. It didn't matter. Whenever new gadgets hit the market, he was like a kid in a cookie store."

Tessa opened her purse and took out Ryan's medical ID bracelet. "But finding this on Walker's boat is what sent me over the edge. You see, Ryan had epilepsy, from the time he was about five years old he suffered from grand mal seizures. He had to wear this medical alert everywhere he went. The thing is as long as Ryan took his anti-seizure medication they were usually under control."

Anniston winced at the sight of Tessa handling what was likely evidence. "How often have you picked that up since you found it?"

Tessa sighed. "I put it in my jeans pocket and then transferred it to my bag. I've taken it out a couple of times since Monday."

Anniston removed a plastic bag from her briefcase. "We might still find microscopic DNA on it yet. Slip it into the baggie and I'll send it to the lab."

Anniston noticed Tessa's reluctance to part with it and laid a hand on the woman's arm. "I'm sorry. Sending it for testing is the only way to know if there's anything of evidentiary value."

"I know. Finding it is why I'm convinced Walker did something to him."

Anniston couldn't afford to get tunnel vision this quickly, so she prompted Tessa to go on. "So without his medication Ryan is at risk for another seizure?"

"Exactly. And since I have yet to locate his car or other belongings, I have no way of knowing if he has his meds." That sent Tessa into a replay of the scene last night at Royce's house. She detailed everything about the argument she'd overheard, everything the six men in the room had said in the heated discussion until she'd backtracked to her car. She took out her cell phone and thumbed through the photos she'd taken. "These are the license plates of the people who were there."

Anniston's jaw dropped. "My God, you're a genius. Who thinks to do that?"

"I'm motivated to find out what happened to my brother."

Jackson cleared his throat. "It's obvious from the plates one of the cars belongs to Sinclair, the main person we went to initially. He's the one who suggested Ryan's case had something to do with Livvy's."

Anniston's brow creased. "Why would the chief of police do that if he's somehow involved?"

Jackson proffered a theory. "Granted, Sinclair seemed fine when we spoke to him on Saturday. He even pointed us in Tessa's direction. His cooperation was either a clever ruse or something changed between then and Monday night. I'm guessing he conned us, otherwise he wouldn't have been hanging out at Royce's house in a fierce disagreement. That's why we put our heads together before you got here and came up with a way to jumpstart your investigation."

Lenore reached to open a photo album. "When you've lived in a small town for as long as we have, you get to know most of the residents on a personal level. Since Jackson says Tessa can ID the men belonging to those cars. It should begin with the guys who showed up at our house yesterday to get us to believe Livvy took off." She flipped through church photos they'd taken over the years at all kinds of events. "Here's Boone Dandridge officiating at Livvy's wedding."

Lenore handed it off to Tessa, who studied the photo.

"That explains the collar he wore."

Lenore's heart dropped. "I've known Boone Dandridge since he first got to town. The man had trouble getting people to come to services back then. I felt sorry for him so I rallied neighbors and coworkers to church. I took the kids to the Sunday school class he used to teach." She shook her head. "I guess you never really know who your friends are until you go through something like this."

"I'm sorry," Tessa said.

"Don't be. It's better to know than to go on pretending." She picked up another photograph. "Here's one that shows Carson Frawley handing out doughnuts to a group of kids at a Christmas party two years ago."

Tessa took one look and nodded. "He wasn't as vocal as the others, but yeah, he was there."

Lenore had one of Dave Oakerson in his scuba gear showing a group of teens how to work the oxygen tanks. "Now this is a lot trickier. This was taken years ago before Oakerson became mayor. He owned the dive shop in town, taught all my kids how to dive."

"That's the man I saw driving the BMW. He arrived last."

Anniston smiled. "I'm impressed. You guys are doing all my work for me."

Tanner studied the images of the plates. "Not quite. That still leaves two men a mystery. It could be Roger Baskin. Baskin was one of the men who stood here yesterday and stoked Boone's theory."

"I don't have a picture of Roger," Lenore admitted. "You see Roger doesn't attend Life Stone. I'm not sure where he goes to church if at all. But his connection to Royce goes way back. He's the person Royce trusts to fix those expensive cars he owns. Whenever they need tinkering with, it's Roger's responsibility to keep them all running. You sometimes see Roger driving Royce around town, acting like his chauffeur."

"Especially that Maybach sedan Royce has," Tanner finished. "You'd think a decent mechanic like Roger would find it beneath him to haul Royce all over town like that."

Anniston waved away any concern. "No need to speculate on the remaining guys. I'll run the plates for all the vehicles in those photos and get a definitive list. But let's get back to basics. It may seem like a lame cop question, but I have to ask. Did your sister have any known enemies? Did Walker?"

Garret let out a low moan. "That's a loaded question. They both grew up here on the Key. I'm sure they've pissed people off a time or two, but nothing that would cause this kind of circumstance. For the most part, everyone loved Livvy and they tolerated Walker."

Anniston chewed her lip, knowing she was about to hit a nerve. "Okay. Then how about the marriage? Was either of them having an affair?"

It was Lenore who went over Livvy's suspicions. "After Ally came along there was a time when Livvy thought so. I'm not so sure about recently."

"Walker often acted distant at family functions," Tanner added. "We attributed the attitude to thinking that he was better than all of us."

Anniston took note of the protective father. "That doesn't necessarily mean he was unfaithful."

Tessa sat there listening to the back and forth and wondered if she should mention Raine's disclosure over lunch. She didn't want to break a confidence. But after an awkward silence hung in the room, Tessa thought of a way around that. "Over the past two days I've tried to talk to as many locals as I could. It seems there were rumors around town that Walker was seeing someone."

The room fell absolutely silent. Beginning to feel remorse for bringing it up, Tessa reminded them, "They were just rumors."

Lenore dropped her head in her hands.

Anniston reached over, patted the woman's shoulder. "Don't worry. By the end of the week, I'll be able to give you an answer and tell you definitively whether it's true or not."

Jackson decided it was time to bring up what he'd found out at the bank from Nathan. "I'd like to know how you intend to work around the fact that the investigators have already snatched up all their financial data?"

Anniston held up a hand. "I'll cover that in a minute. For now, does anyone have anything pertinent to get out on the table, anything of value? Now's the time." When no one offered up a new topic, she went on, "Okay then, this is the plan. I'm approaching these two cases from the ground floor. As I said earlier, I've already done backgrounds on your daughter and Walker." She turned to Tessa. "That includes Ryan."

When she heard mumblings, Anniston continued, "Don't even ask what I've discovered so far because I'll hold off until the reports are complete. You've already given me additional information and reasons to dig further. I will tell you this much. I've barely scratched the surface. Second, and this is a big one, I'll try to get my hands on any and all security surveillance tapes that cover both time frames going back to Labor Day for Ryan and then leading up to the Thursday the family went missing. That will take time. If it turns up a dead end, the Marcelli Agency has a very good reputation with various law enforcement agencies throughout Florida. That also includes the state investigative team. Even though detectives aren't allowed to share anything from an ongoing case, we have ways around that hitch." She turned to Jackson. "That covers financial records. So, that's the game plan. Any questions? If not, I need to head to the Mainsail Lodge and check in."

Anniston picked up her briefcase. "Don't worry, we'll touch base tomorrow. By the way, how are the searches going?"

It was Garret who explained that today's event had a low turnout. "Thanks to Dandridge sending out that email, it sandbagged the whole thing."

Anniston's eyes grew wide. "I'm not sure I've ever worked a case where a pastor would do such a thing. Do you have any objections to calling in organizations like Equusearch to get the job done?"

Garret shook his head. "None at all. In fact, that's an additional resource."

On her way to the front door, Anniston picked up her computer bag. "Good. In the meantime, I think your family and friends need to get out there tomorrow and make every effort to continue on your own."

Mitch stuck his hands in his pockets. "We'll go out every day, even if it's just the six of us scouring the neighborhoods." He took a step closer so his mother wouldn't overhear. "My crew and salvage boat's due in tomorrow. At some point over the next few days we'll make plans to take *The Black Rum* out. We'll use divers and utilize side scan sonar to cover the bay, the ocean, the surrounding lakes, and any water between here and Tampa Bay where the van was found. You understand what that means, right?"

Anniston nodded, knowing they were talking about recovery instead of rescue. She leaned in to whisper, "Even if your mother isn't ready, it's a good idea." For everyone else's ears, she raised her voice. "I'll follow up with the investigator in charge of the case, hopefully get some updated info regarding the van."

Jackson was impressed with her savvy demeanor and willingness to work fast. But she didn't know Dack Hawkins. "You think you can get info out of Hawkins? Good luck there."

Anniston sent him a wide smile. "I'm persistent. Plus, my daddy knows his daddy. Right now, I have a lot on my plate, so you guys get some rest. We'll talk tomorrow."

Garret followed her out of the house to her SUV, and opened the driver's side door of the Ford Explorer. "I have to say, you certainly came prepared."

Anniston eyed the tall, good-looking man who made his living in riding the next big wave competition. "I read about you. You wouldn't dream of surfing the Banzai Pipeline without several years of training and preparation. I don't take on a case without doing the same."

"Fair enough. You impressed my family."

"And what about you?"

"Absolutely. I wouldn't be standing here if you hadn't. You should be a cop."

She frowned. "How do you know I wasn't?"

"I guess I need to do my homework on you. But since I thought I was getting your father...you have the advantage. For now, anyway."

"I'll save you the trouble. I was two years out of the academy when my dad had his heart attack. Since then my brother and I, who was also a cop at the time, couldn't stand to see dad's business slide into oblivion. So we made a pact to keep it going."

"That's a huge sacrifice."

She casually lifted a shoulder. "What can I say? Italian families stick together. Mama spends her days taking care of Daddy while Sebastian and I keep Marcelli Investigations in the black. You must be pretty close to yours or you wouldn't be here helping your parents through this terrible ordeal."

"There are times my dad drives me crazy. But what're you gonna do? He's just as hard on Mitch and Jackson as he is on me. So, I have to believe it's nothing personal. Do you regret giving up your badge, giving up what you worked so hard to achieve?"

"Not really. I'm happy taking a bigger role in cases, otherwise I'd likely still be a beat cop in South Beach handing out parking tickets." She tapped his chest. "This way I get to help people like you and your family."

"We're grateful."

"I could see that. What else is on your mind?" Anniston saw him swallow hard. She thought she knew the reason.

Garret looked up at the sky. The stars were just beginning to pop out. "I don't think this will have the happy ending my mom and dad are hoping for. I need to know you're aware of that and won't play games with their emotions. At some point, dancing around reality will get old and become pointless. Because my brothers and I are pretty sure Olivia, Blake, and Ally, maybe even Walker are...you know...not around anymore."

"You're that certain your sister wouldn't take off?"

"Positive. She's the most dependable person I've ever known."

"Well, I follow the evidence. Period. If the evidence tells me there's little hope the four are alive, I'm prepared to tell your parents the truth. It goes with the job."

"Okay then. That's all I wanted to hear."

After Anniston took off, Tessa helped Jackson and Mitch fix supper, which they'd volunteered to do while Lenore got some rest.

"What did you think of Anniston?" she asked.

Jackson stood at the counter dipping pork chops into an egg batter before dusting the meat with flour. "She's sharp. I like that she'd already done her homework before getting here."

Tessa nodded in agreement as she broke up lettuce for a salad. "I think she knows what she's doing. I feel a little better knowing she's involved. I like her."

Mitch snickered as he peeled his next potato. "So does our baby brother. He even followed her out to the car."

"I noticed that," Jackson said. "She's way too smart to get involved with Garret."

Tessa thought otherwise since the private eye seemed just as smitten. But she said nothing and turned her attention to the way Jackson handled himself at the stove. His eyes danced with devilish glints of gold as he showed off his culinary skills. "Where did you guys learn to cook?"

Jackson somehow managed to arrange all the pieces of meat to fit in the huge fry pan. "Standing right here. My mom worked full-time keeping the books for several businesses. Even though she wasn't a CPA she used to do tax returns at a bookkeeping service to bring in extra cash. Anyway, Olivia and I used to take turns making supper and having it ready when Mom and Dad got home. We couldn't have been more than eleven or twelve at the time. We started out with the basics—hot ham and cheese sandwiches, mac and cheese—then progressed to tuna casseroles and chili Frito pies. When we got fed up doing all the cooking, we schooled Mitch and Garret on how to whip together your basic scrambled eggs."

"More like tricked," Mitch quipped. "They initially told us if we beat enough eggs into a bowl we'd get to use them to make batches of sugar cookies."

At the stove, Jackson sent a pork chop in the air, neatly flipping it in the skillet. "So gullible."

That insult prompted Mitch to pick up the mess of potato peels on the counter and sling them in Jackson's direction.

The cook ducked the incoming stream of skins. To retaliate, Jackson picked up the leftover flour and tossed it toward Mitch. The dust hit him full in the face.

Both men dug into Tessa's salad bowl. Lettuce flew across the kitchen. Cherry tomatoes sailed through the air. Black olives whizzed past Tessa's ear. Rolling laughter erupted from all three as they tried to dodge and weave the flying food.

"Stop that!" Lenore shouted from the doorway. "Look what you've done to my nice clean kitchen. Honestly, I can't let you boys out of my sight for a minute. You'd think you were eight years old."

Standing behind his wife, Tanner surveyed the damage. "Just blowing off a little steam. They wouldn't be mine if they didn't."

Hands on her hips, Lenore sent her husband a scowl and shoved him back through the door. "That's no excuse. Blowing off steam indeed, more like making a mess. You're grown men. Start cleaning this up right this minute. And don't let the meat burn while you're doing it."

Dutifully Mitch grabbed a mop from the laundry room.

Lenore eyed the red stains from the tomatoes on Tessa's blouse. "Now look what you've done to Tessa's clothes. Take off that top and I'll toss it into the wash for you."

Tessa shook her head. "That's not necessary. I've got to be going anyway. Raine Manning invited me to stay with her and it's almost time to meet her there."

Mitch couldn't believe his ears. He whirled around from the mess on the floor. "You're staying with Raine?"

"I met her today at lunch. Her invitation comes at a time when I could really use a place to crash."

With a fork, Jackson stabbed a piece of sizzling pork in the pan before it turned black. "I thought you were staying for dinner."

Tessa glanced over at Jackson and the meat getting browner by the minute and grinned. "I'll sample your cooking another time. Right now, I'd like to get settled in at Raine's before it gets any later. Plus, I'm really tired. The meeting took a lot out of me. And trying to sleep in my car the last couple of nights really wasn't the smartest thing I've ever done."

"You should've said something," Jackson pointed out.

"I should have. I'm sorry for not trusting you."

"Well, there's no denying she doesn't trust your cooking," Mitch cracked.

Tessa smiled at that but tried to change the subject. "Make sure to count me in for the search tomorrow. And I'm sure when I let Raine know, she'll be there, too."

Mitch's pulse picked up. "I doubt she'll show."

Tessa tilted her head to study Mitch. "Why do you say that?"

"She wasn't there Sunday or Monday, now was she?"

"Maybe she had to work."

"Not Sunday morning she didn't."

Tessa decided this thing between Raine and Mitch was an obstacle course with too many years of hurt feelings for her to try to navigate. When Jackson offered to walk her to the car, she got out of there in a hurry.

They said their goodbyes standing at the curb. But it was the tender way Jackson explained Mitch's testy reaction to Raine that touched her heart.

"I'm not sure what happened between those two. I was busy finishing up my second year at Columbia, trying to bring up my grades, and contemplating how I could get a jump on summer classes. But Livvy, bless her heart, always tried to keep me in the loop with all the family gossip. She told me Mitch had acted like an ass. That could cover quite a bit. So, I'm guessing after all this time Raine still carries a grudge about something. To my brother's credit, I think he's attempted to make amends several times. But maybe some actions can never be forgiven."

"It's admirable the way you see both sides. You're big on family loyalty. I like that."

He stepped closer, slipped his hand around the back of her neck. She anticipated the moment when he pulled her in, when their lips met. The ugly world they'd been dealing with fell away, replaced by familiar urges between man and woman. The kiss started slow, a little pop for pleasure before building the heat, fire for fire.

She yielded to the sensations and the playful way he used his tongue. His mouth left her breathless and wanting more. She pulled back. "I have to go, Raine's expecting me."

"Soon we'll have to finish this. You want to as much as I do."

She grinned. "I do. But timing is everything. And so far, ours has been lousy."

"That'll change. I'll see to it."

Chapter Eleven

Tessa swung her Toyota into the designated marina parking area very near where the Indigos had held their press conference on Sunday.

Raine's home turned out to be a twelve-hundred-square-foot, two-bedroom, one bath houseboat located right on Sugar Bay within walking distance of a dozen boutiques, shops, and restaurants.

Tessa immediately spotted the blonde standing outside a boathouse waiting for her. Shoving out of the car, she sent Raine a wave. "What a beautiful spot!"

"Thanks. I love it here."

"I just came from the Indigo house and an intense session with a woman who says she's gonna get to the bottom of this whole thing."

"That's a pretty big promise. Maybe she's a scam artist. Some of those private detectives just take your money and do nothing."

"I don't think so. You've got to meet her. She's…a go-getter." Tessa went around to unlock the trunk where she'd stowed her stuff. "I'll unload my crap out of the car and then tell you everything. How's that sound?"

"Here, I'll give you a hand," Raine offered, running down the dock in bare feet.

"Luckily, I didn't bring all that much. It never occurred to me that I'd be here this long." Tessa set out two pieces of luggage and reached to close the trunk.

"Travel light. I like that," Raine said as she hefted one of the bags and led the way into the house.

"I thought by this time I would've already located Ryan and been back living my normal life."

"I'm so sorry," Raine reiterated as she made her way into the living room.

Tessa took in the décor—the tongue and groove pine floor and the sunny paint on the walls. The shabby chic furniture told her that Raine had a Bohemian side to her. "You never mentioned your house floated."

"Didn't I? Will that be a problem?" Raine said, heaving the bag on top of a full-sized bed and plopping down next to it.

"Not for me. It's roomier than it looks from the outside." Tessa stood back admiring the pale turquoise paint Raine had slapped on the walls. "This is so cute." In that moment, she decided she had a lot in common with her new roomie. Maybe it was her love for all things do-it-yourself that made her appreciate another's flashy expression of color, but she felt an immediate connection to her hostess and her generous spirit.

The mismatched furniture—a bed painted bluish green and a yellow French country dresser—only endeared her more to the obvious beachy theme that prevailed. Sitting next to the bed was a smallish nightstand with a tabletop that had been coated with decoupage cleverly using a map of the Florida Keys. The shelves on the wall held a library of paperback romance novels. Any other time she would've loved to delve into each one.

Raine tilted her head to study her guest. "So you're okay with staying here now?"

"I'm grateful, very appreciative. I'm sorry if it seemed like I had a problem with it earlier."

"Don't worry about it. But I did see that proud look on your face and wondered if you'd even bother showing up tonight."

"To tell you the truth, I think I'll enjoy staying here and bouncing ideas off another female."

"Feel free." Raine jumped up and started out. "Let me show you the rest of the place. The bathroom's in the middle of the hallway so we'll have to share. A heads up, though, it only has a shower, no tub."

"That's fine. But you have to let me pay. I can't just move in here and..."

Raine waved her off. "When you can, you'll contribute. You're paying rent on an apartment back home. That has to strain the budget. Plus, I'm not desperate for rent money. This houseboat belonged to Danny. It's paid for. He left it to me. I have a good job at the taco shack because my mom owns the place. One day, it'll be mine outright. And last summer, the business had a really good run. Tourists love a cheap taco. And like I said earlier, I understand these are extraordinary circumstances beyond your control. You came to town looking for your brother. I know how I'd feel if the same thing happened to me and I was desperate to find someone I cared about, but strapped for cash. I'd give anything if Danny were still around so that I could go look for him if he ever went missing. Maybe that doesn't make sense to you but..."

"No, it does. It makes perfect sense."

Raine led the way into another small bedroom where she'd been just as generous with color but incorporated much softer shades. Pale greens complemented the pop of peach and the wave of dockside teal. The tones gave the room a definite feminine feel while still keeping with the coastal, nautical theme.

"If you want, you can unpack and settle in while I change my clothes. Around this time of day, I have to get out of these jeans and top and put on something that doesn't smell like grease and fish, the downside of working around food all day. Then we'll have a glass of wine and I'll start dinner."

"I'm happy to help with supper," Tessa offered as she walked back to her own room. "I'm handy in the kitchen."

"Good to know."

Inside her space, Tessa opened a suitcase and began tossing her things into drawers. She took her toiletries and arranged them on top of the dresser so they wouldn't take up space in Raine's tiny bathroom.

It took her all of twenty minutes to pull everything out of her luggage and get her second wind. When she heard Raine rummaging in the kitchen getting out pots and pans, she headed that way.

Forty-five minutes later the two had abandoned the idea of cabernet and were laughing over margaritas that Raine had thrown together in the blender. They sat on the deck under the stars nibbling on nachos and popcorn.

Raine briefly put down her glass and sat back in wonder. "So you helped Jackson and Mitch with dinner prep? That had to be a sight to see."

"I wouldn't say I helped, more like tried to referee an ongoing sibling rivalry that turned into a food fight."

A round of laughter escaped Raine's lips. "The sad thing is I didn't even know Mitch could boil water. Although, I guess there's a lot about him I don't know these days."

Remembering what Raine had admitted at the taco shop, Tessa explored it more. "How long have you known Mitch?"

Looking up at the night sky, Raine gulped the tequila concoction, emptying the goblet. "Forever. Middle school crushes that turned into high school sweethearts. And dances. And making out in his car."

Sensing a good story, Tessa angled forward. "Ah, a history together. What happened? Why didn't you two take the big leap into marriage?"

Raine shifted in her seat and poured herself another full glass. "The short answer is Mitch wanted to be somewhere else, anywhere else other than Indigo Key. He copped to that so many times but I was in love. I didn't take him seriously. My mistake. He was telling me the only way he could that he intended to leave as soon as the opportunity presented itself. I suppose he wanted someone else, too. I didn't see that coming either. But the minute he turned eighteen he couldn't wait to get out of here and see the world."

She lifted her drink and sipped the slushy liquid. "Mitch dumped me so fast after graduation I barely had time to take off my cap and gown. Anyway, to get at the why, you'd have to ask Mitch Indigo."

"Do you want to talk about it?"

Raine rolled her eyes. "I thought I just did. I haven't been sitting around pining for the asshole if that's what you're getting at."

Tessa realized she'd almost walked through a minefield. Wisely, she pulled back, breathed in the balmy Florida air. A bit bleary-eyed, Tessa suddenly turned more serious. "Before I even got here I spent days calling all the hospitals in case Ryan had been brought in after a car accident. I went with the hope that he might've suffered amnesia or something. I guess that only happens in the movies though because he hadn't been admitted to any of the local facilities."

"Doesn't mean it didn't happen. He might've had an accident on his way back to North Carolina. It could be a simple case of…"

Tessa didn't let her finish. "I called every hospital from here to Nags Head. They didn't have an accident victim fitting Ryan's description. It's as if he and his Honda just vanished into thin air." Tessa tapped the table. "Right here, within a mile or two of where we're sitting right now. The whole thing's been surreal."

Raine gripped her new friend's hand. "He's out there. We'll find him."

"That's what I keep telling myself." She sipped more tropical tequila. "I get the impression from the Indigos and from what you mentioned earlier at the restaurant that Walker isn't very well liked, not even in his own circles. What kind of guy are we really talking about?"

"Honestly, Walker is an ass. There's no other way to describe him. And yeah, everyone pretty much got fed up early on with that arrogant attitude he tossed around. The local rich boy could be the biggest jerk of anyone. Even back in grade school he bullied people. I never understood what Livvy saw in him. To this day, I still don't. I'll give you an example. The two of them went on a cruise for their honeymoon, one of those that sail the Mediterranean around the Greek islands. Anyway, the jackass spent most of his days and nights in the casino onboard the ship instead of with her. Livvy said that during the trip he lost at least twenty grand."

Tessa's hand flew to her mouth. "Holy crap, Taco Girl, that's a lot of gambling."

"It's a lot of losing," Raine corrected.

"Hmm, that makes me wonder if all the rumors about money woes were all about his gambling debts."

"Knowing Walker, that sounds reasonable enough. I think his daddy bailed him out quite a bit, especially when he got in deep with bookies."

"Walker bet on sports?"

"All the time."

Tessa raised a brow. "Chronic gamblers have bookies. You don't suppose while he was here in town Ryan somehow got dragged into Walker's need for cash? Bookies are known to get impatient for their money. My brother had five grand on him the morning he went off the radar."

"We could always go with that angle and run with it, ask around town. Are we still on for Miami tomorrow?"

"Sure. But I promised Jackson I'd show up at the marina first for the search. And I kinda, sorta promised you'd be there, too."

Raine stabbed a finger in the air for emphasis. "I don't have a problem doing that for Livvy and the kids. Hell, I don't even have a problem being around Mitch. That ship sailed a long time ago. So we'll spend the morning trekking the neighborhoods looking for…what exactly are we looking for anyway?"

"I get the sense from the Indigos they're looking for remains. They just don't verbalize it."

Raine made a face. "Well, that's a sobering thought. Not much to look forward to tomorrow. First, we hunt for any sign of Livvy. Then we turn our attention to Walker's stripper, ask around for his bookie."

Tessa tittered with laughter, the alcohol kicking in and pushing reality away for a while. "So let me get this straight, we're going in search of a stripper and a bookie? Sounds like I landed in a B movie."

"Hey, it isn't my fault that the upstanding citizen Walker led a bit of a sleazy life."

"I'm beginning to think that's true. But what if the bookie's right here in town," Tessa surmised. "In fact, what if Walker's girlfriend is living in Indigo Key?"

Raine shook her head. "In such a small town? No way. Walker would get caught in a heartbeat. No, if you're a man bent on cheating, it's a lot smarter to do it someplace other than in your own backyard."

"But is Walker really all that smart?"

It was Raine's turn to hoot with laughter. "You got me there. Walker the genius. Not."

Tessa clinked her glass with Raine's. "I think I'm going to enjoy bunking here."

Chapter Twelve

The Indigo Key marina was a full service boatyard. It could accommodate most average-sized recreational boats except for the mega cruise ships. The port offered first-rate amenities like fueling stations and waste dumps along with plenty of slips and rack storage. Boaters from all over the world often stopped for midway refueling on their way to destinations in the Caribbean or west toward the Gulf States. Mariners could take advantage of the area restaurants and bars or restock supplies from the two convenient grocery stores within walking distance.

Jackson stared out at the hustle of the harbor realizing he'd missed the beauty of this place. He watched as a tugboat pushed a barge loaded down with supplies and maneuvered it safely out to sea.

The small town atmosphere hadn't changed much in all the years he'd been gone. You could still count on the laidback atmosphere, the whiff of fish coming off the bay, the smell of bacon sizzling in a skillet somewhere nearby, and the sound of the surf lapping up against the feathery sand.

There were fond memories here. As a kid, his summer days consisted of any activity in or near the water. Things like snorkeling, fishing, or fighting with his siblings over precious turf on where best to build a sand fort. It made for plenty of hot and sweaty days. Those days of innocence had been filled to the brim with endless carefree pursuits that only children truly appreciated. He'd taken those days for granted and realized now they had been the best times of his life.

No wonder Livvy had decided to stay put and raise a family here. A flood of envy shot through him.

Tessa walked up with Raine in tow and waved a hand in front of Jackson's face. "Where were you just now?"

"Daydreaming," Jackson muttered as he turned to greet the women. "Hey, Raine good to see you. Thanks for coming." To Tessa he couldn't resist leaning in and placing a light kiss on her cheek.

Raine had already scouted out Mitch's position and knew if she hung around Tessa she might be able to avoid him altogether. "Are you in charge?"

Jackson smiled widely. "Not me. That would be your good buddy." He heard a loud sigh. "Just remember, Raine, you're doing this for Livvy and the kids. Try to put up with him. Like the rest of us the pressure is getting to him."

"I know. I know. I promise to be a sweetheart and not give him a hard time." She took off, walking toward Mitch, determined to make nice.

Tessa turned her sharp blue eyes on Jackson. "What were you daydreaming about?"

Why did those eyes of hers always seem to throw him off-balance with their penetrating stare? Why did he feel a sense of relief that she'd shown up? He took in the outfit she had on, khaki shorts and a white knit tank with swingy lace and imagined slowly peeling her out of her clothes. "What was the question?"

She let out a half-laugh. "You said you were daydreaming. Looks like you're still in a fog."

"Ah, a simpler time, I suppose, when Livvy and I were kids. Did I mention how good you look today?"

"You didn't. Maybe that deep fog has rattled your brain. Or maybe the stress is getting to you, too." She slung a friendly arm around his waist. "A girl never gets tired of hearing she knocked it out of the park even if it's just when she threw on a pair of shorts. Is it always this hot here?"

His eyes filled with genuine amusement. "It's the humidity. It's worse in August. Look around, there's no shade to speak of. We'll likely bake. Did you remember sunscreen?"

She smiled, decided to let him keep talking. Mitch wasn't the only one who seemed to be cracking under the pressure. She listened as he rattled on about stats and data about the area and weather. It culminated in what was really bothering him.

"The heat makes me wonder what kind of turnout we'll get today."

Tessa took him by the arm. "The kind that's dedicated, the ones who'll brave the heat and mosquitos because they care about your sister and the kids. For those who don't want to participate, there are plenty of others who'll take up the slack."

"I hope you're right." It was time to clear the air for good. "There's something I need to say. I'm sorry if I gave you the impression Walker wasn't responsible for Ryan's disappearance. Because I think that's the only thing that makes sense."

"It's commendable you wanted to keep an open mind. I'm sorry I didn't understand that before. But I'll take your change of heart. Now if I could just convince Anniston, I'd consider it a triumph."

The measly turnout was a disappointment. Instead of the massive crowd that had gathered on Sunday, Tessa counted ten hearty souls. It might have been the temperature that kept them away, but she wasn't convinced it was the ninety-degree heat.

But luckily, one remaining search and rescue team had stayed behind with their dogs and pledged to stay in town until the end of the week. Another group had volunteered to send ground penetrating radar equipment whenever the family gave the word.

Mitch began organizing the few who'd shown up, handing out alert whistles, banners for tagging, and sticks to use in weeded lots. Everyone spread out and headed to their specific grid points.

Tessa drew a grassy section of wetland near the beach. Taking her stick in hand, she poked drainage ditches, inspected the greenbelt along the bike path, and explored a section of flat glade with plenty of golden creeper and rose mallow.

She fought mosquitos, encountered a scary-looking iguana with eyes that seemed bigger than its head, and happened upon a family of turtles, nesting under a locust berry bush. But those were nothing compared to the cottonmouth she watched slither into the low-lying marsh.

It wasn't until she'd covered her area of sand twice, some fifty yards or so and back again, that she spotted Jackson at the other end of the pathway, head down, looking dejected and sad. She jogged toward him, only to stumble and trip on her own two feet.

Jackson darted over, pulled her upright.

As she stood up, brushing off sand and grime from her clothes, she had to laugh at her own clumsiness. "And I was worried about snakes. At least I didn't fall into the water. What are you doing out here? This is my turf."

"I came to get you. Mitch pulled us all back in."

"Why?"

"At some point, we have to face reality. If we're going to bring them back home, we need help from the outside. And Mitch's crew chief just radioed that he's about five miles out."

"So we give up the land search in exchange for one underwater? That's…disturbing. Talk about reality."

"Yeah." He rubbed her arm. "I'm wondering what we'll do, how we'll feel, when we find some piece of the puzzle we don't want to face."

"I've wondered that same thing. But so far, we haven't found a single piece of fabric, not a torn shirt, not a shoe, not a trace of anything, anywhere. We've come up totally empty. It breaks my heart."

He looked out over the shimmering water in the marina. "I read somewhere that the first sign of a psychopath is that they have zero empathy for anyone else. If we're dealing with that type of personality, we could be looking for a monster walking among us."

"Any person who drags kids away is already a monster in my book. I could understand somewhat targeting Livvy, Walker, even Ryan. They're adults, maybe they pissed someone off. But dragging kids along in a plot of this magnitude is inexcusable. I keep wondering when I'm out here looking, what could Blake and Ally have ever done to warrant this?"

He took her hand in his. "I'm not sure I could get through this without you here."

She smiled. "Funny. I feel the same way about you."

Hand in hand, Jackson and Tessa joined his brothers on the dock to watch Mitch's pride and joy, a salvage boat named *The Black Rum*, make her way into port.

From the wharf, Mitch waved to his crew chief, Walsh Kingston, standing at the helm. Walsh returned the gesture by raising his arm in the air and giving a salute.

Walsh had a crop of light brown hair with the tips bleached from the sun. His olive skin glistened in the sunlight like a polished bronze statue. His pale blue eyes beamed with mischief that promised either a intense adventure or a serious bout of trouble.

From the time Mitch had set sail on his first salvage boat, he'd felt a special kinship toward the older Walsh. On the surface the two men had little in common. Walsh had been married before, but didn't like to talk about it. He had a history that included a military background in Special Forces, and later, a stint in prison. Mitch was convinced it was Walsh's colorful past that kept him tight-lipped. The man could go hours without saying a single word to anyone. But on a crew hundreds of miles from land, the sea had a way of eventually making a man open up.

It had taken Mitch exactly fourteen voyages out of port on somebody else's salvage boat before he finally got Walsh to talk. He'd discovered firsthand, the air of mystery surrounding the ex-military guy had been well earned.

Truth was Mitch didn't care much about Walsh's former life. In him, Mitch had found a kindred spirit, someone who loved taking a boat out and spending weeks in the middle of the ocean surrounded by nothing but water, someone who experienced the same kind of adrenaline rush in that quest for finding the ultimate treasure.

To Mitch, Walsh wasn't just a loyal employee. He wasn't just a friend. Walsh was that third brother, who had a knack for finding the most sought-after treasure that rested on the bottom of the ocean floor, undisturbed for centuries.

Jackson took Mitch's Thermos and sloshed coffee into a cup, sipped the lukewarm contents. "How do you think Walsh feels about abandoning the dive site?"

"I already polled the entire crew. They all said the same thing. They're ready and willing to comb this entire bay and the Atlantic, if necessary."

There was a commotion over Mitch's shoulder that prompted Jackson to ram an elbow into his brother's side.

Mitch flinched and began rubbing his ribs. "What the hell's the matter with you? What'd you do that for?"

Jackson bobbed his head toward the other end of the pier. "We have company."

Mitch glanced over to where a crowd of locals had gathered to watch *The Black Rum* motor into port. He recognized Dandridge, Baskin, and Oakerson. Disgusted, he scowled at the group of onlookers. "Since when does the town send out a welcoming committee?"

"Since they obviously have a stake in whatever is happening here. I'm beginning to think we're the dunderheads kept in the dark while everyone else laughs at the joke."

The group continued to watch as *The Black Rum* dropped anchor and made ready for the crew to disembark.

Mitch greeted his five-man crew like it was old home week. His brethren were of varying ages from twenty to fifty. But regardless of their differences, it was like a family reunion. "I appreciate y'all coming." Mitch introduced his brothers and friends, including Raine. "Lunch is on me…at her place."

Raine sent Mitch a cordial smile. "Thank you. Even on my day off, I always appreciate the business."

But Walsh had turned serious. He narrowed his eyes, stared out at the horizon. "You could've told me there were other salvors in the area."

Mitch fumbled the Thermos of coffee he carried. "What? Where?"

Walsh pointed due south. "She's anchored on the seaward side, equipped with deep-sea gear so she likely came in for refueling."

Mitch squinted into the glare of the sun. "I can't make out the name."

"It's the *Patagonia Pike*." Walsh cut his eyes toward the boss man to catch his reaction.

Mitch's face went blank. "But they never leave South America. Never."

"Well, they're here now," Walsh fired back.

"Why?"

Jackson and Tessa exchanged curious looks. "So? What's the big deal about the *Patagonia Pike* sitting in Sugar Bay?"

"For one, they're in the business as our competitors who don't have a problem using guns to intimidate the competition. The crew fights dirty and often. And it's rumored they have a financial bigwig who equipped that forty-five-foot monster with state of the art everything."

Walsh took exception to that. "Hey, we're not exactly slouches. Thanks to some amazing conversions, *The Black Rum's* been outfitted to the hilt. I'll match our engines and speed any day of the week with what they've got."

Mitch slapped Walsh on the back. "I know and you'd get beaten every time. Do me a favor."

"Mitch boy, you're racking 'em up faster than I'm able to keep a tally."

"I know that too. Get online. Ask around the blog sites. See if you can determine what they're doing in our neck of the woods so far from the South Atlantic. There has to be scuttlebutt somewhere."

"Sheesh, that doesn't take a genius. What else? They're after treasure."

"Yeah, but I want to know which treasure in which location? And get specifics."

"Sure, what else have I got to do?" Walsh pivoted to get a better look at the town. "So this is where you spend Christmas every year, huh? Do I get to meet the parents?"

"Absolutely. But keep in mind it's not the greatest time to catch them at their best. It's day to day. My mom and dad have taken a hit and have yet to bounce back. They're trying to keep it going, but it's been tough."

"Understandable. So when do you want us to get started?"

Mitch scratched his head. "Well, we've been all over town, gone up and down the beaches, explored every empty lot between here and the city limits sign. I'd say now's the time to move it to the water. But first I have to clear it with the authorities. Hopefully, I'll be able to talk them into helping us with diving on the bay. When we branch out to the Atlantic, which we will, I'm hopeful we'll be able to conduct that search ourselves. As to lodging for the crew, there's a hotel across the street."

"Nah, we're bunking on board, same as we always do." Walsh turned to go, but stopped. "You know she isn't out there, not in this harbor. Your sister. Her family. Too busy. My gut tells me you'll be looking in the wrong place. You should concentrate out in open water where there's less boat traffic. Pick a side of the island to start with. Gulf to the west. Atlantic to the east. That's what I'd do."

"I don't disagree. But people have been known to dump bodies in the bay once the sun goes down," Mitch declared. "We have to cover all our bases. The bay is one."

Intrigued with the confident way Walsh had argued his point, Jackson angled toward the crew chief. "What makes you think Livvy is farther out?"

Walsh lifted a shoulder. "Pure instinct." He tapped Mitch on the shoulder. "But he's the boss. And your brother will attest, I'm only right about eighty-five percent of the time."

Mitch coughed for effect. "Unfortunately, it's that fifteen percent that always gets us into trouble."

Chapter Thirteen

By midday, Tessa sat in the passenger seat of Raine's vintage Fiat roadster speeding down the Overseas Highway. Raine didn't seem overly concerned about clipping along fifteen over the limit.

So far, they'd driven through town without a word exchanged between them. Instead of talking, Raine had cranked up the music—a Death Port CD blared from the speakers.

The minute they'd left the marina Raine had used the alternative rock to avoid any attempt at conversation.

The reason didn't escape Tessa. Raine's mood had gone south since spending the better part of her morning around Mitch. After four hours of playing nice, she'd grown downright sullen. Tessa knew it was all on her.

"Look, I'm sorry I made you go. Obviously you don't like being anywhere near the man, even plastering on a fake smile for Livvy's benefit."

"Ha, that's how much you know," Raine shouted over the rock band. "We got along great, like two old foes afraid to talk to each other for fear of pissing each other off and creating a scene. We wouldn't want to create a scene, now would we?"

Raine finally reached over and adjusted the volume. "It isn't your fault. I should've showed up on Sunday. I purposely avoided the damn thing knowing I'd see him, which is silly because it's ancient history."

"History has a way of repeating itself with very little effort," Tessa warned.

"No chance of that. I may not be the smartest person in the room, but I'm a grown woman now. I'm able to recognize a man who has no intentions of ever settling down in Indigo Key, a place where I have deep roots. How about we talk about something else?"

"Sure. This is a cute car."

Raine snorted out a laugh. "It's a piece of crap and doesn't run half the time. But it belonged to Danny, which means I haven't been able to work up enough of a reason to part with it. Every time I try to write out an ad for the classifieds to put it up for sale, I just can't bear to complete the online post and face the prospect of letting it go. So, like a sentimental idiot, I keep it around as a reminder that Danny worked himself silly fixing this old heap up. I ought to hunt down Hudley Slocum, the guy who unloaded it on him."

"Why don't you?" Tessa wanted to know.

"Because it's been a decade ago. Lots of water under the old bridge since that transaction went down."

"It's sweet that you hang onto Danny's car like this. I wonder if I'll..." Tessa's voice hitched before trailing off. "I can't think like that yet. I have to believe Ryan's okay, that he's out there somewhere. But I'm not stupid. I know he'd never walk away from the business he'd worked so hard to get off the ground. He wouldn't disappear like this on his own."

Raine took a deep breath. "I hear ya. For what it's worth, I think something bad's happened to Livvy and the kids."

"Is Walker capable of harming his own children? There's been a lot of speculation."

"Why not? Desperate for money, he might try to collect on a bundle of life insurance and then take off. There's just one problem with that theory."

"Walker isn't around to collect."

"Yeah." Raine glanced from the road long enough to briefly study her passenger. "Something tells me you aren't completely comfortable heading to Key West like this."

"Because we'll be hitting the pavement looking for Walker's girlfriend? No, I'm okay with it, mainly because I'm determined to do anything to help. I am troubled about one thing. Are you sure this is the right time of day to locate a stripper? Don't they do their thing at night?"

Raine lifted a brow. "They don't have daytime strip clubs back in North Carolina?"

"I guess I've led a sheltered life."

"Probably. The thing is Walker used to make his trips to Key West in the middle of the day so he could be back by dinner time."

"How considerate of him."

"Wasn't it though?"

Once they reached Key West the two women started at the string of nightspots along Dumont Street with names like Cherry Dolls and Body Shots and Topless Babes.

At each location Tessa and Raine took turns shoving Walker's picture under as many noses as they could get to look at the photo. But three hours into their outing, after going from club to club, after using whatever story worked to get the dancers to study the snapshot, they had nada to show for their efforts.

None of the scantily clad females had any desire to own up to being Harlow, let alone to dating the guy in the photograph posed with his wife and two adorable kids.

After striking out with the dancers, they decided to aim the picture toward the bartenders and cocktail waitresses and the clientele. But again, after several more hours of walking until their feet hurt, they couldn't find anyone who recognized Walker. They also found it odd that no one had heard of a stripper using Harlow as her stage name.

Around five o'clock, they gave up and headed to the car.

"As rank amateur detectives that was a bust," Tessa admitted. "I expected more out of this."

"It's our first attempt," Raine pointed out with a shrug. "We're bound to get better."

"Couldn't get any worse. But for every time I get my hopes up, it's ripped out from under me. I'm upset that I'm no closer than I was a week ago to finding...something. I fear I'm running out of time. Speaking of time, I have another favor to ask."

Raine threw her a cautious look. "No."

"You haven't even heard it yet. Hear me out."

"I don't have to. Whatever it is it involves Mitchell Taylor Indigo. Let me guess. You want me to spend my Wednesday night off sitting around with some detective I've never met *and* be in the same room with him for longer than I care to be. The answer is no."

Tessa decided to play hardball. "So people disappear around Indigo Key all the time?"

"What? Of course not."

"Then how do you explain the casual way some people in town refuse to help look for Livvy? As I see it, you either participate in some way or you live with the fact that your friend and her kids are missing, maybe for good. I know I couldn't sit around on the sidelines doing nothing."

Raine dug in her heels. "I drove all the way to Key West to look for a stripper. How is that sitting on the sidelines?"

"For one afternoon." Tessa held up a hand. "I'm sorry. But is your resistance to meeting with the detective due solely to how you feel about Mitch?"

Raine chewed the inside of her jaw, beginning to get annoyed. "I have a problem spending time with the guy who dumped me without a backward glance, no postcard, no note. Is that so hard to understand?"

"Not at all. You've been in love with him a long time. It's reasonable to be pissed off when that guy doesn't return the feeling."

"Now you sound like my mother."

Tessa tried again. "Look, couldn't you set aside your feelings long enough to be in the same room with him for this one meeting?"

"They've hired a pro. What possible thing could I bring to the table? I sling hash for a living."

"You also know all the players, have a history with the locals. You knew about the rumors that Walker was seeing someone on the side. Maybe that different perspective is the very thing that could break the case. The more people put their heads together and try to solve this thing the better chance we have of finding out what happened."

Raine let out a huge sigh and looked at her watch. "When's the meeting?"

Tessa smiled. "Jackson's text said six-thirty."

"If we head back to Indigo now, we should be able to make it." When she noted Tessa's smug grin, she added, "Don't look at me like that."

"Like what?"

"Like you won. I'm doing this to shut you up."

"I don't care why. It's one evening."

"After one morning. Besides, what makes you think the Indigos need me tossing in my two cents?"

"I think Tanner and Lenore need to hear what you have to say about Walker. It might reaffirm a few things they've been questioning. Think of it this way. It has less to do with Mitch and more to do with helping Livvy's mom and dad."

"Low blow, appeal to my sense of fairness."

Tessa slipped her arm through Raine's and picked up their pace to the car. "Come on, if you use that leadfoot like you did coming down here, we'll be able to hustle through traffic to make it back there in no time."

Chapter Fourteen

Everyone except Anniston had already settled around Lenore's dining room table by the time Tessa and Raine walked in the door.

The private detective stood in front of a whiteboard she'd set up to review what she'd discovered so far. "I ran the plates from the photos Tessa took."

Anniston began writing the names of each man using the marker as she ticked off the information. "Your police chief's attendance is a given since he drove his squad car to the get-together. The other three vehicles you've already figured out. The Land Rover belongs to Boone Dandridge." She jotted that make of vehicle next to the name on the chart she was building.

"Carson Frawley drives the Lexus, Dave Oakerson, the BMW, and Baskin owns the Infiniti. The fifth car, the Mercedes, is a rental I traced back to a German businessman named Werner Dietrich."

"Why does that name sound so familiar?" Mitch asked, looking around at his brothers for help.

Jackson shrugged. "No idea, but he's not from Indigo Key."

Anniston turned to the whiteboard and wrote down Dietrich's name. She also drew a line connecting the five men to their vehicles. She tapped the board, but circled Dietrich. "This is an important guy who has his hands in some of the top industries in Argentina, everything from banking to mining to oil. And in his spare time, Dietrich likes to dabble in precious gems, collecting art and other memorabilia from the pre-World War II era, with an emphasis on anything belonging to Hitler or Nazi Germany."

Mitch ran his tongue around his teeth, snapped his fingers. "That's it. Dietrich owns one of the biggest salvage vessels operating out of the South Atlantic. Son of a bitch. His *Patagonia Pike* is right here in port. It's the same one Walsh spotted this morning refueling in Sugar Bay. It normally runs out of Buenos Aires, usually never leaves the shores of South America. As far as I know that crew has never ended up this far north."

Jackson made a decisive noise in his throat. "Sounds like maybe Royce and these guys are working on some kind of joint venture, like a salvage operation right in our own backyard."

A sudden memory flashed to life in Tessa's brain. "Oh my God! As a boy Ryan always wondered what it would be like to get involved in a hunt for one of those Spanish galleons. You don't suppose…"

"Let's not jump to conclusions," Anniston cautioned. But her warning was lost in the speculation that followed.

Jackson's eyes flew around the room. "I should go back and have a talk with that old man, get him to talk. I can't believe I fell for his act. He almost had me feeling sorry for him."

Anniston was adamant. "Stop this. No one jeopardizes this investigation any more than it's already been compromised. No one goes rogue. Do we understand each other? Nothing I've told you or will tell you leaves this room. I'm serious. If you guys won't stick to the conditions of our contract, I'll pack up tonight and head back to Miami. That's how it's gonna be. Period."

That threat got reluctant agreements out of each Indigo male, even Tanner. When Anniston did speak it was to keep the topic alive. "This right here is the main reason investigators don't like sharing what they learn with the family. It makes the situation too volatile. I made an exception for you guys because you're dealing with five missing loved ones, a situation that is clearly emotional, and therefore, unpredictable."

"Okay. Okay," Garret said. "We get it. But how do we get answers if we don't go rogue? You need to utilize all your resources better. There's only one of you." He spread his arms out to take in his family and friends. "We're perfectly capable of doing legwork, recon, whatever you cops call it. If you feel the need for total autonomy and decide to shut us out, it'll take you months to get anywhere."

Anniston leveled a sharp gaze on Garret. "A thorough investigation could take months. This is a marathon, not a sprint. A sprint gets you sloppy mistakes. I'm looking down the road at what will hold up in a court of law, not careless supposition." She let out a sigh. "I'm gathering evidence, which I will follow wherever it takes me. Then when I've got a clear picture as to what happened, I'll take it to the proper authorities."

"The proper authorities shouldn't include Sinclair," Tessa threw out. "Whatever Buchanan is working on with this Dietrich person, Sinclair is part of it."

"More like half the town," Jackson groaned.

"That's just it," Anniston began. "We know the ones we shouldn't trust. It's more than we knew yesterday. In fact, anyone outside this room should be considered a risk. That's why what we say here, stays here."

Mitch had to raise his voice over the disgruntled din beginning to grow even louder. "And that's why you should let us in on the routine inquiries because this thing's branched out. Now we have to figure out the underlying reason Frawley, Dandridge, and Oakerson went out of their way to derail the search. Why would Royce be a part of something like that?"

"Because he's a heartless old bastard," Tanner added. "You have no idea what kind of monster you're really dealing with in Royce Buchanan. Everybody knows that man's always been slicker than owl shit."

That accusation only drove the room into their battle positions, each one offering to do what they could to move the investigation along.

After listening to the appeals that came at her in a fevered pitch, Anniston said, "Fair enough, I'm not used to having partners other than my dad and brother. I'll tell you what, I'll keep at the five who are missing, which is what you guys hired me to do, while you guys dig into the meeting between Mr. Buchanan and his cronies." She shuffled some papers around in her briefcase. "If we all agree to that, then is it okay to move on?"

"There's more?" Garret asked.

A snide expression crossed Anniston's face. "There's a lot more. I didn't just call this meeting to talk about vehicle registrations. First, I received notice from Dack Hawkins that he released the house. He feels nothing of evidentiary value is there."

Jackson crossed his arms over his chest. "So that means Hawkins thinks no crime's been committed and we're back to square one."

"Basically. Hawkins determined whatever happened didn't happen inside the house. But here's the good news for our side. Y'all are cleared to go back there and take a look around, get a second look for yourselves, maybe even a third. Releasing the house also indicates to me that the state is officially moving toward the conclusion that the family left voluntarily."

Lenore put her hand over her mouth. "That isn't really a solution, is it? Two days ago I might've believed that without a problem. But now…"

"Not without more proof," Tanner concluded.

Anniston agreed. "I believe it won't be long—possibly by the end of the week—before Hawkins makes a formal announcement that there's no longer an open investigation."

"How's that good news?" Mitch asked.

Garret spoke up. "I think I know where she's headed with this. Without an open case, Hawkins is free to share what he knows. Am I right?"

"Bingo. Give yourself a gold star," Anniston said. "Not only that but once the case is no longer active it paves the way to finding out all the other information that Hawkins obtained over the last week, bank statements, cell phone records, any other legal documents like wills and deeds."

Lenore rubbed her aching forehead. "But what good are cell phone records in the grand scheme of things? My daughter didn't have the time to send me a text message or call me before she vanished. So how will looking at that help?"

Anniston didn't hesitate. "To tell you the truth, I prefer having someone's cell phone records any day over DNA. Give me phone records and mobile GPS tracking evidence and the cell phone towers and I'll have a perfect roadmap to that person's every movement."

Garret sat up straighter. "You're kidding? I thought these days every crime is solved with DNA."

A derisive tone shot out of Anniston's throat. "Get real. You've been watching too many crime shows. In most cases police rarely have the luxury of working with DNA. They build their circumstantial cases by putting together the movements of victim and suspect and then matching them up to a point of connecting the dots. A timeline that links a victim to a suspect is stronger in court and virtually irrefutable. Unless a defendant's phone was stolen, how is he able to explain away his cell phone's location near the victim's house?"

Tessa thought of how difficult it had been to get into Ryan's online carrier. "Like I told Jackson before, that's all well and good for Livvy and Walker, but no one's bothered with finding out Ryan's information, let alone his movements."

Sympathy rushed through Anniston. "You're right. But that all changed today. My father called one of his buddies in Miami homicide for a favor. The guy got a judge to write out a court order for Ryan's phone records. I spent hours capturing a snapshot of Ryan's visit here."

Tessa's mouth dropped open. "And?"

For the first time that evening, Anniston's lips curved. "I'm connecting dots all over the place. Give me another day and I should have a complete picture for you. I may not even need to go in search of surveillance video."

"Really? That's fantastic." Tessa traded glances with Raine. "I suppose one good turn deserves another."

It was Raine who tossed a nod toward Anniston. "You tell her."

"Gee thanks," Tessa muttered, gripping the arm of the chair and sending Jackson an apologetic look. She thought it best to give them the bad news like ripping off a Band-Aid with one yank. "Okay, here's the deal. Raine and I spent the afternoon walking the streets of Key West looking for a stripper named Harlow who supposedly was the woman Walker was having an affair with recently."

The room grew deadly quiet.

Tessa reached across the table and laid a hand on top of Lenore's. "I'm sorry. I don't mean to hurt you with this kind of info."

Mitch turned an accusing glare toward Raine. "So you've known this for how long and didn't think to say anything?"

Raine got to her feet, slapped her hands on her hips in defiance. "We don't exactly talk these days, remember?"

"And whose fault is that?" Mitch shouted as he stood up to face her. "And what the hell was that we did yesterday at lunch, you know, when my dad and brother came into your restaurant? You might've mentioned it then."

Raine bellowed right back as she grabbed her purse. "I knew coming here tonight was a big mistake. You're still the same inconsiderate jerk you were in high school."

"I was eighteen back then. When are you ever going to let that go?"

"Honestly? Probably never."

Lenore shouted for calm.

But it was Anniston who had to step between Raine and Mitch and push them back from each other. "Now kids, let's head to neutral corners. Try to remember this meeting is for one purpose—for us to get on the same page and stay there. This is a major lead that needs checking out before we jump to conclusions."

After Raine took her seat, Anniston turned to Tessa. "So yesterday when I asked everyone about affairs you purposely held back?"

Tessa ignored the remorse she felt. "I alluded to the mysterious stripper because I didn't want to upset anyone. And I felt I owed Raine an allegiance, a loyalty of sorts, for taking me into her confidence."

Raine beamed. "Right back atcha."

"Why don't you ladies pinky swear, get on with it, and then we're all set to move forward," Mitch said sarcastically.

Before Raine could explode in his direction again, Tessa intervened. "That tone is so unnecessary. Raine and I thought we could locate this Harlow woman and bring the info back to Anniston, do our own legwork, additional fieldwork on our own. But we didn't find anyone who had ever heard of her. Maybe she doesn't even exist."

"That they owned up to," Raine pointed out. "Maybe we just didn't find a person willing to talk to total strangers they likely don't trust."

Anniston chewed on that as she began to pack up her things. "It gives me a name to check out, though."

Jackson had heard enough. He tapped Tessa on the shoulder, nodded for her to follow him into the kitchen.

"What's up?" Tessa asked.

"Is there any way we could get out of here?"

"And go where?"

"I don't know. Somewhere people aren't yelling and getting in each other's faces. I want to spend some time alone with you."

"Sure. But what about finishing the meeting?"

"I have a better idea." Jackson tugged her through the back door, slipping away to his dad's truck.

"Where are we going?"

"First stop is Livvy's house." He dangled his mother's spare key in front of her. "It's no longer considered a crime scene, remember? I want to see for myself what's what. After that, we'll find a nice, quiet, peaceful spot to loll away the rest of the night."

It took less than ten minutes to reach the corner house at the intersection of Blue Fin and Windward. Draped in shadows, the cute West Indies style house looked forlorn in the dark. Jackson noted the crime tape had been removed.

He pushed open the front door, flipped on the lights. Slate tile floors in baby-blue teal greeted them as if they'd taken a trip to Nassau. An entryway led them into a stylish family room decorated with plantation furniture that utilized all the natural elements, teak, rattan, and woven cane. Livvy's ebony and beige color choices along with a splash of aqua accessories ran classy, like a stay at the Hilton.

Nautical trappings—a huge aquarium that took up a chunk of the middle wall and a two-foot-long replica of Walker's yacht sitting on top of the fireplace mantel—

were gentle reminders this was coastal living. Gauzy draperies from floor to ceiling on the massive windows were made to take advantage of the tropical breezes and filter the sunlight.

The only sounds in the room were a ceiling fan overhead that still turned in a slow rotation with just a hint of a whirling click and the low hum of the water pump on the fish tank.

Taking it all in, Tessa marveled at the size of the two huge banana trees, one in the living room, one in the dining room, and all the blooming birds of paradise growing to heights she'd only dreamed about. Livvy had used the plants to accessorize the beach theme. "Your sister had a flair for decorating. She must've had a green thumb."

"She and my grandmother. A couple of years back this house appeared in *Southern Living* magazine. You'll want to take a look at the patio. It's like another room addition to the house. Plus, there must be another three dozen kinds of plants sitting out there."

"Jackson, do you notice anything odd? There's damp soil around the plants like they've been watered recently. The fish are still alive. Someone's been feeding them and taking care of the little things."

"Hmm, maybe Mom's been sneaking in here when she wasn't supposed to."

Tessa turned in a circle to scan the house. "Interesting. The downstairs looks perfect, nothing out of order anywhere, not a magazine out of place, not a stick of furniture upside down. Did the cops even dust for fingerprints? Don't they usually leave behind telltale signs of that inky stuff?"

"The place looks like it could still grace the cover of a periodical. Too clean for the cops to have done much. I thought they were in here turning the place inside out. Let's take a look at the kitchen and then make our way upstairs."

In the kitchen, there was signs Livvy had fixed dinner. Little drops of spaghetti sauce still stuck to the range top. But there were no dirty dishes left in the sink as though she'd fixed pasta that night and then cleaned up the mess.

Tessa opened the dishwasher to find it full of spotless dishes. The counters had been wiped clean. Even the floor gleamed like it had been recently mopped.

"I don't have to tell you this is eerie," Tessa said. "It looks like one of those open houses. I keep expecting a realtor to appear with a sales pitch. Does it always look like this?"

Jackson's forehead wrinkled into a frown. "Walker could be a stickler for a tidy house."

"But there are no signs of two small children living here."

"You're right. No wonder Dack Hawkins released it. The place looks like a damn model home."

"What was it Anniston said earlier about Hawkins? That whatever happened, didn't happen here. I'm beginning to think Hawkins is right."

"I'll reserve judgment until I've seen the upstairs." They took the staircase to a small landing that Livvy had fixed up as a play area. Here there were toys scattered around the little space. Legos on one side, dolls on the other, as if brother and sister had split the room in half.

Jackson opened the door to Blake's room and spotted the unmade bed. "Ah, here we go, lived in." His eyes scanned the typical boy's bedroom. In between the sheets he found two action figures—an Incredible Hulk along with Captain America—Blake had left behind. A pile of clothes including an Avengers T-shirt and a pair of jeans had been tossed on the floor. He opened the closet door, found most of Blake's clothes still on hangers.

He went across the hall to Ally's room and found her bed had been slept in. Her pink Barbie comforter had been tossed back as if the little girl had just crawled out from under the warmth of it not five minutes earlier.

Like Blake, Ally had left behind some of her most prized possessions—an assortment of her favorite dolls and her precious Dreamy Eyes Palomino, a gift for her sixth birthday last August. He ought to know, it had been his gift to her to satisfy her growing desire for a real horse. Glancing around the room, the panic and fear that lodged in his throat were as fierce and fresh as that first day he'd taken his mother's phone call.

With heavy feet, Jackson moved down to the master bedroom. Once again, he found a messy bed with covers tossed back as if maybe the pair who'd been sleeping comfortably there had exited the coziness in a sudden call to action. He went to the closet and saw for himself what his mother had already reported.

"Look at this, Livvy left behind her clothes, clothes for the kids. So did Walker. What did they all do, hop on a plane without taking any personal items with them or any of their belongings? What would make them leave like this in the middle of the night?" Jackson asked, truly puzzled.

"Maybe they got an emergency phone call about something. Maybe they had to go check something at the store and didn't want to leave the kids."

"Both of them? Why wouldn't Walker have handled that?"

Tessa touched Jackson's arm. "No idea. I'm guessing here, same as you."

About that time a noise from downstairs had them moving out into the hallway, ready to go on the offensive. Holding hands, they did a double time down the wide front staircase only to run into the entire gang they'd left back at the house.

Lenore gasped. "I knew I heard footsteps overhead. You scared me half to death. So this is where you two went. We wondered when you suddenly up and left."

Jackson went over to his mother. "By any chance have you been coming here when you knew it was off limits?"

All eyes stared at Lenore.

"Lying in bed Sunday night I remembered the plants and the fish. I walked over here and snuck in the back door. I was afraid the fish might die and all the plants would wilt and I wouldn't be able to bring them back if that happened. Livvy put too much work into them to let them die."

Jackson wrapped an arm around her. "It must've taken you two hours to get to every plant in here."

"I didn't mind. I couldn't sleep anyway."

Tessa patted Lenore's shoulder. "Did you do the dishes, too?"

"No. Livvy left that kitchen so you could eat off the floor. I swear I didn't touch anything else, not even the kids' bedrooms."

Raine nodded in agreement as she inspected the living room. "No wonder Livvy went to bed every night exhausted. This place looks frozen in time, the same as it did on that magazine cover some years back. It takes work to keep a place this tidy."

Mitch's eyes drifted to Raine. "Yeah. Nothing's out of place."

"Your mother told you how neat everything was when she walked in a week ago," Tanner grumbled as he took off for another part of the house. "Now that I'm inside, I'm covering every inch of this house starting with Walker's man cave."

"Walker has a man cave?" Jackson asked as he took off after his dad.

"He has a damned room he keeps locked and off limits to everyone, called it his home office."

"I gotta see this," Mitch said as the others trailed after him, curiosity getting to the entourage.

Tanner led the march through the kitchen, past the utility room, and out into an open breezeway that connected the main house to the detached garage. Sandwiched in between was a smaller guesthouse built as an add-on to match the West Indies style and design.

The cabana style getaway had French doors, which Tanner found locked. Infuriated, he was just about to break a pane of glass to get inside when Jackson stilled his arm.

"Here, try the front door key first."

To no one's surprise the key didn't turn the lock.

Garret pushed them both aside. "Let the master do his thing." He proceeded to take out a key ring from his pocket with an assortment of accessories attached. One looked very much like a torque wrench. He slipped the thin blade into the lock and jiggled it until he heard a click. "Voilà. We have access."

Tanner stared at his son. "I could've sworn I tossed that thing in the trash when you were fifteen after you broke into Cones & Scoops ice cream shop to get your geography book back."

Garret's lips curved into a wide grin. "Hey, I used to forget stuff all over town. Without this little handy dandy device I couldn't have retrieved half my gear. Aren't you glad I dug it out?"

Tanner slapped Garret on the back. "My boys always were too quick for their old man." He flicked the light switch and led the way into Walker's retreat.

Tessa hung back, feeling like an intruder, but not so for Anniston and Raine. They followed Lenore into the man cave, ready to scope it out with gusto and a purpose.

As man caves went, this one wasn't your run-of-the-mill basement variety. Tastefully decorated, it bordered on an upscale clubroom. It had charcoal paint on the walls with a contemporary motif.

The eyes tended to drift straight to the focal point, a built-in seventy-inch flat screen TV that took up one wall. Two rich brown leather sofas were positioned in front of a modern fireplace, done in sleek black granite. There was a murphy bed built into the bookcase.

Tanner opened drawers while Jackson wandered over to the wet bar, and took note of at least twenty different types of liquor. He opened a steel-trimmed, counter-high refrigerator and found it well stocked with an expensive

Danish beer. "Anyone feel like trying this crap? The expiration date says 2059."

Garret sauntered over, removed one from the shelf to study the label. "Yeah, I've heard of this, four hundred bucks to grab a taste of barley and peat with a hint of vanilla and cocoa."

Mitch turned up his nose. "No thanks. I'll take a lager any day over that."

Jackson continued to look around, going into an adjoining bathroom. He came out carrying a well-equipped first aid kit. "I'd say Walker was prepared for both an apocalypse and a frat party."

Tanner opened up a drawer and hit the jackpot. He held up several DVDs. "Yeah, well, there's enough pornographic videos here to get the frat party started."

Jackson spotted Tessa still standing in the doorway. He went over, whispered in her ear. "What do you say we try to ditch these people again and get that alone time?"

The laugh she gave him made up for finding out about Walker's man cave. He grabbed her hand and led her past the garage and down the driveway to the pickup, now blocked in by Anniston's SUV and Raine's roadster.

"Damn. They came in a caravan."

Tessa tugged on his sleeve. "Why don't we walk? The marina's practically down the street. I wouldn't mind sitting out near the beach and enjoying the night sky."

The street was quiet when they angled toward the sidewalk. "Anyplace will do as long as we get to spend some time by ourselves." He glanced over, noticed she seemed preoccupied. "You were uncomfortable back there."

"I was. I know y'all are anxious enough to dig right in, that you might even find something that explains their disappearance. But y'all descended on Livvy's house tonight like a swarm of locusts." She held up her hands. "Not criticizing the reason behind it. But it got me to thinking about how I'd feel if people pawed through my things that way when I'm not around to stop them. I mean, it's one thing to want answers but…going through drawers and private things no one else should see. I guess it's a privacy issue for me. It just didn't seem right, kind of sad."

"We're forced to act like a swarm when we don't even know why they left. It almost felt like Walker and Livvy were living separate lives in that house. I swear I never knew she was that unhappy."

"I guess some marriages are more like nightmares than fairy tales."

"But it shouldn't be that way. If only I'd paid closer attention. Maybe I could've done something."

"Livvy could've left, Jackson. Your parents were practically around the corner."

"I know. That's why the whole thing seems so bizarre."

Chapter Fifteen

It was like anticipating a picnic under the stars.

On their way to the beach Jackson stopped to pick up barbecue sandwiches with chips and soft drinks to-go at a local dive along Largo Avenue called Smokin' Sal's. The fast food joint was small but it was the aroma of slow-simmered brisket flavoring the air that drew most of the customers in from the street. The place had a missing poster plastered in the window about Walker, Livvy, and the kids.

Jackson treated the guy behind the counter like an old friend. The two men spoke about an incident that happened in study hall back in middle school before moving on to a litany of questions about family. Keeping to an easy banter and a friendliness that seemed to go back to childhood, they high-fived each other like teammates.

"Sorry about this business with Livvy. I haven't had a chance to make it to any of the searches yet. Meredith and I keep this place going seven days a week just to keep our heads above water. I'm here from seven in the morning doing the books while she gets the girls off to school before coming in to help me with the lunch crowd. I usually don't leave for home until eleven at night because I'm here cleaning up."

"It's okay. We appreciate you putting up the poster."

"It's the least I could do."

"How's Meredith?"

"Expecting our third in December. We're hoping for a boy this time."

"Good luck with that. How much do I owe you?"

"Don't worry about it. This meal's on me and Meredith."

"Thanks," Jackson said, scooping up the bag of food.

"Who was that?" Tessa asked when they started down the sidewalk again.

"Salvador Bartholomew, a distant cousin, twice removed on my mom's side. Sal inherited this place from his dad. You'll find most of the businesses around here go back second and third generations."

"Salvador Bartholomew are two names you rarely hear together."

Jackson chuckled. "What can I say? We're a quirky bunch in the Keys."

"So I've noticed."

"You'll love the barbecue, too. It has a sweet Caribbean zing that you only get on island."

"Personally, back in North Carolina, we favor our pulled pork."

"Sal serves that up as well, but with a cinnamon sauce to die for."

When they reached the shore, they sought out a place to sit, picking a spot under a towering coconut palm with long-reaching feathery branches. There'd been a question brewing at the back of Tessa's mind for several days. "How long do you plan to stay here?"

Jackson dug out a sandwich and handed it off. "My boss is getting antsy for an answer to that same question. Right now, I'm uncertain how long it'll be before I'm willing to give anyone an answer. How about you?"

"Maybe another week if I'm lucky."

He sipped his soda, contemplated her leaving. "Don't go. You'll regret it if you get back to Nags Head without a resolution. You won't be able to focus on anything but Ryan. You'll stay up late at night until one or two in the morning, spend hours online sending out inquiries until you can't sleep. Insomnia will start getting to you."

Tessa smiled and unwrapped her food. "That's a bleak outlook but sounds fairly prophetic. That's exactly how I'd spend my time. Well, Raine offering me a place to stay definitely helps the finances. But there's still the blog I do for the hardware store. Without daily posts, they may decide to can me and get someone else. I mean, what's more important, finding my brother or some stupid blog?"

"That's the way I feel. I love what I do. But how do I go back to work without knowing what happened to Livvy?"

"Like you said, Ryan consumes my every waking thought. I've lost the ability to write a clever post. I have to face the fact that I may not get my creative DIY juices flowing again."

He reached out, his fingers brushing a trail through that mane of Tahitian red. "I get the impression there's no one waiting for you back home."

"Nope. I broke up last year with a guy who had a problem flirting with everything in a skirt that came within twenty feet of him. I've been free and clear ever since. How about you?"

"There's a woman I see every now and then. We're coworkers, different responsibilities, different departments. I travel. So does she. When it's convenient we spend the night with each other."

"Does she see this arrangement as casually as you do?"

"Absolutely. Rachel won't even meet my family. We've known each other for two years and she's never been down here. Not once. This thing with Livvy came up and I haven't heard from her."

"She hasn't called to ask about how the case is progressing?"

"Did I mention Rachel isn't really the warm and fuzzy type? She's all about ambition, getting ahead in her career."

"Ah, the old Type A personality."

"Exactly. Now that I think about it, I don't know what attracted me to her."

"It's the sex," Tessa said with a snicker, elbowing him in the ribs. "Never underestimate the bond that forms from sexual release."

"I'm not sure Rachel and I have any bond other than physical contact. It's certainly nothing like the heat I feel with you."

Again, her lips curved. It felt good to toss around a few flirtations. She pushed up her sleeves and poked him in the ribs again. "Haven't you heard? It's that North Carolina sizzle. It's so special I hauled it all the way down to south Florida just for you."

"Works for me." He took her chin, fastened his mouth to hers. His blood thumped through his veins like a pressure cooker about to explode. He wanted her flat on her back.

The kiss was all tangled tongues and greedy tastes. Her breath hitched as she pulled him in. His mouth did things to her that made her lightheaded. Off balance, she threw caution to the wind. "Seducing me is pointless. I'm bunking with Raine and you're staying with your parents. We have no access to anything but a vehicle."

He let out a sigh. "Even I'm too old for my dad's truck."

"Exactly. So where does that leave us?"

"We have two hotels in this town."

"Come on, Jackson. That option is fairly obvious. You really want to give the people here something else to add to their play list?"

"I don't give a hang."

"Yes, you do. Try to picture the email Dandridge sends out to his flock about us that your mother would likely read."

Jackson puffed out his cheeks. "I truly wouldn't care. But it might hurt Mom in some way. I don't think Dad would care either."

"I don't want to cause Lenore any more pain. Then there's this Rachel thing back in New York. You have to deal with her first. You owe her that much."

"Don't worry. That's the next thing on my to-do list."

By the time he walked Tessa around the marina to Raine's houseboat, he'd had ample time to think. On the trek back to Livvy's to pick up his dad's truck Jackson had already made up his mind. He'd been putting it off long enough.

He took out his cell phone and keyed in a text message to Rachel. It was short, simple, and to the point. *We've had a good run but whatever we had is over.*

Rachel's reply came back in a matter of minutes. *You're on the road now and tired but when you get back to New York, I have no doubt we'll pick up right where we left off.*

The words *on the road* jumped out at him. Didn't Rachel realize he was back in Florida in the midst of the worst crisis he'd ever faced? Did she think he was on a work assignment somewhere? Had Rachel forgotten all about his sister?

By the time he reached the truck, he keyed in his response. *Don't hold your breath. We're finished. I met someone else.*

He almost typed in the rest, the simple truth. Tessa made him feel more alive than he had in years.

Chapter Sixteen

They decided to forego another organized land search, at least for a day or two until they could regroup. Instead, Mitch had been itching to get back on the water. He dragged Jackson and Garret out of bed before the sun came up. They boarded *The Black Rum* before daybreak, before the curious had a chance to show up and gawk.

With coffee in hand, Mitch stood on the deck as the boat swayed under his feet. He watched the sun come up standing between his brothers. The crystal clear sky indicated the weather would provide a perfect day of calm seas.

The blue water rippled onto shore. With each soft foamy whitecap he knew this was his element, the only thing that made sense in his life. The sea had always trumped any other type of relationship. It wasn't lost on

Mitch that he and his brothers had all chosen professions where the ocean played a huge part in their lives. No doubt the roots they'd formed in Indigo Key were deep and lasting, a testament to their upbringing.

If only Livvy could be here to echo that tribute. How had they reached this point? What could the Buchanan family have done to anyone that led them to searching the bay for something no one wanted to consider? Bodies. Remains. What sin could Walker have committed that would have brought down his entire family?

This early in the day, no one voiced those sentiments aloud. They didn't have to.

In Mitch's mind he had the best man at reading side scan sonar in Walsh. But his brother, Jackson, was no slouch in that regard either. As a tech geek, Jackson did more than dabble in his share of marine electronic gadgetry. An oceanographer was used to studying underwater terrain. Using advanced technology was part of the job. So detecting anomalies in the water should be a piece of cake for either man. Mitch just wasn't sure their vast experience covered locating submerged objects that contained bodies.

After getting the sonar wand over the side and into the water, Mitch sent Jackson and Garret to the nav station to join Walsh. The command center of the ship had a satellite system, Wi-Fi capability, VHF radios, two fixed, two hand-held, two Iridium satellite phones, an assortment of walkie-talkies, several laptop computers, a Navtex system, and a demodulator for pulling down weather forecasts and alerts.

In the closed quarters of the ship, Jackson stood next to a computer screen doing his part to finish off a pot of coffee. As if he'd read Mitch's thoughts, he sidestepped to the helm. "The good news is the bay isn't all that deep. The bad news is if I needed to get rid of bodies, I'd go out fifty, maybe sixty miles offshore, which puts us in the Atlantic, and dump them there. On that, I agree with Walsh."

Mitch ran a hand through his thick, longish hair. "Yeah, I would too, make sure I was far enough away from curious eyes not to get spotted."

Garret took a swig of coffee. "So where exactly does that leave us? Covering sixty miles out to sea is impractical and will likely take us into next year."

Jackson chewed the inside of his jaw. "We don't stop to explore every single object we see on the scan, only those that look manmade, anything that might hold a body or look like the shape of a body. Think of it like…"

"A treasure hunt," Mitch supplied. When he got a nasty glare from Garret, he lifted a shoulder. "Sorry. But we have a vast ocean and it's a great deal like looking for a needle in a haystack."

"Then where's our starting point?"

Jackson turned to look at Garret. "Good question. My vote is just before we reach the mouth of the bay, before it opens up to the truly deep part of the Atlantic, and then beyond that in a methodical grid. Guesswork aside, Anniston's working on getting us the GPS settings Walker used to take Ryan out fishing. That's a lot more definitive. But until then we scour the bay first on our way to the mouth."

As he always did, Mitch punched in coordinates into the ship's computer. But it occurred to him as they rolled through the water another issue loomed. He turned to Walsh. "What did you find out about the *Patagonia Pike*?"

His crew chief shrugged. "Not a thing. According to the chat rooms, the *Patagonia Pike* is still anchored in Puerto Nuevo."

"But we know that isn't true."

"Yeah. So what does that tell you? They're likely on the hunt for something big."

Mitch went to a laptop to pull up the Internet. "I don't understand what they could be looking for. I thought I knew all the hotspots offering the big prizes around the Keys, certainly any that would be large enough to bring

Dietrich's crew up from South America and this close to Indigo."

Walsh didn't hesitate. "Obviously they've discovered something we don't know about, something new."

"Or something old," Jackson amended. "Doesn't a pirate's fortune go back centuries?"

Walsh slapped him on the shoulder. "I may like the way you think yet."

"Wait until you've been around him longer than fifteen minutes," Garret offered. "I guarantee he'll eventually hit all your nerves."

"I grow on people," Jackson said evenly as he got back to the job of watching the monitor. That is, until Garret interrupted, complaining about the boredom.

"How do people stand being cooped up in these close quarters for weeks at a time? I know you did it in college aboard that research vessel. It would drive me up the wall if I had to do this on a daily basis. The bunks are too close together, the heads are too small, and the shower stalls are tiny."

Tired of listening to him whine, Jackson patted him on the back. "Now Sally, you could at least wait another hour before bitching again. I wondered if you'd be able to handle the claustrophobic environment. You like freedom and openness. Maybe that's why you surf like you were born in the water and the size of a wave doesn't faze you in the least."

"I'll handle the boat because I have to, but it wouldn't be my first choice of how to spend my day." Garret glanced at the screen, studied the colorful light and dark imaging. It all looked incredibly difficult to read. "So how are we doing? See anything of interest yet?"

Jackson hit a few keys to enhance the pictures. "All we have so far is a bunch of flat-line data. But then, we've only been out for a few hours." He checked another monitor, tapped the screen. "The thing is, the weather is about to change. We're not out of the rainy season yet. May to October it isn't unusual for a cloudburst to form around this time of day and it's not even noon. There's ominous weather forming. Clouds are coming in fast from the open sea. Looks like heavy rain will cut this voyage shorter than we thought."

Feeling edgier, Garret challenged, "It's just a little shower. We could still dive with a little drizzle spitting down on us."

Jackson gritted his teeth. "If it were drizzle I wouldn't have mentioned it. And if we'd found anything to prompt a dive, I might agree. But we haven't. This rainstorm looks like it might hold some punch. You want to rock on this tub in a storm, be my guest. But I'm voting for going in. As claustrophobic as you are, I would, too."

Walsh overheard the chatter and turned on Garret. "Save your bravado for when we find a target area. Now's not the time to buck a squall."

Garret appealed to Mitch for the final ruling. But Mitch deferred to Jackson and his crew chief. "We'll stay out until those clouds get closer, but as soon as the wind picks up, we're heading back to port."

While his sons looked to the sea for answers, down the street within view of the marina, Tanner prepared to carry out his own agenda.

As Tanner stood on the sidewalk looking at the Life Stone Church, he thought back to the first time Lenore had dragged him here. His Sunday mornings were meant for relaxing not for plopping his hardworking butt down on a hard pew in a stifling hot chapel and listening to Boone Dandridge lecture him on how best to live his life. He knew how to live, had done so for all of his adult life without interference from some preacher man.

But over the years that mule-headed attitude of his had morphed into something he looked forward to doing. What started out as an annoyance turned into years of devoted Sundays. He'd done everything he could to make sure the church continued its growth, all the while nurturing his spiritual side, a side he didn't even know he had. Not only that, he'd found good friends along the way.

Or so he'd thought.

Tanner rubbed the whiskers on his chin. He hadn't bothered to shave since Livvy went missing. If he had timed this visit right, this time of day, he hoped to catch Boone Dandridge in his office. Unless the preacher had altered his daily routine, Tanner fully expected to see the man huddled at his desk working on his next sermon.

For more than forty-eight hours, Tanner had stewed over Boone's email. He'd read the message more than twenty times. The idea that Boone's comments had influenced longtime friends to downplay Livvy's disappearance turning it into a frivolous trip infuriated him. For two days, he'd been mulling over how best to deal with what he saw as Boone's betrayal, not just the stabbing in the back aspect, but turning on parishioners. There were kids who attended Sunday school, who'd grown up in the church. If they couldn't depend on their pastor in a time of crisis then what was the point?

As always at this time of day, the double doors remained unlocked, the auditorium empty. He walked past the rows of pews, down the hall into Boone's paneled side office. Sure enough, he sat at his desk in shirtsleeves, minus his collar.

It took the preacher a minute to realize he was no longer alone. "Well, what brings you by?"

Before leaving the house, Tanner had printed out the email and slapped the paper down on Boone's desk. "This is what brings me here. I wanted to ask you man to man what you were thinking when you sent out this outlandish church-wide email suggesting Livvy and Walker took the kids on some whim of a trip without telling anyone? You obviously wrote this garbage the very same day you and your friends stood in my living room spouting the same thing. How could you poison everyone's mind that Livvy wanted to take off to visit every state in the union? How could you do such a thing? Your assumptions put a huge dent in the turnout we got for the search. Somehow I think that was your plan. What I can't figure out is why? Why would you deliberately misdirect the search and chip away at the foundation we built with the media, something we consider to be extremely important."

Tanner waited while Boone adjusted his glasses and stood up. "A search seemed rather silly. After her car was found at the airport, I made a judgment call. It's clear they took off. I'm sorry you don't see it that way. But it would be a waste of time for people to keep looking under every rock from here to the beach. The mayor happens to agree with me."

Tanner showed his teeth, repeated his outrage. "I don't care who agrees with you. It's wrong. I'm not sure what your game is, Boone, but when I find out, I'm standing up in front of the congregation and letting everyone know it. Let's see how long you keep your position here then. What you did to my family, to Livvy and Walker and to those kids is unforgivable. For years, they were regulars in your Sunday school class. Is that the way you treat loyal members of your flock?"

Clearly afraid, Boone's eyes darted around the room. "That isn't very Christian of you, Tanner."

"Right this second, I feel I'm more of a Christian than the man I'm staring at. Looking at you, I've discovered I don't have that much forgiveness inside me."

Boone attempted to calm the situation. "I understand this is difficult for you."

"What? What's difficult, Boone? That I'm unable to accept Livvy took a vacation? It's ridiculous. I do have one question for you, though. What have you gotten yourself into? What sleazy enterprise has Royce talked you into supporting this time?"

Boone acted insulted. "I don't know what you're talking about. I never kept my support of the golf course a secret. It would bring in a lot of money to the town from tourists who want to add that to their itinerary while they're down here."

"I'm not talking about the stupid golf course. If I find out your shady dealings includes hurting Livvy and my grandkids in any way, I'll enjoy making the drive to Raiford each week to see you behind bars."

"What?" Appalled, Boone came around the desk. "Now you're talking just plain crazy. I'd never hurt anyone, let alone Livvy and the children."

"So you say. We'll see, won't we?" Tanner leveled his finger in front of the pastor's face. "Just don't start counting the money you think you'll get quite yet. Sprawling megachurches tend to cost millions. Where do you plan to get that kind of money, Boone? Where? The congregation certainly isn't that wealthy. So whatever bargain you think you've made with the devil, think again."

Having said what was on his mind, Tanner spun on his heels and headed back outside. He didn't wait for Boone to make a mad dash to the phone and get in touch with his associates.

Rain had begun to fall, a downpour that soaked the lawns and sent streams of water flowing down the low-lying streets.

Walking back to his truck, he was so filled with rage the raindrops did nothing to cool off his fierce temper. In fact, Tanner Indigo felt dead inside at the betrayal he was sure was personal.

Chapter Seventeen

By day's end, the storm had turned into a soft rain. For some reason, the weather put Jackson in a foul mood. At least that was his excuse. Edgy and irritable, he'd snapped at a reporter who'd called wanting a comment about another sighting. This time Livvy and the kids had been spotted in Pensacola. Slamming the phone down in the guy's ear, he had to admit it wasn't all due to worry. Sexual frustration played a role in his ill temper.

Not one to sit around the house during the dreary evening, it was Garret's idea to fix his brother's state of mind. "I say we call Tessa, Raine, and Anniston, and get the women on board for an evening out, meet up for drinks or something. Take a break and try to recharge."

Jackson thought that sounded like a plan. "I'll call Tessa."

Mitch shook his head. "Someone other than me will have to let Raine know. If I do it, I doubt she'll even pick up."

"That's okay. Leave it to me. I'll take care of it," Garret offered.

Raine was a tough sell. But with Tessa and Anniston on his side, Garret was able to get all parties to agree to show up at a pub called A Lime in the Coconut. The bar offered happy hour specials, half price appetizers, and live music, just the atmosphere they needed for a breather.

Even though she'd agreed to go, after getting dressed and styling her hair, Tessa ended up the reluctant one. "I'm just not sure about this. It seems wrong to—"

"Enjoy yourself? Have fun for three hours?" Anniston finished. "Tessa, you deserve a night out. We all do. It won't make a bit of difference in the long run if you listen to some music and do your best to spend a few hours kicking back."

"She's right. It's one night," Raine concluded. "You've been keyed up for weeks. It's time to let your hair down and relax."

So after nudging her out the door Tessa was dismayed when they reached the bar. There on one of the streetlamps were the remains of two missing posters—one for the Buchanans and one for Ryan. The paper had been taped to the metal, but the wind had ripped the fringes to a frayed edge and the rain had ruined most of the images.

As her friends pushed through the door, Tessa decided the flyers would have to be replaced. The sight was enough of a reminder that it took almost all the rum in the first hurricane drink she ordered before the buzz set in.

Once the alcohol rushed through her system, it felt good to be out doing something so normal. Having drinks with these new friends was like a nice boost, an extra bonus, a reward for all the anxiety she'd experienced.

The men had already gathered around a table as far away from the band as they could get. But it was impossible to escape the walls reverberating with the beat. Any attempt at conversation had to be either a shout over the noise, or a must-whisper, right next to the other person's ear.

Since the place was packed, three-deep at the bar and every table taken, the noise was deafening. Mitch had given most of his crew, except the one stuck pulling guard duty, a night off. He and Walsh were taking turns buying drinks—the bunch determined to blow off a little steam.

With that in mind, Raine had promised to practice a détente of sorts with her old flame. As long as Mitch agreed not to say anything to piss her off, she planned to have a perfectly lovely evening.

Mitch on the other hand had no intentions of walking on eggshells. To prove it, he came back to the table just to see if he could get a rise out of her. He pointed to an arcade game near the restrooms. "Remember Alien Starfighter? As I recall I beat you nine straight times one Saturday afternoon at Mac Perkell's game center."

"That's not how I remember it. The Plagar warriors ate you alive. I'm the one who fought hard to get myself back to the ship in deep space and out of the clutches of the enemy."

In the background Jackson heard the good-natured clash from the past ramp up. But in truth, he had eyes only for the vision sitting across from him. Tessa. She'd worn a festive fluted skirt with a bright floral print that revealed long, feminine legs and a lacy voile tank in soft cream that showed off lean, toned arms. He stared at her sandals and the bare toes tipped with pale blue nail polish.

Tessa glanced over at Jackson, caught those deep toffee eyes staring at her. Her belly warmed. She was pretty sure it wasn't from the spiced rum. "What are you thinking?"

In a measured move, he picked up his pint of dark ale, never letting his eyes off hers. "That's a loaded question. I'm not sure you want to know."

She could've easily guessed by the feral look in his eyes. "Hmm, the question is what do we plan to do about all this extra heat between us?"

"That's why you don't want to know."

"Maybe I do."

The flirting had him leaning in to whisper in her ear. "Want to know what's on my mind? We need a bed and an evening to ourselves. How's that for honesty?"

"My thoughts exactly. How long are we required to put in an appearance tonight?"

"Long enough so that when the place starts rockin' we'll be able to sneak out of here without anyone missing us. Want another one of those girlie drinks?"

She held up her souvenir glass with the bar's logo. "This? It's yummy. And the pineapple has to be good for you, right? But I'll pass on having a second one. I'd like to be fully functional when we…"

"Hit the sheets?" He grinned. "I'm all for fully functional."

A pre-wedding party wandered in from the mainland and crammed into what little space there was left. At the bride-to-be's request the band started their set with a version of *Into the Mystic*.

"I always liked this song," Jackson said, capturing her hand and leading her out to the overcrowded dance floor. Their bodies bumped, close contact the only option.

She linked her arms around his neck, breathed in his scent, a fragrance that reminded her of verdant forests full of sandalwood and cedar. It made her want to nibble him all over.

They circled and swayed, wrapped around each other, only a breath apart. His hands wandered to her hips. Hers roamed up his back.

The band changed tunes. The lead singer took a stab at the haunting, soulful melody *Peeling off the Layers*.

She let him nibble her ear, her neck, her lips. He felt her relax and knew the minute she surrendered to the moment and the music. Her soft, sweet mouth encouraged him to plunder and take.

All Tessa remembered was floating on the promise of what was to come. Caught up, they drifted without ever moving from their little corner of the dance floor. It would've been nice if they'd had the place all to themselves. But that only happened in fairy tales. She closed off the others and pretended they were the only two people in the world. She'd never leaned toward fantasy. But if this happened to be as close as she ever got, she'd take her Cinderella moment in a dive bar in the arms of this man any day.

The tender theme went off course to a faster beat as *Give it Away* pounded from the stage. The floor full of dancers erupted in a flash mob frenzy. Bodies moved in rhythm, grinding and spinning, thrusting to the beat. When the song drifted into *Nothin' But a Good Time*, the wild throng switched to a chain of down and dirty, flaying arms and fast feet.

The rock atmosphere, humid as a sauna, became unbearably close, the air hot and stale.

Jackson finally gave up bumping elbows with the horde and snatched her hand. He dragged her outside to an overhang that protected them from the drizzle still spitting out of the clouds. Breathing in the cooler air helped him get over the stuffy confines of the bar. But when he turned to catch how flushed Tessa's face looked, how the streetlight made her eyes dance, he decided the wait had to be over. It was time to act, no more coming up with excuses. The next words out of her mouth told him she felt the same way.

"Where do you suggest we go?"

"I know a place," Jackson stated as lightning sliced across the night sky, just before the crack of thunder rumbled overhead.

"Is it far?"

"It's down the street."

"You're kidding? Not that I'm picky at this point but I hope you aren't suggesting we do this at Raine's house."

"There's an idea, but no. I'll go get the truck."

She stuck her hand out from underneath the canopy, palm up. "It's barely coming down. We could walk if it's nearby. I don't mind the mist."

He cupped her face. "That just makes me want to be with you all the more." He took her by the hand and dragged her around the corner and down Waterfront Street until he stopped in front of a beachfront bungalow with a for sale sign in the yard.

Though the house was painted seashell-white, Tessa noted someone must've been fond of the color red. The shutters and front door were bright crimson. And it had a Spanish-tiled roof. She would've described it as looking a lot like a dollop of whipped cream with a cherry on top. The spindled, hand carved balustrades gave it a rural touch. But if Spanish Colonial architecture and farmhouse rustic ever came together to have a baby, it would've been this house. Somehow old world artisan had ended up in the middle of a seaside postcard.

She studied the flowerbeds and decided someone had been watering the honeysuckle and taking care of the cheerful gerbera daisies and purple periwinkles. "Whose house is this?"

Jackson stepped up on the wide covered porch and bent down to reach the mat, brought out the front door key. "This place belonged to my grandmother. My dad decided to put it on the market after she died last spring. But I don't think he has any intentions of letting it leave the family. He's turned down several offers."

Tessa stared at the porch swing and decided this was the most perfect little house she'd ever seen.

Jackson flipped on the lights to reveal a total remodel. "It's tiny, less than eight hundred square feet." He cocked a brow. "But it's fully furnished which means it has a bed. Are we still doing this?"

She latched on to a handful of his shirt, pulled his mouth a breath from hers. "What do you think?"

"I like a woman who knows what she wants."

Eager mouths sought each other. Her fingers explored his hard body and reached to find the skin under his shirt. She used her teeth to nip along his throat, her tongue to trace a trail down his chest.

"You keep doing that and I won't last another minute." He turned the tables, shoving his hands roughly under her top. He nipped his way along her throat and downward, found the shape and feel of her breasts as intoxicating as the booze had been at the bar. His fingers wandered down to frame her ass. As they latched onto each other, he picked her up and hauled her down the hallway.

He plopped her on her feet when they reached the first doorway and shoved into the room, banging the door back against the wall. They stumbled inside, toeing off shoes, fumbling with buttons, clawing at each other's clothes.

She tore at his shirt, ripped the zipper down on his jeans. "This was a really good idea."

"The best," he muttered, yanking off her top, then working her skirt down before spinning her around. He covered her mouth, grazed down her jaw. They tumbled to the mattress in a whirl of urgency. The need winged up, sailed into the electric air on a beam and a shimmer.

He ran a thumb under the front clasp of her bra, used his teeth and tongue to send her into a mad rush to mate. He moved lower to find silk and satin and tugged it down her narrow hips.

Arousal whipped through her like a sudden squall at sea. She felt his hands begin a journey down her body and leaned her head back to enjoy every junket the trip had to offer. Need flashed and roared up in crests and waves, each one bigger than before.

He watched as those jewel sapphire eyes glazed over. Moving above her, he captured each lazy taste with his mouth. The free fall came with a shudder, a sigh. Her body exploded with a thousand sensations on a swirl of greater longing.

The troubled previous weeks and the stress fell away replaced by a rush of wild abandon.

Wanting more, she reversed their positions and shoved him back on the bed. Straddling him, she stoked the fire with her mouth, running her teeth along his muscled shoulders.

Where they'd hurried before, this was a slow mating, reaching, building to that ultimate rapture. Washed in adrenaline, she bent her head, clamped onto his lips in a crushing kiss. She rode him then, rocking fast and hard. Stretching out the buildup, she helped herself to all he was willing to give her.

They arched together, pumped hot, driven by a fierce hunger. They glided toward the edge, carved through each urgent layer, matching stroke for stroke. Greedy thrusts brought them to the same frantic wonder. Release came on a ribbon of pleasure, a starry whirl of delight.

Bathed in radiant afterglow, still tangled as one, Jackson somehow found the energy to roll, the weight of his body now on hers. His teeth nipped her lips as he dropped down beside her, stroked a hand down her back. Relishing the soft, wet feel of her skin, he told her, "You took everything out of me."

"I'll take that as a compliment." In the warmth of knowing they'd truly satisfied each other, she cuddled under his chin.

He dipped his head to kiss her hair, that messy mass that made him want to rake his fingers through the tangles. "I'm pretty sure we hit every critical high point there is to hit. Give me thirty minutes and I'll be able to do it again."

A giggle escaped. She ran a trimmed nail down his chest. "We have all night to play. It's heavenly having a place all to ourselves."

"It is. I should've thought of this sooner."

She shook her head, leaned over to plant a kiss on his mouth. "The timing is perfect tonight. I'm glad we waited until now. At first, we shoved a lot of things in the corner, but now we've dealt with it all to get to this point, to get to here."

"We deserve here."

"That's what I'm thinking."

A few minutes later she heard the sound of soft snoring next to her and realized Jackson had dozed off. So another round would have to wait, she mused. For a few minutes she watched him sleep. But her mind still raced after the rush of sweaty sex.

Restless, unable to settle, her body still revved with those sensations, Tessa shoved out of bed. Without a robe, she put back on her skirt and top, padded down the hallway over the maple plank floors to the bathroom.

When she swung open the door she was surprised to see marble and rich wood tones, plenty of floor to ceiling crannies and storage spaces. The focal point was the glass shower with a frameless door and the beautiful tilework beyond. Done in creamy white it was accented with amber glass and a splash of bronze.

After using the john, she wandered through the rooms and found the house larger than it looked. The palest of blue paint was like a theme, carried out in each area and making the spaces feel open and airy. From front door to back, she inspected each little niche and nook.

She went in search of bottled water, flicked on the light in the kitchen—and decided this room was her favorite. It'd been completely redone with white cabinets, stainless steel appliances, and a farmhouse sink. Opening the fridge, she found it empty, not even a can of pop. But there were dishes in the cupboard so she ran water from the tap and filled up a glass.

Leaning against the counter, she admired the hand-painted Talavera tiles in beachy colors used as a backsplash. The design had Lenore written all over it. The style made her smile as she imagined Jackson's mother putting her personal touches on the project. There was a little island built from a honey walnut wood that held pots and pans. She could see Tanner marking up the plans and building it himself.

But what made the room really rock were all the plants. It looked like an indoor greenhouse the cook could enjoy while prepping dinner. Under a bank of windows on the side wall grew plants and herbs—even a lemon tree. The greenery gave the room an atrium feel, a peaceful Zen quality—quite a tribute to Jackson's late grandmother.

Out of curiosity she went to the back door, flipped the switch, flooding the yard in garlands of light. The sight took her breath away. The gardens were lush and sectioned off in landscaped pathways and raised planter boxes, and urns that stood five feet tall. She recognized vines of climbing honeysuckle, walls of wisteria, and swirls of succulent rhipsales.

And that was what she could make out in the shadows. She couldn't wait to see it in brilliant daylight. Maybe she'd talk Jackson into eating breakfast out here in the morning.

Reluctantly she cut the light out and tiptoed to the front door, letting herself out onto the porch. The drizzle had stopped. But the rain had left its mark. The earthy scent on the air, the smell wafting from the marina, made her think of new beginnings.

She went over to the swing, wiped the seat with her hand to test for dampness. Finding it dry enough, she took a seat where she could take in the night sounds of the harbor and listen to the waves slapping against the shore some twenty yards away. The eaves still dripped lazily with a soft trickle of runoff. She breathed in the humid air laced with magnolia and jasmine.

To her, the weather seemed more like summertime than fall. It was so unlike her native North Carolina, which could dip into the fifties this time of year and get downright cold during the winter months.

She glanced up, and for the second time that night, found Jackson watching her. She returned his stare and smiled. He'd put on jeans but hadn't zipped or buttoned them up. He hadn't bothered with underwear either. She could see tufts of pubic hair in the gap. His bare chest glistened in a stream of moonlight and made her mouth water. The man looked like he belonged on the cover of *Hunk Daily*.

"What are you doing out here?"

"You got me all stirred up. I couldn't sleep."

He gave her a sleepy, sexy grin and held out his hand. "Come back to bed, Tessa."

When her heart fluttered in her chest, a couple of beats too fast, she realized she'd already fallen hard and wasn't sure what to do about it. But denying this night wasn't part of the deal. She got up and went to him, slid her arms around his waist. She tiptoed up so her lips would reach his ear. Using her teeth, she nipped at his neck. "Take me back to bed, Jackson."

Tessa woke, washed in sunlight. She lifted her head, squinted into the glare and realized she was tangled in the sheets alone. She heard sounds coming from the kitchen and assumed Jackson was fixing her breakfast. Although what he'd used for food she couldn't imagine. She tried to remember the last time anyone had poured her a bowl of cereal.

She was getting dressed when he appeared in the doorway holding a tray with a decanter of coffee, two cups, and two plates filled with scrambled eggs and toast.

"Good morning, sleepyhead."

"Where on earth did you get the food?"

"I got up early and went to the market. It's just down the corner. I had to have coffee. How about breakfast in bed?"

Her lips bowed up. "As great as that sounds, and believe me it sounds wonderful because I don't remember anyone ever giving me breakfast in bed before, I have a better idea. The garden out back…"

"Ah, say no more. Follow me."

They backtracked down the hallway and through the kitchen. She ran to open the back door ahead of him and watched while Jackson set the tray down on a round table under a weeping cherry tree. For a moment, they stood together letting the gentle sea breeze dance across their faces. The clear blue sky didn't hold a hint of last night's storm.

It took Tessa several long seconds to come out of her daze. She lifted her head to take in the beauty of it all, staring at what she'd missed last night. Someone had built a trellis out of an old cedar fence and used it to create a place for yellow roses to bud and thrive. Tall, ornate windows had been arranged to form an open-air greenhouse that provided an arbor for the bountiful hydrangeas. The trumpet vines were arranged just so to attract the ruby-throated hummingbirds. The sweet smell of gardenia had her turning in a circle to make sure she didn't miss anything. "Who did all this?"

Jackson poured two mugs of coffee, handed one off. "My grandmother before she became ill. And then later, my mom and dad couldn't stand to see it turn into a weed lot. They put in sweat equity for all this upkeep. It was so much work we all wondered how my seventy-five-year-old grandmother was able to do it in the first place."

She stuck her nose in a patch of sweet-smelling lilies. "I think I know. This kind of garden takes a love of the soil, a passion for growing things that supersedes everything else. Your grandmother obviously put her heart and soul into making this her own peaceful getaway in her own backyard, steps from her kitchen. Not everyone has this kind of vision, or patience, or the green thumb to make it happen."

Tessa ran her hand along a teak chair and an old table, both time-honored pieces weathered with age. "Your grandmother thought of everything. She created a spot just for reading and relaxing. I've never seen anything quite so lovely. It's like a scene out of a movie set. Imagine how long it took for her to carve out this sea of tranquility with flowers and greenery."

Captivated at her reaction, he took hold of her hand, brought it to his lips and kissed the palm. "I'm sure my nana would be pleased you see her talent. Your eggs are getting cold."

Her lips curved up. "Why do I get the impression I'm giving you the perfect opening to make fun of me?"

"Not me. But I'm often blown away by the female response to flowers."

"This is not simply about flowers. It's art. You have only to spend time in her kitchen to see she had a way with plants." She finally took a seat at the table, dug into the meal. But she continued to look around, to breathe in the fragrant backdrop. "I wish we didn't have to leave. I can't imagine walking out here every day. It makes me ashamed I live in a condo that has a tiny balcony not even big enough to hold a row of clay pots. My place looks more like a soulless entity with no character whatsoever, a cookie cutter environment."

"I have to admit I sometimes feel that way when I look out the windows in my loft. The view is all concrete and steel. A few times I've caught myself hoping I'd glance out and get a glimpse of Sugar Bay, longing for the slower pace back home. Do you miss Nags Head?"

"I suppose I do. But right now, I'm caught up in the tropical locale of the Florida Keys. Plus, it's more laid back. I certainly see why Ryan was drawn to coming here."

He squeezed her hand. "I think somewhere along the way I've forgotten my roots."

"It's easy enough to do." She stood up to carry the dishes back into the kitchen. At the sink, he came up behind her, all hands and tongue. Without protest from her, he drew her back down the hallway into the bedroom.

They didn't leave the cottage until almost ten. By that time, *The Black Rum* had already left port several hours earlier without him. So Jackson improvised by paying Paulie Gruden to motor out and deliver him to the boat.

As soon as he boarded, he knew he was in for a good-natured ribbing from his brothers. But he didn't expect the murmurs and whispers from the crew, namely Walsh.

He had to go past Walsh to get to the helm. "You're late, lover boy. You get lucky last night?"

"Dock my pay. And it's none of your business."

Walsh ripped out a snort of laughter. His eyes glistened with merriment. "Oh, to be in your shoes. I've known a redhead or two, fierce tempers. She's a lovely woman that Tessa. If you break her heart I'll whomp you into dirt."

Jackson moved on without a word. It was Mitch and Garret who followed him to the bridge, all questions. "Where'd you two disappear to last night?"

Garret pretended to stick a microphone in front of Jackson's face using a bottle of water. "The more important question on everyone's mind is what happened after you left the bar? We need details. As if we didn't already know but if you could give us the big picture."

"Get back to work," Jackson muttered.

"Not a chance," Mitch said. "At least it isn't that cold fish from work you've been trying to turn into a human being for so long."

Jackson finally looked up. "Nope. That's over and done with. I sent Rachel a text."

Garret's eyes winked in surprise. "You broke up with her via text? That's cold, bro, even for me. You ask me, it was about time, though."

"Under the circumstances I thought it appropriate. Rachel hasn't once asked me about Livvy and the kids or how my family's handling this thing since I've been here."

"Does she even know you have a sister?" Mitch asked, studying his charts.

"Who knows? Who cares? Rachel's history."

"That's good news since she never once saw fit to come down here for a single family holiday event in all the time you two were dating," Mitch pointed out.

"I wouldn't call what they were doing dating," Garret pointed out. "More like a version of *Sex in the City*." He couldn't resist the urge to harsh Jackson's mellow even more. "So now you're banging the vulnerable gorgeous redhead? That's a nice step up from the cold fish."

"Grow up," Jackson snarled. "I'm entitled to a personal life."

"Hey, don't bite my head off. Sheesh, you'd think getting laid would help your disposition a little. It always makes me feel better."

Ribbing aside, Jackson fired back, "Is that so? Is that why you're hot for the detective but not getting any?"

Garret raised a brow but took the comment in stride. "Hey, give me time and we'll talk. Remember, you have a couple days head start with Tessa. At least I don't piss Anniston off, not nearly as often as Mitch does Raine."

Jackson's mouth cracked wide with a grin, getting into the spirit of the put-downs. "Yeah, he probably needs to work on that. Maybe one day he'll share why she hates his guts so much."

Mitch finally looked up from his maps, a gleam in his eye. "We can only hope. Maybe one day Raine will clue me in on the seeds of the grudge she carries. When that happens, I'll be sure to send out an email blast."

Chapter Eighteen

Their third meeting with Anniston got underway that night inside the Indigo house after dinner. In lieu of any other place, Lenore's dining room had been dubbed the "war room."

While Raine and Tessa served coffee and cut Lenore's lemon tarts into squares, Garret finished cleaning up the dining room table while his brothers took turns adding plates to the dishwasher.

Once space on the table opened up, Anniston spread out her notes. "I know everyone's had a long day but I hope you guys stay awake because we have a lot to cover." She turned to Tessa first. "The lab report came back. They found a tiny speck of blood on the medical alert bracelet.

The dot of DNA belonged solely to Ryan. We know that because you provided them a sample for comparison. It didn't match up with an unknown donor. So that's a wash."

Tessa groaned in frustration. "Because that small amount of blood could've gotten there while Ryan reeled in a fish. I'm way ahead of you."

The detective held up a hand. "Exactly. I can see it now. A defense attorney would argue that Ryan could've caught his finger on a hook or something and left that dot of blood. The problem is I don't know how it got there and neither do you. Speculation is all we have. I'm still keeping an open mind."

Anniston directed her attention to the Indigos. "Next, it's about Livvy's minivan. Unlike releasing the house, which the authorities feel is not an integral part of the investigation, Tampa Bay PD is keeping the vehicle in impound. I doubt you'll be getting it back any time soon, if at all. According to my source, they're in the process of Luminol testing the interior. I've also been told that the investigator in that jurisdiction has gone over three-fourths of the available security tapes inside and outside the Tampa Airport."

Garret swore under his breath. "Where everyone believes they hopped on a plane to paradise."

For a brief moment Anniston flicked a glance at the surfer. What was annoyance at first morphed into patience. "I don't believe a trip ever took place. The minivan might've been found at the airport, but the Buchanan family never got on a plane. Tampa Bay PD is convinced of that. They checked all the major airlines and all the charter jets that flew out of there within the time frame in question. Their conclusion is that Livvy and Walker never bought tickets to go anywhere, certainly didn't use their credit cards to do it. They never got on a plane, at least not out of that airport. Unless they flew off in a private jet with cash, there's no indication they left on their own."

Garret felt the need to follow up. "Jackson already checked with every pilot that flies out of the airfield here. No plane is unaccounted for. They didn't leave Indigo Key from there."

Anniston shuffled her notes and looked directly at Lenore first and then at Tanner. She glanced at Garret, gave him an indication of what she was about to say. "I want all of you to know how much I hate having to tell you this. But I don't want to ever mislead you in any way during this investigation. I feel very strongly that Livvy and Walker and the kids met with foul play. I've taken a second tour of the house where I spent about two hours trying to figure things out. I'm convinced that whatever happened started there."

"So you disagree with Hawkins?" Jackson asked.

"I do. I'll tell you why. I think someone either showed up at the house, late, or called in the middle of the night, which can be verified with phone records. I'm waiting to spring that request on Hawkins at the right time. But either way, the knock at the door or the phone call woke Walker and Livvy up and for whatever reason got them out of bed, which prompted them to get the kids out of bed. The house is so clean and tidy, it makes the phone call more probable. Why Walker and Livvy dragged the kids out of bed at that point, I haven't yet figured out. Nor have I come up with what happened next. Keep in mind my theory is subject to change depending on what else pops up on the radar." She looked from face to face and saw nothing but bitter disappointment. "I know it isn't much but…"

Jackson interrupted with an explanation. "It isn't that, it's a starting point. But Tessa said something to me the other night that resonated. What if these people did call and demand that Livvy and Walker meet them at the business? They lured them out of the house on some pretense."

"That's a possibility. The two parties intersected somewhere. Now, I have other news." Anniston turned to Tessa and Raine. "You guys had the right idea about the affair. You just weren't looking in the right place. The woman's name is Harlow Ellerbee and she's no stripper. In fact, she's a Miami corporate lawyer, a high-powered one at that. She's also been married for seven years to one of the partners."

Hearing that, Jackson's hands clenched into a fist. "So Walker *was* having an affair?"

"He was indeed, for almost a year."

"That son of a bitch," Tanner growled. "I wish I'd bashed some sense into his ornery head last Christmas."

Anniston sent the family a measured, sympathetic look. "I'd say looking at Walker's credit card statements that's where most of his debt came from. It seems Ms. Ellerbee has expensive tastes. Very. Whenever Walker could slip away, the two of them dined at the best restaurants, frequented several high-end boutiques, and often spent their afternoons tucked away inside a favorite five-star hotel where they indulged in ordering room service. Walker also bought Ms. Ellerbee an expensive tennis bracelet worth about two grand and a diamond ring that set him back almost ten."

Jackson whistled through his teeth. "And to think he spent a third of that on the ring he gave to the future mother of his kids."

Garret rubbed his chin. "Uh, question. How exactly did you come by Walker's credit card statements?"

Anniston grinned. "Once the state police cleared the Vitamin Hut as a no crime zone, I sweet-talked Jessup Sinclair into letting me inside to take a peek."

Jackson leaned back in his chair. "I don't understand why Sinclair would allow that. If we think he had a hand in some conspiracy or that he's in league with Buchanan, why would he let you in the shop to look around?"

"I asked nicely and your police chief agreed. Again, his cooperation forces me to keep an open mind."

Garret wasn't so bighearted. "I suppose Sinclair would have to keep up appearances without tipping his hand that he's gone over to the dark side. So what happened once you got in?"

"From that point, it was a simple matter of rummaging through Walker's desk to find what I wanted. No way was the cheating bastard going to keep that kind of telltale evidence around for the wife to find, even in his man cave. Sure enough I found his stash of receipts in a lock box in the bottom drawer of his desk at the business. And before you ask, I jimmied the lock."

Garret laid a hand on his chest. "A girl after my own heart."

"We'll see about that," Anniston teased. "But guys, there's more to this part of the puzzle that you need to focus on. This affair was not serious. I talked to Harlow Ellerbee over the phone for about an hour. She readily admitted to the cheating part, but adamantly denied that the two of them were planning to leave their respective spouses. According to her, Walker was a distraction. They were just fooling around, having fun meeting up whenever they could find the time. I couldn't find any evidence that Walker had any plans to divorce your sister. Harlow claims she never encouraged him to do so."

"And you believe that?" Jackson asked. "I don't."

Anniston cut her eyes to the oldest brother. "And that's your prerogative. But I go where the evidence takes me, not from some personal grudge. No doubt Walker cheated, but unless I can find something concrete that tells me Walker did away with your sister and then took off with the kids, I'm forced to consider that your brother-in-law has become a victim along with Livvy and the children."

Tessa spoke up. "But Walker still could have done something to Ryan."

"Another example of why I need to keep my options open." Anniston put a hand on Tessa's shoulder. "Thanks to you accessing your brother's email account, it jumpstarted my getting to read the correspondence between him and Walker and how he ended up agreeing to the fishing trip. You have to give it to Ryan. He agreed to come down here with what really constitutes trusting a total stranger. Ryan had only known Walker through an online business relationship, a tenuous thread for sure. For such limited contact, Ryan put a great deal of trust in Walker. Somehow I think Walker betrayed that trust."

Anniston took out several sheets of paper from her computer bag. "Since accessing Ryan's cell phone records, it gives me a window into his whereabouts while he was here, times his cell phone pinged from which towers."

"There aren't that many cell towers on this island," Garret pointed out.

"True, but it's still essential to pinpoint where Ryan was in town and at what time of day. Once my tech guy gets the last known hit, which translates to the carrier getting us the most recent information, he'll lay out that roadmap I was talking about earlier." She handed one of the pages off to Tessa. "You pretty much already know the basics. Bottom line is that Ryan spent a lot of time with Walker. There are text messages and phone calls between the two men for four straight days before the activity comes to a complete stop. As you can see there are several calls from another number not belonging to Walker or Livvy with a 305 area code. I called that number and discovered it's no longer working, which adds to the mystery and something else my tech guy will try to track down."

Tessa let out a heavy sigh. "So another dead end."

"Not at all. Each day we find out another piece of the puzzle."

"You have more patience at this than I do," Tessa noted.

"That's why you guys are paying me the big bucks. Plus, I forwarded the emails and the phone records to my dad and brother in case I missed anything. It never hurts to have a second pair of eyes go over the information. They do agree with me that Ryan coming here is what kicked this whole thing into high gear." Just as she heard the beginnings of a protest from Tessa, she turned and pointed a finger. "That doesn't mean your brother did anything wrong or illegal."

"Maybe he stumbled onto something wrong or illegal," Tessa proffered. "I still don't understand why we can't locate his car."

Anniston waved a hand in the air toward Mitch. "We have among us one of the best treasure hunters in the world. So says the online biosphere that keeps track of such things."

Mitch sat with his arms crossed over his chest, unimpressed at the praise. He leveled his gaze on Anniston. "I'm hardly the best. However, the owner of the *Patagonia Pike* is a different story. That man and his crew have deep pockets. They routinely do everything to keep the competition out of Argentine waters. They'll do anything to keep a dive secret and won't share in the take even when it comes to getting sued by government entities with rightful claims. Werner Dietrich simply digs in his heels for the long haul with his staff of lawyers and drags it out in court for as long as it takes. Now Dietrich and his salvage vessel are here in the Keys. You need to do all you can to find out why."

Before Anniston could reply, Raine stared at Mitch trying to better understand. "Are you suggesting the ship being here in port has something to do with Livvy and Walker going missing?"

Mitch held out his two hands, brought them together until they touched in an upside down V. "It's rare that circumstances line up to form the perfect storm. It doesn't happen but every hundred years or so." He stopped and searched out Tessa. "Ryan's disappearance kicks this off in some way, but flies under the radar for weeks." He turned back to answer Raine's question. "That is, until a family of four also disappears. Think about it. Nothing much happens in this sleepy little town for decades and then…pow! It's beyond a fluke."

Anniston made some notes on a legal pad before stuffing it into her bag. "Before I head out, does anyone else have anything to add?"

Tanner blurted out, "Boone's hiding something."

Lenore put her hands on her hips and stared at her husband. "You confronted him today, didn't you? Even though I specifically told you not to because of what Anniston said. What happened to nothing leaves this house? That's where you went when you took off this afternoon, isn't it?"

A hangdog look crossed Tanner's face. With his admission, he replayed the skirmish with Boone and the pastor's reaction. "Now, don't go getting all upset. He pissed me off. I had to do something. If you think I'd let that asshole smear Livvy's name by turning something as serious as this into a joke suggesting she's taken off, you don't know me very well."

"Oh, I know you all right, never could talk a lick of sense into your hard head."

Tanner raised his voice. "So you think it's just fine that Boone Dandridge practically singlehandedly took it upon himself to call off the search like he did?"

"No. I don't think it's right," Lenore shouted right back. "In fact, I think what he did is despicable, unexplainable, and downright mean. Ever since she turned eighteen Livvy's taught a Sunday school class there, showed up with the croup one year, the flu the next. I don't understand how Boone could turn on her and Walker like that. But he did." Lenore threw up her hands. "But what's done is done. Doesn't make what you did right, though."

Jackson got up to walk the floor, jingling the loose change in the pockets of his cargo shorts. "If Dad confronted Boone, then maybe one of us should do the same with Jessup Sinclair, find out once and for all whose side he's on."

"I'll do it," Garret offered.

"No, I think Anniston should do it," Tessa suggested. "It's gotta be her. I don't think any of us could detach enough emotionally to approach the subject with him without blowing up. I know I couldn't. It has to be just the right amount of edge along with a pleasant delivery so it doesn't piss him off."

"She's right," Anniston said. "I did get him to let me in the Vitamin Hut. I could have a sit down with him and tiptoe around the subject."

Jackson tried for a grin. "Now see, I was thinking just a plain ol' confrontation would work. Getting in his face would be more enjoyable."

"It's been my experience that kind of confrontation with a cop usually ends badly. And no one in this family should end up in jail or create a public display that the media could use to turn against our cause." Anniston purposely stared at Tanner. "I know you meant well, but there's nothing we have that proves the pastor did anything wrong."

"Give it time. It'll surface," Tanner promised.

Chapter Nineteen

At the Mainsail Lodge, Anniston ran downstairs to take advantage of the generous breakfast buffet the hotel offered before time ran out. Keeping it casual, she threw on a pair of shorts and a pullover hoodie. When she reached the dining area there were a few late risers, but for the most part, she enjoyed the solace of a quiet place to think.

She helped herself to the serving trays, piling her plate high with plenty of protein and carbs to get her through the day. After all, she had a mission to complete.

She found a table and contemplated the best approach to Jessup Sinclair. Exploring the top cop's devotion to his job and finding out where his loyalties were with the Indigos was a tricky tightrope to walk.

When a shadow fell across her spot, she glanced up to see Garret scooting into the extra chair to join her.

Garret decided she looked like an exotic dark violet blooming on a sunny windowsill, basking in the morning light. "Whatcha got there, Anniston?"

He picked up a piece of bacon from her plate and started nibbling it to a nub. "I stayed here a couple times. They go all out for breakfast. My favorite is always the waffles, especially the ones they whip up for Sunday brunch. You know the kind stuffed with pecans, or piled high with blueberries, or fresh strawberries."

"What are you doing here?"

"Looking for a pretty face to make my morning."

"Does that line generally get you laid?"

Garret grinned. "You'd be surprised. How'd you get a name like Anniston, anyway?"

She resigned herself to chatty conversation. "My grandmother, on my mama's side, was born in Anniston, Georgia, 1925. She met my granddad when she was still in high school. Crazy kids ran off and got married at sixteen, started having kids within the year."

"Young love. I can't even imagine being tied down at that age."

"Most of us can't. But it was a different era. Couples did that kind of thing all the time. When I came along Mama stuck with the name. I get asked about it all the time." She picked up her fork, laid a napkin across her lap. "What are you doing here?" she repeated.

"Okay, no more small talk. I'll level with you. I'm wondering if you're overwhelmed yet." He could see that friendly twinkle in her eyes vanish and the deep brown flash red-hot. He held up a hand. "No need to blow a fuse. People—mostly named Indigo—keep piling stuff on your plate. Your to-do list is a mile long. I'm worried you're getting sidetracked."

Her initial reaction was to punch him in that pretty mouth of his. But then she noticed the real concern on his face. "I have a quick Italian temper and I'm not afraid to use it. I don't much like it when anyone questions my ability to do my job."

"Me? Not at all. My family? No way. You impressed the hell out of everyone. Just don't underestimate who and what you're dealing with."

"What *am* I dealing with?"

"Someone who didn't think twice about taking two kids out of their beds at night and doing God knows what to them."

Anniston's anger evaporated. "You Indigos don't hold anything back, do you? You're a passionate bunch. When we solve this thing, I'd hate to be on the receiving end of your wrath. You pool that fury and direct it toward those who took Livvy and the kids, and I almost feel sorry for them."

It warmed him to know she saw that ardent bent in the people he loved. "I never thought of us as tightknit until this past week. Although we have knocked heads since we've been here."

She waved a hand in the air. "That? My family gets together and it's like a free-for-all. We have two volumes, loud and louder, two emotions, intense and zealous."

He'd bet his bank account he could bring out both and would enjoy every second of the effort. "Then you know how this will likely play. My parents are good people, rock solid. But they aren't as convinced that Livvy is coming back as you might think. They're vulnerable. The armor plating isn't as thick as people would like to believe."

It suddenly hit Anniston what he meant. "You're scared."

"Damn straight I am. And you should be, too. I know you promised Tessa and Jackson that you'd feel out Sinclair and try to get a barometer on his good guy, bad guy persona. But don't take that old man lightly."

"Police corruption is nothing new to me," Anniston pointed out. "I'm no longer that raw recruit straight out of the academy."

"No, you aren't. And you're good at research. Use it now to get a handle on the guy before you go to his office."

"Why don't you just tell me?"

"I could do that. But how much of it would you really take at face value?"

"Good point." She tilted her head to study him. "You're more than a pretty face."

"Gee thanks. Now eat. Don't let your eggs get cold. I hate eating them like that. Yuck."

She gave him a half-laugh and dug in. "Something else on your mind."

"You get a good read on people. It would help us a lot if we had the GPS settings Walker used to take Ryan out fishing. It would narrow down the location to a precise spot. Any chance of obtaining those coordinates?"

"There are only so many favors I can call in at a time. I'm working up to that one. I know I promised the information but…"

"What if we snuck on board the *Misty Dawn* and downloaded the info ourselves?"

"Garret, I won't be a party to something like that. I might lose my license."

"Totally understand. But I don't have a license to lose. Neither does Jackson or Mitch."

"Please, don't do anything stupid and get caught. It would just complicate things."

"No need to worry. If I ever give up surfing, I'd make an excellent cat burglar."

"That's what I'm afraid of," she muttered as she watched him push back and start for the door.

Upstairs, she took Garret's advice and got out her laptop. A simple background check on Jessup Sinclair yielded the seventy-year-old had once served his country with three tours in Vietnam.

Impressed, Anniston read deeper, through a routine history with the Florida Highway Patrol, which included nine commendations in the field. But then she noted the long list of complaints—over three hundred during his career. The accusations included extorting drugs and money from people he'd stopped for traffic violations to making false arrests that led to beating handcuffed prisoners.

Five years before leaving the department, Jessup racked up several grievances accusing him of taking cash bribes from at least three dozen motorists. If they paid up and met his demands, he'd let them off with a warning and wouldn't write up a citation. But it seemed the highlight of his career involved a shakedown of a talented college musician who'd supposedly been caught drug trafficking. There'd been an arrest, an indictment, and then the kid had disappeared right out of his dorm room in the middle of the night. The case made Florida headlines for almost a year. But after a period of time the story went away. She couldn't find any mention of an outcome. Shortly after the incident, Jessup and the Highway Patrol came to a parting of the ways.

As she snapped her laptop shut, it was apparent the old man had a darker side that obviously hadn't come to light during the last two decades whenever he ran for reelection. She decided she'd just found the angle to exploit.

After applying her make-up she got dressed in the lowest cut top she'd brought with her. She'd thrown on a pair of skinny, tight-fitting jeans, a pair of strappy sandals that made her four inches taller, and prepared to woo a seventy-year-old man into confessing he'd long ago thrown away his ethics to join the bad guys.

She still hadn't found enough evidence to point to who the bad guys were exactly. That would take a savvy approach and all the patience she could gather. Yes, she had a tablet full of theories, suspicions, a few leads and more than a headful of ideas. But whether real or imagined she had a long way to go before proving Sinclair held the link to Ryan's or Livvy's case. She wasn't even sure what role, if any, Jessup had played in any of it.

So in a town this small, she prepared to take a step toward covert, a direction that would either go well, or break down in a most embarrassing way. Whatever the outcome, she was prepared to give it her best shot.

Anniston walked through the doors at the police station looking like a tart straight out of *Miami Vice*. But since the outfit was thrown together for that very reason, she couldn't whine too much.

And when the sergeant behind the desk looked her up and down in appreciative fashion that made her feel cheap and tawdry she knew the look worked. The man did everything but whistle and sing the first bars to *Dixie*.

She had to wait fifteen minutes before getting an audience with the chief. So when she did stroll into his office, she ramped up the old Marcelli magic. She acted like her IQ dropped twenty points.

"Thanks so much for taking time out of your busy schedule to talk to me. You know I'm on this impossible case trying to find out what happened to Walker and Olivia. I'm getting an awful lot of pressure from my clients to make all sorts of assumptions. I was hoping you could help me out with a few facts." For emphasis, she added, "I think I might be in over my head."

"It's such a pretty head," Jessup said with a wink. "The Indigos are good at making assumptions."

"Don't I know it. You don't like them very much, do you?"

"I don't have a problem with them, just the way they're trying to make a big deal out of this situation with Livvy.

The simple truth is there's not a thing to indicate the Buchanan family was kidnapped or jerked out of their house in the middle of the night. Not a thing."

Anniston chewed her lip to keep from pointing out that the family had left behind everything they owned. Instead, she rolled her eyes and smiled, leaning forward so he could get a good look at her cleavage. "But they say it was you who first thought the two cases were related."

"That was before we found the car. If you ask me, your clients are being unrealistic. Those boys should pack up right now and get back to their own lives, leave Indigo Key like they've done so many times over the years and travel the world. Leave their poor parents to get back to a routine."

"But how can they do that with their grandchildren unaccounted for, their daughter and her husband gone?"

"That's just it, the whole thing is harebrained but just the kind of stunt Walker would pull. You'll see, Walker and Livvy will come strolling back into town when they're damn good and ready."

Anniston knew she needed to keep Jessup venting and worked up. "But in the meantime I get to keep that sweet retainer. A girl's gotta make a living. Surely you don't begrudge me that? I'm not trying to grab the spotlight here or usurp your territory. I mean look, you know the life of a PI."

Jessup came around his desk and parked his butt on the corner of the wood. "Sure I do, you guys soak the clients for a hefty fee upfront, then rack up a ridiculous daily expense all the while never doing much more than taking pictures of a cheating husband."

Good to know what you think of my job, thought Anniston. It sounded like he spoke from experience. Even though she found Jessup's attitude thoroughly condescending, she kept the phony smile plastered on her face as she waded into deeper waters. "So you're convinced Walker pulls a disappearing act and takes off. I got that, but what about Ryan Connelly. What do you think happened to him?"

"Honestly, the guy probably got fed up with his boring life back in North Carolina and took off on a freighter for parts unknown. The guy could be anywhere by now."

Anniston had grown tired of the game, tired of this silly man who passed himself off as law enforcement. She got to her feet, bringing her IQ up to a healthier quotient. "A freighter? Really? What did he do with his car? I ran the plates, his Honda's still registered to him without benefit of selling it to anyone."

She didn't miss the patronizing look Jessup gave her but she ignored it. "Plus, Ryan had a business back in Nags Head that he'd babied along for years. I don't see the connection to giving up what he'd worked for and setting sail on a freighter."

"People get fed up with their lives all the time and decide to try something else. That's what Alaska's for. The sister admitted the business wasn't doing that well. If you don't believe me, ask her."

The defiant attitude had Anniston turning for the door. "I think I'll do that."

It was a balmy eighty degrees when Anniston ended the skirmish with Sinclair and christened it a standoff. Calling it that was the only way she could live with the fact that she hadn't dug in and battled him more. But the goal had been to learn how much he disliked the Indigos. After her twenty minutes with the chief of police, he'd left no doubt.

She changed clothes and brought that news into The Blue Taco looking for lunch. It was crowded, so she stood in line to place her order behind a young mom with two cranky toddlers who wanted nothing more than a sugary churro. The kids cried so loud through the woman's order Anniston couldn't think straight. When it was her turn, she took one look at Raine behind the counter and felt instant empathy.

"How do you put up with this chaos?"

"I've been working here since I was old enough to stand at the register." Raine lifted a shoulder. "Danny and I were raised by a single mom. This place didn't run itself. We pitched in, learned the ropes. You deal with the public every day. What can I get you?"

"I'll take the steak burrito plate with a Diet Coke," Anniston said, removing her debit card from the pocket of her jeans. "Here's a thought. Why don't you give Tessa a job here? She could use the cash."

Raine's eyebrows formed an arch. "That's not a bad idea. I wonder if she'd be insulted by the offer?"

"There's only one way to find out," Anniston declared before moving along so the next person in line could order.

After finding a table on the patio, she took out her iPad and started organizing the major points about the meeting with the police chief into an email for the Indigos. She was deep in thought when Raine arrived with the food and dropped into a chair next to her.

The sunny blonde clasped her hands together, all excited. "I have an idea. Let's get together tonight at my place, just us girls. I'll bring home takeout, some enchiladas and fajitas, and we'll make a party out of it. Maybe I'll get Tessa plastered and hit her with the job idea. You could back me up on that."

"Sounds like a plan. Besides, I need an opening to tell her that…" Anniston shifted forward and whispered, "I don't think Jessup has done a thing to look for Ryan. Absolutely nothing."

"Oh, she's figured that out already."

"Suspicion is one thing, confirmation another. Jessup thinks Ryan jumped on the first freighter out of port and took off. Sound familiar?"

Raine settled back in the chair, stumped. "He actually said that?"

"Yup."

"Funny isn't it, so many people around here suddenly deciding to take off?"

"Well, it makes me wonder how safe visitors are with a man like Jessup running the show. What if I went missing? I'm an outsider. This island gets thousands of tourists every season. It makes me wonder if I should dig into the town's history a little farther back. You know, see how many tourists have disappeared during their vacations."

"Do it. See what you can find out by tonight. Be at my place around six-thirty. I'll make sure Tessa knows to expect company."

At that very moment the only person Tessa intended to entertain was Jackson Indigo. Jackson had been able to detour from his duties on *The Black Rum* long enough to spend two hours with Tessa inside the tiny bungalow.

So far, they'd made the most of every minute. From the moment they'd burst through the front door they hadn't been able to keep their hands off each other.

Her fingers fisted in his hair. She plundered his mouth while he devoured hers. They couldn't get out of their clothes fast enough to ravage each other.

Her naked body was like hallowed ground, he thought as he worked his way from her luscious mouth down to her lovely curves. He lingered over the texture and shape of her breasts, pleased when he felt her quiver, her heart pick up its pace. There was shock and awe as he licked his way down her belly, kissed the silky skin of her thighs.

With each touch, her blood heated. With each nibble and nip, she wanted more. Erotic sensations blinded her. Passion and hunger shifted back and forth as he did things to her no one else ever had.

He swept over her, brushed her cheek with his lips and whispered, "Look at me, Tessa. I want you to look at me when I'm inside you."

She met his deep brown eyes. Her head was spinning as she shuddered at the joining. Pleasure flowed down like gentle rain as he raised her arms above her head, locked his fingers with hers. He began to move, slow and deliberate, over her, inside her.

The frenzy had her wrapping her legs around him. She felt the power in his muscles as he drove them higher. He left her heart skidding and her body quivering as they vaulted up, rocking through the satiny dance, the bond as old as time.

Heat curled and circled between them like steam rising. The climax shattered, white-hot, like a rocket in the night sky.

There were still tremors pulsing through her when he rolled to the side and brought her with him. Snuggling into his chest, she rested her head on his heart, listened to it thud in her ear. "I like jumping you in the middle of the day."

He let out a laugh and raked his fingers through the strands of her copper hair. "I like being jumped. Sneaking away from the guys took some planning."

She raised her arms in the air that signaled a touchdown. "But you did it."

"I aim to please."

"Now you're just bragging. I'm starving. How about you?"

"Yeah, smelling the stuff only made me work harder."

"Hmm, food as an incentive, I'll have to remember that. It's time to break for fuel. I left the sack on the coffee table."

"I'll get it." He got up, didn't bother putting on his boxers as he padded out to the front room to retrieve the Kung Pao chicken takeout Tessa had brought from Lee Fong's Palace on Pearl Street.

"We could nuke it warm," he said when he brought the bag back.

"Can't wait."

"You want to eat here in bed?"

"Sure. Why not?"

They set the Styrofoam tray between their bodies, took turns dipping into the veggies, munching on the tender meat.

Jackson had his mind on making plans for later. "I could pick you up and we could go out for dinner at that little French bistro by the marina."

But Tessa had already picked up her phone to check her messages. "I don't know. It looks like Raine's having a little get together tonight at six-thirty. Girls only. She wants me there."

"What for?"

"No idea. But I'm bound to go. It has to be somewhere in the roommate code, right?"

Obviously disappointed, he grumbled, "I suppose."

She stroked a finger down his cheek, leaving a trail of Kung Pao sauce. She used her tongue to trace the path off his face. "How about we come back here after that?"

He pinned her to the mattress. "I don't want to wait that long."

Chapter Twenty

Girls' night out at Raine's rippled out like a pebble on a pond. Anniston tossed out an invitation to Lenore, who in turn invited her best friend, Jule Mae Harriman, who brought along her daughter-in-law, Cara.

As promised, Raine provided the appetizers and entrées. For dessert, Lenore baked her decadent chocolate cake she'd laced with coffee liqueur. Anniston had stopped by the liquor store and picked up enough wine to buzz a sorority house. Jule Mae and Cara contributed a tasty guacamole and a Crock-pot queso dip along with bags of chips.

The spread looked like it could feed twenty people. It prompted Tessa to go in search of Raine's dishes and glassware to brighten up the table. It made her long for her cramped kitchen back home. But then she realized these same friends wouldn't be back in Nags Head.

Willing to try for another normal evening, Tessa listened to the houseboat rock with the welcome sounds of laughter and merriment. For the first time in days, she noticed a difference in Jackson's mom. Lenore's spirits seemed to lift. Maybe everyone needed another chance for the worry and tension to drain away. She concluded it was worth a shot.

Tessa opened a bottle of white wine, poured until she'd drained every drop into their six glasses. As she went to discard the empty into the recycling bin, she hesitated. "You know, back home I would've found a use for this wine bottle."

Without a crafty bone in her body, Anniston let out an easy laugh. "Really? Why?"

"Because this one's a DIY genius," Raine explained. "You should read her blog sometime. It's under the name of the hardware store, The Toolbox."

"Catchy name," Anniston noted, taking out her cell phone to check it out. She used the search engine to land on a site with a picture of Tessa on the sidebar. "So how exactly would you reuse a wine bottle?"

Tessa found Anniston's reaction amusing. "Paint it, decoupage it, or sprinkle it with glitter. If you're truly creative you could design a mosaic pattern and turn it into a lamp. Or just leave all that stuff off and tie a pretty ribbon around the top, use the bottle to hold candy or flowers and give it as a gift."

"Huh, learn something new every day." Anniston sat back, tipped her glass toward Tessa. "I like a woman who thinks on her feet. Although I'm not sure I have the patience for turning around a wine bottle." She turned to Lenore. "Do you do this kind of stuff?"

"Oh yeah, had to. Raising four kids on a tight budget, I used to save all kinds of stuff. I even made the kids' birthday cards. Then when Livvy became a mom, we'd pool our resources and make some of the best projects for the annual church bazaar. Halloween and Christmas items were our specialty." Lenore scowled into her drink. "Come to think of it Walker made her get rid of all her craft supplies and move them out of the corner of the kitchen and into the utility room, said it junked the place up too much."

Jule Mae reached across the table and snatched up a jalapeño popper. "Walker's an ass, always was."

Raine tittered with laughter. "That's the consensus. Who else but Walker would build himself a generous man cave that caters to all his hobbies and then relegate Livvy's to one counter in the laundry room."

Anniston stuck a chip into the guacamole. "I don't think I like this guy very much."

Cara shifted her weight in her chair and snagged a chicken taquito, dipped it into the salsa. "Once in high school he stole the answers to the chemistry midterm. It was common knowledge. Back then, I think Livvy liked the aspect of the bad boy in him."

Lenore acknowledged that with a bob of her head. "I think you're right. Livvy seemed to be attracted to everything he did. She even crossed that line herself a time or two by shoplifting a blouse he wanted her to buy. He was right there encouraging her to do it. God knows her father and I tried to talk some sense into her head. We tried to dissuade her from dating him, but nothing we said mattered. Typical teenager behavior I suppose."

Raine wanted to leap to her friend's defense, but the truth prevented her from doing it. "Walker and Livvy dated for more than two years before they got married. That was plenty of time for her to see all his warts. And let's face it, there were plenty of red flags. Like the time he took off with his friends to Daytona for spring break and had a one-night stand with one of the coeds there. I couldn't believe it when Livvy forgave him."

Lenore nodded. "That was three months before the wedding."

Raine took a sip of wine. "Exactly. I kept thinking she'd come to her senses and back out. But I think she liked the idea of having Walker's family money. There, I've said it." To Lenore, she added, "I'm sorry. It's what I've always believed."

Lenore brushed a hand over Raine's arm. "It's okay. Tanner and I decided a long time ago that was part of it. As parents we tend to think our children are perfect. We know they aren't. But we overlook their flaws and their mistakes and hope everything will turn out for the best. I'm still hoping for that."

Jule Mae poured herself another glass of vino. "We all are. You know, this is exactly the kind of get-together Livvy would have loved."

In agreement, Raine leaned over and clinked her glass to Lenore's. "Damn straight." She turned to Tessa, looked her straight in the eye. "How would you like a job at the restaurant, manning the counter, taking orders? It was Anniston's idea."

Tessa sat back and grinned at the group of women. "Are you sure you won't get sick of having me for a roommate *and* an employee?"

"Nope. We clicked, girlfriend. Who knows? Maybe you're the new blood that will liven up the place."

Tessa scooted around the table to give Raine a hug first before she moved on to Anniston. "I'm definitely feeling the love here tonight."

Anniston snickered as the wine mellowed her out. "Oh you're feeling the love all right. You've been in such a good mood ever since you and Jackson started having hot and sweaty sex."

Tessa almost choked on her nacho. Her cheeks flushed bright red. She put her hands up to her face to try to hide the blushing. She finally dropped her hands and stared right at Lenore. "I don't know what to say."

Lenore waved her off. "I'm no prude. I would hope my boys have sex. And Jackson? The fact that he's having it with you is pure joy to me. It means he finally called it quits with that cold-hearted New Yorker."

Jule Mae bumped her friend's shoulder. "That female who never even bothered to come south to meet you and Tanner? Woohoo, that a boy, Jackson!" The older woman shifted closer to Tessa. "I'll tell you what everyone else around here already knows. Those Indigo boys know how to fill out a pair of jeans, now don't they? You ask Raine about Mitchell. She should know. They were an item all through high school."

Raine rolled her eyes. "The only good thing I have to say about Mitchell Indigo is that he takes care of himself. No offense, Lenore, but your middle boy is a bit of a big head with an ego out to here." She spread her arms wide.

Cara hooted with approval. "Back in the day when I dated Garret, whew!" Cara fanned herself. "Let me tell you that man knows what to do with a lot more than a surfboard. If you know what I mean."

Amused, Anniston decided then and there she might like to get to know Garret a whole lot better.

While the women gossiped at Raine's, down the block and around the corner, the Indigo men hosted poker night in the backyard. They sat under the stars at the picnic table, drinking Pabst Blue Ribbon that Tanner kept for just such occasions in an old steel cool box, the vintage cooler so ancient that the lettering from the soft drink advertising had faded off decades ago.

With Lenore out for the evening, Tanner had brought out his full box of cigars, the one he'd been hoarding, and passed them around.

Mitch had asked Walsh to join the game in a friendly gesture in an attempt to dupe new prey. So far the plan had worked. Between Mitch and his crew chief, the two men had cleaned up, winning almost every hand.

Which meant Jackson had gone winless all night. His mind had been on Tessa and how he intended to get her alone later. And Mitch had given him hell about his losing streak and lousy luck.

Tanner sat back and tossed in a quarter for his ante. "Jackson's got his mind on a woman. That's no way to play cards."

Mitch shuffled and dealt the next hand. "Ah, so that's his problem? Could've fooled me. I thought maybe he confused five card draw with Go Fish."

Garret threw in his coin and decided it was his turn to take a dig. "Even before his mind was on a certain redhead, Jackson never could play cards worth a damn anyway."

Tired of the insults, Jackson simply lifted his middle finger in the direction of both brothers.

"Are we in a serious card game here or at a frat party?" Tanner grumbled. "It's hard to tell with all this stupid back and forth."

"My thoughts exactly, who could concentrate with all the gum-flapping going on?" Jackson pointed out, picking up his cards and studying the prospects. He discarded two, waited for Mitch to deal him new. He fought the urge to show his pleasure when he picked up another six to make it three of a kind. With the best hand he'd held all night, he upped his bet by fifty cents and sat back to see the others take the bait. The betting went around the table until Walsh, Tanner, and Garret folded, each deciding the round was getting too rich for them. It came down to Mitch and Jackson.

"Okay, Brother Jackson, I call," Mitch noted. "Show me whatcha got."

Jackson grinned and slapped his cards on the table. "Read 'em and weep."

Mitch groaned and threw down his paltry three deuces. "I should've known when you hung in there so long you had something better. I thought you were bluffing."

"And I thought you were smarter than that," Jackson said as he scooped up his winnings.

Mitch rubbed his hands together. "Okay, so we finally have us a game now."

Walsh shook his head at the banter. "You guys always been this competitive and tough on each other?"

"Yes," Tanner answered quickly. "Drove their mother and me crazy. One day I took all of them, including Livvy, to a remodel site I was working on."

"How old were they?" Walsh wanted to know.

"Probably ranged in age from thirteen to nine. I told them to paint a wall. I thought that should keep them busy. Plus, how could you find anything to argue about by painting a stupid wall? Same color, using the same rollers. But damned if they didn't find a way to squabble over how to do it the right way and then tried to see who could finish it first."

"You got your room painted, didn't you?" Garret said in remembrance.

"I did. And you guys were paid five dollars apiece to do it."

Jackson picked up his can of beer. "As I recall Livvy bargained for more."

"That she did," Tanner said with a faraway look in his eye.

Taking that as a cue to change the subject, Garret wisely altered their course. "Did you read Anniston's latest email? She laid out the high points from her meeting with Jessup. I think we should follow up."

Mitch let out a whoop of laughter. "Yeah, I bet you do. Don't you think you should play a little hard to get once in a while?"

"Why would I want to do that? With so many things swirling around in her head about this case, she could use a distraction."

Tanner angled his head toward his youngest son. "Leave the woman alone until she finds your sister."

"Is that an order?" Garret wondered with a glint in his eye.

"Can't you tell?" Jackson said. "It's a strongly worded suggestion."

Tanner turned back to Garret. "But like all things you'll go your own way. All of you do that. I expect nothing less. But you can thank your mother and me for instilling that individual spirit in all of you. Got four kids and none of them ever ask for a damn thing from their old man."

Jackson suddenly realized his father was on the verge of tears. He got out of his seat and went over, put his arm around his dad's shoulder. "None of this with Livvy is your fault. You're not a mind reader. Don't go blaming yourself. We didn't even stick around here. So if you feel like passing out blame, aim it at the three of us."

Tanner scrubbed his hands over his face. "That's just it. You guys were off in other parts of the world living your lives. I was right here, living practically down the street. I should've done something, should've seen something. She's my daughter."

"And our sister. We'll find out what happened, Dad," Jackson promised. He skirted the table, plopping down just as Walsh began dealing the cards again.

Garret took that opening to kick his brother under the table. "Uh, Jackson, could I see you for a minute in the kitchen. You too, Mitch."

"Now?" Mitch complained. "I haven't even looked at my hand yet."

But Tanner immediately suspected something was up. "No point in running off to the kitchen, Garret Davis. I'm not a child. Might as well say what you got to say in front of me."

Garret shifted in his chair. "It may take Anniston some time before she gets her hands on the GPS settings Walker used to take Ryan fishing. I was thinking we could board the *Misty Dawn*, download the info, and leave out the middle man entirely."

Tanner grinned. "Now there's an idea. Nothing I'd like better. And since the women are otherwise occupied, there's no better time like the present. Do you guys know how to do that kind of thing?"

Jackson thumbed the air toward his baby brother. "He does. Garret's a whiz at this sort of thing."

"Walker might've been a total ass, but he was a techie in every sense of the word. Last Christmas, I got a look at the system he uses when he invited me to go for a beer. He has a transponder that tracks each time that yacht comes within range of a wireless signal. It uploads all its data automatically. The beauty is, that if I can get in, crack his password, we'll have every single place this ship's been and when. But here's the excellent part. Walker set it up with a Bluetooth connection. There should also be videos and a voice diary."

"Holy shit," Jackson said. He glanced around the table. "That could crack this case wide open on many levels, answer a lot of questions. So who's in or out?"

"Well, hell," Walsh said, throwing down the cards he'd just picked up. "I guess that puts an end to poker."

The men piled into a Nissan Titan pickup Mitch had leased to use to get around town.

"Nice wheels," Tanner said, riding shotgun in the passenger seat while the others jammed into the rear. "Wouldn't mind having one of these myself."

"Don't you think someone should stay behind in case we get busted?" Walsh suggested from the backseat.

Garret agreed. "Not a bad idea. I think it should be Dad."

Jackson tapped his father on the shoulder. "Somebody has to hang back to bail us out of jail in the event we get caught."

Tanner glanced over at Mitch behind the wheel. "So you boys think your old man is too old for this sort of thing, is that it?"

Mitch did, but he didn't it was a good idea to verbalize it. "Not at all. But it makes sense because you live here. We'd need a local to put up bond. Am I right?"

"That's BS. The solution to that is, don't get caught," Tanner chided.

"This must be the wild heathen ways Sinclair told us about," Jackson muttered as they climbed out of the truck.

The marina was quiet. The only noise seemed to be coming from Raine's houseboat, lit up like a Christmas tree.

"Any advice for us?" Mitch asked Walsh. "I know you've done this sort of thing before."

"Yeah, get in and get out, don't linger."

Mitch turned to Garret. "Did you bring the cables and flash drive?"

"I'm not an idiot," Garret snarled. "I brought everything I need. Since this was my idea, I'll do the downloading. All I need is for you guys to stand guard, let me know if anyone gets too close and too curious."

It was a simple plan.

The four men stationed themselves along the pier leading up to Walker's yacht while Garret slipped on board. At the helm, he had trouble accessing the ship's computer without knowing Walker's password. After playing around with several combinations, he smiled to himself when he finally figured it out. He booted up the GPS software, brought up the main menu, selected the tracklog feature, and highlighted the time frame he needed. He plugged in the flash drive, and hit save.

"What the hell is taking you so long," Jackson whispered when he came up behind Garret. "Everyone's getting antsy out here. Hurry it up."

"Almost finished. Had a hard time figuring out Walker's password. That's what took the longest."

"Ah. What was it?"

"The word harlow, no caps, and the numbers three-four-nine."

"Son of a bitch."

"Yeah, that's what I said. I need a beer," Garret grumbled as he made his way past Jackson and out into the night.

From start to finish the entire covert operation had taken less than an hour. But learning Walker's password put a damper on the rest of the night's festive mood.

Chapter Twenty-One

Fishing on the Key had always been a popular pastime. An angler could catch speckled trout by using shrimp as bait, or bag several redfish if you were willing to stay to the grass flats.

Thirteen-year-old Clint Sayer and his running buddy, Wedge Crowder, had a plan. They'd waited all week for Friday to get here to go fishing. They'd stowed their gear in their school lockers, ready for when the final bell rang at the end of the day that signaled the beginning of the weekend. They'd already bragged to everyone who would listen that they'd catch enough mangrove snapper for a fish fry on the beach that very night.

Their favorite fishing hole was a small back bay off the beaten path known as Rumrunner Cove. It offered a shallow channel where you could snag snapper, tarpon, snook, or redfish in four feet of water without too much effort.

After scrambling to get to their lockers, the boys exchanged binders and heavy textbooks for their beloved fishing gear. Arms full of equipment—rods and reels and tackle boxes—they flew out the double doors and into the bright sunshine ready for whatever the weekend had to offer.

The two young teens set off down the street for the convenience store that sold bait, chattering like two magpies.

Walking fast across the playground, Wedge recounted his day. "Did you see Katie Sutcliffe puke her guts out this morning in the hallway outside Mr. Bell's English class?"

"Nah, I heard about it though."

"I was three feet away when the chunks started flying. Some of the spew almost landed on my shoes."

"Gross."

"No, it was kinda cool to see how green Katie's face turned when she tried to bring up that last little bit. I thought she was gonna choke or something right there."

Not to be outdone, Clint contributed his own story. "Did you hear Sarah Gellman got herself a size thirty-four bra? Thirty-four!"

"Be glad. When she cheers at the football games like she did last night, her tits bounce up and down all over the place."

"Yeah, but I'm sure gonna miss that sight. None of the others jump down off that pyramid like Sarah."

Wedge poked Clint in the ribs with his elbow. "Judd Trimble told me Lisa Garfield gave him her panties after gym class."

"No way! How'd he get her to do that?"

"He gave her five bucks and promised he'd take her to the movies."

Wedge pulled up short near Willie DeSoto's bait shop called Fast Willie's. "We gotta stop and get the bait. I'm not relying on no artificial lures this time to catch me a fifteen pounder."

"Everybody knows live bait's the best thing for drawing 'em in."

Once they reached Fast Willie's they left their gear outside on the open-air patio long enough to fill their grocery list. They pooled their money and bought a bucket of live bait—finger mullet and mud minnows—two Snickers bars, two cans of soda, and a big bag of Cheetos.

It wasn't until Willie rang up their tab that the teens realized they had no cash left to buy ice or the Styrofoam cooler that would keep the fish fresh.

"What are we gonna do without the ice chest?" Clint wondered.

Wedge had it covered. "No problem. I brought my keep sack. We'll let them dangle in the water until it's time to head home."

The boys set out again, arms loaded down with even more goodies, in the direction of Rumrunner Cove, a mere dash around the bend. They trekked down sloped terrain to the water's edge and found their favorite spot blessedly deserted.

Once they reached the surf, Wedge freed up his overburdened arms by kneeling down on the ground to let his fishing rod drop gingerly to the sand. He picked up his spinning rod, tested it out with a flick of his wrist, making sure the bow was still prime. "I was worried about cramming it into my locker. But it looks like it survived just fine."

"Told you the bamboo would flex back okay." While Clint gathered up his fly rod, the one his dad had given him last birthday, he started toeing off his Nikes.

Wedge did the same with his shoes and got rid of his socks, prepared to wade out into the water. Just as he'd hoped, the channel was calm, the waves barely drifting to shore in a slow glide.

"If we're lucky we might catch us some good-sized shrimp for gumbo."

That prompted Clint to dig out three squirming mullets and thread them one by one on the hook. He tossed his line in, used those same fingers to unwrap his candy bar, and finished it off in four bites.

The Cheetos would have to wait otherwise the crunching might scare off the fish.

Thirsty, Wedge popped the top off his soda and gulped the cold liquid before letting out a showy belch loud enough to wake a bear.

"Shhh!" Clint cautioned. But before he could scold too much, his mouth stopped moving. His jaw fell open. "Wedge, look over there near that bunch of marsh grass."

Wedge rolled his eyes and returned the same sound his friend had directed at him. "Shhh, yourself. You're screeching like a little girl."

"Wedge, I'm telling you, check out that spot over there. What is that hung up in the maiden cane? That looks like a body to me, still wearing a shirt that's all tattered and stuck in the bramble."

Wedge let out a holler. "Holy shit. Or all that's left of one." He took a few steps to get a better look as his feet sunk into the sandy bottom. "It's his middle half, Clint. It don't have no head. We gotta tell somebody."

"Dang it! This place will be crawling with cops. And you know what that means."

"Yeah. No snapper. No fish fry for us. And now we're stuck with all this bait."

The news spread like a wildfire's inferno. Neighbors came out of their houses to gawk and try to look at what the boys had discovered. Cars showed up, drivers slowing down to see if they could catch a glimpse of the body from the roadway.

By the time Jackson and Tessa pulled up they had to park on the other side of Willie's convenience store because the onlookers had gathered and tested the boundaries of the crime scene tape.

The Florida Fish and Wildlife Commission were already there. No doubt due to Jessup Sinclair calling it in. Deputies had promptly sealed off the area with yellow tape. From the sidewalk down to water's edge the roped-off area kept news crews back near the curb. Reporters and cameramen edged toward the rope trying to get an on-air interview with anyone who would talk to them.

Because they couldn't get anywhere near Rumrunner Cove, Jackson took Tessa's hand in his and ambled up to where Jessup stood guarding the pathway.

It was the first time in almost two weeks that Tessa had spoken directly to the police chief. Not since reporting Ryan missing had she bothered. Now anger boiled to the surface at the man's lack of interest in finding her brother. "Anything you want to share with us?"

Jessup adjusted his gun belt. "Not much. Boys found a partial body, a torso, hung up between the rose mallow and maiden cane. That's all I know."

"Is it Ryan?" Tessa asked.

Jessup's face didn't hide his annoyance at the question. "I don't know that for sure yet." He cast an eye toward the crime scene techs and coroner. "And neither do they. The body's so decomposed it may take weeks to get an ID."

Tessa found his callousness rude and unnecessary. "You never really wanted to find Ryan, did you? Why is that? What did my brother ever do to you that kept you from looking for him?"

In a defensive posture Jessup crossed his arms over his chest. "I put out a BOLO. That's standard procedure, same thing any other agency would've done. I made calls to other states. That's also standard. What else did you figure I should do?"

The chief's coldness pissed Jackson off. "What the hell did Ryan Connelly ever do to you?"

Jessup met Jackson's anger with stone-cold silence.

The two men glared at each other until Jackson finally muttered, "I see why the state didn't think you were up to handling a high-profile case like Livvy's disappearance. After all, this woman's brother's been missing for almost a month and you barely went through the minimum. We won't take up any more of your precious time since we see how busy you are, relegated to traffic detail."

That last part hit a nerve. "You keep that attitude up, I'll find a way to jerk a knot in your tail, boy. You wait and see if I don't. You Indigos think because the town carries your name, you run this place, but you don't."

Jackson leveled a deadly stare. "But you and Oakerson do, is that it? Right there with your buddies, Royce and Dandridge. Do me a favor. Give your pals a message for me. You'll screw up eventually and when you do the Indigos will be right there waiting for it to happen. My brothers and I aren't going anywhere anytime soon. At least not until we get some answers. Sooner or later, you'll have to deal with us."

"Is that a threat? Are you threatening a member of law enforcement?"

Without another word, Jackson spun on his heels, Tessa's hand grasped tightly in his. "I'd like to pop his face."

"I know the feeling. His apathy has always bugged me. The day I got here, I went to see him before I even checked into the hotel. My initial impression then was that he was hiding something. I thought I might be overreacting due to my state of mind at the time. I was fearful for Ryan. But now I'm sure I wasn't dramatizing the situation. Is that usual? Is it normal for law enforcement to be so…uncaring, so unfeeling?"

"It seems to be Jessup's. I wonder why that is?"

"I almost asked him outright what he was doing at Royce Buchanan's that night. But I was afraid I'd tip our hand."

"As soon as Dad confronted Dandridge that ship already sailed."

Chapter Twenty-Two

Confronting Jessup did nothing to alleviate the overwhelming sadness she felt that Ryan had likely been found.

Tessa had been sitting on the Indigos' porch watching the light fade as the sun dropped behind a bank of clouds. The crickets and tree frogs serenaded her. The fireflies came out to show off.

It had only been a matter of hours—it wasn't even official yet, but she was pretty certain those boys had come across Ryan's remains.

She thought back to what she could have done differently? If the body turned out to be his, he'd likely been dead since the day he checked out of the hotel to come home. That meant by the time she got curious enough to start getting concerned, he'd already been taken from her. Someone had prevented him from leaving town. But who? And why? What clue had she missed? She still put Walker at the top of the list. But was she suffering from tunnel vision? Anniston kept reminding her that a good investigator kept an open mind.

As she sat there, a fresh resolve moved through her. She would find Ryan's killer no matter what she had to do or how long it took.

She wavered about making the phone call to her dad. Although she had to do it before the news hit the wire that a body had been found. She didn't want reporters showing up on his doorstep bombarding him with stupid questions. There was just one problem with that. She didn't want to hit her father with bad news without definitive proof that it was Ryan. Even though she might be convinced, was it fair to her dad to crush whatever hope still remained in his mind?

She sighed into the night air.

Jackson joined her on the porch and hunkered down in front of her. "Do you need anything? Is there anything I can do? Mom's making you some hot tea and fixing a plate of sandwiches."

"Thanks, but right now I couldn't eat a thing. I'll have to call my dad before word gets out. The thing is do I give him hope or do I tell him straight out what I really think? I don't want him seeing it on the news and thinking I shut him out. What a horrible way to learn that you've lost your only son."

"It's too early to think like that."

Tessa thought otherwise. "No, it has to be Ryan. When you were bugging Sinclair, I heard one of the techs from the medical examiner's office say that the body had likely been in the water for three weeks or longer. That fits the time frame."

Jackson set his jaw. There was no denying the span of time might match up to the state of decomposition. But the look on Tessa's face told him she wasn't completely prepared to accept it. "It was an extraordinary step you took coming down here alone to find your brother. I should've told you that before now."

"That's what families do."

Jackson thought of his own situation. He could be walking in Tessa's shoes at any moment. When his mother appeared with a plate of sandwiches and a pitcher of lemonade on a tray, he could tell the thought had crossed her mind, too.

"What happened to the hot tea?" Jackson asked.

Lenore set the tray down next to Tessa and took a seat in one of the rattan chairs. She fanned her face. "It's way too warm out here for that. Tessa needs something cool and refreshing and full of protein. That's why I made my specialty, egg salad sandwiches fixed with yogurt and smeared with avocado and topped with sliced tomato from my garden."

"Thanks, Lenore. But..."

She laid a hand on Tessa's shoulder. "No buts. You want to find out what happened to your brother, you have to keep up your strength. No doing without. You'll get through this. We'll all help you and see to it."

Anniston's SUV screeched to a halt at the curb. Raine jumped out of the passenger side and ran up to the porch. "We got here as soon as we heard. Do you know for certain if it's Ryan?"

Tessa shook her head. "Jessup was adamant about that. The coroner doesn't know yet and won't for quite some time. I feel so much better having you guys around though." She picked up a sandwich off the tray. "I'll eat because I want to know how Ryan died and who did it. Damn it, I want answers."

Lenore filled a glass with lemonade, handed it off. "If I know my boys, they won't quit until they get answers. So that part will come." She cut her eyes toward Raine and Anniston. "And these two are your reinforcements."

Tessa couldn't deny it.

Later, they banded together again in a brainstorming session around the dining room table.

Anniston crossed her arms over her chest and leaned back against the tall hutch that took up one wall. "Over the next few days I know we'll be anxious for news. But until then there's another matter I need to bring up. I delved into Indigo's crime history over the years on island and came up with an interesting tidbit that at least needs to be explored."

Garret stretched out his legs. "That research probably took ten minutes or less. I'm not sure we've ever had a crime wave before now."

"Oh really? Then what can you tell me about the other missing persons case that happened on island?"

Garret looked puzzled. "I don't understand. Tessa's brother may no longer be missing. She may finally get a resolution so I'm not sure that counts."

Anniston sent him a strange look. "I'm not talking about Ryan, but the one that happened two decades ago. In fact, it's one for the record books. I first discovered it online and then ended up at the public library going through newspaper articles on microfiche. It's an old missing persons case from twenty-five years earlier. A woman by the name of Darla Pendleton was last seen here. She wasn't a local. What struck me about it were the similarities to Ryan's case. You see, it was rumored that Darla was in town to meet a person who'd offered her a job. This was 1992. Back then Internet wasn't widely used by the general population. So Darla used old-fashioned correspondence to communicate with her potential employer. She apparently answered a classified ad. Got here in town and her family never heard from her again."

Raine piped up. "Wait. Could that be the one my mom mentioned when Livvy first went missing? Mom brings it up from time to time. There were rumors that this woman was Royce Buchanan's mistress."

Anniston's eyebrows rose. She tossed a thick file folder on the dining room table. "That would be another layer to the puzzle. I discovered Darla Pendleton is the sister of Braden Pendleton." She saw blank faces staring back at her.

But it was Garret who voiced what they were all thinking. "Who?"

"You're kidding? Don't you guys ever pick up a newspaper? Pendleton is the state senator from Miami who mysteriously disappeared two years ago after going out to sea on a fishing trip. It's been an unsolved cold case back there ever since. What no one ever talks about, though, is his sister vanished right here on Indigo Key long before her younger brother became a politician. My dad also found out Braden once had a connection to Royce Buchanan."

Tanner grunted. "You could've saved yourself some time on that one. You want to know the last bill Braden Pendleton rammed through the legislature in Tallahassee at the midnight hour right before he went missing? Ask me, I'll tell you everything there is to know about it. That bill took away the conservation designation on the marshland south of town. Taking away that favored Royce's golf course and gave it a chance for clear sailing through the city council. It stunk to high heaven two years ago when it happened and it still does today."

"Politics and developers make for strange bedfellows," Anniston said aloud. "I'm beginning to wonder how far back this thing goes. Getting rid of the designation must've come at a high price."

"That's a shame to hear the designation's been snatched," Jackson noted. "I worked on the wetlands project when I was in high school, was part of the team of people who fought for that area to stay protected. Even back then it was Dad's idea to fight the developers."

Tanner nodded. "I took you out there to appreciate the natural beauty of the place. Just like my daddy took me when I was barely out of diapers. Put a protest sign in my hand. My dad and I sat in front of a big old road grader that looked to me like an ugly monster at the time. Back then the developers wanted to turn the land into a shopping mall. We fought and we won that battle. After I met your mother, we used that remote location to go out there and make out."

Lenore slapped her hubby on the shoulder. "No one wants to hear about that."

"I do," Garret said with a twinkle in his eyes.

Mitch, who'd been standing in the far corner of the room, whacked his little brother on the head with a rolled up magazine. "You've always been weird and a whole lot warped."

Tanner ignored the byplay and jabbed a finger in the air. "Who knew it would take a bunch of shady political backroom deals and bribes from the corporate bigwigs to take away that beautiful spot? The same spot where Koda Indigo first landed on island with his woman. Which just goes to show you why I didn't go down without a fight. This Key's been part of my family's history and still means something to me." He put a hand over his heart. "In here. So I got me one of those environmental lawyers out of Key West. He used a few legal maneuverings to put a ding in Royce's plans over the last two years. I don't know how much Braden Pendleton got paid to try and get rid of the conservation status, but I can tell you this much. Buchanan didn't count on me stonewalling him with a crafty attorney of my own. We came up with a strategy and proved that area is prime wetlands, home to an assortment of whooping cranes and broad-wing hawks. Those birds have made that area a nesting place for centuries. We used that to our advantage to stop the golf course."

Jackson grinned. "Good for you. I'd hate to see the area become just another fairway."

"That's just it. If Royce gets his way he'll drain the marsh, fill it in with packed dirt, and then pour concrete for an ugly clubhouse. That's just the beginning. They'll bring in architects to build a resort and we'll never get it back. Never. That land will be gone for good." Tanner's voice cracked with emotion. "My grandkids will never get to enjoy the beauty of the place, like it's been for centuries."

Jackson felt the sudden blow of remorse. "You took me out there as a kid so I'd appreciate the flora and fauna. It's one reason I work with ecosystems today. I should've helped you more. Why didn't you mention it two years ago? I could've found more lawyers to help or written an opinion on the damage Buchanan's plans would do to the environment. It seems I've turned my back on so much that's happened here over the years."

"You're not alone," Mitch said with a grimace. "I barely take time out to show up for Christmases. I'd forgotten I'd promised Blake to take him out to hunt for treasure."

Garret raised his hand, midway up. "Guilty. Some time back, I promised to teach Blake and Ally to surf but I never carved out the time to do it. We're sorry, Dad."

Tanner waved them off. "You boys have the right to live your own lives as you see fit. I raised you to find the thing you loved doing and go for it. You've all done that. I don't expect you to come back and fight my battles for me."

"But we're family," Jackson said, looking around at his brothers. "The island's our home, too. We should've done more."

Anniston took a seat at the table, began to make notes in her iPad before looking Tanner's way. "So who in town were the people in your corner? Who were the opposing players other than Buchanan and Pendleton?"

"Initially, I had the support of the town council. But that started falling away little by little about six months ago when Dandridge stood up and made a speech at one of the meetings then used his pulpit to do the same on Sunday morning. His support for Buchanan caught me off guard. Boone said the idea of playing eighteen holes every day ultimately won him over."

Mitch sat down next to Jackson. "So where did Walker stand on all this?"

Tanner made a growling sound in his throat. "Where do you think? Right where you'd expect. He wanted that golf course, thought it would help him turn the Vitamin Hut into a multi-million dollar outfit wining and dining fancy backers."

"I wish I had my whiteboard," Anniston grumbled as she began to assemble her thoughts. "So let's go over what we know. During the month of September five people go missing without a trace. We have a salvage boat that never leaves South America sitting offshore. We don't have a clue why it's here. We have a group of locals led by Walker's father that will definitely benefit from turning a marshland preserve into a high-end golf course. Not sure why Livvy and Walker would have to go missing for that to happen but somehow Ryan fits into all this. I'm just not sure where. But he comes to town…meets Walker in person and then…disappears."

Garret had his own suspicions. And it was as good a time as any to bring up what they'd discovered in the tracking log from Walker's boat. "Walker and Ryan never got out of Sugar Bay to the open sea. You don't go deep-sea fishing out in the harbor. The currents wouldn't have carried Ryan's body to where it was found if he'd been dumped in the Atlantic. They never went fishing. So says the GPS coordinates."

Anniston shot him a look. "And you know this because…?"

"Garret downloaded the information from the transponder," Jackson declared. "It would explain why Ryan's body washed up at the cove where it did. I ran the tide and current analysis from Labor Day weekend. It jives."

Tessa had been listening from the doorway. "You're saying the digital print proves Walker didn't take him fishing? At all? Then what was Ryan doing all those days from Saturday to Wednesday when he was last seen? With Walker, I might add."

Jackson sent her a sympathetic look. "We suspect Walker tried to pull Ryan into some kind of shady scheme, maybe spending a few days to butter him up and build up his pitch into a solid bait and hook. Ryan either resisted, or discovered the plan was a scam, threatened to go to the authorities, and Walker had to get rid of him. So he tossed him overboard on his yacht. During Labor Day weekend, the *Misty Dawn* never got farther from the dock than a thousand feet."

"That would explain why his ID bracelet was found on the boat," Raine chimed in.

Tessa glanced around the room. "How do y'all feel about that?"

"Awful," Lenore answered. "For more reasons than you think. If Walker did that to Ryan, then anything is possible."

"So y'all don't think Ryan's car is in the ocean?"

"Not likely. Not practical," Mitch answered. "Could be stored in a warehouse somewhere to keep it out of sight, or someone put it in one of those containers and shipped it out of the country. Happens all the time in ports of entry where the island's small and really hard to conceal a big ticket item like a vehicle."

Mitch scratched his chin and looked at Tessa. "Something else has been bothering me. How tall was Ryan?"

"Five-ten, weighed about one-fifty-five. Why?"

"Walker was six-feet. He could've overpowered Ryan because it was likely a surprise attack from behind. But if we apply that same principle to Walker, it means someone had to surprise him, take him down enough to get to Livvy and the kids, then make all of them disappear. Walker wasn't exactly a small guy. And Livvy? Livvy would've clawed like a tiger at anyone who touched her kids."

"So what's your point?" Anniston wanted to know. "Anyone can use a stun gun if they get close enough. That'll disable anyone long enough to take them down." She felt it her duty to mention a critical point. "Keep this in mind. It takes a special kind of mindset, a certain amount of boldness, along with an arrogance to breach someone's home and gain access. I talked to the neighbors. No one reported hearing a disturbance. No screams. No gunshots. If they were taken against their will, it was a clean, quiet entry. Since nothing in the house indicates that a struggle took place there, Walker didn't open the door and freak out about who had come calling at a late hour. If that is what happened, then we're looking at a highly organized individual who came to the house with one purpose in mind."

"Or it was someone Walker and Livvy knew well enough that they didn't consider it a threat," Garret offered. "It has to be someone they knew. That's how they got in the house. Walker or Livvy just opened the door and let them inside."

Raine had been standing back, unwilling to contribute an opinion until now. "What if it's a her? Anniston pointed out the other night we shouldn't get tunnel vision. I tend to think she's right."

"As far as I'm concerned anyone could be a suspect," Anniston said, sorting through her notes. "The thing is, and something I'm having a difficult time getting past is this. If I'm in bed late at night and my husband or bedmate is beside me, if the doorbell rings, what's the first thing you do? Lenore?"

"I shake Tanner awake if he isn't already and make him get up to answer the door."

"Exactly. Whatever made them leave the house, it was a simple matter of the person or persons ringing the doorbell and getting Walker to come to the door. After that, our unknown sub or subs had all the access they needed to the family. For that reason, I don't think this was a stranger abduction." She searched the gazes around the room for confirmation.

"I agree," Raine added.

"Sounds plausible to me," Tanner said. "All the more reason we shouldn't trust anyone outside this room."

Lenore ran a hand over her husband's. "That's a sad fact, but one I'm beginning to accept."

Anniston had made her point and went on, "Whatever the reason, it wasn't robbery. But they might have had something someone wanted bad enough to use the kids as leverage to get them to comply."

Jackson was beginning to think they were heading in the right direction. "That would explain why the perpetrator had them wake up the kids."

Anniston agreed. "Which means, if we find why Ryan had to be killed and not allowed to leave the island, if we discover what was in play and how it correlates to the abduction, then we'll be able to make sense of all this."

After listening to the talk, Tessa cleared her throat, leveled her gaze on Jackson. "I want to go look for Ryan's Honda. Tomorrow. First thing. I think it's time. I know you usually go out on *The Black Rum* at first light but I'm asking you to help me. You know all the places where someone might hide a car. I could drive around looking by myself for hours but I doubt it'd be as effective."

"I know this area like the back of my hand. Good idea. We'll drive around and see what we can find."

Mitch had a better plan. "Take Anniston. Hell, take Garret. Use two vehicles, split up, cover more ground. I'll take the boat out, pick up where we left off this afternoon with Walsh while you guys do a search on land."

"That'll work." With a wink, Jackson crossed the room to his mom, placed a kiss on her cheek. "Now that we have that settled, today is someone's birthday. Lately, things have been super crazy, but your sons wouldn't let this auspicious day pass without a little birthday celebration. We've worked out a surprise for you, Mom."

Mitch sat down at the piano and started tickling the keys. "Tessa, I know this is a sad day for you. But I hope you'll understand the people in this room care about you. And because we do, we want you to help us wish our mom a happy birthday."

Tears welled up in Tessa's eyes at the sentiment. "I think it's a perfect idea."

Jackson squeezed her hand before going over to help Garret drag a set of drums from a hall closet out into the living room. The surfer took a seat behind the snare and waited for Jackson to pick up the guitar he hadn't touched in three years.

"I'm a little rusty," Jackson admitted as he hit the first chords of *Trip Around the Sun.* "Since it's Mom's birthday we honor her tonight with our music, if you can call it that. For years, she and Dad spent their hard-earned money on music lessons. God knows why."

"I wanted musicians," Lenore fired back, pleased with the turn of events.

Jackson's lips curved up. "That might be true, but unfortunately what you're about to hear is the result of seven years of trying. Mom, this is for you, your favorite song and then some. And while Livvy might not be here to sing for us tonight, or Blake and Ally to help us with the chorus, we'll do our best to make this a good time the only way we know how."

The trio blended melody and rhythm as they sang the lyrics, strong and deep. Soon the toe tapping started and everyone's mood seemed to mellow out. They went into a rendition of *Happy Birthday*, Beatles style, until they segued into *I Gotta a Feeling*.

In the corner, Tessa nudged Raine. "Why didn't you tell me they could play and sing like this?"

"Been a while since I've heard them. I just assumed they'd given it up entirely." But she had to admit Mitch's chorus reminded her of other nights, nights when he'd played a symphony just for her. She reminded herself she'd been nothing more than an impressionable kid. She changed the subject. "I'm thinking we should get Chinese takeout. Lenore loves the stuff but Livvy says she never orders it for herself."

Tessa cocked a curious brow. "You're not suggesting food from The Blue Taco?"

"Hey, who doesn't love eating at Lee Fong's? He makes the best Szechwan dishes around with the freshest veggies."

"Then we should call it in." Tessa came out of her funk. "I don't see a cake around here anywhere either. Why don't we run out and get her one of those with buttercream frosting?"

"Good idea, if we leave now we'll make it before the bakery in town closes," Raine suggested. "We'll probably have to settle for whatever they have on hand, but hey, she won't celebrate her birthday without cake."

Tessa and Raine reached the bakeshop five minutes before closing. They found the only item left in the glass display case that could serve a mass of people was a multi-layer strawberry cake. Luckily it was covered in the buttercream icing Tessa craved. They paid for it and headed to Lee Fong's where they ordered from his buffet-style hot pot selections—dumplings, prawns, scallops, clams, wontons, mushrooms, bok choy, and a variety of other veggies.

While they waited for their order, Raine kept checking Tessa's face for any signs she was about to break down in tears. But so far the woman had showed a steel composure. "Does it feel funny to, you know, be out buying food and planning a party on the day that body was found at the cove?"

Tessa sighed and lifted her shoulders. "I'm okay. Lenore's been good to me. I had no idea today was her special day until Jackson's impromptu music tribute. Things have been coming at all of us so fast lately we haven't had time for anything but craziness. So I'd like her to enjoy herself tonight. Besides, I don't like thinking about Ryan left there like that…for so long…in the water. How many times did I go near the marina and never thought to look along Rumrunner Cove?"

"How could you possibly have known to look there?"

"I should've done something...more."

Raine gave her a look of disbelief. "Unless you're psychic you wouldn't even know about Rumrunner Cove, let alone that's where his body would turn up. What did your dad say? I know you called him."

"About what I expected. He's still holding out hope it isn't Ryan. He'd like to believe Jessup's theory that Ryan took off. But deep down my dad knows it isn't like Ryan to do anything so spur of the moment and abandon the business he'd worked so hard to get off the ground."

Raine touched Tessa's hand. "Whatever the outcome, I want you to know I'll be here for you."

"This sounds crazy but I've come to think of you like a close friend. Jackson, too."

Raine bumped Tessa's shoulder. "Oh, come on. You think of him as something other than a friend. You didn't come home the other night after going out to the bar. I'm not your keeper, but I'm able to figure out where you ended up."

"I ended up right where I wanted to be. It was special and exactly what we both needed, a little sexual release."

"Is that all it is?"

Tessa sighed and decided to come clean. But before she could fully disclose what was in her heart, Mr. Fong finished bagging the order and called their name.

They took the fare back to Quay Avenue and spread the goodies out in the kitchen for a buffet-style banquet.

They discovered the merriment already in full force. Mitch had popped the cork on several bottles of merlot and chardonnay. The festive mood rubbed off almost immediately. Tessa felt as though everyone else had a head start on a good buzz. She decided she needed to loosen up and play catch up. So before she dived into the food, she downed two glasses of white wine.

Jackson took notice. But after the day she'd had he wasn't going to judge her if she got a little tanked tonight.

He glanced at the faces around the table. "Not bad for an unplanned birthday blast."

Lenore raised her glass. "Thanks to Raine and Tessa for grabbing the meal and the cake."

"It was our pleasure," Tessa said, her words slurring a bit.

They partied until midnight and by the time it broke up, Tessa had polished off a bottle of wine all by herself.

Since Raine hitched a ride with Anniston back to her houseboat, Jackson helped Tessa out to her Toyota. If they were planning to get an early start in the morning looking for Ryan's car, it made sense to spend the night together at the Waterfront bungalow.

Tessa was all for that. She took out her keys but Jackson snatched them out of her fist.

"You can't drive in your condition."

Her lips bowed with the grin of the very plowed. "'Kay." She pointed a finger at him, tapped his chest. "I designate you as my good-looking chauffeur. Fetch me to the castle, my handsome hunk."

Once Jackson folded her into the little sports car, she became a talkative chatterbox. "That was so sweet what you and your brothers did for your mom. Why didn't you tell me you could sing like that? You're a sweetie pie, that's what you are, Jackson Indigo."

"It's not the first time we've cheered her up with a song or two. We thought it might be awkward without Livvy. For a few minutes there it was."

"No, it was wonderful," she breathed out, leaning her head back against the headrest.

He pulled into the driveway about the time she swayed in her seat. He was beginning to think she'd have trouble maneuvering out of the car and standing upright.

But she surprised him by nimbly dancing in a circle on her way up to the front porch. Into the spin though, she missed the second step and stumbled into the flowerbed.

He caught her right before she fell. "You've had way too much wine."

"I believe I have. But…the day your brother's body is found and used for fish food, you're entitled to get wasted."

"Aw, baby. I'm so sorry."

She shunned the words of sympathy but turned into his arms. "You have a beautiful singing voice and play the guitar like Springsteen."

Jackson hooted with laughter as he unlocked the front door. "Now I'm certain you're full-on drunk." He helped her inside, pushing her onto the sofa before she lost her footing and took a tumble.

But she was persistent. She tugged on his hand to keep him from getting up. Shoving her hair out of her face, she started pressing her body against his. "I want you, Jackson."

"Tessa, you're plastered."

"Sure I am. But I still want you."

"You have me, darling." More than she knew, thought Jackson. "Let's get you to bed." He scooped her up, headed down the hallway.

"See, this is what I wanted all along," she murmured into his ear. Linking her arms around his neck, she held on tight and went after his mouth in a sloppy effort, woozy at the movement.

He laid her on the mattress, took a seat next to her. "You okay? Your face looks a little green."

"I'm fine. Please, Jackson. Make me forget these images I have in my head about how Ryan could've died. I keep thinking about him out there on that beach, cold and alone. I should've been the one to find him."

"Don't do this to yourself."

"And something else…he was already dead by the time I got here." She leveled her finger at him. "No sense in denying what I already know. He was gone. I sensed something bad had happened. But I didn't do enough."

"You did everything you could. I told my dad the same thing. Don't let guilt eat at you like this."

She tried to kiss him again. "I don't want to beg, but could you take me somewhere else tonight, Jackson? Please. I'm not so far gone that I don't know what I'm asking." She ran a manicured nail from his throat to his chin in an attempt at seduction.

Maybe that was his undoing, or the sultry way her eyes sought out his. He took her in his arms, and rocked her. "It'll be okay, baby. I promise."

Moonlight and shadows danced through the curtains as he began to undress her, getting her out of the shoes first and then her top. He worked the jeans down over her narrow hips.

He removed his own shirt and shorts, tucked her under the covers and crawled in after her. Tenderly, he spread kisses along her jaw.

If the goal was to take her somewhere else, he intended to send her to the highest mountain, high enough where nothing bad could touch her, at least, not tonight.

He lingered a breath away, indulged himself in the smoothness of her skin, the softness of her lips. As she turned in his arms, he slipped his hand under the sheets and moved past the silky lace. He found her warm and wet. He took pleasure in her gasp and moan, the way she arched her back to ride out each crest and wave. He watched her give in to the quakes and tremors, her body erupting and shuddering until finally she went limp in surrender. Still clinging to him, her lids grew heavy and she finally dozed off.

He kissed her forehead and locked his arms around her in a tight embrace. "Sleep now, baby. I'm here. And I won't let anything bad happen to you."

Chapter Twenty-Three

Tessa woke curled against Jackson's side. Nestled in safety, she tried to lift her head, but the dizziness from the hangover slapped her back into her pillow. She let her woozy state even out before snuggling deeper into the warmth of his body.

Her befuddled brain fought to remember the previous day's events—the body at Rumrunner Cove she thought was Ryan's, the fear and sadness she'd heard in her dad's voice over the phone, the grief at losing her only brother. It all came rushing back in a montage of emotions leading up to Lenore's birthday party and all the wine she'd consumed to help her deal.

In response to the sheets rustling beside him, Jackson's arms came around her in a protective embrace.

She placed a kiss on his throat. "Sorry I woke you. Go back to sleep."

"Don't be. We have a busy day ahead of us. We should probably get moving." He pressed his lips to her forehead, started to stick a leg out from under the cover to get up.

But she pulled him back to nibble at the corner of his mouth. "I do need a shower, but not before I take care of you the way you took care of me last night."

"You remember? I'm surprised."

Her blue eyes sparkled with mischief. Her lips formed in a wide sunny arch. Playfully, she poked him in the ribs. "I drank too much last night, I didn't suffer a massive case of amnesia. Plus, my head's beginning to feel a whole lot better. My thoughts are very clear."

He cocked a brow. "No one could blame you for guzzling the wine."

She winced. "Your parents probably think I'm such a lush."

"No. They knew you were upset. You had a right to be." He tucked strands of red hair behind her ears. "How much better do you feel exactly? What did you have in mind to start the day?"

She glided up determined to show him and forged a trail of kisses down his bare chest. "How much time do we have?"

Jackson breathed out a satisfied sigh. "We'll make time."

Behind the wheel of Tessa's car, Jackson drove past wooded countryside—flat landscape with narrow stretches full of short-leaf fig that grew alongside thatch palm. These areas were too populated for hiding a car, unless the parties involved did so behind gated walls. In this section of the Keys people tended to spend the money they'd brought with them from frigid places like Caribou, Minnesota, or Madison, Wisconsin, on luxury and privacy.

Since they wanted out of the deep freeze of winter once and for all, relocating and experiencing Florida life to its fullest meant they'd sought out stately houses with gorgeous views and private boat access.

The island itself was less than three and a half miles long, which meant it didn't hold a lot of hiding places within the city limits. But south of town was a different story.

There were dozens of places along the back roads and canals outside Indigo Key where Ryan's Honda might have ended up. Jackson and Tessa checked out each spot while Garret and Anniston trailed after them, Anniston behind the wheel of her SUV.

Like a mini caravan the four had driven up and down the coast twice, combing basins, searching low-lying marshes and salt ponds located off the main blacktop. Some were in the middle of thick groves with acres and acres of Spanish lime trees and coastal shrub. The brush made it a likely cover for anyone to dump a vehicle in the bog, away from the prying eyes of traffic from the roadway.

The Toyota and Explorer parted company off the main route. Once Anniston took the fork to the west side of the island, Jackson veered off in the opposite direction heading southeast.

"Where are we going?" Tessa asked.

"I want to check out the restoration project, see the preserve my dad's been involved in trying to save from Buchanan and his developers."

"You talk as though you haven't been out there recently."

A pained look crossed his face. "I haven't. It's been years."

He pointed to a tidal basin with vegetation in various stages of overgrowth. "Back during high school this place was someone's private marina. The house and the forty acres belonged to an old woman who'd moved here sometime in the late thirties. When she died at the ripe old age of ninety-five, she owed a ton of back taxes. It fell to the state. I think even then my dad was afraid Buchanan would get his hands on the property. So he started lobbying to make it a natural preserve. The politicians in Tallahassee agreed with him and a conservation effort was born. But the legislators wouldn't pump any tax dollars into the project. My dad rounded up donations, assigned teams of volunteers to work and bring it back to its glory days. The old house could be used as a decent museum but the project was always low on cash. We spent what we had on hand to bring in truckloads of fill dirt to build up the bog floor so it would hold native mangrove again and hardwood hammock. After years of neglect, the area began to come back, bringing with it the natural way of rebirth and regrowth."

Tessa turned her head and thought she saw something slither into the blackish green water. "Uh, Jackson. Any chance we'll run into alligators out here?"

"Highly probable. Snakes, too. There are all kinds of reptiles and birdlife that you won't find in any other part of the state. Birds like white-eyed vireo and ruby–throated hummingbirds make their home here."

"I'm not too concerned about cute little hummingbirds. It's the alligators that are cause for alarm."

Jackson grinned. "I've got your back."

"What about my front? Do people actually live out here?"

"Sure. There are probably ten shacks in this marsh where swamp folk live off the land. Been that way for hundreds of years. They live off the grid." He parked the car under a bank of drooping cypress and shoved out of the car. Looking up, he studied the charcoal clouds bunched together and rolling in fast from the east, gobbling up the blue sky. "It'll be raining soon, we need to pick up the pace and finish exploring before the downpour hits."

They roamed forty yards or so off the road before hitting softer ground toward the edge of the murky green waters of the bog.

It didn't take long for the humidity to get to them. Winded and out of breath, they crisscrossed past horsetail reed and sedge.

Among the middle of the undergrowth, she stopped for a breather. Scanning for snakes, her eyes landed on the tail end of a silver Honda sticking out at an awkward angle. The front end was buried up to the hood, the windshield barely visible. The sedan sat in the slough, mud up to the rims, surrounded by patches of pondweed. It was so deep in the muck, there was no way you could wrench open any of the four doors.

Tessa's face went pale. She drew in the muggy air, her heart thudding in her chest. It beat so fast she could barely get out the words. She didn't actually remember reeling from the sight, only that Jackson kept her from falling. "That's his car." She shifted her body toward the trunk end of the car, squinted to make out the license plate. "And look at the North Carolina 'First in Flight' Kitty Hawk emblem. If that's not enough the plate frame is his college alma mater, North Carolina State."

Her head began to spin. Her mouth had gone cotton dry. "What's the car doing this far out of town?"

"You stay put," Jackson said quietly. "I'll go check it out."

"No way. I'm coming with you."

"Tessa, there are all kinds of critters out here... You said so yourself."

She did her best to ignore the swarm of mosquitos the size of bumblebees and the croaking of what sounded like a hundred bullfrogs all at once. Determined to go on, she held up a hand, waved him off. "Don't even suggest it. I haven't stuck around this long without realizing the implications. I know what I might be dealing with. I want to see for myself what's in that car."

"You've got a spine of steel, you know that? I think you'd see this thing through no matter what size 'gator we run into."

She slapped his arm. "Putting that image into my head isn't helping the situation."

With Jackson clutching her hand in a vise grip, she had to make her feet move to get close enough to peer inside the car's interior. But they still had to slog a good fifteen more yards through the boggy landscape to do it. The sludge was thick like glue as they trudged past a forest of sweet bay and pop ash. They ducked under the gigantic bald cypress branches, trekked around gnarly vines that twisted to touch the ground and block their way.

"We should've brought a machete," Jackson groaned as he pushed past the stubborn arm of a dead birch.

"I'll say it again, why would his car be way out here? Ryan wouldn't even know this place existed."

"Exactly." Jackson deliberately avoided any more conversation until they reached the mud-spattered Honda.

When she tried to cup her eyes over the glass she heard Jackson warn, "Try not to touch anything. This is the best evidence we've had since we started this thing."

It took every ounce of mettle she could muster to squint her eyes into the glare of the windows. "That looks like Ryan's luggage and computer bag still on the floorboard. See?"

"We know he was packed and ready to head back home until he was spotted with Walker at the burger place." Jackson studied the angle of the car. "You found his medical alert bracelet on Walker's boat."

Her pulse jumped. "What are you thinking?"

"We already suspect someone dumped Ryan in the ocean from the deck of the *Misty Dawn*. That's why the body eventually washed up where it did onshore, almost ten miles from here. Whoever did that to Ryan, realized they had to get rid of his car so they tried to sink it here. Big mistake. The swamp's too shallow so it belched it back up in the mud."

"Lucky for us," Tessa muttered.

"I'm calling the state police and then Anniston. I don't trust Sinclair." With a shaky hand Jackson took out his cell phone from the pocket of his shorts. His knuckles were bone white as he punched in the number.

But before he could hit send, an echo of gunfire burst out of the trees. The repeated tat-tat-tat-tat-tat-tat-tat was so sudden Jackson thought they'd wandered onto a gun range.

Bullets whizzed past where they were standing in knee-deep water. Jackson dropped and brought Tessa down with him into the muck.

Pings hit the Honda's metal as they tried to use the car as a shield. Their place to hide became an open-air shooting gallery. All around them the air zinged with a rapid barrage, every bullet aimed at them. Even the calm water of the bog rippled with shots. Water lilies exploded as the bullets found a home shattering the delicate greenery.

Off in the distance Jackson heard someone running, then the sound of an engine starting up. Tires screeched. Just as quickly as the hail of bullets had started, it ended with silence descending over the preserve.

"Are you all right?"

Afraid to move, Tessa puffed out a grunt.

"Whoever it was is gone now."

"What was that all about?"

The sky began to spit down drizzle.

Jackson gripped his cell phone again and scanned the wetlands for any sign of activity. "I'd say someone took exception to us finding Ryan's car."

"Enough to try and kill us."

"Yeah. That's why I'm calling Garret and Anniston first. The private eye carries a Smith & Wesson."

Anniston didn't need to take out the handgun as she stood in a driving rainstorm huddled beside Tessa. The two women, along with Jackson and Garret, watched as investigators supervised Ryan's Honda getting dragged out of the bayou.

The car, now bullet-ridden, was towed under the watchful eyes of Dack Hawkins. The detective wasn't one bit happy about being called out in such bad weather to an alligator-infested pond. He hadn't even had time to change his shoes. The expression on his face said it all.

Tessa sensed the man's petulant attitude. It didn't sit well with her. She decided she was done with the passive role she'd played so far. With that in mind, she confronted the investigator head on. "By now you know they found my brother's body yesterday."

Hawkins adjusted his umbrella so the rain wouldn't soak his pricey Ferragamo loafers. "The medical examiner hasn't confirmed that yet. In fact, he hasn't even finished the autopsy. If I were you…"

"You aren't me," Tessa fired back, taking a step toward Hawkins and shoving the umbrella to the side so she could see the cop's face. "No more jerking me around, okay? My brother's dead and you know it. The police chief in this town let it be known he thought my brother left on his own accord, had jumped a freighter and just took off."

She threw her drenched arms out wide for emphasis. "Does it look to you like he drove his own car into a murky swamp like this because he decided to take an excursion around the world? It's a ridiculous notion. The only trip he took was on Walker's yacht. I want to know what you plan to do about finding out if Walker killed my brother before Walker went missing."

"And while you're at it, maybe find out who the hell emptied a rifle in our direction," Jackson said, his mood boosted with snarky undertones. "That ought to give you enough incentive to hang around town and do Sinclair's job for him."

As rain poured down and into the cop's eyes, Hawkins moved the umbrella back over his head. "I can't comment about an active investigation."

"Blah, blah, blah," Tessa snapped. "We've heard that before. Sinclair didn't think it was too active. In fact, he declined to do much work into Ryan's disappearance. He even put forth a stupid idea that Ryan jumped a freighter. Now I've already given DNA to help the coroner ID Ryan, anything to jumpstart getting answers for my family. But finding the car says you guys were way off base."

Reluctantly Hawkins squinted into the distance and muttered, "I'll see what I can do. By the way, who knew you planned to come out here to look for the car?"

Jackson decided to shelve the attitude and make some headway. "As far as I know, just the family. Something else you should keep in mind, though. I know you aren't from around here. But attempting to hide a vehicle in this spot doesn't make any sense. Most locals would know this place is too shallow to sink a car. It's less than six feet deep at the edges, no more than fifteen feet deeper in the middle."

Garret spoke up. "As soon as I got Jackson's phone call that was a giant red flag for me. Dumping the car here would indicate whoever did this was just looking for any watering hole he came to first, maybe on his way out of town heading south toward Key West. The asshole had no idea the water level wouldn't be deep enough to bury a car."

A wide-eyed look crossed Hawkins face. "You're saying it wasn't a local?"

Jackson wiped his face with the end of his shirttail. "We're saying if Walker is responsible for Ryan's death, he obviously had outside help getting rid of the car."

"You guys are letting your imaginations run wild," Hawkins proclaimed before cutting his eyes over to Anniston. "You hired a competent private investigator. Let her take the lead."

But Anniston took the opportunity to tout the theory. "That's just it, I agree with them." She decided to hold back having Ryan's medical alert bracelet for now. "What if I could prove Ryan was on board the *Misty Dawn*?"

"You're kidding? I already know that much. Even Sinclair acknowledges Ryan went fishing with Walker. That's why he came down here." Hawkins narrowed his eyes. "What are you holding back?" Hawkins pointed a stern finger at Anniston. "If you're withholding evidence...I could see to it you lost your license."

"Playing hardball won't work with me, Dack. So you won't. Let's just say, what I have is in a very safe place. You might want to take it up with Sinclair that no member of law enforcement checked Walker's boat or sent a crime scene team there."

Hawkins couldn't believe his ears. "Damn it. Ever since I set foot in this town, I'm dealing with gross incompetence. We haven't even found Walker yet and you're accusing him of murder. I want that evidence," he shouted over the clap of thunder that rang out.

Anniston briefly described the bracelet and how she'd obtained it. "I submitted it to the same lab the state uses. I'll gladly send you the results. But you have to promise me to stay on top of Ryan's case. None of this announcing 'there's no crime scene' crap before moving on."

"I don't need your promise. I want that lab report." But with his demand, Hawkins dropped his head. "It isn't my fault there wasn't a shred of evidence in the Buchanan house."

"That's just it, they didn't leave without their personal belongings. Who does that? You have to admit they never hopped a plane." When Hawkins started to explode in protest, Anniston quickly went on, "Just promise me, you'll work Ryan's case. You have an unidentified body, a male, lying in the morgue. You now have Ryan's car with his belongings still in the backseat. You're bound to comb over the vehicle for DNA, fingerprints. You're standing here now because someone opened fire on my clients. Potential evidence just keeps piling up. We intend to be part of this whether you like it or not. Find out what happened to Ryan Connelly, that's all we're asking. Plus, since you've deemed Livvy's case no longer active, I want you to share what you know. I'd like your full cooperation on both." She held out a hand in peaceful accord.

Hawkins wavered before stretching out his hand. Drenched skin-to-skin, they shook on the deal. "But I want every piece of evidence you have, no holding back, and all your theories documented."

Anniston chewed her lip. "Sorry. No can do. I'm not sharing my theories, let alone putting them in writing. At least not until I know the people I can fully trust around here. Sinclair's a problem. On that we agree. Correct?"

"Yeah. I'm getting soaked here, Anniston. Could we negotiate this somewhere else, like the nearest coffee shop?"

"No need. I want to know who the coroner has lying on that slab in the morgue as soon as you do, okay?"

Hawkins sighed. "Your old man would be proud. You're as tough as he is."

"I'll take that as a yes, and a compliment. Your first latte's on me."

The cop looked from one Indigo face to another. "For what it's worth, I don't think your sister left on her own. The thing is the higher ups are pressuring me to move on. If I could turn up something, anything at all that points to foul play, I'd dig in and fight them. The truth is the van was my last hope. Without a break there, I don't have a choice in the matter but to focus on other cases."

Just as Tessa was about to speak up in protest, Hawkins added, "I'm here, aren't I? On site. At the moment, my priority is your brother."

Jackson took a step closer. "We appreciate you leveling with us. But since we think Ryan's case leads straight back to Walker, we're hoping, at some point, you'll turn up a reason to rethink Livvy's situation."

"Fair enough. As long as Anniston keeps me in the loop, I'll return the favor. I expect all of you to keep this detail out of the public domain."

Tessa glanced around at the group for confirmation. With a nod from Jackson, she turned to Hawkins. "You got it. As long as you're honest with us about Ryan, and consider keeping an open mind about Livvy, we'll keep our mouths shut and our eyes open."

"And it would be great if you could find out who tried to kill us, the sooner the better," Jackson noted, before everyone broke up and started making a mad dash for their cars.

But later, after the group had cleaned up and dried out, they sat around the kitchen table eating Lenore's crab and corn soup, going over the events of the day.

"I've never been shot at before. It's an experience I'd rather not have happen again," Jackson said. "And if things weren't bad enough, there's Tessa finally getting a good look at Ryan's car and dodging bullets in mud up to her knees."

Tanner couldn't believe what he was hearing. "What the hell is going on in my town? We're coming unraveled at the hinges."

Jackson's voice had turned cold, sharp. "I've never been one to carry a gun before but from now on I think it'd be a good idea if we did."

"I still have my old .22 rifle," Tanner pointed out.

"That's a start," Jackson said. "But I had a little more firepower in mind." He sent Mitch a knowing look.

Mitch responded with a nod. "I keep weapons on *The Black Rum*. But if you want something for yourself we'd need to hit up Michael Tang down at the wharf. What are we talking about?"

"Shotguns would do. Nine millimeters would be better."

Anniston drilled holes in Jackson. "Do you guys even know anything about guns?"

Jackson shrugged. "What's to know? Point and shoot?"

The detective sent him a withering stare. "There's a little more to it than that, safety for one. I suggest after you've made your purchases we find a gun range and I'll give you a quick lesson in the art of lock and load."

"It was just an idea," Jackson admitted. "If Mitch

provides what we need, I'll settle for that."

Anniston wanted to make her point. "The offer still goes if you need the down and dirty how-to."

Garret took that opening and ran with it. "I wouldn't mind taking a look at that down and dirty how-to."

Anniston sent him a sultry look. "That surprises me. I heard you didn't need much of a how-to instruction guide."

With a wink, he grinned. "Then my reputation precedes me."

She slapped him lightly on the shoulder. "Along with your ego."

Chapter Twenty-Four

The Atlantic waters churned, deep and green, as Jackson stood on the deck of *The Black Rum* looking out over the sea of foamy whitecaps. Slightly overcast, the sun hid behind low drifting clouds. He breathed in the salty air, the moisture hitting his face and making him remember another time, another boat.

That summer day, he'd stepped up as Livvy's caretaker. He recalled that little girl who loved the sea almost as much as he had. But while he didn't mind sailing, Livvy mostly enjoyed swimming and snorkeling in shallower waters. Her first experience fishing off the deck of a boat had not started off well at all.

It had been a lazy warm July day right before the fireworks on the Fourth. Their dad had taken them out deep-sea fishing not along the shores of Sugar Bay but to the open sea. With no land in sight, Jackson remembered Livvy puking her guts out at the up and down sway of the boat. Instead of buckling under to the seasick feeling though, she'd sucked up her courage and insisted on trying to catch a fish. He'd baited her line until she'd gotten the hang of touching those wiggly worms and threading them on the hook. Focusing on the fish, she'd forgotten all about her queasy stomach.

But there had been plenty of other times when she'd been there for him, like the time he'd gotten into a fight with Jimmy Blakely. Like a she-bear, Livvy had swept in and clocked Jimmy in the nose with one blow. Taking up for her kid brother—that was the sister he knew and loved.

How could anyone back then have predicted this moment, this future turn of events, this hellish path to uncertainty? Reality meant he and his brothers were out here at this juncture looking at an ocean dump.

As he stretched on his wetsuit, Jackson remembered something Tessa had said. It was the not knowing part that tore her up on the inside, the idea that she might never know what really happened to her brother. They had that in common, a bond neither one wanted.

She'd handled this entire journey on her own, with no family nearby to lean on. Like him, she'd been determined not to give up.

He'd spent every morning for a week on the boat staring at the computer monitor, scrutinizing images, trying to find that one singular spot that might lead him to a body. All the while hoping like hell he didn't find a single trace of anything on the bottom of the ocean floor.

• He couldn't do much more than rely on the wide range of technology Mitch had provided—an underwater remote-operated vehicle, a slew of state of the art cameras, the latest mapping software, and sophisticated sensors.

• Utilizing the hardware, he'd pinpointed an anomaly a hundred and twenty feet below the surface. The object had gotten his attention the moment he spotted it. After dropping the rotating wand at several depths in various locations around it, he'd stared at the tinted screen focusing on what appeared to be an eight-foot-long object. It looked like a rectangular block that could very well be several bodies wrapped together in some kind of plastic tarp and tied with rope. If he wasn't letting his imagination take over, it was the right shape and size for a body.

The spray hit his face, which caused Jackson to turn and check the dials on his tank. Under any other circumstances getting ready for a dive was always an exhilarating feeling, but not today. The anticipation of this terrified him.

"It's the closest thing we've seen that resembled a likely prospect. It damn sure isn't a natural part of the ocean floor," Jackson explained to his brothers as they stood next to each other making sure the oxygen tanks were in perfect working order.

Neither Mitch nor Garret seemed convinced, though.

"I know it's a longshot but...it's definitely worth a look."

"It seems too narrow for four bodies," Mitch pointed out. "Shouldn't it be...I don't know, rounder, heftier?"

Jackson stuck to the facts as he shouldered his tank in place. "I've gone over the ocean currents on and around September 24th. I've done the math and the estimates for weight and drift, it all adds up to this spot." He used his finger to circle the area in question. "And check out the length of this thing. Believe me, it's long enough to contain...bodies."

Garret winced. "At this point I'm antsy enough that I'm willing to go down and check out anything. At least we'd be doing something. We've been out here for days and what do we have to show for it? Zip. Nada. I say it's about time we got lucky."

Mitch loosened up his tense muscles by rolling his head from side to side. "Lucky? To find the bodies of our sister and her kids we call it luck? Doing this, I feel as though I'm in a surreal world that never ends." He finished stretching his shoulders and added, "Are we really ready for this? Walsh offered to go down first and do the recon."

"No," Jackson muttered. At the railing, he spit into his mask, rubbed the lenses, and then dipped it into a bucket of seawater to rinse off. "It should be one of us who finds her."

Garret went through the same ritual with his mask and said, "I agree with Jackson. But what do we do once we get down there? Do we haul up this thing and check it out on the deck of the boat, or do we see what's what at the bottom?"

"Good question." Jackson turned to Mitch. "Any ideas?"

"I say we play it by ear until we see what we've got. If it looks like it holds what we're looking for, then we surface and bring it up slowly with a crane. If we're unsure, we bust it open down there without the bother of dragging it to the top."

Jackson glanced out to the horizon, watched the sun pop out behind the billowing clouds. It streamed down in a gilded ribbon across the sky turning the water into a sea of gold. "Makes sense. Let's get this over with." He checked the time on his diver's watch, noted the readings on his wrist compass. With a nod of his head, he was the first to roll backward over the side of the boat and into the water, disappearing into its depths.

His heading was straight down into a cavernous, shadowy Atlantic. He swam like an agile dolphin, cutting a swath on the way to the bottom.

As he'd expected, at seventy-five feet below the surface, the water became a deep cerulean and with it, poorer visibility. That's why each brother had clipped a light to his vest.

The light meant Jackson could get a better look at the organ pipe sponges and other soft corals with their delicate limbs fluttering to the tune of the drifting currents. A school of amberjack swam by and into an overhang where a stealth three-foot blacktip shark waited for his lunch.

At one hundred feet they used what air they had in the tank four times faster than they had earlier. At this point they were on the clock before they ran out of air completely.

Jackson cleared his mind and dived toward the limestone bedrock where the silt shifted and allowed him to study the anomaly that lay at a depth of almost one hundred and twenty feet. He ran his hand over what turned out to be a thick roll of carpet tied with fraying rope.

Up to this point, the brothers had communicated very little and only when necessary using hand signals. Jackson gestured to Mitch and took out his knife, snipped the binding.

Elation shot out like cannon fire when all three men realized it was nothing more than a bundle of carpeting that probably fell off a freighter a year or two earlier. Once he cut the twine from around the roll, the carpet shredded into huge chunks.

The trip to the top seemed to take forever. But as soon as they broke the surface, it was Jackson who had the most frustration stored up. "Why the hell can't we locate them? Where the hell could they be?"

Yanking up his mask, Mitch reached to grab hold of the ladder and hoist himself over and onto the deck. "It's one dive spot. It could take two dozen more tries before we find anything at all. Hell, they may not even be out here. It's possible we aren't even looking in the right spot. Do you know how many thousands of square miles of the Atlantic there are? And we haven't even touched the west side between here and Tampa Bay."

Jackson scaled the rungs behind his brother, swung onto the deck, scrubbed the water off his face. Anger raged inside him and he flung his mask against the railing. "Why aren't we able to find them? I'm sick of the worry. I'm sick of the look in Mom and Dad's eyes every day that goes by with no word."

Garret followed him over the railing and crossed to where Jackson stood. He wrapped him up in a bear hug.

"It's okay. We'll get through this. We'll get Mom and Dad through this."

Jackson let himself hug back. But it didn't last long before he got sentimental. "Tell me the truth. When we were ushers at their wedding, did it ever occur to either one of you then that Walker could ever do anything to hurt Livvy like this? All those times we were sitting around unwrapping Christmas presents, did you consider the possibility that he was enough of a lowlife to ever hurt his kids? Did he do away with her and the kids? Is he sipping a piña colada in Maldives with another girlfriend? I'm not so sure."

"What are you saying?"

"That we played poker with the guy. We ate the burgers and steaks he cooked on the grill. We drank his whiskey. We tossed a football around at the beach. We all put up with his attempt at stupid jokes. Sometimes I got the impression he was trying too hard. Were there signs that he was dangerous, violent, signs we missed?"

Garret bristled. "People have different sides to them. We never knew about the office he kept off limits or the affair, maybe affairs as in plural. If a guy cheats once, he's likely to serial cheat. Isn't that how the statistics read? If we couldn't trust him to do right by Livvy then how do we give him the benefit of the doubt now? Where are you going with this, Jackson?"

It was Mitch who completed the thought. "I think what Jackson's getting at is he thinks Walker is a victim."

Jackson puffed out a breath. "Walker was certainly no saint. But he loved those kids."

"When did you change your mind?"

"Seventy feet under water. A conversation I had with Blake last spring. It hit me about halfway down."

"And?"

"It was after Nana's funeral. Blake told me his daddy read to him and Ally every night when he was home. That he set up a telescope so they could take turns looking at the stars in the backyard. Like any eight-year-old Blake was looking forward to a carefree summer. Walker had promised to take him camping. To get him ready for it, Walker put up tents in the backyard so they could sleep outdoors. Does that sound like a guy who could do harm to his own kids?"

"Tessa thinks he killed her brother," Garret reminded them.

"I know she does. That's a possibility. However, I'm leaning toward the category that's not what happened. I want to know if Walker could do away with his own wife and kids? That's the thing I'm having the most trouble with. I go back and forth."

"We don't have anything definitive. That's what's so frustrating for all of us. Right now, it's all speculation. Who knows what was going through Walker's head? Who knows how deep his feelings ran toward this Ellerbee woman? Who's to say he was even still in love with Livvy at all? Who knows what mess he got tangled up with in Royce's schemes? If he was facing financial ruin, who knows what Walker was capable of doing on any given day?"

"So we're chasing our tails?" Jackson said, rubbing his eyes.

"Jackson, we've been doing that since we picked up the phone and found Mom on the other end."

Tessa stood behind the cash register at The Blue Taco taking the food orders. Unfamiliar with the menu items, she was having trouble with speed. Slow to ring up the customers, the line was out the door. There were even a few who left the counter grumbling, but most gave her time to peck the keys and get their orders straight.

It was early afternoon when Tessa glanced up and saw Dack Hawkins making his way to the counter. As soon as she looked into his face, she knew why he was there. The news wouldn't be good.

In spite of all the talks she'd had with herself in preparing for this moment, she couldn't prevent her lips from trembling as Hawkins delivered the blow.

"I'm sorry. But you already knew it was a grim possibility that the remains the boys found on the beach would turn out to be your brother. I'm sorry," he repeated.

"I did. But... I need to call my dad, make arrangements to take Ryan back home."

"It'll be days yet before we're able to release his remains."

"That long? May I ask why?"

Hawkins cut his eyes down to the floor before looking back at Tessa. "The coroner hasn't yet determined the manner of death. You should probably consider the possibility that you might never know how Ryan died exactly. I can tell you it wasn't a drowning. There was no water found in his lungs. He was dead when he went in the water. But since we don't have...all of the body..."

Tessa rubbed her forehead, the first signs of a headache forming. "I hadn't thought of that."

"The medical examiner isn't ready to give up yet." Hawkins reached across the counter and took hold of Tessa's hand. "I won't give up on this either."

When Tessa saw the sincerity on the cop's face, her eyes welled up. "Thank you," she muttered and meant it.

"If you need anything, call me," Hawkins said, before reaching in his pocket and pulling out a business card. "I'm staying at the Mainsail Lodge so I'm able to answer any questions that come up." With that, the detective turned on his heels and headed for the door.

Raine came up behind Tessa then and wrapped an arm around the woman's shoulders. "Go back to the houseboat. Relax for the rest of the day."

"There's no need. I need to stay busy."

"I'm not letting you hang around work with this kind of news. Where's Jackson?"

"On *The Black Rum*. He's in the middle of a dive. And you know what that means."

Raine's face went white. "Oh, no. We're just now dealing with this and now we may have to face the reality of Livvy's fate. This is a nightmare." As the lunch crowd continued to stream through the door, she reached out to Tessa, took her hand. "Will you be okay? I'll take over for you here."

Stubborn to the end, Tessa plastered a smile on her face. "This is my second day on the job. I'm not…"

"For God's sakes, this is a taco stand not a sickbay where you're expected to stay at your post no matter what happens during a life and death crisis situation. You need to go call your dad."

"You're right. I guess I'm not thinking straight." Tessa gathered up her purse and walked out to her Toyota, still in a daze. As she sat behind the wheel she punched in the number back home. The call lasted no more than fifteen minutes but drained her emotionally. After hanging up, instead of heading for the houseboat, Tessa decided to walk. She let the light breeze dance over her face to dry her tears as she made her way down to the shores of Sugar Bay.

She found a bench and sat there looking at the water. It was smooth as glass, the boats barely bobbing on the tides. Jackson was out there somewhere trying to locate a body, no, more like four of them. Even though she could've texted him to get an update, she wasn't sure she could handle more bad news. She might not have known Livvy and her kids, wasn't even certain Walker was the villain she'd made him out to be all these weeks, but she felt a kinship to the family. That connection made her unsure of everything.

Feeling vulnerable and dejected, she stayed glued to the same spot mulling over the last days of Ryan's life. He'd come down here to this paradise to enjoy himself. Before he could leave, he'd crossed paths with his killer. How had he died? How long had it taken? Had it been quick and painless? Or had he suffered? Of course he'd suffered, she decided. Had it been a gunshot wound to the head? Or had he been beaten to death and his body thrown into the water?

Thank God she'd had the sense to check things out for herself instead of staying put in Nags Head.

She wasn't sure whether she was angry or furious. How could Ryan have posed a threat to anyone, enough for the killer to take his life? He was always such an affable person willing to help out anyone who needed a hand. Had he been murdered over five thousand dollars? Jackson was right. The sum seemed measly now.

The more questions that whizzed through her head, the more she fumed. But did getting mad really do any good? She should turn the outrage into solid determination. After all, she wasn't alone in this. She had friends with like-minded goals, friends who were willing to try for answers. Look how Jackson had leaned on Sinclair and how Anniston had pushed Hawkins into a corner to get his cooperation.

Tessa glanced up at the heavens. The sun broke out through billowy clouds streaking the sky with rosy orange stripes. The scene resembled an inspirational postcard she'd picked up for others back home when she'd been trying to comfort friends.

But it seemed there was no chance of comfort.

Sitting there she felt aimless. Staring out at the horizon she watched the sun drop slowly into the afternoon sky. The harbor was alive with activity. There were sailboats returning to port having tested the wind and currents. Yachts were motoring out with the sole purpose of taking advantage of dinner and a sunset. Fishing trawlers brought in their end-of-the-day catches, their holds brimming with shrimp or crabs. Schooners were filled to capacity with vacationers anticipating trophy barracudas for their walls.

Life, it seemed, went on around her.

But not for Ryan. Never again for Ryan.

A burst of sadness swept through her. The sobs erupted and she couldn't seem to stop the flow of tears.

As soon as he stepped off *The Black Rum*, Jackson spotted her like that, sitting forlorn and lost. Head tossed back, she looked like a fiery red-haired mermaid waiting to cast her spell over the nearest male.

Which would be him, he thought now. He sat down on the bench next to her, tossed an arm around her shoulders. "Raine called Mitch with the news. I'm so very sorry, baby."

Her head dropped to the comfort of his shoulder. "Deep down I already knew."

She wiped her nose on a napkin she'd stuffed in her jeans pocket from the taco shop. "What about you? Did you find anything?"

"Nah, just a roll of carpet that probably fell off a freighter a long time ago."

"I'm sorry." Her breath hitched. "They don't even know a cause of death. How is that possible? He could've been shot in the head, but…"

"Don't do this to yourself," Jackson pleaded. "Don't think about how he died, not now."

"No, right this minute my grief is so deep and wide, I almost feel as though it's a living thing that I could reach out and touch, or hold this giant ball of heartache in my hands. I have something to ask you. I know it's a lot, but…you can say no because the timing really sucks. But when I leave to bring Ryan's remains back to North Carolina will you…?"

Jackson didn't let her finish. "I'll go back with you."

"You will? I know it's an imposition."

"Don't be silly. I'm not doing anyone any good here. That's a fact. Besides, I don't want you having to go through this without me. Let me take you to the cottage. We'll spend the night there just the two of us. I'll pick up some more groceries and make you a meal. I want to be with you tonight."

"I was hoping you'd offer because, right now, there's no other place I'd rather be."

Chapter Twenty-Five

They stopped at Raine's to let Tessa leave a note for her roommate and pick up a few things she'd need for an overnight stay. She collected her toothbrush and toiletries, a change of clothes, and stuffed a robe down into her bag.

At the market they browsed for fresh yellowtail snapper and settled on a fifteen pounder Jackson could pan grill. He grabbed eggs and milk while Tessa headed down the produce aisle, picking out a bundle of asparagus and the makings for a salad.

Even weighed down with the shopping bags, the easy stroll to the cottage took less than five minutes. But before reaching the front door, Jackson pulled up short and pointed to the *Patagonia Pike* moored practically across the street from the bungalow. "Look how low she sits in the water. They're loaded with supplies and gearing up for an expedition to somewhere."

"You don't think that's odd for them to anchor so close?"

He did, but sending alarm bells running through her was the last thing he wanted, especially today. "It's a free country. During the last week, I've seen the crew come and go in the harbor." He unlocked the door and carried the groceries into the tiny kitchen. Heaving the bags on top of the counter, they began to unload the sacks.

The salvage boat forgotten, he tried to pamper her by plopping her down at the table to watch him cook. But that didn't last longer than the need to throw a salad together.

"I'm not an invalid. I can help with dinner," she insisted as she took out a knife to slice and dice the vegetables.

"You aren't used to being coddled, are you?"

Had she ever been coddled? she wondered. "I guess not. My mom died when Ryan and I were still in middle school. There was no one around after that to spoil us about anything. Dad worked long hours to pay Mom's mounting medical bills. Ryan usually tried to ease his burden while I kept the home fires burning, cooking, cleaning, that sort of thing. I guess by the time my mom had been dead several years and he joined that online dating site, he thought he deserved a little attention of his own."

Jackson dumped rice into a boiling pot, lowered the burner. "It's a shame he didn't get it with Suzanne. I'm looking forward to meeting this infamous femme fatale."

"You shouldn't be. She's a viper. It's funny how people think she's so charming and normal. Of course those are members of the country club she joined. She acts like she's from old money when in truth she's more of a phony than anyone I've ever met."

"You don't think she had anything to do with Ryan's death, do you? How did Suzanne feel about Ryan? How does she feel about you?"

The question had her fumbling the knife she used to chop up the peppers. "As much as I detest my stepmother that's how much she detests us. The feeling is quite mutual."

"But you mentioned something about when your dad dies all his money will go to her, right?"

"I did say that, but it was an assumption, an off the cuff attempt at humor. In truth, I'm sure my dad would never even consider leaving his children out of his will."

Jackson dropped the fish into a skillet. "Just how greedy is this woman?"

A sick look crossed Tessa's face. "Greedy enough to insist on my father taking out life insurance to the tune of two million dollars and making her the beneficiary."

"With you and Ryan out of the way, she'd get his entire estate. I don't want to freak you out or anything, but if we're making a list of suspects, it's something to consider."

"Maybe she hired someone to follow Ryan down here from Nags Head."

"Would she do something like that?"

"I don't know." Tessa took out dishes from the cupboard to set the table. "But once when Suzanne got mad at a neighbor she told us she knew the right people who could make things happen. About a month later, the lady's house caught fire. Luckily, the woman and her children managed to get out in time and escaped without any injuries. But I always wondered if Suzanne's threat was connected in some way. When I mentioned it to Dad he dismissed it, said Suzanne was just trying to impress us with a lot of big talk. Believe me, it had the opposite effect on everyone but Dad."

Jackson removed the pan-seared snapper onto their plates and dished out the rice. "I'm curious. What had the neighbor done to piss her off?"

"She let her little boy wander over the property line with his dog and the dog pooped on Suzanne's prize tea roses."

"You're kidding? That's it? This woman sounds like a piece of work. How did Suzanne act when you announced you were coming down here to look for Ryan?"

A slow moving fear spread to the pit of Tessa's stomach. "Suzanne was against it, told me it was a waste of time, that he probably just wanted a break. Now that I think about it, she did everything she could to keep me from coming here."

With that charge hanging in the air, Jackson got out two beers from the fridge. They sat down to supper under a cloud of doubt.

When he realized the mood had darkened, he laid a hand over hers. "Look, we're probably letting our imaginations take off into the irrational and the wild. Something you definitely don't need right now. I hate it that you have to go through this. But we don't dare deny that the situation calls for thinking outside the realm of normal."

"Granted I might have a wild imagination, but just in case, I'm asking Anniston to look into Suzanne's background."

"There you go, an even better plan."

"Jackson, do you really think Walker murdered my brother?"

An unsuitable topic for sure, Jackson decided. "I've been thinking about that and I don't know. If I believe Walker killed Ryan, then I have to consider the possibility he did the same thing to Livvy and the kids."

She wanted to be mad at his change of heart, but understood the logic of that. "You know what? I think we should table any further discussions about murder and enjoy the food you fixed."

He locked his fingers into hers and kissed the top of her hand. "An excellent suggestion. Did you know my grandmother was a combat nurse assigned to a MASH unit during the Vietnam War? Her sister, Tansy Williamson, a photojournalist, got the idea to travel over there and take photographs of my nana in action."

He stood up and crossed over to where an older photo hung on the wall. "This is the shot Tansy took of my grandmother in her nurses outfit tending to an injured soldier that made the cover of *Time* magazine." He tapped the glass. "Tansy behind the lens, my nana in front."

"You come from interesting stock, Jackson."

He chugged his beer and smiled. "I really do. You know, when I'm around you, you get me to thinking about things I'd forgotten."

"I wish I could've met your nana."

"Me too. She was a feisty individual long before anyone ever heard of the feminist movement. She used to wear these crazy hats around town so she wouldn't get too much sun. That's before all the warnings came out and every kind of sun screen hit the market."

"Sounds like your nana was ahead of her time." Tessa leaned over and began to nibble his jaw. "Let's hurry and clean up the dishes and go to bed. What do you say?"

"I like the way you think."

Jackson was fast asleep with Tessa nestled beside him when he heard what sounded like a thud hitting the front of the house. He sat up, rummaged through the nightstand drawer, grabbed a hefty two-foot-long flashlight he found there and tossed back the covers. The floor creaked as he made his way to the bedroom door, wishing he'd followed through with Michael Tang and bought a gun.

The minute he turned the handle, Tessa shot up like a rocket, still in a sleepy stupor. "What's wrong?"

He put a finger to his lips for quiet and motioned that he'd heard a noise and intended to check it out.

In spite of his protests, Tessa crawled out of bed to follow on his heels. "I'm going out there with you," she whispered.

"That stubborn side to you is annoying," Jackson muttered.

"Get used to it," she said, and grabbed her robe.

They tiptoed down the hallway, past the bathroom to the living room. He crossed to the window, peered out onto the lawn.

"See anything?"

"No." He went to the front door, opened it up enough to see if anyone was on the porch.

The brown envelope, the nine by twelve variety, had been propped up against the front door and fell into the open doorway. In bold letters printed across the width, it was addressed to "Livvy's Surviving Family."

Jackson leaned down to scoop it off the mat, but before he could, Tessa warned, "You don't want to handle it. Maybe they left fingerprints or DNA. Let me find something to use to protect it." She dashed off to the kitchen to grab a potholder or dishtowel.

While Tessa did her thing, Jackson used the time to scan the street and the harbor from the doorway. There were no cars moving, no shapes or shadows lingering anywhere near the house. He squinted in the direction of the harbor and noticed the *Patagonia Pike* had its running lights on, motoring out of the bay.

When Tessa reappeared, she handed off two potholders for Jackson to use to grasp both sides of the packet.

They treated the envelope as if it were an explosive device, using a pair of tweezers to undo the metal clasp and pull out the document—a single sheet of paper, computer-generated, three paragraphs long.

The letter read like someone had ripped the pages out of the middle chapter of a thriller. Jackson stared at the words, unable to focus.

It was Tessa who began the gut-wrenching narration.

As soon as she'd finished the last word, Jackson felt like he might be sick. "Call everyone, get them rounded up. They need to know about this."

"Jackson, it's four-thirty in the morning."

"I don't care. Either we go to them or they come here."

Tessa dug out her cell phone. "With limited space here, I'd say it's better if we do this at your Mom and Dad's. But that would mean we'd have to transport the note and use additional care handling it. I think that's a bad idea. We should get everyone over here."

"Fine, just do it," Jackson muttered. "When will this nightmare ever end?"

Chapter Twenty-Six

An hour later, they'd thrown on clothes and made coffee and got ready to greet their sleepy band of sleuths.

Anniston arrived first, half-awake and cranky. She was still trying to wrap her mind around the fact someone had left a note when Jackson handed her a mug.

"Thank God for caffeine." Using both hands to grip the cup, Anniston took a seat on the couch, the whole time eyeing the document still on the coffee table. "This case just keeps getting weirder."

Jackson took a sip from his own cup, playing lookout at the front door for the rest of the family. Too angry, too upset to sit, he railed into the early morning dawn. "We've suspected from the start sick people scuttling around in the dark is pretty much how this whole thing got started. I just don't think we were prepared for a blow by blow detail like this."

"Who would write such a thing?" Tessa asked.

"The same person who murders little kids," Jackson barked. He rubbed his forehead. "I'm sorry. I didn't mean to snap at you."

She rubbed his back. "It's okay. I know it hurts."

When Anniston got too close with her coffee, Tessa took up guard around the note. "Try not to spill anything on it. And before you ask, we never touched it with our bare fingers."

"Good thinking. It hadn't crossed my mind because it's a little early for me. At this hour I'm barely able to form a cognizant thought."

Lenore walked in, gave her son a big hug. "So this is where you two have been hiding out." She patted Jackson on the back and whispered in his ear, "You should buy this place, move back home and get out of that concrete jungle you call Manhattan."

"Mom, not the time or the place."

"Just saying."

Tanner grumbled as he came in behind his wife, followed by Mitch and Garret. "What's this all about anyway? Where's the damned coffee?"

Lenore pushed her husband and sons toward the kitchen. "I'm sure it's not in the living room." She pointed toward Jackson. "We still have to wait for Raine. We don't start without her."

Raine showed up last, but she'd stopped to pick up a dozen pastries and croissants from the French bakery on Seafarer Way. "After Tessa's phone call I thought we might need butter-laden dough with our sugar high."

Mitch took the box and flipped up the lid. He made a sound in his throat that sounded like pure pleasure. He picked out a cruller, took a generous bite. Showing his gratitude for the food, he bent his head, placed a kiss on Raine's forehead, then her cheek. "Good call. You always did think of everyone else first."

Raine tilted her head at the compliment. "Have you been drinking? If not, you must still be half asleep."

"Now Blondie, that's just mean. It's too early for that kind of wanton aggression." He watched as she pushed past him into the kitchen.

"If I have to put up with your attempt at being nice, I'll need a gallon of coffee."

After everyone served themselves coffee and sweet rolls, dragged chairs in from the other rooms, they huddled together in a circle in the small den as Tessa used the tweezers again to hold the paper in place. She began to reread the chilling account of how Walker, Livvy, and the kids had supposedly died.

"'Your sister suffered. I made sure of that. I beat her before putting a bag over her head and strangling her just as I did Walker. I suffocated him first, though, made sure he was dead. I did the same thing to the bratty kids. The little boy begged me not to hurt his daddy. The boy was so scared he wet his pants. The girl wasn't much better but at least she showed some gumption. She tried to kick at me. She was still screaming and fighting when I put the bag over her head and watched her slowly die. I watched each one take their last breath and enjoyed every minute of it. Although it was over too quick to suit me.'"

Tessa stopped, put her hand on her stomach. "Someone else has to finish. I think I drank my coffee too fast or something. I feel sick." She dashed down the hall to the bathroom.

Anniston leaned over the table to read without bothering to pick up the note and continue where Tessa had left off.

"'They didn't live long after I took them. But did I mention your sister tried to get away? She crawled on her belly before I hit her in the head and crushed her skull. She still wasn't dead though and begged for her life. Don't think you'll ever find me. And you're wasting time looking for the bodies. You'll never find their makeshift graves. The swamp is a very unforgiving place.

Decomposition begins immediately. It tears at the skin. And the 'gators use them for food. You might as well accept they're gone for good.'"

Anniston let those last disturbing words hang in the air before she took inventory. Lenore had leaned her head on Tanner's shoulder and softly sobbed. He put his arms around his wife, unable to find any words of comfort.

Raine had tears streaming down her face. It warmed Anniston to see Mitch reach over and take Raine's hand in his.

She searched out Garret's eyes, eyes that were cold and distant. Anniston could almost see the guy plotting revenge. She finally cleared her throat to get everyone on the same page with what had to be done. "After we've thoroughly vetted this thing and spent hours discussing the way this asshole formed his thoughts, we'll need to tag and bag the letter and envelope as evidence and send it off to the lab for analysis."

It was the athlete who was forced to put on his game face. Garret needed to explore every avenue. "The thing is, how do we determine if we're dealing with someone who's simply yanking our chain or making a genuine confession?"

Raine gently removed her hand from Mitch's grasp to wipe away tears. "But who would make something like this up if it wasn't true?"

Mitch sipped his coffee. "There are plenty of crazies out there who get their rocks off doing exactly that. Look at the poor mother back in Chicago in 1957 whose two daughters disappeared. For weeks afterward before the bodies were discovered the mother received a host of crank calls and ransom demands even though later it was determined her girls died within five hours of going missing. During times like this, a few rotten apples rise to the occasion with all the malicious intent of predators."

"But who knew there would be so many rotten apples in the place where we grew up?" Garret pondered, pushing his remaining pastry to the side. Either the rush of sugar made him queasy or it was the idea that his sister and her kids might've suffered a horrible fate. His stomach felt tied in knots. "Mom and Dad have already received a few disturbing phone calls in the middle of the night, heavy breathing to boot. I'm surprised the phony ransom demands haven't kicked in yet."

Raine absorbed the sickness in that. "So you don't think this note is for real? I'm not sure I agree. It sounds real enough to me."

While Jackson listened to the discussion ramp up, unlike the others, he could see it in his head, could see Livvy's fear, could almost touch her suffering for himself, and knew the terror she must have felt at knowing she was about to die.

There was something raw and primal that simmered inside him. His hands clenched in fists at his sides. He'd never been a violent man, but now, he wanted to get his hands on the person who'd brought such devastation to his family.

After washing her face, Tessa had joined the others and felt a little better. But she took one look at Jackson's face and realized there was something wrong. The note had hit him hard. He seemed to be in his own world. She crouched in front of him, talking to him softly, reassuring him that everything would be okay. He seemed so troubled that she did her best to get through to him by touching his face, squeezing his leg, until he came back to himself.

Her heart went out to him because she could tell the depth of his fury went deep. "It's okay to be furious, Jackson, pissed off."

He framed her face with his hands, stroked her cheeks with his long fingers. He lowered his voice so no one else could hear. "From anyone else that might be nothing more than a platitude. But you know what I feel inside. I've never felt closer to anyone than I do you right this moment."

Tessa pressed her lips into both his palms. "I'm here for you."

Jackson flung an arm around Tessa's shoulders for support and looked around the room. "I think the note is the real deal. This sick bastard wanted to beat his chest and he thought the best way to do that was in writing. Doesn't mean he stuck to the facts. But we have to treat this the same way we would if we happened upon any other lead on our own. We parse every cruel word this bastard used. Hope like hell he was making most of it up."

"But you don't think so?" Garret asked.

"No. I also saw something odd. It might be nothing more than a coincidence but about the same time the packet showed up on the doorstep, the *Patagonia Pike* left port. I think we should find out where it's headed."

"I did some research on that," Mitch told him. "Turns out the owner Werner Dietrich has an interesting past. During World War II, his father was a ranking officer in the SS."

Jackson rubbed his forehead, a headache beginning to thud. "He was a Nazi?"

"An important one. The *Patagonia Pike* has a habit of looking for U-boats that reportedly carried Nazi gold from war-torn Germany to South America and sunk on the way. It's the company's one specialty."

"And have they found any?"

"Two, one back in 2005 and again in 2010, which means they're likely hungry for a hit."

"Then what are they doing off the Florida Keys?" Mitch's silence had Jackson's jaw dropping. "Are you suggesting they're here looking for Nazi gold?"

"I'm telling you what I found out. Why they'd leave South American waters when as many as eighteen German subs were sunk off the coast there I don't know. Is it possible a German U-boat went down off the Florida coast? Absolutely. In 2014 divers located U-576 in the waters off North Carolina. It was found near a merchant tanker on its way to Key West in 1942. And in 2012, U-550 was discovered off the waters of Nantucket. All told, some twenty U-boats sank in coastal waters off the U.S.

Were they all laden down with gold? Of course not, just a lot of fantastic history. But for the record, there's still about fifty U-boats out there somewhere unaccounted for, some that were rumored to carry gold bullion hidden in the ship's supply hold."

Jackson angled his chin. "It's either way too early in the morning to have this discussion or I'm just not seeing the connection. What would the *Patagonia Pike* have to do with Walker and Livvy, literally a guy who was deep into running a supplement business, and a typical soccer-mom wife?"

Mitch chewed his lip. "That's what we need to find out. Did they get pulled into some treasure-hunting scheme they thought would solve their money woes?" His eyes sought out Tessa's. "Did Ryan get suckered into the same deal for the same reason?"

Tessa exchanged looks with Jackson. "That's a distinct possibility. As I said before Ryan had a childhood dream. He didn't talk about becoming a superhero, but he did mention that someday he'd go looking for treasure. I'm afraid it might've been his undoing."

"Maybe all their undoing," Jackson determined, considering that grim realization.

Chapter Twenty-Seven

Jackson spent his days on the water, his nights wrapped around Tessa at the cottage. They took turns doing the cooking, whether breakfast or dinner. Or they'd go out to one of the island's restaurants, sample the local cuisine. They often took walks around the harbor or they might veer off along the strand to explore the shops.

They'd gotten into a routine where they spent the evening bouncing theories off each other. Or simply nurturing the growing bond happening between them. They tried to make each other laugh during the bad times when all thoughts turned to Ryan, or to Livvy and her family.

They both felt pressure that their days together were numbered. While Tessa waited for a call that would send her back to Nags Head, Jackson went out each morning with his brothers wondering when and how it would all change.

Anguish and worry had brought them together. But something deeper had to be what made it all stick.

That's one reason Jackson pushed himself.

After a long day on the water, running on too little sleep, Jackson was bone tired and starving when Tessa sent word that Anniston had summoned them all to the Mainsail Lodge. The PI had booked a conference room that came with a generous spread. The deal included appetizers, sandwiches, chips, drinks, and a dessert tray piled high with butter tarts and gooey muffins.

The guys packed around the buffet, filling their plates like they hadn't seen food in two days.

"Beer's over there," Anniston said, directing them to another serving station.

Lenore looked at all the food. "I'm glad I didn't have to throw all this together."

Tessa handed her a plate. "Lenore, you've been cooking for the lot of us every time we get together. Let someone else serve you for a change."

"I like the sound of that. I'll take one of those lobster rolls for starters. They look exactly like the ones from Raine's place."

Raine patted her arm. "That's because they are. Those are filled with fresh lobster, caught this morning."

Mitch helped himself to one off the serving tray. "I love the way you make these with your special blend of mayo, sprinkling the meat mixture with a little paprika on top."

Raine's cynical heart cracked a little. "It's my mom's recipe and you know it."

Mitch bobbed his head. "I do. But she's no longer running the place. You are."

Lenore glanced at Raine's plate. "I see you're turning up your nose at the fish."

"I'm staying away from the stuff I brought," Raine said as she chose a vegetarian hoagie piled high with greens and avocado and cheese. "You work around the same foods long enough and before you know it you're sick of smelling fish and tacos, let alone eating that same thing twice a day."

"I can vouch for that," Tessa added. "Just the few days I've been working there I'm sick of smelling the fish frying and rolled tacos."

"Totally understand," Raine said as she snatched a bag of chips from the tabletop.

"I want you to know I hate leaving my job," Tessa admitted.

Raine sent her a wide smile. "You don't have to say that on my account. It takes a brutal schedule to keep the restaurant running. I'm used to it. You don't have to be. Besides, it's time for you to head back home with your brother and put him to rest."

Tessa wiped back tears that spilled down her cheeks. "I know. But I will miss being here. I've come to think of y'all as family."

"And us you," Lenore assured her. "Tanner and I were thinking about going with you and Jackson back to Nags Head for the funeral."

Tessa's face brightened. "Oh, I wish you would. I hated to ask, but I was hoping you might come."

"Honey, all you had to do was let us know you wanted us there."

"But with the search for Livvy—"

"Don't you worry, we'll make plans to be there. It might be good for us to get out of here for a few days. We won't stay that long, a couple days at the most. Mitch and Garret will hold down the fort while we're gone."

"That's wonderful." Tessa turned to Jackson. "Did you hear that? Your parents are coming to Nags Head for the funeral."

"I heard." Jackson slapped his dad on the back. "Nice gesture. What brought that on?"

"Tessa's been through a lot. It's the least your mother and I can do for all the work she's done to help find Livvy.

If not for her we wouldn't know about Jessup's little meeting with Royce."

Jackson bobbed his head in agreement. "It's a good thing to do. It means a lot to her."

Anniston cleared her throat. "Once you all get your food and get settled, I have a long list of things we need to go over."

"The gang's all here. Might as well throw it at us now," Jackson stated wearily as he took a seat at one of the tables.

"First of all, the lab found the note and envelope had been wiped completely clean, no fingerprints whatsoever, no touch DNA, nothing."

Jackson suddenly lost his appetite and pushed his plate away. "We pretty much already knew the person who left it wouldn't make it that easy."

"That's the bad news," Anniston said. "Now for the good. The lab was able to ID the printer used, an HP Laser Jet 9500."

"They can do that?" Garret dug into one of the lobster rolls and took a swig of beer, sat back in his chair.

"Oh yeah. But the HP 9500 is a fairly common model widely used in commercial offices, which makes the printer one we might be able to track." Anniston turned her attention to Jackson. "Try to think back when you found the note. Did you hear a car in the area?"

"No. I heard a thump like someone stepped up on the porch and hit the swing up against the house. Maybe that means they looked in the window first before dropping the envelope and then took off on foot. If that's the case, it doesn't make sense that it was anyone associated with the *Patagonia Pike*. The boat was already motoring out of the bay by the time I opened the door." He ran a hand through his hair. "If only we had just one thing in this mess that made sense."

Mitch pushed his plate away as well. "Especially since whoever did this got away with making an entire family disappear. In my book, we have two options. We check out every printer in town or narrow it down right away to the five people Tessa saw at Royce's house."

"I vote for confronting the men who tried to misdirect the search," Lenore said before sending her hubby a stern look. "Only this time we go as a group or in pairs to talk to Dandridge and the others."

Tanner snorted. "Why? Boone will simply deny it. Just because he's a pastor doesn't mean he's above lying. You think he'll admit to being the author of that note? Think again. I'd rather spend my time digging deeper into what Walker and Royce are involved in."

Anniston prompted them to move on. "Let's finish the agenda completely before we decide on a strategy. We have a lot still to cover. For starters, my source inside the Tampa Bay PD tells me when the crime scene techs went over the minivan they reported it smelled like the interior had been gone over with bleach. As for the Luminol test, it came back with a hit. They found trace blood in the cargo hold. Not a lot—and it might be explainable if it belonged there from a nosebleed or something equally innocent."

"But they smelled bleach," Jackson pointed out.

"Exactly. Put the two together—bleach and a dab of blood and it's never a good sign, my friends."

Lenore tried to keep from crying. Once again, she reiterated her resolve. "We should start by talking to the four who didn't want us searching for Livvy. They might know something. We should find out where they were that Wednesday night."

"An excellent idea," Anniston echoed. "Now to the other matter. My tech guy discovered that phone call Ryan received from the 305 area code came from what's known as a throw away phone, or sometimes called a burner phone."

"So there's no way to trace it?" Tessa questioned.

"The feds have a better chance at it if the person buys fifty or more at a time because retailers are supposed to report that kind of purchase. But let's face it. If a person buys one or two and stays under the radar, pays cash at the register, uses it for under two weeks, and then tosses it in the trash, the activity is gone. Since I already know it's a nonworking number, I'm sure it's been disposed of by this time, probably discarded in the bay or some dumpster around town."

Tessa let out a sigh. "And that was more than three weeks ago. We'd never locate it. We keep striking out at every turn."

"Not exactly." Anniston decided it was time to remind the clients that patience could be a virtue. "That day at the preserve I made a pact with Hawkins about sharing information. This morning I was able to prod Hawkins into telling me what the forensic team found in Ryan's Civic. He wouldn't give me the entire list, but one of the things they came across was the five grand, minus about forty bucks."

Tessa scrubbed her hands over her face. "So if Ryan wasn't killed for the cash then why?"

Jackson pulled his chair next to Tessa's, took her hand. "I'd like to point out that no one uses a burner phone unless they're involved in criminal activity. And Ryan did end up deceased. We just have to keep digging."

"Kidnapping and murder tend to be the ultimate in illegal activity," Garret stated, polishing off his sandwich.

"Aside from that, the other night Tessa asked me to run a background check on her stepmother." Anniston dug out a thick packet from her satchel. "This is what I found. Suzanne Connelly is an interesting woman. She's been married four times. Your father is number four. Two of her husbands died, number two and number three. One died as a result of a still-unsolved mugging in downtown Charlotte, the other in what was listed on the death certificate as cardiac arrest. Both men were heavily insured. Suzanne was the beneficiary to the tune of two million dollars."

Tessa's jaw dropped. "That's downright scary. It doesn't exactly make me feel one bit warmer or fuzzier about the woman."

"I'm sure it doesn't. When you go back to North Carolina for the funeral you might want to sit down with your dad and have a heart to heart with him."

"If only it were that easy. When Ryan was alive we couldn't talk any sense into our dad before the wedding. I doubt knowing about her past will make a difference. I think in some weird way my dad actually loves Suzanne."

"It won't hurt to try," Jackson advised. "I'll be there with you."

Lenore traded looks with Tanner. "When do you two leave?"

"As soon as the coroner releases the body we're off to Nags Head," Jackson said.

Anniston went over to Tessa. "If you think it would help, I'm happy to talk to your dad myself."

"I may take you up on that."

"Your call." Anniston kept to the business at hand. "Hawkins also agreed to share the Buchanans' phone activity with me, landline and cell records. Do you remember when we discussed that this all started at the house with someone ringing the doorbell in the middle of the night and Livvy getting Walker to answer the door?" Anniston paused long enough to make sure they were all on the same page. "Well, it seems that's more likely than a mysterious phone call luring them outside their house and to the Vitamin Hut. That night only two calls came in, one on Walker's cell phone from Harlow Ellerbee."

"The other woman," Jackson finished.

Anniston nodded. "I've already contacted Ms. Ellerbee to ask her about it. She claims she phoned Walker that night to cancel their rendezvous scheduled for the following Tuesday. She said she had to go out of town. Which prompted me to check with her law firm. I was able to confirm her trip to Atlanta where she went to take a deposition. She was there for two days. The only other call that came in took place at eight twenty-five that evening. That was from Walker's father, landline to landline. I talked to Royce before I got here. He claims the reason for the call was nothing sinister. Royce wanted Walker to arrange to take Nathan Hollister out on the boat that weekend to try and catch swordfish."

Jackson's expression hardened into a frown. That excuse didn't add up. "Since when does Nathan Hollister have any interest in catching a trophy fish? The Nathan I knew didn't even like setting foot on a boat. He's worse than Garret. That's the one place where Nathan and I went our separate ways. I loved the water. He didn't, had a fear of it so much that he usually distanced himself from anything aquatic, preferring instead to stay on dry land."

"Are we talking about the banker?" Tessa asked.

Jackson got up to pace, no longer able to sit in one place. "Yeah, and childhood friend. I didn't realize he and Royce were so tight these days."

"As president of a bank, Nathan would have to mingle with the large account holders," Tessa pointed out. "And maybe he simply got over his fear over the years."

"Maybe." But Jackson didn't buy it. "Garret never got over his dislike of boats."

Anniston chose to move on. "Hawkins also provided us with a little bonus. He turned up a surveillance video of Livvy making a withdrawal the day she disappeared. He sent me a copy. It seems the Wednesday she went missing, at ten forty-eight in the morning, she walked to the ATM on the corner of Pearl Street and Seafarer Way where she took out five hundred dollars, the maximum she could take without going inside the bank. Not exactly a break in the case, but it's significant because if you watch the video, Livvy seems...distracted. You might even say nervous."

Anniston clicked the keys on her laptop as everyone crowded around to peer at the screen, all hoping it would lead to further insight into Livvy's actions that day that might break the case wide open.

"Watch and tell me what you think." Anniston hit the button to show Livvy walking along the sidewalk leading up to the bank. "This is from the camera across the street. Some of you may not know it but this intersection is the busiest in town. Keep watching. Right there in the middle of the block is where she comes into camera range."

Jackson's eyes remained riveted to the monitor while the scene played out. "This can't be right. Are you sure this happened that morning?"

"The time stamp has been verified." Curious, Anniston wanted to know, "Why do you say that?"

"Because I went to the bank and talked to Nathan myself. Remember? Nathan never said a word about Livvy withdrawing that kind of money."

Anniston eyed Jackson with open distress. She'd seen that same look on Garret's face several days before, a look that had retribution written all over it. She wanted to tamp it down before it had a chance to take root. "Could've been Mr. Hollister wasn't aware of the transaction until much later. Or it was overlooked in all the other activities. I know at the time the authorities focused on releasing the surveillance of her at the supermarket that Wednesday afternoon with the kids. That's standard police procedure for getting the last known sighting out to the media. That video was responsible for jumpstarting the public's awareness about the family going missing. That's initially what created the firestorm that brought the reporters knocking."

Jackson wasn't so sure. "Nathan's the bank president, nothing goes on there that he doesn't know about firsthand." But instead of saying more, his eyes drifted back to the screen where the frame showed his sister standing in front of the building, swiping her card and waiting for the machine to spit out the cash. "She really has lost a lot of weight since I saw her last spring."

Mitch nodded in agreement. "She's so much thinner than she was at Christmas."

"Look at the dark circles under her eyes. To me, she looks tired, like she hasn't been getting a whole lot of sleep," Garret added. "And what's with the guarded way she moves. Do you see that? Watch her look around as if she doesn't want to get caught."

"That's my take." Anniston swung the laptop back around to where she could key in another site. "And her last post on social media occurred shortly thereafter when she posted a picture of a pug at the local shelter she was thinking of getting for the kids."

Lenore put her hands over her mouth. "I didn't even think of checking online. Let me see the entire post." Her eyes darted from word to word. "That's so strange because Walker had nixed that idea several months back."

"Really? Well, according to Hawkins, that afternoon before she left work, Livvy went online and made several online purchases, specialty coffee from an online retailer, and several books about housebreaking a dog. She buys a few video games for the kids before hitting a home goods site where she selects a rug and a set of towels from the same vendor. All those items were delivered to the house the day after the first search, a Monday, five days after she went missing."

Jackson made a frustrating growl in his throat. "Which is further proof she didn't plan on leaving."

Anniston pointed to the monitor. "When you put it all together, it seems like no big deal, like Livvy had a fairly routine day in the ordinary life of a wife and mom, just taking care of business."

"Except for the cautious way she acts at the ATM machine," Garret pointed out.

Anniston blew out a frustrated puff. "I'm not sure what any of it means. Keep in mind there might be a simple explanation for her demeanor. She could've been wary of withdrawing that kind of cash and was simply making sure no one was standing behind her."

Jackson thought of something. "I'm curious. Was the five hundred dollars found in the purse she left behind at the house?"

"Good question. I checked the handbag. It contained zero cash."

"So what happened to the money? Livvy didn't load five hundred dollars' worth of groceries into the minivan at the Winn-Dixie."

Anniston picked up a can of Coke and popped the top. "No she didn't. Besides, she used her debit card at the market. For me, all this adds up to Livvy and Walker were taken out of the house for some unknown reason. My take is, for what it's worth, this abduction took weeks of precise planning. But in the end, the stars had to line up just right in order to pull it off without leaving behind any witnesses. I've gone door to door in the neighborhood. I can't find a single person who saw the couple leave with their kids."

"So where does that leave us? It sounds like we're right back where we started with more questions than answers."

While the statement was fairly accurate, it didn't sit well with the private detective. "On the contrary, I believe we've made incredible inroads. I know it seems slow going, but we've been able to come up with a full circle of suspects."

Jackson shifted his gaze around the room to find his brothers. "We need to talk about what happens next. I've come to a decision. I should've said this some time back but…now's the time. You guys should feel free to go back to what you were doing before all this happened, regardless of what you committed to when you got here. It's not the same for me. Once I go back to work, I'll likely end up sitting in my office twenty stories above the city looking out at traffic or draw an assignment half a world away. I don't have the freedom you guys have. Mitch, the treasure hunter, and Garret, the globe-trotting, world-renowned surfer."

Jackson ran his hands through his hair. "Livvy and I grew up close. Ask Mom and Dad. At least I thought we were. Obviously I let our relationship slide over the years. I should've listened more when she called, answered her emails sooner and in more depth. I should've been a greater part of the kids' lives. Maybe that's the reason I'm not willing to go back to my job without having all the answers. It'll drive me crazy not knowing what happened to her."

Mitch shoved out of his chair, a muscle in his jaw twitching. "You realize it could take months to find those answers, if we ever get them at all."

"I do, that's why I've already asked my boss for an indefinite leave of absence. He wasn't happy about giving it to me. I wouldn't take no for an answer. Because of my precarious work situation, I wouldn't ask either one of you to give up more time here. This could turn into an indefinite period where nothing's resolved."

Garret stood up, thumbed a wave toward his older brother. "You don't have to ask me. If you're staying, then so will I. I'm not leaving my family in the lurch."

Mitch wandered the room until he came back full circle near his brothers. "I told you the day I picked you up from the airport that I'm in this thing till the finish. As long as we're able to give this our all, then we'll be okay. I'd already decided to stay on island. I even told my crew they could start looking for another gig on a boat somewhere else if they wanted."

"Will Walsh stay?" Jackson wondered.

"You bet, as long as we need him. That's the kind of guy he is. I'm not sure about the rest of the crew, though."

Garret pushed his way into the middle, stretched an arm out, slung it over first Mitch's shoulder then Jackson's. "The Indigo brothers are up to the task."

"Damn straight," Jackson muttered as he grabbed Tessa's hand. "There's something we need to take care of. I'll meet you all back at the house later."

Chapter Twenty-Eight

Jackson and Tessa made their way outside to the Mainsail parking lot. He took out his cell phone, all the while trying to bank his gnawing suspicion. But it wouldn't go away. He tapped into his email account, skimmed through a bunch of saved messages in his inbox from last year. His gut instinct told him he needed to go ahead and follow through. He'd already decided to confront Nathan and wasn't surprised when Tessa seemed to already know the plan.

"We'll take my car," she offered. "You seem to have a lot on your mind."

"Are you sure you're up to this? We haven't been getting a whole lot of sleep since the night that note showed up. Maybe you'd rather take a pass on coming with me."

Tessa had studied Jackson's face during the meeting and could tell the wheels were turning. "No need to try and ditch me. I'm fine. Better still, since I decided to keep busy and keep my mind off the visual of that horrible letter. This way, I'll have a purpose. I know something got to you in there." She tilted her head to try and read his demeanor. "Whatever's bothering you, involves the bank president. So out with it."

"I'll feel better after I ask Nathan a couple of questions."

"Ah. About his need to get a trophy fish for his wall when he has a deep fear of the water?"

"That too."

When Tessa realized that was about all she would get out of him, she yanked the car into gear. "Do you want to tell me how to get to the Hollister house?"

"It's a few blocks from my grandmother's cottage on the other side of Sugar Bay. Follow the loop from the marina around to where the houses start getting a lot bigger."

She followed his directions, heading past the wharf, driving the short distance without asking any more curious questions. When they reached a bend in the road, he pointed to a grand Southern style home with a spectacular waterfront view and dock access.

"Wow, you weren't kidding. For a guy who doesn't like the water your friend lives practically on top of it."

"Yeah, but that's Wendy's doing. The big house, the big mortgage, the important contacts. It seems banking's been real good to Nathan over the years."

"Want me to go with you?"

"Nah, if I make an ass of myself, I prefer doing it without witnesses."

Stubborn man, she decided as she watched him get out of the car.

The sophisticated digs were draped in early evening shadows as Jackson stepped under the portico and rapped on the door.

Wendy Hollister, a dark-haired beauty, had class written all over her. At least that's the way Jackson had always thought of her. She answered the door wearing a pair of rose-pink silk pajamas.

"Hi Wendy, I'm looking for Nathan,"

"Nathan isn't here. He went out of town yesterday on business. Bank convention."

Jackson narrowed his gaze on Wendy, noted what sounded like a party coming from inside the house. He didn't think the festive music was from the television. "I didn't realize Nathan's job took him out of town quite so often."

Upbeat Wendy shook her head. "It doesn't really. This is the first time in over a year."

"When's he due back?"

"I'm not sure exactly. His note didn't give me a lot of detail."

"He left a note to tell you he was going out of town? He didn't tell you this in person?" Jackson asked, scratching his chin. "I don't understand. Could I see the note?"

Wendy's look turned sheepish. "Okay, so it wasn't exactly a note. He sent me an email yesterday afternoon. By the time I got home from work he'd already packed and was on his way to Miami International to catch a flight to Denver."

"You didn't think that was strange?"

With each question Wendy's chipper attitude began to wane. "Look, I have my own busy career at city hall. Nathan often goes his way and I go mine. I have company right now and I need to get back to my…guest."

Jackson wanted to keep her talking, at least until he figured out what might be going on inside the house. "That's right, you're Mayor Oakerson's assistant. How long?"

Wendy beamed. "Three years now."

It occurred to Jackson that he'd never noticed Wendy Hollister was a bit of an airhead. "Will you call me when Nathan gets back in town? In the meantime I'll try to touch base with him via email or his cell phone."

"Sure. That's a great idea." With that, cheerful Wendy shut the door in his face.

Jackson headed back to the car disheartened but a lot more curious.

As soon as he settled into the passenger seat, Tessa wanted to know, "What was that all about?"

"It seems Nathan's taken a side trip to Denver." Perplexed, he pulled the seat belt across his lap as Tessa pulled away from the curb. From his pocket, he took out his phone, dialed his old friend's number.

He held the device out so she could hear. "Going straight to voicemail." He left a message. "Nathan, this is Jackson. Give me a call first chance you get." He rattled off the number for his cell. "It's about Livvy. I'd appreciate hearing from you as soon as possible."

Out of the corner of her eye, Tessa watched him. "Are you gonna tell me what this is all about? You aren't this worked up over an ATM transaction that Nathan kept to himself."

Jackson should have known she'd be able to read him. "Remember that day right after I got here I went to see Nathan at the bank to find out about the finances. He mentioned to me in a funny, offhand sort of way that he had a thing for Livvy. I didn't think anything of it at the time."

"So?"

"My hunch is the two were having an affair, a wild, heat-of-the-heart affair."

Tessa tapped the brake and slowed the car down to a crawl. "That's pretty weak, Jackson. I mean you and Livvy go back years with this guy. From what you've said he was your best friend. What makes you think…?"

"There's more. I went back and looked at several emails Livvy sent me over a year ago. In quite a few she never failed to mention Nathan. She had lunch with Nathan. She spent a Saturday going to an antique mall with Nathan. I didn't think much about it at the time, just thought two friends sharing a meal, an afternoon together. No big deal. In other words, I blew her off. I think she was trying to tell me something even then, and I was too preoccupied to listen. Livvy was unhappy, Tessa. I suspect she'd finally reached her limit with Walker at least a year ago, and was ready for something new, maybe even ready to divorce him and move on. I think on the days Walker took off for Miami, Livvy and Nathan spent a great deal of time together."

Tessa chewed her bottom lip. "We could really use Livvy's address book right about now, something with a list of her contacts, a calendar she kept, that sort of thing. It would be a snap if we had access to her computer. That would likely be a goldmine. We should work on Hawkins to get the desktop back."

"We'll give Anniston that chore. She seems to have a way with the cop."

"I'm getting a sense there was a relationship there between those two once upon a time."

"I got that same feeling. So the other day aboard *The Black Rum*, I did some snooping on Hawkins. He grew up in the Miami area and was at the police academy as an instructor during the same time Anniston was there as a recruit."

"Ah, so the plot thickens. Hawkins and Anniston had a fling."

"Don't tell Garret. He has a thing for her."

"So I've noticed. But in case you haven't been paying attention, it looks to me like the feeling is mutual. She's quite taken with Garret. There's a lot of sexual tension between those two."

"Anniston's interested in him? Really? Weird. I wouldn't have figured that."

"Me either. I seriously doubt her type is a surfer who travels the globe to exotic places looking to catch the next big wave. But there you go." Tessa pulled to a stop in front of the house on Quay Avenue and cut the engine. "Attraction rarely confines itself to boundaries or limitations. Opposites do attract. Look at my father and Suzanne."

"Are we opposites?" Jackson asked, taking her hand.

This was one of those things that made her sad about heading home. "I guess we'll find out if it's possible for us to keep this going between us long distance. Is it really possible for a blogger and a guy who holds a doctorate, to find common ground?"

"I think we already have."

And that was the painful truth. "Do you intend to tell your parents about your suspicions?"

"I think for now I'll keep it just between the two of us, mainly because my parents have had to deal with quite a bit lately. And then there's Mitch, who'll likely go off the deep end at hearing Livvy would stray. In case you haven't noticed, Mitch holds Livvy up there on a pedestal."

"I don't know, Jackson. I think it's better to be one hundred percent upfront in all this with everyone. I know it might be painful to absorb, but I think they'd prefer to hear the truth now instead of down the road, that includes Mitch."

"Then I guess I'll have to figure it out as I go, pick the best time to land the blow." He looked off in the distance as if contemplating life, like he was trying to figure out how to frame his next words.

The Nissan Titan screeched to a stop in front of the Toyota. It was Walsh Kingston behind the wheel. The crew chief got out and ran up to the car window. "Jackson, where's Mitch?"

"I don't know. We just got here. Why? What's up?"

"I tried calling him, left several messages, but Mitch isn't picking up his cell. Someone planted explosives aboard *The Black Rum*."

While Walsh had been anxious to find him, Mitch had detoured to the public library and shut himself off in the corner to do his own research on Werner Dietrich and his arrival in Argentina. He'd discovered that during the aftermath of the Second World War, Werner Dietrich's father had been suspected of smuggling millions in gold out of Germany before the fall of the Third Reich.

Up to 1945, the elite SS unit had spent years plundering the property and possessions of millions in order to bankroll the war effort. That included yanking out fillings from the mouths of victims who'd lost their lives during the Holocaust and whatever else the Nazis fancied. They'd looted everything they could from French, Czech, and Polish banks—bags of gold, coins, silver, and platinum. Although suspicions were rampant the proof of such transactions were left vague and remained elusive, leaving one burning question. Where had all that pillaged loot ended up?

Mitch had been so wrapped up in finding out how many of the U-boats had been suspected of carrying bullion that he'd missed his cell phone igniting in a series of texts and calls.

By the time he reached the harbor he found *The Black Rum* still anchored and looking no worse for wear. Jackson and Garret were already on the scene going over every inch of the boat with the crew making sure all the devices had been located.

But as soon Mitch reached the deck, he grilled Walsh for answers. "You're telling me someone got close enough to leave plastic explosives on board my ship? How could that happen? The crew has always been vigilant about posting guards whenever we're in port. Those are the rules. When did we abandon that process?"

Walsh pushed back. "No one left this ship unattended. I guarantee it. We've taken leave together as a unit only once since we got here and even then we assigned a guard. That was the night we went to the bar."

"Then one of the crew fell asleep on lookout."

Walsh shook his head and fired back. "You know these men. I'm telling you that isn't the case."

"Then tell me how it happened?"

"Whoever did this swam up to the side of the boat and tossed several devices over the railing, fast and quick. The IEDs landed on deck near the helm but didn't detonate."

"And you're saying no one heard that? Scary thought. Who was on guard duty?"

"Prentiss was on the starboard side."

"Are you certain he never left his post?"

"I've asked him. He swears he didn't even take a break to go to the bathroom."

"Then how'd you find it?"

"After eating supper I went up on deck for a smoke and to take Prentiss a plate of food. I almost stumbled over one of the damn things. We managed to find two more about ten feet apart."

Mitch scrubbed his hands over his face at the thought of it. "Thank God no one was hurt. I want to talk to Prentiss myself. From now on we make sure each side is covered. If morale is a problem, double their pay."

When Walsh continued to eye him with curiosity, Mitch returned the gaze. "What now?"

"What exactly have we gotten into here, Mitch? We've been a team for almost ten years. We've been in some pretty tight scrapes, from the shores off Morocco to the waters in the Congo, even had to draw our guns on another boat in the West Indies in a standoff once. But no one's ever tried to blow us out of the water until now."

Mitch blew out a breath. "I have no idea. If I knew, I'd let you in on it. Is the crew ready to bolt?"

"No, no, they're sticking. But I'd be lying if I said they weren't nervous."

"They have every right to be," Jackson tossed out, as he came around the port side, and stood next to his brother.

"Maybe that's why I'm having second thoughts about leaving for North Carolina with Tessa. I think I should stay here."

"I'll leave you two to hash this out in private," Walsh said sending his captain a mock salute and turned on his heels.

Mitch did his best to put on a brave front. "If you're considering disappointing Tessa because of this little incident, my advice would be not to. When the time comes Tessa will need you there with her. You're sleeping with the woman. That should mean supporting her through one of the toughest times of her life."

Jackson wasn't buying the bravado. Mainly because his brother gripped the railing so tight his knuckles were white. "I know that. But she could fly up with Mom and Dad so she wouldn't be alone. I could take another flight in time to make the funeral, be gone no longer than overnight. You don't fool me, little brother. *The Black Rum* and all on board could've ended up toast this evening. Using C-4 is a serious indication someone is worried about us. And for whatever reason, they're scared. We keep pissing these people off. Maybe Anniston's right, we're getting closer than we think to the answers."

"I'm beginning to believe that. I'm sure Garret and I should be able to handle whatever comes up here."

"Okay then, I'm counting on y'all to solve this thing while I'm gone."

For the first time in hours, Mitch's lips bowed into a grin. "We'll do our best." When Jackson started to walk away, Mitch grunted in that direction. "But Jackson…"

"What?"

"I wouldn't mind if you wanted to cut the trip a couple of days shorter that what you'd planned."

Jackson chuckled, gave his brother a salute of his own. "No problem. That sounds like a plan I can keep to."

Later that evening after things had settled down, Jackson took Tessa for a walk around the bay. It seemed like a romantic stroll but it was also a decent vantage point where he could scan the harbor and keep an eye on *The Black Rum*. From this point forward, they'd need to be extra vigilant. But right now his focus had to be on the woman walking beside him. Not ten minutes earlier, she'd finally received that call from the medical examiner she'd been dreading.

"You let your dad know?"

"It broke my heart, but yeah. Dad's taking care of the funeral arrangements." She stopped to look up at Jackson. "You know, I had a long talk with Raine and Anniston about what happened on Mitch's boat. The three of us are aware the situation has changed dramatically. Obviously someone thinks we've hit a nerve." She tightened her hold on Jackson's hand. "Enough that someone wants us dead. They shot at us out at the preserve. Now they're trying to scare us with explosives."

She had such worry in her eyes he tried to downplay the whole thing. "But no Indigos were on board the boat tonight."

"That just means they were sloppy. Tonight. My point is, if you should decide to stay here and not go with me to Nags Head, if you need to stay behind and be with your brothers, I totally understand."

He tucked several strands of copper hair behind her ear. "That's good to know. But I'm still going with you. The thing is, before heading back to North Carolina, I have a favor to ask. I'll go with you back to Ryan's funeral. But when it's over and you've spent a few days with your family, I want you to come back here with me. Come back with me to Indigo Key, Tessa. You still haven't found out how Ryan died. The answers you want are right here within these shores."

"Is that the only reason you want me to come back with you, Jackson, to find out who killed Ryan?"

He cupped her neck, brought her closer. "No. I want you here with me, back where all this started, where I started." An almost needy emotion landed in the pit of his stomach. "I'd like you here with me to be with me, for me. We aren't opposites, Tessa."

That made her smile. "No, we aren't. Are you asking me to come back because you feel sorry for me? Because of the lousy situation I have with my stepmother? Because once I go back home to my empty apartment, I'll miss you like mad."

She was going to make him say it. "I've fallen in love with you. Through all this madness, you and I seemed to be the only thing that makes any sense at all around here. I'm not sure how it went down. I come back home to a crisis like this and end up finding the best thing that's ever happened to me right here. But that's how upside down things are right now. Go figure."

She threw her arms around his neck, covered his throat with kisses. "I fell in love with you that night on the dance floor, the night we made love in your grandmother's cottage."

He framed her face with his hands. "I'm glad to hear it because I bought it, the cottage. I figure whatever happens, the house will stay in the family. But what I'd like, what I'm hoping for, is that you'll move out of Raine's place and stay with me at the bungalow. It already has a bed and furniture and you seem to like it there."

"I adore it. I adore you."

"Then I'm hoping we'll figure this thing out. Together."

Anticipation rose in her chest replacing the despair of recent weeks. "It's hard to believe I'm feeling this elated with so much sadness around us."

"Don't think about the sadness, not tonight. You and I deserve this, Tessa."

"We do. I want happiness again, Jackson."

They bumped bodies, pressed their lips together—the promise of faith and hope on the horizon. They had to believe better days were yet to come.

Turn the page for a sneak preview
of the second book in the trilogy

Indigo Heat

Indigo Heat

Skeeter Bronson loved the ocean. All he'd ever wanted to do in his life was to become a shrimper like his daddy. As a child, during the summers and on weekends, he'd worked on his father's boat from the time he'd turned eight.

So when he somehow managed to scrape enough money together to buy his own shrimp boat, it was the happiest day of his life. Course, he would never admit that to his wife, Adele.

Skeeter named his pride and joy the *Southern Star*, painted the name on her himself. The first time Skeeter had laid eyes on her, she was a beat-up old beauty, a double-rigged trawler with a two hundred horsepower engine. It took him almost two months of hard work to get her in seaworthy condition.

In thirty years of shrimping, she'd always been good to him, always brought him back to port in one piece, no matter how bad the weather.

The years had come and gone, some good, some not so good, but his home away from home would always be the sea. And God help him he loved the *Southern Star* almost as much as he did Adele.

During the good years he would upgrade the trawler with new engines, rigging, and every piece of equipment he could afford, including the latest and greatest fish-finding echo sounders. It had taken him forever to learn to read the damn thing and all the instrumentation that came with it.

In those early months with the modern technology, he'd felt like a blind man with his first guide dog. He'd been the first to install state of the art gear and immediately became the butt of jokes from the other shrimpers. For about two months he endured the ribbing. That is, until he was able to bring in twice the catch that the other shrimpers brought in.

These days, he could tell if the shrimp were large or small or where they schooled in massive quantities at the precise location on the bottom of the sea floor. With his knowledge of the ocean, he rarely bothered with tide charts because he knew the area around the Keys like an old familiar lover. No one was better at it than Skeeter Bronson. He'd shrimped in the west in the cooler Atlantic but preferred the warmer waters to the east in the Gulf of Mexico.

Tonight, he was after pink shrimp and maybe if things went well, he'd take a run around the Tortugas for some Royal Red. That would bring in some extra cash he could use to remodel the second bedroom his wife wanted to turn into her hobby room. The money would go a long way to getting her off his back.

He was two hours into his run, eyes glued to the fish finder, looking out for the telltale signs of the larger schools when an unusual echo popped up. For now, he ignored the strange blob on his screen and focused on the massive school of shrimp swimming along the sandy bottom.

Skeeter directed his crew to drop the tickler chain to get the shrimp moving and to avoid a large by-catch.

But the echo kept repeating. He realized his nets were about to get tangled up in whatever it was so he maneuvered the boat into position, avoiding the echo as much as he could but still aiming for the schooling shrimp. He ordered the outrigger lowered, the nets, and the bag line.

Everything was running smoothly until he felt the long line jerk, caught on something. God, he hoped he hadn't ripped another net. He should've heeded the echo and avoided the area altogether. Reluctantly he powered down the engine and ran to the winch, hoping like hell he hadn't torn a hole in the net too badly. In all his years of shrimping, he'd dragged up just about everything you could think of, tires, fishing gear, half a lifeboat, a buoy, a car hood, and even an old World War II mine that gave him gray hairs until the Coast Guard took it off his hands.

The winch began to strain with the load as it brought up some type of large cylinder-shaped object. Skeeter elbowed his crew chief, Bobby Joe Wylie, in the ribs and bet him five bucks that they'd snagged their first washing machine.

"Maybe it's one of those old bells. You know, like from the Titanic," Bobby Joe said hopefully. "Wouldn't that be something?"

"I don't think it's a bell. Too small," Skeeter declared with some maritime knowledge of such things.

So when a fifty-five-gallon drum surfaced in the net—a dull black barrel with silver markings, the kind used in chemical storage facilities—the two men traded annoyed looks.

"Damn illegal dumpers," Skeeter muttered. Every time someone dumped waste into the gulf it screwed with his livelihood. If the markings on the drum could be traced back to an owner, he wanted to know who and what they'd dumped. But as he took a closer look he noticed all the key numbers had been sanded off, leaving nothing to identify the vendor.

"What the hell have we got here?" Skeeter asked as he angled the winch holding the drum and carefully lowered it onto the deck so Bobby Joe could work it out of the net.

"Check the net for damage," Skeeter called out as he grabbed his crowbar and tapped the drum a few times to determine if it might be empty or full. He decided the only thing to do was to pop off the lid to see what was inside.

He used the crowbar to chisel around the rim and pry off the sealed top. As soon as he was able to inch up the cover, the odor hit him and knocked him back a step. He recognized the smell of death from his two tours of duty in 'Nam. Fearing what was inside, he knew he had to finish getting the lid off.

He raised the heavy top high enough to get a peek in. The first thing he spotted was the long hair that signaled an adult female body and the plastic bag over her head. He took a few steps back to gain his composure and took a deep breath of fresh air before returning to the drum to open it the rest of the way. By this time the crew had gathered around the barrel to watch.

Skeeter had to find the mettle to take a good long look at what was in there. When he peered in, he saw immediately an additional smaller body, the petite head, a child's head with dark hair that obviously belonged to a little girl. Large chunks of concrete had been dumped in the bottom of the barrel and used to weigh it down to make it sink. If not for getting tangled in the nets, it might never have surfaced at all.

Skeeter stepped back in horror as realization hit him. He knew then exactly what he had on his boat. He choked back tears, but tried to hold it together enough to get his mind right. "Bobby Joe, get on the radio and call the Coast Guard, give them our location and tell them we may have found that missing lady and her daughter."

While the night spun out around him, Skeeter heard Bobby Joe's rattled voice in the distance. "This is the *Southern Star* calling the Coast Guard, this is the *Southern Star* calling the Coast Guard, Mayday, Mayday."

Dear Reader:

If you enjoyed *Indigo Fire* please take the time to leave a review.
A review shows others how you feel about the work.
By recommending it to your friends and family it helps spread the word.

For a complete list of my other books visit my website.
www.vickiemckeehan.com

Want to connect with me and leave a comment?
Go to Facebook
www.facebook.com/VickieMcKeehan

I'd love to hear from you!

Don't miss these other exciting titles by bestselling author

Vickie McKeehan

The Pelican Pointe Series
PROMISE COVE
HIDDEN MOON BAY
DANCING TIDES
LIGHTHOUSE REEF
STARLIGHT DUNES
LAST CHANCE HARBOR
SEA GLASS COTTAGE
LAVENDER BEACH

The Evil Secrets Trilogy
JUST EVIL Book One
DEEPER EVIL Book Two
ENDING EVIL Book Three

The Skye Cree Novels
THE BONES OF OTHERS
THE BONES WILL TELL
THE BOX OF BONES
HIS GARDEN OF BONES

The Indigo Brothers Trilogy
INDIGO FIRE
INDIGO HEAT
INDIGO JUSTICE

ABOUT THE AUTHOR

Indigo Fire is Vickie McKeehan's sixteenth novel. She writes romantic suspense and makes her home in Southern California.

You can find Vickie online at
https://www.facebook.com/VickieMcKeehan
http://www.vickiemckeehan.com/
https://vickiemckeehan.wordpress.com